Fragments

Felicity Hawes

For everybody who has listened to me talk about doing this for years.

CONTENTS

Twenty

Twenty-One

Twenty-Two

Twenty-Three

Twenty-Four

Twenty-Five

Twenty-Six

Twenty-Seven

Twenty-Eight

Twenty-Nine

Thirty

Thirty-One

Thirty-Two

Eighteen months later

PART ONE

ONE

Her breath was steaming up the window as she screamed soundlessly, so terrified that she could no longer make a noise. Her chubby little fists, exhausted from banging helplessly against the glass, stilled as she desperately tried to make out the figure lying on the ground. It was no use; the crowd surrounding it was only getting bigger and suddenly the November air was filled with sirens and flashing blue lights.

"Mum. Mum! Teddy won't give me the iPad back, and it's MY iPad. Mum. Mum. Mum, Mum, Mum!" I pulled the pillow further over my face, counting silently to ten before I lost it with her.

"Ok. Ok! I'll sort it Rose, just stop, will you? I don't need this first thing every single morning." I waited a beat before deciding I was safe from more diatribes from my daughter. The coast seeming clear, I poked my head out of the pillow to be greeted by a furious seven-year-old.

"It's not my fault," she said moodily as soon as I made eye contact. "It's so unfair, he always takes it, and he NEVER gets told off." Despite myself I couldn't help grinning at her.

"You are SO dramatic, Rose." I said, mirroring her intonation. "Honestly, do all your friends behave like this too?"

"THEY don't have annoying little brothers who steal ALL their stuff," Rose replied, her tone still angry but her actions at odds as she crawled onto my bed to snuggle into me. I held her tightly, savouring the moment. They didn't happen very often anymore; Rose was normally way too cool for much affection nowadays. For a minute or so we both stayed silent, enjoying the calm. I felt myself beginning to drop off into a doze again when thundering footsteps alerted us both.

"Oh GREAT," said Rose sarcastically, this time being the one to bury her head into my pillow. My bedroom door flung open and over the threshold came a whirlwind, the constant thorn in Rose's side. Within seconds I was being devoured in kisses, a pair of arms strung tightly around my neck.

"Hi, mummy!" Three-year-old Teddy greeted me enthusiastically, following it up with another kiss on the lips. A very wet kiss. Lovely. Nevertheless, I hugged him back hard before releasing him a little so I could see his face.

"Morning Teddy bear. Have you been taking Rosie's iPad again?" Ted grinned at me mischievously. His little cheeks were still chubbily adorable with baby fat.

"I only LOOKED at it," he replied, his imitation of Rose absolutely spot on. As he looked angelically back at us it was suddenly too funny not to, and Rose and I burst into laughter.

"Right, well don't touch it if she's said no, ok? Come on guys," I continued, glancing at my phone. "I need to drop you to your dads' houses in an hour. Let's get moving!" Ignoring Rose's delighted shout at the thought of going, I began to chivvy them along to get clothes out, shouting instructions as I went. Already that trapped little girl of my dream was forgotten.

We pulled up at my ex-husband's house first, with Teddy almost pressed up against the window in his eagerness to get out. Teddy adored his daddy with every part of his little heart. Daddy was the best person in Ted's whole wide world, and always had been. On cue, and as if he was watching (which was quite likely, Steve adored his son even more than Ted did him) for our car to pull in, Steve rushed out. He opened Teddy's car door, unstrapping him and lifting him into a bear hug almost before I'd come to a complete stop. I smiled indulgently before getting out myself to grab his bag from the boot.

By the time I'd got it and walked round to the pavement Steve had the front passenger door ajar and was chatting to Rose. She was already in fits over whatever story he'd been telling, her newly acquired pre-teen attitude disappearing and leaving my loveable seven-year-old back in her place again for a moment.

"Hi darling," Steve said, noticing me and treating me to my own bear hug whilst peering into my face. "You look tired. Want to come in for a cuppa?"

"Oh, thanks very much," I retorted, trying but failing to look offended. "I won't stay. I need to drop Rose over to Dan's before ten. They're going out somewhere, apparently." Steve's eyes immediately shuttered, and his mouth was working to control his thoughts. I knew exactly what he was thinking because I felt the same. "I know I know, but he says he's definitely around this weekend," I said, pre-empting his question and darting my eyes exaggeratedly over in Rose's direction as a warning to Steve not to say anything negative. He got the hint.

"Ok. Well, if, you know, things *don't work out*, then let me know. We'd love to have her here for the weekend with us. Wouldn't we Ted?" My son, now trying to clamber up his dad's leg to get his attention, shook his head and stuck his tongue out at Rose.

"Don't want Rosie. MY daddy." Rose's smile dropped for a moment, and she looked incredibly young.

"That's really unkind, Ted." Steve had bent down and was looking our son in the eye while he spoke. "I'm part of Rose's family too, just like you. Now what do you say to Rosie?" Teddy looked seriously back at Steve before trotting over to his sister.

"Sorry," he said, giving her a big cuddle. She sighed dramatically and hugged him back.

"That's ok. Come on Mum. Dad'll be waiting for me!" Steve gave me an understanding smile and made a silent gesture to call him. I nodded before bending down to say goodbye to Ted. "Mum! Come ON!"

"I'm coming! Bye boys, have a lovely weekend and I'll see you tomorrow evening, ok?" Steve waited until Rose had shut her door before bending forwards to give me a kiss on the cheek.

"Shame we didn't meet earlier really, isn't it? It would have made your life easier for sure, just having me." Steve's whispered parting comment floated over to me on the wind. I paused before double checking Rose was out of earshot and gave him a look, to which he simply shrugged his shoulders, his eyes dark and unreadable. I smiled and shrugged slightly, a hint of apology crossing my face. He was right after all; life would be much easier had both my children gotten to have Steve as their father.

I got into the car and began to reverse with Steve and Ted waving enthusiastically at us, before beginning an impromptu game of Tag on the way back to the front door. Our last glimpse of them before we drove past the hedge was of Steve catching Ted up and burying his face into his stomach, making my little boy laugh uncontrollably. It was so nice to be able to leave your child with someone you knew loved them like you did, I reflected, as I drove away. Glancing at Rose, now quiet and gazing out of the window with a smile on her face, I wished I could say the same for my daughter's second parent.

"You ok babe?" I asked, as we turned into Rose's dad's road. Or more precisely, her grandparent's road, because Dan was back living with his mum now. Rose didn't answer apart from to nod, but I could feel the tension beginning to mount in the car, and I gently squeezed her knee in understanding. "Listen, if he's not there do you still want to stay with Nanna?" No answer. "Or you can come home with me. Or you could go to Steve's. Whatever you want, ok?" Rose still didn't reply, and her dainty little chin wobbled a little bit. She's already anticipating being disappointed, I realised. God, why did Dan have to be such an awful parent? He didn't seem to understand what a treasure Rose's love for him was, and how fragile and temporary it would be if he kept disappointing her. We pulled up outside, both of us automatically glancing down the road for his car, which wasn't in sight. Rose turned to me with sad eyes.

"Let's see what's going on first, hey? He said he's got something exciting planned. Maybe he had to go and sort some stuff out for it. And anyway, I'm sure Nanna will be pleased to see you." Rose rolled her eyes at that but began to walk up the small back path to the kitchen door. Dan's mum lived in one of those roads where you only ever went in through the back. I followed her as she opened the door and called out.

"Nanna?" She called as she slipped her shoes off. I followed suit just as Dan's mum appeared in the doorway.

"Hello, love," she said, bending down to kiss the top of Rose's head. "Hi Marnie, how are you?" Sarah directed a warm smile at me. I'd always liked Dan's mum; she'd been the closest thing I'd had to a mother figure in my teenage years. I knew it still disappointed her that I hadn't stuck around with her son though.

"I'm ok thanks, how are you?" I replied, distracted by Rose, who was peering through into the rest of the house.

"Where's Daddy, Nanna?" She asked, clearly not able to see him in the front room. Sarah met my eyes defensively before answering.

"Ah. Well, the thing is love, that Daddy's got a new job, and he's got to work today. But he has promised me," she hurriedly continued, noticing as I did that Rose's face had drooped, "that he'll be back by five and then he'll take you out to the cinema, how does that sound?" Rose was trying to hide her disappointment and instead tried her best to smile.

"Oh. Well, that's good that he's got a job again isn't it, Nanna? Shall I stay here with you for today then? Shall we go out to the park?" I already knew what Sarah's answer was going to be, but it didn't make it any less painful, my heart hurting for Rose when she confirmed it.

"I'm sorry darling, just with my legs…you know? But we can stay here and watch some films, just 'til Daddy's back?" Sarah couldn't cope with going out alone with Rose; she was growing increasingly frail, a lifetime of bad diet and no exercise catching up with her.

"I could always drop her back later. When Dan's home I mean?" I offered, trying to give Rose an out.

"That's ok Mum," she said, going over and giving Sarah a gentle hug. "I'll stay here and keep Nanna company instead. Daddy won't be long, I'm sure."

"Ok babe." I leant down to give her a kiss. "Why don't you go and find something to watch while I speak to Nanna quickly?" Rose gave me a knowing look but nodded and left the room.

"Is he actually at work?" I asked in a piercing whisper. "Or is that code for the pub again?" Sarah, her face flaming, shrugged in embarrassment.

"He was supposed to be starting a new job this week. And I'm sure he went on Wednesday and Thursday. But I've not seen him since yesterday morning. I rang him last night and he was just having a couple in the Goose. He'll have gone straight into work today before I got up!" She ended defiantly, still defensive of him even when we both knew there was no chance of that. I sighed.

"Ok. It's just if he doesn't come back this evening, she'll be devastated. You know she will, Sarah. Can you ring him, just to make sure he remembers she's here this weekend? Otherwise, I might as well take her back with me now because it's not fair. Or Steve's invited her to stay with him and Teddy?" Sarah bristled a little, making me wish I hadn't mentioned that. No matter how much Dan had messed up, Sarah was always quick to remind Rose that she was his child and had always resented Steve's presence in her life a little. I think the way that Steve had taken Rose on made her feel badly about her own son's lack of fatherly duty.

"She'll be fine here, Marnie. We are her family, you know."

"I know I know. I just meant that he's got Ted, so he offered, that's all. Anyway, can you let her ring me later to say goodnight please?"

"I always do. Bye love, take care." Sarah leant in for a kiss, stiffer than she usually was. I sighed inwardly. Now I'd offended her.

"Well, ok. Bye Rosie, love you." I called through to the living room, getting a muffled response in return. Closing the kitchen door behind me, I began to walk back down towards my car, trying to keep my anger in check. It was impossible. He was so bloody useless. Why could he never just put her first? Before his mates. Before the pub. Before the drink and the drugs.

It seemed incredible that once upon a time I'd loved him more than I'd ever loved anyone. That was until I was eighteen and began to feel sick. I grew up in the three minutes it took for the positive line to show on the test, realising from that moment that baby Rose was going to be the most important thing in my world. Dan had never got the memo, it seemed. Even now he was still the same teenager I'd been obsessed with years ago, the cool boy two years older than me and party mad. He was the life and soul back then, always the joker that everyone wanted to hang around and have a good time with, while I was a broken, motherless mess who just craved someone who was going to look after me.

TWO

"Marnie! Marnie, over here!" My baby sister's loud voice was unmistakeable over the bustle of the rest of the Saturday lunchtime crowd. I glanced in the direction of the shouting and was immediately drawn to a splash of bright colours amid the sea of beige and cream. Lula was not a person you could ever miss, even if you wanted to. She was outrageous, both in personality as well as lifestyle, and proud of it. It had always been that way; we were absolute polar opposites in pretty much every aspect of our lives. Our parents always used to laugh indulgently at our differences. I, as the older sister, was sensible and took my responsibilities seriously even as a child, while Lula was an extrovert to whom anything vaguely run of the mill was horrifying. I grinned over at her, still waving frantically at me, and returned the gesture. As I reached the table Lula stood to embrace me.

"Hi Loopy," I said, wrapping her up in my arms and breathing in her familiar smell. She hugged me back before releasing me with a groan.

"Marnie, how many times? Don't call me that!" She was laughing as she said it, but it had been a sticking point throughout our lives. Not that she ever believed me, but I actually had tried to stop calling her by her childhood nickname. For as long as I could remember, she had been 'Loopy' to us all. Mum used to say 'loopy by name, loopy by nature', and up until she was about six, she more than played up to it for laughs. And now there was only me left to remind her of the nickname. What a sad thought. To get my mind back to the present day, I pasted a smile on my face and leaned in towards Lula.

"So, where's my gorgeous nephew then? I thought you might have brought him along."

"No, Rashid's not at work so they've gone to the park. What about yours? Don't tell me that Dan actually remembered he was having Rose today?" My little sister had never shared any of my affection for Dan, even when we were together.

When I first brought him home to meet my family, she'd turned into an absolute devil, constantly bursting in on us or antagonising Dan by making suggestive comments about what we must be up to in front of Dad.

Although Dan remained good natured at the time, I knew it stung that she could be so horrible when he was so used to being universally loved by all. And the fact that I never stood up for him as I felt too bad on my little sister had always been a bone of contention between us. I privately thought that a lot of it was to do with the fact that I had dropped Lula for Dan's company and was nothing more but good old-fashioned jealousy. In hindsight I almost wished I'd listened to her when she used to tell me what a deadbeat he was. Only almost though, Rose was a pretty good outcome as far as old relationships go.

"No, he wasn't there. I left her with Sarah, they both seemed happy with that. Apparently he was at work." I didn't dare tell her that he had actually more than likely been in the pub for days; there was no point in giving her yet more ammunition. I already felt like I spent most of the time that Lula was anywhere near Rose running interference to stop her from bad mouthing her dad. Let kids make up their own mind was my motto.

"Ah. Sounds believable," Lula responded, rolling her eyes. "Honestly he's such an idiot, I can't believe you ever thought that having a baby with him was a good idea."

"I didn't exactly plan it, as you well know. Now can we change the subject please? Have you seen Dad this week?" Our father had been moved to a care home for dementia sufferers a couple of months ago, which was the main reason that I had recently moved back to our hometown. Now I was here I tried to go and see him a few times a week, but recently I'd banned the kids from going. It was getting too painful for them that Grandpa didn't recognise them anymore, especially for Rose.

"Yeah, I went Thursday. I thought I might have seen you. I'll tell you what though, next time I'm too busy to go, I'm sending in an actor. He'll think it's me anyway."

"Lula!" I said, pretending to be outraged but unable to help smiling. "You can't say things like that." Lula laughed at me.

"True though, and worth serious consideration." She grinned. "Let's get drunk. What do you fancy? Wine?" I laughed. "What?"

"I thought Buddhists didn't drink to get drunk?" I teased, smiling indulgently at my little sister. Lula, true to form, had gone in the opposite direction to me after university. She'd packed up and gone travelling as soon as she'd finished, desperate to get away from ordinary suburbia (and quite possibly me and Dad) as soon as she could.

She'd spent her student years working part time in the local Tesco to save, and it then fell to a reluctant me to drop both her and her best mate, Zara, at Heathrow to begin their voyage around the world by flying to Thailand. From there, the girls spent a good six months roaming Southeast Asia and immersing themselves in Buddhism before landing in Australia to begin a working visa on a remote cattle station in the Outback. The plan, apparently, was to complete that before heading to the Gold Coast for some hedonistic fun prior to returning home.

Rashid was already on the cattle station when they arrived, doing the same thing with his brother. According to Rashid it was love at first sight, and they got married in a simple Christian ceremony out there before we even met him, Lula's Buddhist practices suddenly forgotten. Luckily, he was probably the nicest guy you'd ever meet, and both Dad and I now love him.

"Yeah, ok. I might only have the one though. I'm worried I'll have to go and pick Rose up later when Dan doesn't come home from work.'" Lula raised a wry eyebrow, but uncharacteristically said nothing. I busied myself behind the menu as I heard her order a bottle of red for us. Once we were alone again and the wine was poured, Lula raised a glass to me before taking a deep sip.

"Can I ask you something, Marnie?" She looked a little wary, and immediately my heart began to beat faster.

"What's wrong? Has something happened to Ruben?"

"No nothing like that!" My little sister was quick to reassure me. "It's just, well, did you know that Dad's got a woman visitor who goes to see him most weeks? One of the nurses told me in passing. She assumed it was another sister of ours. She's around our age apparently." I frowned and took a sip of my own drink.

"That's a bit weird. I didn't know anyone else was visiting. I wonder who it could be? Shouldn't they have told us someone was seeing him?"

"Dunno. Maybe they don't have to? It's not like he's not supervised or anything. Maybe it's one of his friend's daughters, or someone who used to work for him in the city?" I was still frowning.

"Hmm maybe. But I'm not sure I like the thought of him being seen like that by anyone else. And he definitely wouldn't like it. Well, if he could still remember how he would feel, that is." I pondered for a moment. "I'm going there tomorrow. I'll ask the nurses for a bit more information then." Lula looked relieved that as usual I was assuming responsibility for the situation.

"So, tell me," She said, leaning in. "Been on any more dates yet?" I groaned and downed my drink before pouring myself a second glass. I'd need it for this conversation. And I could always walk to get Rose if I needed to.

The lunch with Lula turned into an all-afternoon affair. We decided to go shopping afterwards as I was desperate for some new clothes now that the weather was turning colder. Dan had actually paid me maintenance for once this month, which was basically unheard of, so I had a bit of extra cash. Maybe he really did have a job.

When I finally arrived home, I glanced at my phone to see it was already six o'clock. I decided to call both kids now to say goodnight. That way I could check that Rose was happy to stay at her dad's before it got too late to walk and grab her. I decided to ring Ted first in case he was going up to bed soon, and idly slipping my shoes off, I padded through to the big kitchen-family room at the back of the house that spanned the entire width of our property. I'd chosen this house mainly for this open living space, although when I was here on my own or it had grown dark, I preferred the small snug room at the front. The blackness on the other side of the huge glass patio doors had always made me feel uneasy, as if someone was lingering just out of sight.

As it was only dusk for the moment I pottered around on the wooden floor, getting impatient for Steve to answer the phone.

"Hi darling!" I rolled my eyes at the endearment. Honestly, he was such a flirt, and I dreaded to think how his wife Addy felt about the way spoke to me. She'd always seemed completely fine with it though, and so I supposed I should be too; it was so clearly harmless.

"Hi Steve. Just ringing to speak to Ted before bed. I thought you weren't even going to answer, you took so long!"

"Oh, great I'll just grab him for you. I know sorry, we were playing on the trampoline. Teddy!" He shouted for our son at full volume, still with the phone attached to his ear.

"Steve!" I grimaced, wincing at the loudness. He laughed.

"Sorry babe, didn't mean to deafen you. Hey, did Rose get off alright? Dan was there, was he?" I sighed, anticipating having to explain all about Dan and his possibly fictitious job again.

"I dropped her with Sarah, but Dan should be back by now. I'm ringing Rosie next to check she's ok." I hoped that was sufficient; Steve loved Rose just as much as he loved Teddy, and it killed him a little that he didn't have the right to have her every other weekend, particularly when he knew Dan and his habits of old.

"Ah, ok." His tone told me he wasn't impressed by this. "Well, she's still welcome over tonight, or even tomorrow if she wants to. You will tell her that, won't you?" I sighed guiltily. It really did hurt my heart sometimes. Here was a fantastic dad for both of my kids, and I just hadn't been able to make myself love him enough to stay. Now only Teddy reaped the benefits.

And Rose did love Dan. No, actually, adored would be more fitting. In her eyes he was the best person in the world, and the saddest part was that the more he let her down, the more she wanted to please him.

In contrast she had begun to fight a little against Steve's open offering of love and care for her in recent months, and I wondered if it was some sort of guilt trip that was making her behave that way because she'd always loved spending time with him before. Rose had only been one when Steve moved in with us. Her existence had been the catalyst that had made me finally break away from the notoriety that had followed me around my hometown, and leaving Dan to his stale fate, I had moved an hour away to somewhere completely new in the hopes of a fresh start for me and my baby girl. Instead, I found myself with no money, no support, and no way that I could see to make anything get better.

Steve saved me from drowning in a life of single parenthood, and he'd brought her up as if she were his own. She called him Daddy Steve or 'Staddy,' her own personal take on it, practically from the moment she met him, and he would dread the weekends that she went to her 'other' dad's. In fact, it was Rose's reaction to Steve that initially persuaded me to carry on seeing him, and the two of them were thick as thieves from the start. Even when Teddy came along Steve went out of his way not to let Rose feel left out in any way, and for a few years everything was great. Suddenly Rose and I were a part of the stable family unit that I'd always craved. Until I went and ruined it for all of us, that is.

The problem was that Steve appeared when I had nothing. I was nineteen with a one-year-old daughter in tow who I adored, but with no stable family unit. Dad was working all the hours he could, a strategy I've since realised was the only coping method he could come up with, and Lula had her own life to be getting on with. I'd moved away from them both when I left Dan, desperate for a new beginning and to leave the bad memories behind.

When Steve and I met that day in the park I hadn't been sure about him. He was there with his niece, and we began talking when Rose had toddled over to the little girl and whacked her on the head. Steve laughed off my apologies and made me laugh about it too, even while I stood there bright red with embarrassment. The girls ended up playing for ages while we chatted, or more accurately, Steve chatted to me, and for the first time since leaving Dan I gave someone my number. I didn't expect him to call at all, so when he texted that same evening, I was a little unsure.

Maybe he was a murderer? Or a psycho who prayed on young mothers? After all, who struck up a conversation that quickly with a stranger they'd met in the park? But for some reason I did reply, and things went from there. He was the perfect gentleman, who loved both Rose and I to distraction. The only problem was that there wasn't much of a fire between us. My teenage relationship with Dan had been if anything a little too full of the hot stuff; tempestuous and not built to last, but full of a passion which I now knew existed. Poor Steve, I did love him. I just wasn't *in* love with him.

Steve was desperate for marriage and kids of his own right from the start, and he roped Rose into his fantasy too. He started talking to Rose about her future brothers and sisters as if it was a foregone conclusion, so that when she asked me in her little plaintive voice when 'her baby' was going to come out of my tummy, I found myself wracked with guilt at depriving them both. And I also began to talk myself into it; maybe a baby was exactly what I needed to feel more connected to Steve?

Watching him with Rose had made me stay, so it wouldn't be stupid to think that watching him become a father would make me fall in love with him. When I unexpectedly found myself pregnant with Ted it felt like fate had made the decision for me. Steve and Rose were both over the moon, and once I'd gotten used to the idea, I decided I needed to fully embrace my new trajectory in life. I said yes when Steve proposed, using Rose to unveil a T-shirt emblazoned with the words, 'Mummy, will you marry Staddy' on it in the middle of a crowded town 'picnic in the park.' As the people surrounding us clapped, I told myself this was what I'd always wanted. Ted was born a few months later, and my path was set.

But about eighteen months ago I'd gotten to the point of no return. I was biting my tongue at every opportunity, feeling trapped in my idyllic family, and having to endure sex rather than enjoy it. Steve was everything I should have been grateful for, but he took care of me too much, if you can believe that.

Having met me when I was broken and vulnerable, he took me straight to the doctors and got me on some medication that changed my life. Suddenly I felt strong. Suddenly I felt like me again. But then he continued to micromanage my life until I felt incapable of achieving anything. I'd go shopping to cook a healthy dinner from scratch, and then when Steve got home from work, he and Rose would laugh at my inevitable cooking failure, conspiratorially rolling their eyes at 'silly mummy.' Then there was the time we went on holiday after Ted was born, and Steve insisted I wasn't to get in the pool alone with the children. I wouldn't 'be able to keep them both safe.' I knew he meant well and that all he wanted was to take care of us all, but honestly, towards the end it grated on me so much I had to stop myself from screaming.

And so I had *the conversation*. It took just one hour to devastate the three people I cared for the most, but I had no choice. Rose took it the hardest, and no matter how many times I explained that Steve did nothing wrong, she started to pull away from him, to talk about her 'real daddy' only, and to refuse to hang out with him. So here we were, with Rose desperate to have the same relationship she'd experienced with Steve, with Dan. I didn't know how to break it to her that Dan was never going to be what she needed.

"Hi Mummy guess what? I've been bouncing!" Ted's little voice brought me back to the present and made me smile.

"Ah that sounds fun! Are you having a good time at Daddy's? Are you being good?"

"Yeah, got to go now Mummy. Bye!" I could hear Steve laughing in the background as he persuaded our son to stay still.

"Ok, be good Teddy! Speak to you in the morning, love you lots."

"Bye mummy," followed by a sloppy kissing sound.

"Sorry I couldn't keep him still!" Steve was back.

"No worries, I know what it's like. So, I'll come and pick him up about five tomorrow, yeah? Or I can come and get him earlier if you like?"

"No definitely not, five is fine. In fact, I can drop him if it makes your life easier?" I shook my head before realising he couldn't see me.

"Don't worry I'll be out getting Rosie anyway. Hopefully. See you then, Steve."

"Bye babe. Let me know if Rose wants to come here before that though, yeah?" I murmured a reply and hung up the phone. I don't know why I did that; got the easy conversation out of the way first. I should really do it the other way so that I had something to look forward to. Dan's phone rang and rang with no reply. Fixing myself a cup of coffee, I let it ring for at least a minute before hanging up. It was hopeless, I would have to ring Sarah's house phone and deal with her blustering defence of that dickhead instead. Padding over to the table and wincing as I sipped too hot coffee, I put the phone to my ear, ready for battle.

"Hello?" came Sarah's panting voice. She had obviously shot up from the living room sofa to snatch the phone up before Rose did.

"Hi Sarah, it's Marnie." I paused to a wall of silence. "Just checking in and wanted to say goodnight to Rosie. She there?"

"Of course she's here. Where else would she be? I'll get her." Sarah was as grumpy as expected. I waited while the phone clattered down, and Sarah went to get my daughter.

"Hi Mummy." Rose sounded defeated, which could only mean that Dan had not made an appearance.

"Hi babe, you ok?" I waited, not wanting to ask outright and upset her even more.

"Yeah I'm ok. Mummy," I could barely hear her as she dropped to a whisper. "Daddy hasn't come back yet. I think Nanna's really cross." I couldn't work out how closely Sarah would be standing, and whether she could hear me, so I picked my words carefully.

"Oh Rose. She's not cross with you though. You know that don't you?" She didn't answer but I knew she was probably nodding; a habit obviously picked up from me. "Nanna's just a bit sad that Daddy can't spend the time with you this weekend. Do you still want to stay there? Or I can come and get you? Whatever you want." There was a little pause before my little, wise-beyond-her-years daughter answered.

"I'll stay with Nanna, Mum. We have lots of fun even when Daddy's at work." I smiled sadly. Even at seven she knew diplomacy.

"Ok then, if you're sure. Shall I come and get you in the morning instead then?"

"No, five as normal will be fine, thank you. Dan will be home shortly, and he'll want tomorrow to spend with his Rosie girl." Sarah's voice clattered down the line towards me; I knew she'd been listening.

"Rose it's up to you. You can decide how you feel in the morning. Nanna will let you use her phone if you want to come home, or if Daddy has to 'work' again, ok?" I ignored Sarah's huff as she recognised in my tone the air quotes. He bloody deserved it.

"Ok mum. Love you. I'll ring you if Daddy has to work."

"Love you too darling, sleep tight. Bye Sarah, have a nice evening." I finished the conversation politely, not wanting to leave Rosie with a grandparent on the defensive.

"Bye love," she said, her voice a little softer now that she knew I wasn't going to put my foot down and whisk Rose away. "See you tomorrow." The phone was hung up and I was left alone with the dialling tone. I decided to switch my coffee with a wine; it was Saturday night after all, and I still felt the pleasant buzz from my lunchtime wines lingering. Maybe I'd even splash out and order a takeaway.

Just as I was pouring an overly large glass my mobile rang. It made me jump, a sudden noise in the silence, and I splashed wine over my hands and the kitchen worktop. *Shit.* Briskly wiping the worst up with a t-towel, I snatched up the phone again in case it was Rose. It wasn't.

"Hi Marns, what you doing? Fancy going out tonight? It's your kid free weekend, isn't it? I thought we could go down The Crown for a few, and then into town. Aaron's being a right pain in the neck; I need to go out! Shall I come to yours now while you get ready?" I rolled my eyes even as I smiled. It was Martha, who'd been my very best mate back at school, when things like that meant everything.

In the Dan years she'd dropped out of my world a little bit, and once I moved out of town I may as well have gone to Australia for all the contact we had. But I was back now, and we seemed to have reverted to being sixteen years old. She was the only old friend of mine who'd not only insisted on contacting me on my return but had just simply turned up on the doorstep expecting to come in, with wine for me and toys for the kids.

"Martha!" I almost shouted down the phone, worried she was going to hang up without my go ahead and turn up on my doorstep in two minutes time. "I'm not really in the mood tonight to be honest. I might need to go and get Rose, so it's not a good idea to be out all night. Come round here for a drink if you like though?" Martha snorted derisively on the other end.

"Marns I want to go *out*. I need a break from that arsehole." The arsehole in question, Aaron, was a four-year-old terror, who had run rings around both of his exhausted parents from the moment he was born. I laughed.

"Stop calling him an arsehole. He'll know what that means soon, and you'll damage him." This was met with an even bigger snort.

"Damage him? Marnie, that child has a stronger skin than titanium. Believe me, I would *love* to make him feel bad about his behaviour occasionally. And he knows more swear words than me. Arsehole probably doesn't even register," she finished as an afterthought. This time we both laughed and then I sighed.

"I'll tell you what, how about we go to The Crown for one, and then we can come back to mine for a takeaway. Deal?"

"You are so boring Marnie! Honestly, you'd think you were the married one not me. Well, if that's the best you can do I suppose it'll have to be enough. See you there in twenty?"

"Yep, see you then. And just 'cos I'm single doesn't mean I've got the time or energy for any more of that relationship rubbish, so don't bother trying to persuade me into another set-up, ok? Ok, bye."

I carried my wine upstairs with me, aiming to change my top for a more exciting one. What I'd just said to Martha was true; I didn't want a new relationship, but sometimes it was nice to be appreciated from afar. In that spirit I decided to get out my good make up too. Most of my stuff was Maybelline at best, but over the years I'd carefully curated a tiny amount of MAC and Charlotte Tilbury too. Allowing myself the luxury of time for once, I called out to Alexa to play my favourites.

Old R&B filled the room; in my humble opinion the best uplifting music to get ready to, and I hummed along happily, stroking creamy browns and creams over my face to sculpt it into something not entirely me anymore.

I had almost finished when I heard a faint knock at the door. I sighed a little. Martha had obviously decided to collect me on route and although she knew to come round to the side door that we always left unlocked when we were home, she must have forgotten. Or maybe I'd forgotten to unlock it with the kid's phone calls and everything. I waited a moment in case she let herself in, but another knock propelled me towards the stairs. Taking them in two's, I was at the bottom and skidding along the hardwood floor in my socks in no time.

The silhouette on the other side of the front door looked larger than Martha's petite frame, and immediately I panicked that it was Steve or Dan and that something had gone wrong. Wrenching the door open, I was faced with a strange man. Dark haired and covered in facial hair, he stood at least six feet tall and without a smile on his face, he was more than a little menacing. I automatically closed the door a little to give me more of a chance to slam it, my innate female suspicion of every unknown man working furiously even while I tried to keep it off my face.

"Hi," I said, endeavouring to look unconcerned but probably only managing to grimace at him.

"Hi. Package to sign for," he replied, only then drawing my attention to the box he was holding out, so concerned was I with his face.

"Oh! Sorry," I said, apologising for no reason other than my unspoken suspicion that he was a serial killer. I took the electronic pad out of his hand clumsily and signed, a blurry line that was apparently good enough for all delivery drivers. He handed me the box without another word and turned back to his van. "Thanks!" I called after him, hoping I hadn't offended him with the blatant assessment that was probably written all over my face.

I was just about to shut the door when a car pulled up and Martha speedily got out, shouting back towards her family, and trotting up my front path in the highest heeled boots I'd ever seen. I grinned and waved at her long-suffering husband, Sam, although it was too dark to see if he was waving back. The car pulled off just as Martha reached me.

"Fucking bastard," she greeted me with as she leaned in to kiss my cheek and I was enveloped in a puff of something strong and sweet. She moved past and into my hallway, leaving me to close the door as she continued. "Do you know what that little brat's done now? He emptied my entire top drawer of makeup onto my new bed sheets and drew a massive willy on them with my new Chanel lipstick! Honestly, I'm putting him up for adoption." I reached the kitchen just after her and she was already in my fridge helping herself to the wine.

"He did not?" I laughed, going to get her a glass out before she began to swig from the bottle. "He's only four, he's obviously going to be an artist if he drew a recognisable penis. You should be proud of him!" Martha gave me a withering look before gulping her drink.

"Very funny. How am I supposed to get it out? And it definitely was a penis. I'm raising a delinquent. What's that?" She changed the subject, pointing to the box still in my hand.

"Dunno, it's just been delivered." I crossed over to the utensil drawer where I knew I'd find my sharpest scissors. "Pour me another one please. Oh damn, my glass is upstairs, hang on." I clattered the scissors down onto the countertop and ran back up to my room to get it. By the time I'd gotten back to the kitchen, Martha was holding something in her hand, the box flaps untidily sticking up where she had hacked at it with the scissors. She looked at me white faced.

"Sorry," she said. "I thought it would be something stupid and I was being nosy. Marns I'm really sorry. Here." She held her hand out and, bemused, I reached over to take it. A small heavy weight was transferred into the palm of my hand and automatically I opened it to see. It was a cream lump of material with a thin black strip. A fridge magnet. I turned it over and my heart thumped heavily, just once.

The clay was in the shape of a London tube station sign, a red circle with a blue rectangle running horizontally through it. But it was the name of the station that had caused my heart to beat so painfully. Wimbledon. A thousand memories assaulted me in the space of thirty seconds, all of them containing Her. I looked up at Martha's stricken face, and suddenly came back to the present.

"Martha, don't worry. Honestly, it's fine." She almost looked as if she wanted to cry, an emotion so far removed from Martha's general demeanour that I was worried.

"I'm really sorry, Marnie. It's none of my business but..." she trailed off, confused by my confusion. "Is everything ok?" I was staring down at the magnet, my mind trying to work furiously.

"Not sure. I don't know where this has come from. Who would send me it?"

"Have you looked for a note?" I shook my head and began to rummage in the box. Pulling out the stiff grey paper stuff that had obviously provided padding, I shook it all out to make sure there was nothing else tucked in.

"There's nothing. Not even a return address. I don't understand." We looked at one another before I carelessly chucked it back into the box and purposefully strode to the side door, dumping the entire thing in the black bin outside. "Must be someone having a sick joke. Let's forget it. So, tell me more about Aaron, did you take a picture of the penis masterpiece?" I pasted a fake smile on my face and waited desperately for her to launch into a story again. After a moment, she did, with all the gusto she could manage. Neither of us could miss the weird atmosphere that had entered the room with the magnet.

THREE

I made the taxi pull up at the end of the road rather than go all the way down the cul-de-sac as it would be a pain to try and turn around at the bottom. My neighbours seemed to think nothing of parking wherever they pleased, and I also didn't really want the car to alert any of them and have them peering out at me stumbling in so late.

It was hard enough being judged for being a single parent, let alone being thought of as an irresponsible one. A few of the streetlights were out and I got my phone ready to use the torch, glancing at the time as I did. Jesus, it was twenty to three in the morning. I picked up my pace, suddenly shivering in the early morning chill. I had only taken my fake leather jacket out with me, and my wine coat was wearing off.

My house in the distance was almost indistinguishable from the others in the complete dark and silence, apart from the porch light I'd left on. It was eerie how different even the most familiar was at night, as if something evil was exposed, waiting just out of sight to grab you and squirrel you away. I hated the darkness. After I left Steve and moved back here, I couldn't bear coming home to a dark and empty house. A light on sometimes had the power to trick me into thinking someone who loved me would be there, patiently waiting.

Letting myself in I shuddered involuntarily as I slipped off my jacket. My new-build and normally baking house was freezing. I played around with the thermometer on the hallway wall, trying to turn it up before noticing it was already on the toasty twenty-two degrees I liked. How weird.

Aching with thirst and realising my hangover was about to kick in massively, I stumbled down the hallway to get a drink of water and some painkillers. The quiet evening in the pub had turned into a manic session in town, with shots and dancing galore. I knew that allowing the escalation from my one drink deal with Martha was probably all a reaction to the receipt of that magnet earlier, but I refused to probe that situation even internally. Some things were better left in the past. I knew already that I would be dreaming of her again tonight, and that was more than enough to be getting on with.

The kitchen was noticeably colder even than the hallway, and flicking on the light, I was confronted by a shimmering floor. I grasped how drunk I must be, about to take a step to cross to the sink before my brain registered what it was. Shards of shattered glass were scattered all about, and looking wildly around, I found the cause of both glass and temperature, a broken pane in the side door. Right there in the centre of the glittering floor was a small fridge magnet, landed the right way up and brazen. I felt frozen to the spot for a moment, fear filling my blood and not knowing what to do next. Instinctively I backed out, moving swiftly to the front door again and called the only person I knew would come to rescue me without hesitation.

I was sitting in my car on the driveway when he pulled up, the ignition on to use the heating. I knew it was technically illegal given my drunken state, but quite frankly I was happy to take the risk, it was so cold. I chose not to think about whether this was fear or temperature induced. He jumped out and so I did too.

"Show me," he said tersely, indicating for me to unlock the front door. I did as he asked but decided to wait where I was rather than go in. I was freaked out enough by the magnet; I didn't need to see it again. He was only gone a few minutes when he returned, a look of anger on his face.

"Where did you get that thing from?" On closer reflection, it wasn't anger but worry distorting Steve's features.

"I don't know," I whispered. "I mean, it was sent to me today in the post. But there wasn't a note. I threw it in the black bin."

"In the outside bin?" he said, looking at me sharply. I nodded. "Right, let's get you in the car. I don't want you staying here tonight. We'll ring the police, but I doubt they'll do anything 'til the morning now." I wanted to protest, to assert my independence, to not be that pathetic woman who can't cope alone. Until I remembered that I was shit-scared of staying here alone, because someone was clearly on the psycho-train tonight and directing it all at me.

"Ok," I said, my dry mouth making the words sound strange and unfamiliar to me. "But I'm staying in the spare room, no funny business." At this he broke into a smile, and I was relieved to see he was still there and ok underneath.

"You sure Marns? I reckon we could talk Addy into it if you're game?" I punched him playfully and got into the passenger seat of his car. Steve gave me one last smile before pulling smoothly away, dialling 101, the non-emergency police line, on his car phone as he did.

Her chubby fists were sliding along the steamed up glass, the condensation making it difficult for her to hit it properly. Beside her the other girl watched in silence, her thumb firmly in her mouth as she sucked away and tried to make sense of what was going on.

She could see more clearly now, the pool of blood spreading ever further outwards, like the ripples when you threw a stone. There were lots of people milling around, but the crowd had been pushed back, and there was one man who kept pressing something strange against her lips.

"Get off her! Help her!" The little girl screamed as she banged again and again, the glass refusing to give way whilst every single person watching the scene unfold steadfastly ignored her, too busy gawping at the spectacle of the woman dying in front of them to care about two little girls trapped in the car.

My breathing was abruptly cut off as someone pushed vigorously on my windpipe. My eyes shot open in panic; the dream still very much present in my mind, and I started to fight them off.

"Mummy!" cried Ted gleefully, his weight shifting from where he was sitting on my throat so that he could throw his arms around me tightly. I panted, enjoying the sensation of air flowing freely to my brain again.

"Hello Teddy!" I said, hugging him tightly back.

"Why're you here, Mummy?" Ted sat back on his heels and looked thoughtfully at me. He was too young to remember living with both of us and took it in his stride that he had two houses and two sets of parents. Even with Steve not being her biological dad, Rose had been the one who had struggled most with the divorce.

"Oh, I just wanted to see you!" I lied, unwilling to tell him the truth, which was that someone was targeting our house. The lie brought back to the forefront what had happened last night, and uneasiness rose with a vengeance. I needed to get the window sorted before the kids came home, I realised. "Where's Daddy, is he awake yet?" Teddy shook his head, his thumb firmly wedged into his mouth. Out of habit, I pulled the offending digit gently out again. He and I had Battle Royale's over it daily. Today he didn't really react, apart from to give me a withering look and stick it back in. I was too on edge to argue.

"Addy downstairs," he offered through a full mouth

"Oh great. Let's go down and see her, shall we? Have you had breakfast Teddy Bear?" My son nodded.

"Coco pops. Can I have more though?" I laughed. He would eat twenty-four-seven if I let him; people kept telling me it was a boy thing.

"Ok, lead the way!" I said, whipping the cover off of me and wedging my feet into the spare slippers that Addy had obviously gotten out for me, along with the pyjamas I was wearing. She was an absolute treasure, and much better at the wife thing than I'd ever been.

I entered the kitchen after Teddy, who was prancing just ahead of me like a mini pied piper. Sitting at the square farmhouse-style table in the middle of the room was Addy, her long dark hair chucked on top of her head in a messy bun, and her beautifully slender fingers wrapped round a steaming mug. The table was heavily laid with pastries, toast, spreads, cereals, and fruit. You name it, Addy had it. It was like looking at a magazine shoot, and feeling suddenly awkward, I hung back in the doorway. But she had looked up, alerted by the noise we were making, and smiled serenely in my direction while expertly grabbing the box of coco pops from Teddy and pouring them for him before they went all over the floor.

"Morning Marnie, how did you sleep? Sit down. Can I pour you a coffee?" I smiled back gratefully and sunk onto one of the wooden benches that ran along either side of the table.

"That would be lovely, thanks Addy. I slept ok, considering. Thank you so much for letting me stay. I'm sorry I got Steve out in the middle of the night." I felt the need to apologise to her, his actual wife, for using her husband as my 'in case of emergency'. She glanced at me from the coffee pot and shook her head.

"Don't be silly! We're happy to help, you know that. What happened? Steve only said you'd had a break in. Was anything taken?" It was my turn to shake my head as I thought about how much to tell her. Did she know about mum? Maybe Steve had mentioned it. Swallowing, and checking that Teddy's eyes were glued to the flickering screen in the corner of the room, I whispered in reply.

"No nothing was taken, but my kitchen window was smashed by a fridge magnet." Addy looked bemused so I carried on. "I got a delivery last night, and it was this fridge magnet in the shape of a London tube sign. It had Wimbledon written on it." I paused and searched her face for any sign of comprehension. She still looked confused; Steve had obviously not filled her in on my history. I sighed.

"It's a long story, but when I was eight my mum was killed outside Wimbledon tube station. There was an argument, and she was stabbed. I was there; I saw the whole thing from our car." Now I'd shocked poor Addy, who for the first time since I'd known her, looked unsure about how to respond.

"Oh my God. Marnie I'm so sorry, that's horrendous!" I nodded but answered matter-of-factly.

"Yes, it was awful, but it was a long time ago now. The worrying thing is that someone obviously wanted to remind me of it for some reason and sent the magnet. I chucked it in the outside bin and went to the pub. When I came back, someone had thrown it through my kitchen window. I think that's why Steve insisted I didn't stay there. I really hope you don't mind." Addy looked outraged at the thought.

"Of *course* I don't mind! You can stay as long as you want, and Ted and Rose too, obviously!"

"No, it's ok. I'll get the glass replaced today, and we'll be fine. It was probably just a coincidence anyway; just kids, who found the easiest thing to smash a window with." I didn't believe that, and neither would she, but what was I supposed to do? I couldn't move my family in with my ex-husband and his wife, could I? I supposed I could ask Lula to stay with her, Rashid, and Ruben, but that didn't sit quite right either.

"The police are going to come round there later this morning, so I'd better get a wriggle on actually, it'll take me half an hour to walk home." Addy looked scathing.

"Don't be stupid, me or Steve will drop you home. We'll drop Teddy later too, it'll save you coming out if you're still trying to sort it."

"Thanks," I said gratefully. I wasn't relishing the thought of walking all the way across town in my high heeled boots and a full face of smudged make up on a Sunday morning. It screamed 'stop out,' and I had enough going on without the entire town talking about who I was sleeping with now.

By the time Addy had force-fed me a couple of pain-au-chocolat's Steve was up and insisted on driving me home so that he could check for himself that the house was empty. Too hungover to argue that I could look after myself I let him do what he needed to, and once he'd left, I rung a glazier, swallowed the quoted astronomical callout fee, and ran a deep and boiling bath. To make things even better, I realised I still needed to get to the nursing home before the kids were back. I glanced at the kitchen clock; it was already quarter to two. Rosie hadn't rung my mobile, but I worried that she'd tried our house phone this morning and I hadn't been here to answer it. I'd already rung Sarah's house phone and her and Dan's mobiles, to no reply. Vainly I hoped that this meant they were all having a nice day out and were too busy to talk to me, but I wasn't holding my breath. I decided to ring Lula. If she was going to see Dad today, then maybe I could skip. While I waited for her to answer, I smiled a little at the thought of sending a stand-in like we had joked about yesterday.

"Hi Lula, listen, are you going to see Dad today? Oh bugger. Ok, no worries. No, it's fine I'll go. I've just had a busy morning and as the kids will be back soon, I thought...no honestly it's fine! Ok, love you, bye." They were already at the coast for the day. Picking up the dustpan to empty it, I spoke to the silent stranger in my kitchen.

"Hi, sorry to interrupt you." Briefly I wondered why all British people did this, starting every sentence with an apology. "I was just wondering how long you think you'll be? It's just I need to see my dad; he's in a nursing home because...erm, so how long?" I caught myself just in time. That was another talent of mine; over-explaining to people who couldn't have cared less.

"Five minutes love, and I'll be done," he replied. "Don't suppose there's a cuppa going though, is there?" I'd already made him one when he arrived twenty minutes ago, but immediately felt rude.

"Oh sorry, of course! Tea? Coffee? Biscuits?" I busied myself at the kettle, mentally berating myself over my need to please, instead of just telling him that if he just hurried up, he could have his next cuppa in the comfort of his own home.

I was fuming as I swept up the broken glass once the glazier had gone. Not only had it cost me a small fortune to get it fixed on a Sunday, but the police had finally got back to me and been completely and utterly uninterested in the whole thing. I asked why they hadn't attended last night, but apparently unless the suspect is actually on-site and I was calling about a break-in in progress, they don't have the staff to attend every callout in person. Instead, I needed to fill in a form online that would give me a crime number for insurance. "Blame the government cuts," I was told. Even after I'd spelt out the connection of the magnet to Mum's death, the officer brushed it aside, saying that there was nothing illegal in sending a present. And to make matters one hundred times worse, my gorgeous bath was now sitting untouched and freezing cold just up the stairs.

It was over thirty minutes later that I was pulling into the nursing home car park hungover and hating responsibilities to other people. I began making slow loops around, looking for an empty space. Typically for Sunday it was full; it seemed to be the one day of the week where everyone remembers they've got an old person. After five minutes of aimlessly driving around, I was tempted to simply leave. I needed a McDonald's cheeseburger, and Dad really didn't know much about anything anymore; he wouldn't know or care if I was there or not. Only the fact that his carers would know that no one had turned up made me persevere. Glancing at the car clock, I realised I had exactly half an hour before I needed to leave again to pick Rose up, thanks to the slow glazier. It might have taken him five minutes to finish the work, but he then proceeded to stand chatting and eating all my biscuits for another twenty.

I was clearly out of luck today though, and despite the impending bad daughter guilt, I was just preparing to accelerate out of the carpark when someone began to reverse out right before I passed them. Adrenaline kicked in and I indicated, making sure the other car park crawlers knew that I was staking my claim, with the universal car park politics and rules now protecting me from being undercut. I jogged through the building after signing in and found Dad sitting in a big armchair in his room.

"Hi Dad," I said breezily, kissing his cheek and sitting down next to him to take his hand in mine. His skin was papery under my touch, and he looked vacantly at me for a long while before speaking.

"Judy?" he said, slurring a little. The pang of hurt when he didn't recognise me never went away.

"No Dad, it's Marnie," I replied gently. "I'm your daughter. Don't worry though. It's hard to remember everyone." I forced myself to grin at him. "Ooh, nice flowers!" I said, changing the subject and pointing towards the vase filled with purples, blues, and yellows on his small coffee table.

"Judy," Dad said again, seeming set on the confirmation.

"Marnie," I said again while squeezing his hand gently. Blinking rapidly, I managed to dispel the tears before they started. There were only so many times you could take being called your dead mum's name. Before I had a chance to desperately scramble for another topic, one of the nurse's popped his head in.

"Hi Marnie, how are you today?" It was Devon, Dad's favourite, and mine too. Quite often recently he'd been the only one who could calm Dad down. He came fully into the room with some clean sheets, obviously about to change the bed. "Hi George," he said, leaning down and making eye contact with him. "I need to change your bed. How about you go and take this lovely young lady of yours for a coffee in the social room? I hear," he dropped to a whisper, "that there's even *cake*." Devon's eyes twinkled and Dad smiled back at him, a rough noise that I identified as a laugh coming from his throat. As he stood up, he gently pulled Dad to his feet too, their arms linked so that he could support him. I hurried to the other side. "You want some help getting him down there?" Devon asked and I shook my head.

"No it's fine, I can manage." We were just shuffling slowly out of the door when my conversation with Lula popped into my mind. "Hey Devon." He turned round from the bed to look at me. "I've heard Dad's been having another visitor. Do you know who she is? I wondered if the flowers were from her." I gestured to the table, and Devon looked puzzled but answered easily.

"No sorry. I've only seen you with George recently. Are you sure it wasn't someone visiting someone else? Just someone who happened to speak to him? And I'm not sure about the flowers. Maybe you've got a secret admirer George, being the silver fox you are?" I laughed and nodded in understanding. That must be it. But then Lula said that they had thought it was another sister of ours. And there was still the flower question lingering. I opened my mouth to say this to Devon, but instead I shook my head and carried on walking with Dad. He hadn't seen whoever it was anyway. I'd just ask to see the sign in book at reception when I left instead.

FOUR

It was ten past four by the time I pulled up at Sarah's. Naturally I'd managed to get stuck behind a little old mini driving at fifteen miles per hour all the way from the nursing home, and the one-way streets through town meant I had no chance of overtaking. Instead I passed the time banging my hands on the steering wheel, and swearing under my breath about revoking people's licences once they got old.

I'd also found it really hard to concentrate on anything in the present on the drive; seeing Dad did that to me. All I could think about was him; this bull of a man who had seemed so physically remote to my life before Mum died, and then after she went, someone who lived in the same house as me but was never there emotionally or mentally again. I felt really angry at him in my teenage years, desperate for a tether to normality and feeling like he never provided it. But once Rose was born and I had experienced firsthand how difficult parenthood was, I began to understand just how much of a lethal blow losing Mum must have been. To suddenly be in sole charge of two little girls, neither of whom you'd ever spent much alone time with, must have been terrifying. And now, seeing him as nothing but a shell of who he used to be felt even more unfair. For someone to lose their whole concept of life once, only to rebuild it in the only way he knew how to, it felt particularly cruel of fate to deal him dementia.

Finally entering Sarah's estate, I pulled up in a space directly outside her house and could see my little girl sitting on the kitchen windowsill and looking out. Waving as I got out, I hurried towards the back door. It was unlocked as usual, and I swung it open at just the same moment that Rose pulled it from the other side. She flew into my arms and squeezed my neck in a tight cuddle.

"Hi baby," I said, kissing the top of her head. She pulled away in childish disgust.

"Muuum," she moaned. "Don't call me that!" I grinned, glad that she was clearly her normal self. Just then, Sarah came bustling through from the living room.

"Hi Marnie love, I didn't hear you come in." She came over, also giving me a cuddle, I understood that I was forgiven for yesterday's lack of discretion. "All ok?" She asked, searching my face. That was the trouble with Sarah. She had been the closest thing to a mother throughout my teenage years when I spent all of my time in this house, and so she knew me better than most. I nodded, keen to keep the break-in from Rose.

"Yes everything's fine. Sorry I'm a bit late, the traffic from the nursing home was a nightmare." I grimaced and Sarah immediately looked sympathetic.

"How's your dad?" She asked, moving over to switch the kettle on. It was tradition that every other Sunday I would stay for a coffee and catch up with her. I resisted the urge to look at my watch, eager now to be back in my own house with both kids. I wasn't altogether happy with the fact that I had been out all afternoon, and I was secretly dreading what I was going to find when I finally got home.

"He's ok. Well, the same as he always is nowadays anyway. They say he's not distressed or in pain or anything though, so that's good." My eyes filled a little. "That's the most important thing, isn't it? I'd hate it if he knew what was happening to him. He'd be so scared." Sarah left the mugs for a second and came to give me another squeeze.

"Yes that's the main thing," she said. "It's a cruel disease, and I know it's been hard on you, love. But you're doing as much as you can for him, now you're back." She turned from me again. "Right. Miss Rosie, how about we get out some of the biscuits we made?" She changed the subject briskly, at the same time reminding me that Rose was listening to everything I said about her Granddad. My daughter grinned and ran over to the 'treat' cupboard.

"I decorated them mummy," she said proudly as she handed me a dubiously green and slightly burnt biscuit.

"Lovely!" I said with true enthusiasm. I loved it when the kids made me stuff, even if it was going to give me a bad stomach later. We took the mugs and biscuits through to the living room, where, not totally surprisingly, Dan was curled up on the sofa and fast asleep.

"He was exhausted from work," Sarah said warningly, obviously worried I would start an argument. She didn't need to worry. It broke my heart that he didn't care about Rose like I did but, while she worshipped him, I would never stop trying to encourage the relationship between the two. Instead I just nodded and perched on one of the armchairs, Rose snaking about my back. Trying to lighten the mood, I told Sarah about the 'new sister' I appeared to have. As I did, I remembered that I hadn't checked the signing in book, being in too much of a rush to get the kids. Sarah and Rose laughed at my efforts to make it seem funny.

"Imagine there being more of you running around!" she said.

"I know, imagine another Aunty!" I joined in, widening my eyes comically at Rose, who paused before she giggled, clearly trying to work out what I meant. My sister and my daughter got on like a house on fire, but sometimes Lula was a little too pally for my liking and they referred to one another as 'besties'; they had all these in-jokes that I wasn't party to, and sad as it was, sometimes it made me feel left out. I finished my coffee while Rose told us both a ridiculous story about something that happened at the park. Apparently Dan's nineteen year old sister, Sophie, had turned up with the latest boyfriend in tow. Rose, a tough customer to impress at the best of times, was describing him. She took after my own sister rather than me personality wise; they were both dramatic but hilarious. As she eventually came to the end of the anecdote and took a breath, I jumped on the opportunity.

"Come on Rosie, we need to go and get Teddy bear." Rose rolled her eyes but got to her feet, trying not to show her eagerness to see her little brother.

"Mum, your nicknames are *ridiculous*. Ted won't want to be called Teddy bear forever you know!" With that she raced out of the room to grab her stuff. Sarah looked happily after her.

"Oh, love her! I really do enjoy having her around, you know Marnie. I'd hate it if we didn't get to see her as much as we do now." Sarah was clearly skirting around the big sleeping elephant in the room, who at that moment chose to give a big grunt and pull the blanket up further. I resisted the urge to copy my daughter and roll my eyes.

"I know you do, Sarah, and Rose loves coming here. But it would be even better if she was able to spend more time with Dan, that's all." Sarah's faced clouded and I knew she was annoyed, but quite frankly, what else did she expect? I glanced at the door, desperate for Rose to make an appearance. Finally, we heard her footsteps thundering down the stairs. *Thank you.* I stood up. "Ok, well thanks for the coffee. Rose," I addressed my daughter as she came through the doorway. "Give Nanna a kiss and say thank you for having you." As Rose obeyed my order Sarah glared at me as she spoke.

"He's just not as used to it as he will be, what with you running away with her and everything. Still. You're here now I suppose. Say goodbye to your dad, Rosie love." Rose released her grandparent and, realising Daniel was still fast asleep in a heap on the sofa, shot me a confused look. Sarah intercepted it and raised her voice. "Danny! Rose's going now; she wants to give you a kiss goodbye." No answer from the father of my firstborn. "Daniel!" His mother said sharply, this time accompanying it with a shake. He groaned and pulled the blanket further over his head. Sarah ripped it off. Rose glanced at me again, this time trying to stop herself from laughing. I smiled conspiratorially and jerked my head in Dan's direction to encourage her to get on with it. She crossed over and climbed onto the heap of a dad, burrowing until she found his face.

"Bye Daddy," she said, following it up with a kiss on his cheek. Daniel opened an eye blearily.

"Oh! Bye Rose. Why are you going so early?"

"She's not," I answered curtly before anyone else could, fed up all at once with his substandard parenting. "It's half past four Dan." Now he sat up, so quickly that Rose slipped down into his lap.

"Marnie! I didn't know you were here. Sorry about this," he gestured to the blanket whilst wiping a bit of dribble off his lip. What did I *ever* find attractive about him? "I've just been flat out at work; did Mum tell you?" I found it hard to smile and nod at this blatant lie, but I'd always tried to be civil in front of Rose.

"Yeah, she did." I had a sudden thought. "So, when shall we start the support payments from again then? Do you need me to sort it out, or will your boss do it?" Daniel flushed. Ha, I thought. Serves him right, if he's going to plead exhaustion from all his hard work then he can start paying for his daughter. Sarah glared at me and I turned, suddenly fed up with the pair of them. "C'mon Rose, let's go and get Ted." Rose bounced along ahead of me to the kitchen door, calling a quick "bye" over her shoulder. Sarah came to see us out and just before I left, grabbed my shoulder to stop me.

"He will start paying you," she said in an urgent whisper, obviously not wanting Rose to hear. "Just give him a chance please, Marnie. He can't be expected to hand over everything he earns to you straightaway." I gave her a stony stare, not trusting myself to answer. Never mind that in the over six years that we'd been split up, he'd probably paid a couple of hundred pounds in total towards her upbringing. I was clearly not to ask for what was rightfully Rosie's, as the golden boy must never be upset.

"Bye Sarah," I said, neither of us moving in for our customary hug. I sighed and turned away. I was halfway down the path behind Rose when I felt an arm around my shoulders. It was Sarah of course, enveloping me in a cuddle. I breathed in deeply, relieved even though I didn't want to be. As much as I hated the way she was sometimes, I couldn't bare being at odds with her.

"Look let's not fall out," she said. "All I meant was that he will help you out as soon as he can, ok?" I nodded against her shoulder. She pulled away to look at me. "Don't keep our girl away from us if it's not right away though, will you?" Ah. The real reason for the hug.

"I've never not let you see Rose in all the years he hasn't paid," I said, stung. "Why would you think I'd start now?" Sarah smiled, relieved that I wouldn't stop the visits and clearly not listening to the second part of my comment.

"Well, great. I knew you wouldn't do that to Danny; you've always been a nice girl really. Have a good week and tell Rosie we'll see her on Tuesday, ok?" I nodded and turned on my heel, eager to get away. Rose was waiting impatiently in the front seat, already strapped in and ready to go. I climbed in heavily, suddenly wearied by my interlude with Sarah. Turning the key in the ignition, I pasted a smile on my face and turned to my daughter.

"So? How was it? What did you and Daddy do today?" She gave me such a look of understanding that it made me want to cry, and I turned to concentrate on the road rather than let her see.

"It was ok. Me and Daddy went to the café for breakfast, and I had sausages and beans. Then I wanted to stop in the park on the way back, so he said yes. But then he was really, really tired when we got home 'cos he's been working so hard, so me and Nanna made the biscuits." God, she reminded me of her grandparent, excusing his faults already.

"I'm glad you had a good time," I said in a measuredly even voice. There was no point in pointing out the obvious flaws in her big weekend with Daddy; namely that he'd barely spent any time with her. Rose was fierce in her defence of Daniel, and to be fair to her, I remembered from our younger years that when he was on form there was no one more fun to be around. And after all, it was clear to anyone who met him he simply hadn't grown out of being a teenager yet.

We pulled up at Steve's and Rose rolled her eyes at Teddy's beaming face and frantic waving in the front window. He disappeared, obviously to come to the door, and Rose shot out of the car. I smiled as she ran to scoop her little brother up on the doorstep. She behaved as if he was such an inconvenience to her, but they really did miss each other on their separate weekends; yet another reason to feel guilty for my life choices. Addy appeared in the doorway behind my two kids, smiling at me welcomingly.

"All ok, Marnie?" She said lightly. That's what I loved about her; she knew instinctively not to put any emphasis on her question, knowing that little ears were listening to every word.

"Yep, all good thanks Addy. No Steve?" I peered around her, expecting my ex-husband to reveal himself.

"No, he's popped out to fill my car up before I get in it tomorrow morning and end up running late."

"He's such a sweetheart, isn't he? Why did I ever let him go?" I joked, grinning at Steve's new wife.

"Lucky for me that you did," she replied, smiling back companionably. "Right." She knelt down to scoop both of my children into her arms and give them a hug. "Be good for Mummy, you two!" She planted a kiss on each child's forehead, laughing as Ted rubbed his energetically off. "See you Wednesday, Teddy Bear! Bye Rosie!"

Pulling up at home with my by-now-tired children, I was relieved to see that our house looked just the same as it ever did.

"Out we get then guys. Rosie, straight in the kitchen to do your homework please."

"Muuum," my seven-year-old groaned, already with a very teenage mentality about these things.

"Don't mum me," I replied. "I told you to do it Friday after school so that it was out of the way. Maybe next week you'll listen to me." I chivvied her along gently with my foot whilst unstrapping Ted. Rose groaned and started up the short path to the front door. Joining her with a deflated Ted in my arms, I unlocked the door with difficulty, and she went to push it open. It caught on an envelope lying on the mat. Rose picked it up and glanced at the front before handing it to me.

"This one's for you, Mum," she said, as if either she or Ted received mail on a regular basis. I rolled my eyes playfully at her.

"No way!" I said, making her giggle as I attempted to shift her brother, who was point blank refusing to let go of my neck, so that I could take it. As Rose sauntered off, I raced through to the living room to dump Ted on the sofa before my arms completely dropped off. He grabbed the remote and put some cartoons on, oblivious now to my leaving.

Following in Rose's wake, I slid my finger under the corner of the envelope. The paper ripped apart too easily and something chunky fell out. I knew what it was before I even picked it up off the ground. Before I had a chance, Rose was beside me, her hand outstretched to get it.

"Don't!" I shouted, knocking her hand away. She flinched at the suddenness of both my movement and my voice, looking worriedly at me. My fingers closed about the cold, hate-filled object and I quickly bundled her into my side.

"Sorry babe," I said, giving her a quick hug before releasing her. "I thought it was sharp.

"What is it?" She asked, reasonably expecting me to show her.

"Nothing," I replied, clamming up. The kids didn't know about Wimbledon. "It's rubbish. Is your homework done? No? Why not? Get on with it!" Rose looked hurt at my abrupt tone and turned back towards the dining room table without a word, immediately making me feel guilty.

In a bad mood now, I wrenched the back door open, about to chuck both the magnet and envelope in the wheely bin once again when I realised there was a note in there. For a moment I was still tempted to throw them away without further investigation when my curiosity overcame me. Unfolding it warily, I quickly scanned the typewritten words.

Marnie,

Please don't throw my present away again, I didn't want to have to break your window. I think you should put it on your fridge to remind you of her. Memories are important you know. Does Lula remember what happened like you do? Take care of yourself, won't you?

That was it. Shivers raced up and down my spine and I glanced through the gaping opening of the side door into the quickly darkening evening, suddenly sure someone was out there. Even as I checked for a postmark, I already knew that it would have been hand delivered. What self-respecting psychopath relies on Royal Mail to deliver their threatening letters on a Sunday, after all? I slammed the door and turned the key, fumbling a little in my eagerness to get it secure.

Resolving to ring the police again I turned, suddenly remembering Rosie slogging through adverbs at the kitchen table. I was nervously aware that there was a lot of glass in this room, a lot of opportunities for watching.

"You've done enough Rosie," I trilled, my nerves making my voice high pitched and strange sounding. She stared up at me nonplussed, her pen poised over only the second question on the worksheet. "Come on," I continued, almost lifting her out of her seat in my eagerness to get her hidden. "Go and watch TV with Teddy. I'll explain to Mrs Davies in the morning." I didn't need to ask my daughter twice. With a last incredulous look at me, she sprinted from the room, and I heard shrieks of delight as her and Teddy greeted one another, probably by bundling.

Quickly double checking that the door handles were locked, I too left the danger of the kitchen and closed the door behind me before perching on the stairs with my mobile in my hand. I had just dialled 101 when the note registered properly. *Does Lula remember like you do?* What did that even mean? Changing my mind I rang my little sister instead, impatiently picking at the edge of the carpet as I waited.

"Hi Marnie, you ok?" It was Rashid, my brother-in-law. I smiled despite myself, calmed by his voice as soon as I heard it. He had that rare quality of making you feel safe as soon as he was in your vicinity. Lots of people were puzzled by their relationship when they first met Lula and Rashid. With her exuberant personality and loud voice, on the face of it they seemed polar opposites, never destined to be together. I knew better though; he was Lula's safety, her mooring when she became too wild for her own good.

"Hi Rashid, I'm good thanks, are you ok?" He replied that he was and began to tell me a story about Ruben at the park. Normally I would sit back and soak up any story told in his voice, allowing the calm and warmth to wash over me. Today however, I needed answers.

"Rashid I'm sorry but is Lula there by any chance? It's just I really need to speak to her." A brief silence was immediately filled with his rushed apologies, making me feel bad again. "No, no, don't say sorry, I'm the one who's being rude! I just need a quick word. It's about Mum." I heard him shout for Lula, listening to her running down the stairs and snatching the phone up breathlessly.

"Marnie? What's wrong?" I took a deep breath, urging the panic to leave my voice so as not to worry her, forever the protective big sister.

"Oh nothing's wrong! Sorry. I didn't mean to be rude to Rashid, can you apologise for me?" I heard Lula's derisive snort.

"Don't be silly, Marns, he's fine. He said it was about Mum though. What's up?" Mum was the only topic where Lula's normally loud, opinionated tone would grow soft and sensitive.

"Honestly nothing's wrong. It's just, well...look, have you received a weird package recently? Like a fridge magnet? Or something else?"

"Erm no, don't think so. Babe, have we received a fridge magnet in the post?" I heard her asking Rashid too. "He says no. Why, what's going on? I thought this was about Mum?"

"It's not, not really," I said, keen to downplay the strangeness. "Just, yesterday after I got home from seeing you, I had a package delivered. It had a fridge magnet inside." I paused and was met with dumbfounded silence until…

"So?" Lula, never one for waiting around, prompted me.

"It was in the shape of the tube station sign. It said Wimbledon on the front." I waited, but again was met with uncharacteristic silence. "Lula?" I began to panic that she'd hung up on me. "Hello?"

"I'm still here," she eventually said, now speaking in hushed tones. "Wimbledon? You're sure?"

"Well of course I'm bloody sure!" I snapped. "Sorry," I sighed after a beat. "It's shaken me up a bit, that's all. So you didn't get one?"

"No," Lula replied stonily. She always hated to be spoken to in anything other than a loving tone. Again, why her and Rashid worked so well.

"Lula, I said I was sorry. Lula? Forgive me?" My voice took on the ingratiating tone it always did when I wanted her forgiveness; I couldn't bear to be at outs with her. My much-indulged little sister gave a martyred sigh.

"It's ok, Marns. But I didn't get one though. Why would you get sent one and not me? Is it just because you're older do you think?" Lula was already speaking in an injured voice, the chip on her shoulder at being the younger and less-remembered sister in Mum's murder as ever just under the surface. Unusually I was struggling to keep my cool with her today. I must have been panicking more than I thought.

"I don't know," I replied, matching her clipped tones. "Surely it doesn't matter right now. The point is that it's a bit weird, don't you think?" I didn't tell her about the broken window or the letter; I didn't know why but suddenly I didn't want to talk to her anymore.

"Dunno," she responded huffily. "Probably just one of the usual weirdos, isn't it? Remember them from when we were kids? They were like 'fans' of the crime, weren't they? Harmless though." It was my turn to get annoyed now.

"I wouldn't say harmless, Lula, no. Look don't worry about it. Like you say it'll be nothing. Make sure you go and see dad this week, yeah? Love you, bye." I didn't wait for a reply before I ended the call. Sitting stewing for a moment, it was a surprise to see Rose and Ted standing in front of me looking curious.

"Who was that?" Rose asked uncertainly; clearly my abrupt hanging up was throwing her off. When I didn't reply, she looked annoyed instead. "Was it Martha? Why didn't you let us talk to her?" I decided to let them think Martha had been on the phone; they found her hilarious but harmless and I didn't want to get into questions about why I'd been arguing with Lula on the phone.

"I just had to check something quickly, and Aaron was in the bath, so she had to go. Speaking of which," I stood and scooped Teddy up, who shrieked with delight. "We'd better get you two mucky pups clean for school tomorrow. Come on!" I chucked Ted onto my back and began to race up the stairs, Rosie following and laughing in my wake. Already thoughts of calling the police were receding. It would be the same as last night, I reasoned. No one was hurting me, were they? And Lula was probably right anyway, it would be one of the 'fans' who'd managed to track me down again.

FIVE

After a restless night's sleep I went through the motions of Monday morning, dropping Rosie to school and Ted to nursery before heading over to the nursing home. As an ambulance driver I tended to do shift work, a huge problem when you were a single parent. Luckily for me, the scheduler at our station was a parent himself and was sympathetic to my plight, giving me more or less the same hours week in, week out, and I was off until Tuesday night.

As I pulled into a space in the care home car park and got out, I noticed a group of patients being both lead on foot and pushed in wheelchairs over the tarmac towards the gardens. The Home was an old manor house, and one of the main reasons Lula and I had chosen it for Dad was the gorgeous outdoor space, with landscaped gardens and even a lake to be found on site. We'd naively imagined that Dad, being a keen walker and all-around nature lover, would be able to enjoy his last years soaking up the surroundings on his daily strolls. Unluckily for him, the disease had gathered almost unprecedented speed, and mercilessly swept his mobility along with it.

Shaking my head, I strode towards the entrance. It really annoyed me that the planners for this place had been short sighted enough not to amend the driveway to the carpark, which crossed between the house itself and its grounds, so that any patient would need to be accompanied by a carer to safely reach the gardens. I hurried up the stone steps to avoid the busy accessibility ramp and was signing myself in just as Devon came past, pushing a wheelchair with an old man in it.

"Hi Marnie," he greeted me sunnily. "I've just been in to get George up; he was awake bright and early this morning. He's in a really good mood!" He waved as he and the gentleman moved smoothly off out of the door and down the ramp to the side of the steps, to go and join the others. I smiled after them. Devon was now the main reason that Lula and I wouldn't move Dad from here, despite the other things that might annoy us. He had the most incredible way with the patients, and especially Dad, who despite being in a complete fantasy world nowadays actually seemed to respond more to the young carer than he had to us in years. Signing my name in the Visitors book reminded me about Dad's mysterious friend.

"Excuse me," I said to the receptionist, who had left me to it after a brief glance of recognition of me when I entered. Now she looked up enquiringly. "Are you able to let me know who my father's visitors are? Like a list of names?" She looked a little confused. Clearly it wasn't a question asked often.

"Yeah, sure. We keep a database of visitors and who they visited on here. What's your father's name?"

"George South," I said, waiting for the recognition. There wasn't even a flicker, and I was slightly impressed; even in this small town our notoriety was beginning to fade. The woman clicked a few buttons and then read quickly down the short list.

"Right, so these are kept in historic date order, and looks like George has had five different ones since he's been with us." I nodded silently, willing her to carry on. "Marnie South, Steven Houghton, Rudi Evans, Paul Scunthorpe." Here she stopped talking and I began to get impatient; was she working on her dramatic timing or something? That was four by my count; me and my ex-husband, and two of dad's old friends who were still compos mentis.

"What about my sister and her husband? Tallulah and Rashid Singh?" She glanced down again at her screen and shook her head.

"Not on the list, sorry. Maybe they forgot to sign in?" I raised my eyes to the heavens for a moment. Sounded about right.

"Ok, what about the fifth name?" I asked, forcing myself to stay polite through gritted teeth.

"Erm...oh yeah, sorry, she was right down at the bottom, obviously hasn't been coming long. Judy South." I froze, feeling my face turn bright red and hot.

"Sorry?" I whispered.

"Judy South," she repeated, beginning to look at me with a little concern. "Are you ok? You look a bit flushed."

"I'm fine," I said hoarsely, backing away a little. "I'll just go and see my dad now. Thanks." As I walked off down the corridor towards Dad's room, I felt shivery and weak. Judy South.

"Hi Dad," I said faux cheerily, entering his room after a swift knock to find him seated at his little coffee table and focused on the morning TV programme. He didn't show any sign of hearing my greeting. "Dad?" I said a little louder, touching his shoulder gently. Very slowly he turned to focus on me, even his reflexes dying a slow death in front of my eyes.

"Judy," he said, the corners of his mouth sliding upwards into a wonky smile. The pang I always got was doubled today and I felt a little nauseous as I stroked his arm and smiled back.

"Marnie, Dad. I'm Marnie, remember? Judy's dead." As I watched his face fall at my bald words, I felt hugely guilty. I wasn't normally as blunt as that, instead preferring to remind him who I was instead of who she no longer was. I touched his cheek gently to say sorry, and after a few seconds his smile was back.

"Judy," he confirmed, smiling beatifically at me. I sighed and picked up his wizened hand, placing it against my overly warm cheek and relishing, even now, in a parent's reassuring touch.

"Judy," I agreed, watching his eyes light up momentarily before the fires burned out once more.

I managed to draw out my visit with Dad for just over an hour, which is quite an achievement when the person you're talking to has absolutely no idea who you are, and instead thinks you're your dead mother. I told him all about what Rose and Teddy had been up to. I'd had to stop them coming to see Grandad after he forgot who Rose was and then got upset when she got upset. He listened politely to my drivel now though, nodding away and smiling when I did. At least his manners were still intact.

After getting into my car, I thought for a moment before reversing. My first instinct was to drive over to Lula's work and continue the conversation about the magnet. But last night's phone conversation still rankled, and I was unwilling to be told it was nothing to worry my silly little head about. Instead, I swung the car around and headed in the opposite direction, sure of someone who would be as keen as me to solve the mystery, and as worried about what was going on as I was too.

Crawling along the main thoroughfare of town, I tried to type a quick message of warning with one hand, while attempting to look like a diligent driver. It wasn't best practice for an NHS worker obviously, but it did save time doing these sorts of things in traffic. Risking a glance down, I checked what I had written before I sent it.

'I com to yr worl now'

Hmm, probably not my best efforts but possibly decode-able. Suddenly the traffic began to flow again, and I hastily pressed send and chucked the phone onto the passenger seat. It'd have to do. If not, I'd just be a surprise.

Pulling into the bland car park in front of the school, I was pleased to see that there was a space right at the front, and, as good as a golden ticket, it was not a disabled one. I parked my little golf in one seamless manoeuvre and got out, feeling triumphant. I loved it when that happened. The smallest of victories could brighten my day.

The reception area was as bright and airy as I remembered from when I used to visit frequently, and I strode up to the huge desk, waiting for someone to look at me. Both of the women were on the phone, although one glanced up. A moment too late I realised it was Hayley, fellow attendee of St Paul's from 2004-2009, and not one I ever got along with. Puzzling as to why anyone would give such a haughty bitch as her a job, I immediately adjusted my features into a stony countenance to match hers. I just couldn't resist being petty. She didn't look at me again until she finished the phone call.

"Marnie," she said, a statement of fact rather than a greeting.

"Hayley," I replied, mimicking her tone and even her hair flick. The other receptionist was clearly hurrying her conversation along to a conclusion while eying us interestedly, picking up on the sudden tension and keen to listen properly.

"How can I help you?" She asked haughtily, bound by her employment to be civil.

"I'd like to speak to Steve Houghton, please." She smiled sharkily at me.

"I'm afraid that's impossible. Mr Houghton is teaching at the moment and can't be interrupted. I can take a message for him?" She sat with her pen poised, as if I would really impart information to that cow.

"Could you please go along to his classroom and tell him his ex-wife needs to speak to him urgently? I'm sure he'll be glad of the interruption if he knows I'm here." Hayley looked as though she was about to refuse when the other receptionist intervened.

"Hayley, it's obviously important, you go along quickly now, and I'll hold the fort, ok? It's break time in a moment anyway." With no other choice, and with one last poisonous look at me, Hayley pressed the security button and let herself into the main school.

"Sorry about that," her colleague said. "She's new and trying to get to grips with all the little exceptions we make to the rules, if you know what I mean." I grinned. As childish as it was, her being on my side was making my soul a little happier.

"No problem at all, I know what it's like having to train new people." She smiled back before continuing with her work, while I idly began to read the framed newspaper clippings posted along the walls, articles on different things that the school had achieved. It was a few minutes before a flurry of activity behind the glass security doors caught my eye, and a steady trickle, then a stream, of huge teenage boys began to fill the corridor. It must already be break time, I realised.

"Marnie?" Lost in thought, I hadn't noticed Steve appear into the reception, striding straight up to me and giving me a hug before pulling away but still holding me and looking into my eyes. "What's wrong? Teddy? Rose?" I shook my head, keen to dispel him of his panic as soon as possible.

"No, no, they're fine. I just really needed to talk to you about something. In private," I added, raising my voice and widening my eyes in her direction to shame the clearly listening Hayley. Steve followed my eyes to the woman's reddening forehead.

"Let's go out the front," he decided, taking my hand lightly and towing me out. For once I wasn't concentrating enough to take it back with a lightly humoured reprimand. "So; what's going on?" He asked, now out of earshot of anyone. "Are you ok?"

"Not really," I admitted, proceeding to fill him in about the note, Dad's mystery visitor's name, and both Lula and Martha's dismissiveness. "I'm a little freaked out to be honest. The others seem to think it's not worth worrying about." Steve didn't speak for a moment, deep in thought.

"I think you're right to find it all weird. I mean I know there've been those strange people before who think they know your family. But from what you used to say, they were always well-wishers who thought they were helping. Whereas all of this together is a little threatening. Have you rung the police again and told them about the note?"

"No, Lula talked me out of it. Do you think I should then?" Steve nodded.

"I would. Listen," his head shot up as the bell went. "I've got to get back in there, I'm teaching again now. But ring the police, let them know. And tell the nursing home not to let anyone see your dad except you maybe? It's your right to decide if you don't think he's safe. Speak later," he was already running off. "Bye, love you."

"Your wife wouldn't like that," I called after him, trying to lighten the mood. It worked and he turned and grinned at me.

"She thinks it's funny," he said, with a final wave before disappearing into the building. Shaking my head but smiling properly now, I went back to my car.

I did take Steve's advice and rang the police but got the impression that they thought I was time wasting. They promised to log it, but whatever way you looked at it, posting a note or having the same name as someone's dead parent didn't constitute a crime. Very helpfully though, they suggested that I invest in some CCTV. They hung up on me right about the point I asked who was going to fund my new security measures, what with being a single mother on health worker wages.

I grumpily stalked about the house putting washing away and attempting to tidy up enough so that it didn't quite resemble a hovel. By school pick up it was back to looking semi-decent - just in time for the kids to come home and wreck it again. The phone rang just as I was about to leave.

"Hello?" Nothing. "Hello?" I tried again, cradling the handset between my shoulder and ear as I attempted to fold yet another load of sheets. I was about to hang up when I heard something on the end, some sort of rushing noise. Stopping the folding, I used my hand to press the phone to my ear. It was heavy breathing. Jesus, I thought, as prickles of panic began running up and down my spine, this was straight out of stalkers 101. "Look, whoever you are, you need to leave me alone, ok? I don't want any trouble." I was just about to hang up when faintly I heard;

"Marnie? Marnie, love?" In an instant I recognised the voice.

"Sarah?" My pulse began to drop back down to its base rate. "What's happened? Why are you so out of breath? Are you ok?"

"I'm fine, just been getting the washing in, it's about to rain. Got the kids yet?" A bit flabbergasted at the banality of the conversation when I'd been expecting a psycho, it took me a moment to reply.

"Erm, no, I need to leave now actually," I replied, glancing at my watch.

"Ok love, can you tell Rosie I'll ring her when she's back? I've got a surprise for her."

"Oh. Yeah sure. Speak to you later then."

"Bye, love. Take care of yourself, won't you?" It wasn't until I'd pulled up at school that her last phrase resonated in my brain. It was the same as the note. I turned off the engine and grabbed my hoodless fluffy coat that would do nothing to protect against the rain that Sarah had prophesied, before laughing under my breath. Imagining Sarah as a crazed stalker would be like thinking Dan was going to suddenly become father of the year; on the scale of likely to unlikely it dropped straight off the end.

I joined the gaggle of parents waiting for the gates to open and peered around for a familiar face to talk to, preferably one that had been organised enough to bring an umbrella. As I scanned the crowd a voice began shouting.

"Marnie! Marnie, over here!" Martha was standing with a group of reception mums I knew were your typical PTFA types; career women who no longer had to work, instead pouring all of their unspent energy and time into school fundraisers and governors' meetings. They weren't my kind of people; they made me feel inferior and young just by their presence. However they all had umbrellas and dry hair, so I swallowed my discomfort and headed over to join them. Martha caught me in a hug more akin to a rugby tackle and drew me under shelter. "Girls, this is Marnie. She was my best friend at school, how funny that we've both ended up back here! She's got Rose in year three and Teddy at the nursery." I mumbled a 'hi' and smiled at the nearest woman, who returned the greeting while the others glanced smiles in my direction before carrying on their conversation. Martha moved her head closer to mine. "So, how are things? Did you manage to find out who sent you the package? I'm telling you, I'd be so freaked out if it was me!" Martha was never one to regulate her volume, and I could tell by the small stillness of the woman closest to me that she was listening.

"No, I've chucked it away," I replied, not wanting to divulge any detail in front of strangers. In the hectic aftermath of Saturday night, I realised I hadn't even filled Martha in on the broken window or Dad's mysterious visitor. "I'll ring you later," I continued, hoping she got the message. She grabbed my hand and squeezed it lightly to show she understood.

"Ok," she said, before turning to the group at large. "So have we decided on a DJ for the disco next month?" She asked, igniting a passionate debate about the cost implications of using a proper DJ versus one of the parents making a playlist. I listened half-heartedly for the next few minutes, wondering at the vigour some people had, until finally the scraping of metal on metal signalled it was time to move.

SIX

I was busily shovelling spaghetti bolognaise down everyone's throats before Rosie had Brownies when the house phone rang again.

"Don't!" I shouted as Rose went to answer it, basically knocking her hand away in my effort to snatch it up.

"*Chill*, Mum," she said, in such a perfect imitation of the way Dan used to speak to me that it made me feel sixteen. I snatched it to my ear.

"Hello?" I made myself sound confident; a single-mother-force to be reckoned with. There was silence the other end, but this time I was prepared for it. "Sarah? Is that you?" Suddenly the dialling tone was ringing insistently in my ear. So not Sarah, I realised, as I became aware that my back was slick with perspiration. On the off chance that my psycho was a stupid one, I quickly dialled 1471. It was withheld. Adversely a little relieved that whoever they were they weren't that much of an idiot, I calmly put the phone back on the table and looked up to meet Rose's glare with a smile. "Eat up, Rosie," I cajoled as if nothing had happened. "Brown Owl waits for no one." She unwillingly smiled at me, and I smiled back, forcing my eyes to go nowhere near the dark windows.

Sarah didn't ring back that night even though Rosie didn't ring her. Admittedly it had completely slipped my mind, which made me feel awful the next day when Dan rung me to say accusingly that she'd had a fall, and he didn't find her until he came back this morning from a mate's. She'd been admitted to our local hospital to recover.

"She said Rosie was ringing her last night, didn't you call?" I bit my tongue so hard I think I swallowed a piece, but managed to point out that I wasn't actually the one who lived with her, and where was Dan until this morning? "Not that it's any of your business," he said haughtily, "but I was at Banjo's house; his missus says she's had enough of his drinking, and she's left him." I rolled my eyes on the other end of the phone and refrained from being sucked into a conversation about one of Dan's oddly named friends.

"Ok. Which ward is your mum in, do you know?" I'm working the late shift tonight, so I'll pop in before. Well," I paused as I realised that my childcare for Rosie was now in hospital. "I'm supposed to be, if Steve can have Rose too." Thundering silence galloped over me from the end of the phone before Dan icily retorted.

"No need to ask Him." Dan always put special emphasis on the H as if one was talking about some sort of deity. There was absolutely no love lost between my two exes. "She's my daughter. I'll have her here overnight. Like Mum does."

"Really? Erm, ok." I was definitely not comfortable with that idea, but what choice did I have? Work was as flexible as they could be, but calling in the day of a shift really messed things up for everyone. Before he had time to get offended by my less than enthusiastic response, I continued. "I'm sure Steve won't mind having her though, if you're busy? He's already got Ted, after all."

"Of course I'll have her. You drop her with everything she needs right? And she can go to the toilet without me and all that stuff?" For God's sake! Trying not to scorn him too much I replied through gritted teeth.

"Yes, Dan. She's seven. She can do all that stuff on her own. I'll drop her at five and feed her first, ok? Now what ward is your mum on?"

Eventually hanging up, I took a deep breath to steady the frustration that had built up over the course of the conversation before turning to a bright-eyed Rose, who had clearly been listening.

"I'm staying with just Daddy tonight?" she guessed correctly. At my nod she gave a shriek of glee, and, abandoning her breakfast, thundered up the stairs while shouting about needing to pack. It was so sad how much she worshipped that twat, it really was. I let her go, just thankful that she hadn't clicked onto the fact that Dan was having her alone because her grandparent was in hospital. I glanced down at Ted, his eyes on the TV as he steadily chowed through yet another bowl of cereal without a care, secure in his own stable family set up.

For someone who worked in the realms of healthcare, it was odd how much I really hated the smell of hospital wards. As I padded quietly past the mini reception, I had the biggest urge to run back out. They reminded me so much of the past, and even of the present too, with the amount of times Dad was admitted for falls before he went into the Home. Almost all my memories in hospitals were sad ones, but then I supposed that was probably true of most people. In my opinion, the only good thing to happen in hospitals were babies being born, and as I was knocked out for Rose's birth and Teddy was born at home because he came so quickly, I didn't even have that. We had joked about how typical that was of Steve's genes; everything was so easy and straightforward when he was involved.

I swallowed the urge to run and instead scanned the small ward of six beds for my surrogate mother. I couldn't see her, but there was a bed in the far corner with the curtains drawn round it. I wanted to go over, but just knew that if I was to go and poke my head round the material, I'd be greeted by a stranger and their family staring accusingly at me. A middle-aged nurse walked by, and I seized my opportunity.

"Excuse me? Can you tell me if that's Sarah Dewey's bed?"

"Yes it is, love. Her daughter are you?"

"Erm, kind of daughter-in-law. Is she ok for visitors?" I gestured to the closed curtains that surrounded Sarah.

"Yeah, she's fine. Apparently everyone else is distracting her though, so she asked us to shut them." The nurses grinned conspiratorially at me. "Is she always such a character?" I smiled. Sarah had obviously been making her presence felt.

"Oh yes," I replied, grinning back and thanking the nurse before turning towards the elder woman's bed. My shoes squeaked on the floor as I walked, making me wish I'd put my rubber soled work shoes on. Taking a deep breath and adjusting my face into a big smile, I pulled back the curtain to be greeted by Sarah sleeping. Tiptoeing over to the large chair by her bed, I lay the magazines I had brought for her on the small bedside locker and sat down. Just as I was wondering whether I should gently wake her, I noticed a beady eye was watching me from the pillow, shutting as soon as she thought I saw her. Such a faker.

"Hi, Sarah," I said, expecting a response. Nothing. I rolled my eyes; she could be so dramatic. "Hello? Sarah?" I accompanied my words with a shake of her shoulder this time, and Sarah gave a hugely affected snort, her eyes flying and making a little 'oh', as if I'd surprised her. With huge effort I refrained from laughing.

"So, how're you feeling?" She was struggling to sit up onto her pillows, and I moved swiftly to help her before sitting down.

"Hi love, no Rosie?" She peered behind me as if my daughter was going to pop out. I shook my head.

"She's at school."

"Ah. Yes, of course she is." Sarah's face fell a little in disappointment, and I hastily grabbed the magazines and tilted them towards her.

"I brought you these though, I thought you might be feeling a little bored. So," I placed them across her lap. "What happened then? Dan rang this morning and said you'd had a fall?"

"Oh, it was awful, Marnie!" Sarah began, unconsciously settling herself back into the pillows to enjoy retelling the story. "I'd just been getting the washing in, and I rung you, do you remember?" She didn't wait for me to reply. "So, after I got off the phone, I thought I'd make myself a coffee while I waited for Rose to call back. The next thing I knew I was lying on the floor of the kitchen in the pitch black. They think I must have fainted and banged my head on the table. I've got a lump the size of an egg, feel!" Sarah offered her head towards me, and reluctantly I skimmed the surface of her scalp.

"Oh yeah. It's massive," I said as she obviously wanted a response.

"Yes, it's very sore. So anyway, for some reason I couldn't get myself back onto my feet and thought I'd just have to wait for Danny to get home." I nodded along, pettily pleased that there was no way she could explain away the Golden Boy not coming home or even checking in on her. "My fault really, but I forgot he was working nights yesterday. He came in at eight this morning, and absolutely exhausted, to find me lying there. And I was really cold, and couldn't really hear him properly, even when he put me in bed. So, he rang an ambulance, such a love!"

What a hero, I thought snidely. It really got to me that she was so unbelievably blind in worshipping her son that she refused to ever acknowledge any of his shortcomings. I decided not to voice my frustrations and waited for her to finish so I could ask my next question.

"So what do they think caused the faint? Do you know how long you'll be in for?" I felt sorry for Sarah, really, I did, but I worked two to three night shifts a week. I needed to know when she'd be back in the game to have Rose before I threw myself on Lula or Steve's mercy.

"They think it's to do with my blood pressure, something medical. Erm, orto...orthe"

"Orthostatic hypotension?"

"That's the one! You are clever Marnie. And they want to keep me here for today at least to monitor me." I nodded. It was about what I expected. I decided to break the news that would make her day a whole lot brighter before I left.

"Ok, well you just concentrate on getting better. And don't worry about Rose, Dan's having her tonight while I work." She transformed with a wide brimmed beam, and I struggled not to propel myself out of the ward there and then.

"Oh, that is so like Danny," she gushed, seemingly unaware that as the child's father, it shouldn't be such a big deal for him to have her. "Rose'll be over the moon!"

"She is," I agreed, deciding to give the older woman what she wanted; she was in hospital after all. "She ran up to pack her stuff as soon as I told her this morning. Well, I'll leave you to rest now, I need to go and see Dad today too. And I'm sure Dan will be in soon to see you, won't he?" She flushed, and I felt a sweet little pang of victory that immediately made me feel ashamed.

"I'm sure he will if he has time," she replied, making us both aware that he obviously hadn't thought to check in on her after ringing the ambulance. "Thanks for coming to see me love." I bent down to give her a kiss, and as I rose, she gripped my hand to still me. "And thank you for trusting Danny with her. I know it's not easy for you, given the past." She gently released me, leaving me astonished by her admission that Dan was possibly not the best father that ever lived, and I smiled before leaving her.

The visit to Dad was as uneventful as they always were these days; his powers of conversation had disintegrated, with only small reminders, such as remembering his dead wife's name, to keep him going. I held his hand instead and told him all about Sarah's fall, and that Dan would be having Rose alone tonight. As stupid as it sounded, I just wanted him to give me a little cuddle and agree that while it was hard to let it happen, Rose deserved the chance to find out for herself what her father was like. But for him to do that he would have to remember that he had a grandchild, or even a daughter to give him a grandchild for that matter. I had to face the possibility that for the rest of his life, my dad would believe that I was my dead mum.

After picking the kids up from school and nursery, I did my best to answer Rosie's one thousand questions about 'what I thought her dad would have planned' while hoping with all I had that he'd remembered he was having her and hadn't gone out instead. Deciding to drop her first just in case she needed to go to Steve's with Ted, I trudged through rush hour traffic before finally turning into the council estate where Sarah and Dan lived.

Typically, there was no parking anywhere near their back gate and I was forced to bring Teddy with me instead of just running Rose up the path. A glance at the car clock told me I was cutting it fine to get back home and changed after Steve's too, and I silently cursed myself for not getting ready before the drop offs.

A swift turn of the kitchen handle proved the door to be locked, and I almost growled in frustration. Knocking sharply, I tried to placate Rose's wide, worried eyes with a reassuring smile.

"I'm sure he's just upstairs or something, babe." She looked back, wanting to believe me but obviously finding it a little hard.

"Yeah, or he's gone to the shop for sweets? Nanna never locks the door though." She replied as I whipped my phone out while knocking harshly again. Teddy was now copying my banging action with his head, giving me the possibility of brain damage to worry about too. I had stopped knocking and was using my free arm to hold him back when the ringing tone finally stopped.

"Hello?" Dan answered my phone call croakily, immediately alerting me to the fact that I had woken him up.

"Dan. We're at the back door. I'm dropping Rose for the night. Remember?" A small pause told me he'd forgotten.

"*Of course* I remember," he said scornfully, the bed springs creaking as he sat up and giving the game away. "I'm just sorting her room out and obviously didn't hear the door. Hold on." The line went dead, and we waited impatiently. Rose's eyes were still a little blue and my hands were busy firmly trying to stop Teddy from his new favourite game of ramming his head against a hard wooden door. After what seemed like at least five minutes we heard the lock scraping on the other side and the door was wrenched open.

"Daddy!" Rose flew into Dan's arms and snuggled deeply into his chest. I wrinkled my nose. I would put money on him smelling a little rancid. He definitely looked like he hadn't washed since coming home this morning.

"Hello my angel," he said, cuddling her back and smirking at me. I looked stonily back at him. Dan seemed to think Rose's affection was a game of one-upmanship.

"Right, here's your backpack babe," I said, ignoring Dan and refusing to get irate. "Remember you need to put your hair up for school and brush your teeth, yes?" Luckily Rose had gotten 'into' hair recently and could do a basic ponytail fairly neatly.

"We know that obviously, Marnie!" blustered Dan as Rose nodded and came to give me a hug. I caught her up, letting Teddy continue his quest for concussion for a second as I breathed her in, trying to quell my discomfort at leaving her here. I used a kiss as cover to whisper in her ear.

"If anything goes wrong or you're worried I've written my mobile number, Auntie's number and Steve's number in your notebook in the bag. Ring any of us and we'll sort out coming to get you, ok? Nanna won't mind you using her phone for that," I finished, pre-empting her next question. Putting her down I gave her one last squeeze, and made myself turn, hold out a hand to Teddy, and call a breezy goodbye as the door shut behind me.

The drop off at Steve's was the complete opposite; prompt, easy, and with no worry burrowing deeply in the pit of my stomach. Both Addy and Steve had come to the door to greet him, the smells of baking wafting into the cool air and making me want to swap places with my son.

Finally pulling up at home, I realised that I had less than ten minutes to get changed and make a quick packed dinner before I would have to be out of the door again. Bloody Dan, always messing up my life.

The house was in darkness as I entered, which I hated. I kept forgetting that the nights were closing in now that it was early October, and that even if it wasn't dark when I left, it was bound to be when I came back. As I switched on the hallway light while slipping off my shoes, a bright white envelope on the doormat caught my eye. Dread immediately filled me, and I snatched it up while glancing down the corridor towards the dark kitchen and wondering what might be waiting for me. A faint beep, a little like a text alert, went off in the kitchen's direction. I reached into the hallway closet for the baseball bat I kept there; a must have for any single woman. Armed with that and the letter, I made my footsteps as loud as I could and called out.

"Hello? Who's there?" There was no response and I continued, desperately trying to sound as scary as I could. "I have a bat, I'm warning you." No one answered but I heard the rustle of them shift their position slightly. Oh God, someone was actually there. I hadn't truly believed it when I said it. For the smallest moment I considered just running out of the house and banging on my neighbour Lydia's door for safety. But my stupid urge for independence reared its head. No way could I be scared in my own home; I was the only adult here and I needed to act like it. Whoever it was clearly wanted to dredge up the past, so let them get it over with now.

"I will hit you!" Summoning all my remaining courage I ran the last few steps into the dark kitchen, my bat over my shoulder and ready to swing. Fully expecting something to come out of the blackness and grab me, I circled around several times. Nothing happened. I felt behind me with my spare hand and I flicked the switch. The room was instantly bathed in brightness. And it was empty. The dishwasher sang its little tune to tell me the cycle had finished.

My breathing was ragged as I gave the entire space one more detailed look, feeling hot and foolish. I lowered the bat and leant against the wall for a moment trying to regulate my breaths. Feeling thoroughly stupid now, I turned back around to face the hallway, the shuffling noise I'd heard was right behind me. Whipping around, I swung the bat out in front of me, a primal scream exiting my body as I did. I realised it was the blinds shimmying together from the open fanlight window. I'd opened it this morning before the school run to get rid of the smell of burnt toast. Both foolish and glad I was alone with no one to witness the craziness, I strode over, and with some difficulty in leaning over the sink, closed it firmly. Immediately the house was still, with only the faintest strains of Lydia next door's TV and the ticking wall clock breaking the silence.

My watch told me I should have left five minutes ago. I chucked the baseball bat back in the cupboard and was already thundering up the stairs when I noticed the white envelope scrunched up and sticking awkwardly out of my pocket. I really, really didn't have time to open it now. Especially as I instinctively knew it was from my friendly neighbourhood psychopath.

This wasn't the first time that Lula and I, or even Dad for that matter, had gained a groupie. You didn't lose your mum in a horrific murder without some publicity and coupled with the fact that even I could see that Lula and I were very sweet looking (mum used to dress us the same and dad carried the tradition on until I rebelled at ten), and easy to feel sympathetic for, we were the perfect fixation for the slightly mentally fragile. Although to be fair only about seventy percent were harmlessly insane. The rest were your genuine well-wishers; parents of our childhood friends who had known Mum, and now took on the role of 'helping' poor old Dad bring us up, as well as the professionals we came across in the course of time, teachers and counsellors and the like.

Even at eight I knew that it was awe-inspiring to have lost your mum. Losing your dad didn't have the same effect on the adults for some reason. Maybe because mums were traditionally the ones wrapped up in the care of the whole family – it had certainly been the case in mine. Or maybe it had more to do with the manner in which the parent died. Cancer was too common-place to be treated with reverence for long. The dad of a boy in the year above me at school died of it about six months after my mum did. He got sympathy too, but nothing on the scale of me and Lula. And his mum got special treatment for perhaps a term before she was clearly expected to just get on with things. And of course, she did.

Our dad fell apart when Mum died. He'd spent the whole of our short lives up until that point working long hours in the City (apart from the traditional earlyish pick up on a Friday) and he didn't know where the washing machine stuff was or even how to work it. He was useless at remembering the stuff we needed for different days at school. He never even attempted to cook food from scratch, suddenly we were having the takeaways we'd always futilely begged for when Mum was alive, to the point we were sick of it. The school mums looked after him, offering free childcare and food, and the school itself were lenient to the point of bending over backwards when he'd sheepishly confess he'd forgotten the packed lunches or the wellies that had been asked for . Never again did a stiff note arrive home with us to point out something had been forgotten, the way it had on the few occasions that Mum had dropped one of the thousand balls she was juggling.

Even those genuinely crazy followers were kind too, in the main. Complete strangers, feeling sorry for the family of the poor murdered woman, would write little notes for us and leave them alongside some sweets or magazines on the doorstep. It was nice in a way to realise that the world hadn't forgotten our tragedy. But back in the present, it was costing me time that I didn't have and so, chucking my uniform on, I resolved to take the letter with me and read it on my break.

Michal was leaning against our ambulance when I bombed it into the staff car park, waiting with a coffee in his hand. He was an experienced paramedic, assigned to me when I surprised myself by successfully getting taken on through the local paramedic apprenticeship programme six months ago. Now, he grinned when we made eye contact, his teeth starkly bright against his dark skin and his hair falling about his forehead in its corkscrew tendrils. He was probably the most beautiful man I'd ever seen in the flesh, I thought abstractly, as I had done thousands of times before.

When we'd first been put on shift together there had been a little spark, that weirdly sweet tension of attraction between us. I let myself enjoy it for a few weeks, until sensing he was on the point of asking me out, I recoiled from the idea and loudly began to talk about my relief at being happily single, also concerned that starting something with my mentor would get too messy. He took the hints with good grace, and instead we began to form a genuine friendship of camaraderie. Locking my car, I smiled back and headed over.

"What time d'you call this, slacker?" he called as soon as I was close enough. "Here," he said, proffering another cup of coffee towards me. "We'd better get moving, my bet is within..." he looked at his watch, "twenty minutes."

"Nah," I shook my head. "It's Tuesday. People are over the weekend by now and they're out drinking or messing about on a football pitch again. I'm saying six minutes." He shrugged and began to walk around to the passenger side to get in.

"Fine. Closest buys breakfast, yeah?"

"Yeah, and I'll be making sure I order the biggest on the menu too!" I started the vehicle and carefully began to drive out of the ambulance station, giving Mia and Sheridan a wave as I passed them. "And I need a larger coffee than that," I said, answering Michal's un-voiced question as to where we were going. "Been a busy couple of days."

"Oh yeah? Finally got your end away, did you?" Michal grinned and momentarily I wished he'd let me get my end away with him. A bit of no strings sex with a gorgeous man I actually liked seemed extremely appealing suddenly. Instead, I tutted and looked mock-offended.

"Oi, it's not been that long! Well," I admitted, faltering under his knowing smirk, "ok it has. But I'm not bothered," I lied. "Sex is overrated." Just then the radio shot into life and our first call came in. After we both listened with the utmost attention and I had swung the van round to face the other way, the adrenalin already pumping, we both glanced down at the dashboard clock.

"Shit," Michal exclaimed. "Breakfast's on me then. Again." I grinned as I gunned the engine.

"You should know by now I *always* win," I said, the note in my inner jacket pocket already completely compartmentalised as I concentrated on the job in hand. "Right, you ready? Everything sorted in the back? Let's go."

SEVEN

I had literally crawled, exhausted from the busy shift, into my bed when I remembered the note. For a moment and with my eyes shut, I kidded myself that I would be able to ignore it and just read it when I woke up this afternoon.

Of course that wasn't going to happen. Instead, sighing and kicking back the covers, I padded across the darkened room to my work jacket and fumbled until I found the correct pocket. Vaulting back into bed, I pulled the covers up to cover my lap before taking a deep breath and slicing it open.

Two things fell out, one a folded over piece of white paper, the other a thicker rectangle. Thoroughly confused, I turned the card over first, my eyes immediately drawn to the emblem in the corner. It was the double headed black eagle that followed me wherever I went; the badge of Wimbledon football club. My blood seemed to freeze as I made myself study the rest of what I now recognised as a ticket stub, already knowing in some way what information I would find.

Wimbledon F.C VS Sheffield United F.C

Friday 09.11.2001

Kick off 5pm

The day mum died. I held the ticket gently in my hands, forcing myself not to rip it into the thousand tiny pieces that my instinct was telling me to. Feeling incredibly nauseous and not at all like I could sleep again, I apprehensively opened the folded paper and read the type written note.

Dearest Marnie,

Just a little note to ask how Sarah is after her fall? Did she like the magazines you took her? You know, you should probably tell her to be a bit more careful, especially as she insists on pretending to be your mum. You've already got a mum, remember? In case it slipped your mind, I've enclosed a little keepsake for you. She loved you that day, she even died because of you. Don't forget her now.

That was it. Every hair on my body was standing to attention. I realised I was shivering, the pieces of paper shaking in my hands. With a lot of effort to hold the note still, I reread it three more times as I tried desperately to glean any more information about who had sent it. There was nothing that I could identify; just that it was someone who knew where and when Mum was killed, and that I was close to Daniel's mum.

Forcing myself to take deep breaths in an attempt to calm down, I went through who knew about my relationship with Sarah; Daniel, Steven, Lula, Rashid, Sarah herself. Dad? The last one was ludicrous of course. Dad thought I was his dead wife, so there was no chance he was going to be punishing me for 'forgetting her.' And after a moment or so I dismissed the others too. Not one of those people would be going out of their way to hurt me, not even Dan. They all loved me in one way or another.

I reached over to my phone, fully intending to call the police again and log it, when it began ringing in my hand. Glancing down and seeing Lula's name pop up, I was relieved. Not only would I be able to offload this most recent development, but she had obviously forgiven me for our frosty conversation the other night. As I swiped across to answer, I realised that this just might have been a first; Lula reaching out before I did after an argument.

"Hello?" I said eagerly, relief washing through me as Lula's usual happy tones floated through the earpiece. "Lula, I'm so glad you called, how are you? How's your week been so far?" My sister began to tell me all about Ruben's latest dirty protest and we both shrieked with laughter while I basked in the normality, already feeling my heart rate drop back to normal. As her story came to an end, and she began making noises about having to go, I took a deep breath.

"Lula, listen. I got another note last night. It's really starting to freak me out so I'm going to tell the police." There was a pause as my sister digested what I'd said.

"Another note?" she asked in a faintly hostile tone. "Why, what does it say? Look, are you sure this isn't just you overreacting? We all get notes you know. I got a card the other week from Mrs Dee." Her voice had taken on a sullen tone, and her competing with a card from Mrs Dee momentarily made me smile. If she was bringing up our old next-door neighbour, who was loony as they come, she must be jealous. It was odd, but I supposed that siblings found competition wherever they could. A murder in the family just meant that sometimes ours were more morbid than other peoples.

"Lula, it's not a competition! I'm not talking about the usual stuff. This is threatening. It was a note that was warning Sarah to stop acting like my mum. And a ticket stub from the Wimbledon football match the night she died. It's all a bit too much, Lula, don't you think?" When I paused for her reply and was only greeted with petulant silence, I felt my temper slipping. "Oh, forget it. I've got to go. I need to report it." I had taken the phone away from my ear when I heard her shouting.

"No, don't go. Sorry Marnie." Astounded at not only a phone call but an actual audible 'sorry' from my sister, I rebuffed her apology pathetically eagerly.

"No, I'm sorry, Lu. I know it's hard on all of us when these freaks crawl out of the woodwork. I've just got a bad feeling about this one. It seems sinister compared to the others." She sighed before replying, and I could tell she was trying to keep her frustration under control.

"Yeah, maybe. Still just sounds like a fan to me. But if you want to waste the police's time then go ahead. Are you seeing Dad today?" She suddenly changed the subject, leaving me feeling like a drama queen.

"Oh, erm, no not today I don't think. I'm on nights and need to see the kids for a bit before they go back to Steve and Dan's. I feel like I never see them anymore." Lula laughed, a little unkindly to my sensitive ears.

"Ah yes," she said. "The two fathers of the year." Weirdly Lula had never particularly liked Steve, who was, in everyone else's opinion, the nicest person who ever lived. In all the time I'd been away from here, living with Steve and the kids, we'd barely had a real relationship; I rang her once a week to check in while she often sat in petulant silence on the other end. When she did speak she told me he wasn't authentic, and his aura was all wrong, whatever that meant. "I take it you rung the school this morning to check Dan even remembered to drop Rosie?"

My heart dropped. I'd been so stupidly preoccupied that I'd forgotten to even ring the kids on my way home this morning. Feeling like the world's most neglectful mother, I gabbled a farewell to Lula and hung up, ringing Dan's mobile immediately. It rang out as it inevitably always did, and, heart still banging, I rang the home phone with no response either. With the panic beginning to bubble in my throat, I called Rose's school. There was no reason at all to think that Dan hadn't taken her, or that something had happened. Surely they'd have rung me if so? Before I'd gotten any further in my reasoning, a cool and calm voice answered.

"Good morning, St Agatha's School."

"Hi, this is Rose Dewey's mum, Marnie South?"

"Oh, hello Mrs South. That's good timing, I was just about to ring you." Fear gripped me in the moment she took to take a breath, and Rose had been hit by a car or abducted ten times over before she spoke again. "Rose appears to have forgotten her lunchbox this morning. Shall we give her a hot dinner, or will you be dropping it in?" In the relief that filled me I forgot to even be mortified that Dan sent her in with no lunch.

"Oh! So she is at school? Actually in the classroom?" A strange pause followed before the woman spoke.

"Well yes of course she is. Is something wrong Mrs South?" The tone had become a little more alert and immediately I realised that I had inadvertently raised her suspicions.

"Oh no, no, nothing's wrong," I tittered nervously, keen to downplay Dan's flaws as a father. "She stayed at her dad's last night, and I just realised I hadn't dropped her lunchbox, silly me." I took the blame rather than let her suspect that Rose was definitely not in the safest of hands when Dan was solely in charge. "If you wouldn't mind giving her a hot dinner today? I'm really sorry, I'll log on and pay for it now."

"Ok, no problem!" The receptionist's voice had mellowed again. "Can I help with anything else, Mrs South?" I didn't bother to correct her about my marital status in my eagerness to get her off the phone.

"Oh no! Thanks for your time, and sorry again, bye then!" I pressed to hang up and let out a relieved sigh. All was good, Rose was at school and Lula had almost convinced me that I was being over-dramatic. Cheered, I snuggled down under my duvet to catch a few hours of sleep before the cycle began again.

EIGHT

The next couple of days passed in a whirl of shifts, visits to the recuperating Sarah, and Dad in the care home, whilst looking after the kids. Nothing more untoward happened, and I started to relax. Whoever it was had obviously finished their joke now.

As we trudged towards the weekend, I began to feel relief spread through me; it was my weekend to have the kids so there was no reason for us to be separated, and the post this morning had contained only the usual terror of bills to pay. I was waiting in the playground on Friday afternoon for the kids to come out of school when I was jolted as someone grabbed my elbow. I swung around to confront my attacker, my hands raised defensively. I was greeted by Grace, the mum of Rose's best friend, Ruby. She looked a little taken aback as we locked eyes, and I realised I must be looking more than a little manic.

"Marnie? Sorry, I didn't mean to startle you," she began, her hand on my elbow turning gentle and comforting. "Are you ok? You seem a little..." she trailed off, as polite suburban mothers do, before she called me crazy.

"Crazy?" I finished her sentence as light-heartedly as I could, even giving a little chuckle as I did. "Night shifts all week, that's all. Bit of a zombie; I was in a daze!" Her face broke out into a relieved smile that she wouldn't be forced to deal with any personal woes from a woman that she only interacted with because her offspring happened to like mine.

"Oh, poor you, I bet those are tough!" she said. "I just wanted to grab you quickly to ask whether Rose would like to come and play soon? Or even tonight if she's free?"

"Tonight?" I repeated, playing for time as I tried to think of an excuse. It had been a long week, and I just wanted us all to be safe and sound at home. With a stranger obsessing over my life, the last thing I wanted was Rose to be elsewhere, somewhere I couldn't protect her if I needed to. "Oh, I don't know...that's a lot for you, isn't it? With your kids too?"

"It's no trouble," she replied lightly. "Max, my eldest, has got someone coming too, so really, it'll be doing me a favour. It just means that Ruby will stay out of their hair! You know what they're like when they've got friends over; little sisters become enemy number one!" Almost too late I pasted a conspiratorial grin on my face to match hers while my stupid brain tried to keep up. I didn't know how to refuse, cursing myself for not just saying we were busy in the first place. I opened my mouth to backtrack.

Just then, movement at the school doors distracted us both as Rose and Ruby's class began to file out, the two girls at the front of the line, laughing and chattering exuberantly. It had made me feel so much better that Rose's overnight stays with Dan this week had caused her none of the tears or distress I'd been imagining, and happily I watched my little girl and her best friend come to a stop by the teacher, still clasping each other's hands. They spotted us both at the same time and frantically pointed at us, waiting for the teacher to recognise us and send them our way. She did so with a wave, and the two little girls ran over delightedly, shoving bags, drinks and bookbags at us as they did.

"Hi Mummy, can I please go to Ruby's house if her mum says so, *please*? We've got a new dance we want to learn before Monday and it's really important!" I could vaguely hear Ruby making the same petition to her own mother and knew without a doubt that I didn't have the mental strength to say no to all three of them. I turned, a resigned smile on my face as Ruby's mum matched it with a delighted one.

"Ok with you for tonight then, Marnie?" She grinned conspiratorially. "They know how to wrap us round their fingers, don't they?" I nodded dumbly, the worry flooding my body again. Turning to Rose, I bent down and whispered to her on the pretence of taking her lunchbox too.

"Are you sure you want to go tonight? This week's been a bit crazy, with Nanna's fall and everything. Are you sure you're not a bit too tired?" She looked at me with seven-year-old disgust.

"OF COURSE I'm not tired, Mum. Please let me go, we really want to do this dance. We're having a competition with Layla and Mia on Monday!" I nodded at her, powerless to be the bad guy when all I really wanted was to wrap her up in the safety of home. The girls shrieked delightedly and hugged one another before dashing off across the playground.

"Rose! ROSE!" I shouted after her, and she came back, pausing in front of me enquiringly. I bent down and hugged her briefly too, breathing in her head as I kissed it lightly. "Have a good time then," I said. "And be good! I'll pick you up later."

"Oh, don't worry," Ruby's mum said. "I'm dropping Max's friend off about six, and he lives in your estate. I'll bring her home too. Save you getting Ted out in the cold."

"Oh. Thanks," I said, my eyes still on Rose and her friend as they twirled around one another. "Thanks," I repeated more warmly, aware I was sounding rude. "That's really kind of you, if you don't mind?"

"I don't mind at all!" Ruby's mum replied. "Now go home and put your feet up, you look ready for bed!" With one last wave, they joined the throng of parents and children leaving to begin their weekend, and then they were swallowed up and gone. I stood clutching Rose's bags and lunchbox for a moment and wondering why I hadn't just put my foot down. Sighing instead and feeling deflated, I changed direction and trudged across the tarmac towards Teddy's nursery. At least no one would want to steal him for the evening. If anyone did, they'd soon bring him back anyway.

Friday was freezer food night in our house, and I'd opted to shove a pizza in the oven for me and Ted. While it was cooking, we slouched on the sofa together, his elbows jamming painfully into my stomach as he rested on me. It wasn't painful enough for me to tell him to get off though, and I relished the heat of his small body against mine. My eyes were fixed on yet another episode of Paw Patrol, while my son murmured the script under his breath.

My mind was elsewhere. Absently I picked the skin around my fingertips and stared at the black screen of the phone resting on the arm of the sofa. It was five pm now, and Ruby's mum hadn't contacted me to say there were any problems. Not that there would be, I corrected my brain. She'd been there several times after school in the months since we'd moved back, and the worst that had ever happened was the time both girls decided to give one another a fringe. I remembered how Grace and I had howled with laughter at the state of them over a glass of wine in their cosy kitchen while the girls tried to front it out as it being the style they were going for. But tonight, I just wanted there to be a reason for her to come home early. The oven timer went off and I moved a reluctant Ted off of me.

"Shall I bring the pizza in here, Teddy bear? We can have it on the sofa for a treat." I wasn't even willing to admit it to myself out loud, but the back of the house with its widely exposed windows and doors was still making me uncomfortable as darkness swept in. All week I had been making sure that everything was done in the kitchen before dark, which was a lot easier when I was on night shift and the kids were out early. But today there was nothing for it; I would have to be brave. I walked quickly through the door and to the oven, purposely not even looking towards the darkening garden. Keeping my head down, I concentrated on slicing the pizza up and carried it back through.

Ted still had his eyes on the TV but obviously heard me come in, as without looking, he spoke.

"Juice." I rolled my eyes, a smile playing on my lips. I tried not to give them juice apart from at dinnertime, and Ted never let me forget it.

"Juice what?"

"Juice please," he replied, his eyes still on the cartoon. I put the pizza on the table by the sofa, and he reached down to grab a piece. I swooped in and balanced a plate under it on his lap before padding swiftly back to the kitchen. Repeating the process of not looking at the staring eyes that must be trained on me from the garden, I made us both a squash. A distant vibrating noise immediately made me run back to the living room, drinks half spilt across the wooden hallway as I chucked them onto the coffee table and snatched up my phone.

"Hello? Hello?" The number was one I didn't recognise, and I had the worst premonition that Rose had been involved in something bad.

"Hello, Marnie? It's Grace, Ruby's mum."

"Oh God, is Rose ok? Has something happened?" There was a brief pause, as even Ted looked up at my panicked tone of voice. I tried to smile reassuringly, but only succeeded in grimacing at him.

"Oh no, nothing like that, Rose is fine!"

"Oh. Good! That's great!" My hand had relaxed on the phone, but I couldn't help feeling a little angry that she'd worried me like that. "Did you want me to come and get her after all?" I was already moving to turn the TV off and haul Ted out, dinner forgotten now.

"No, it's completely the opposite actually. The girls want to have a sleepover here, is that ok?" Now that I wasn't panicking as much, I could actually hear my daughter squeaking happily next to the phone.

"No!" I tried to adjust my tone to acceptable levels. "No, but thank you," I started again. "We've got people round tonight I'm afraid. My sister and her family."

"Oh, ok, no worries!" I heard her murmur something to the girls, obviously answering their clamouring questions. Rose's indignant huff was audible, and she began gabbling an argument directed at me as I listened, feeling guilty. "Right, so I'll drop her at six as arranged, ok?" Ruby's mum was back, and I muttered a response before hanging up. I felt like shit now; Rose was going to be in a bad mood with me, especially when she realised that her aunty, uncle and cousin weren't actually coming. I turned my attention back to the TV and Ted, not hungry for pizza.

I was right; Rose was in a foul mood when she was dropped home, her gorgeous face pouting and miserable. After saying goodbye to Ruby's mum, she slammed the front door and ran up to her bedroom, not even stopping to speak to us. Ted gave me a look as if to say' you're in trouble' and I smiled ruefully back before following in her wake.

"Rose?" I pushed her door open a little to see that she was lying on her bed, curled onto one side so that I couldn't see her face. "How was Ruby's, babe?" I sat down on the bed and leant over so that I could see her cross little face.

"I'm not talking to you," she replied angrily, sticking her bottom lip out at me. "Why couldn't I stay?" she blurted out after a moment, unable to keep it in. "Why did you say people were coming?"

"I'm sorry Rosie," I began, stroking her hair as I did. "It's just I haven't seen much of you this week with work and everything. I missed you." I'd kept all the craziness of the week away from the kids. I hadn't wanted them, and especially Rose, to be worrying about anything. She sat up and rolled her eyes even while she edged a little closer.

"Mum, you see me all the time. And Ruby's got bunk beds, *and* I was going to sleep on the top one!"

"Sorry, babe." I gathered her up to me, and after a moment she relaxed into my arms. "Tonight just wasn't good. But I promise another night, ok? And we can have Ruby here next week maybe? I'm not working Fridays anymore, remember?" I felt her head nodding against my chest. I decided to come completely clean while she was being magnanimous. "And I expect Ruby's mum told you Auntie's coming? Well she's not; I just said that as an excuse."

"Erm...ok." Rose gave me a quizzical look, but to my surprise didn't make a big deal out of it. "Shall we go and watch TV with Teddy?" Completely out of her funk now and bouncing out of my arms and off the bed, I grinned at her retreating back and followed in her dancing wake back down the stairs.

NINE

Saturday and Sunday passed peacefully, and I began to hope that all of the crazy stuff was over and done with. Lula and Rashid were not contactable all weekend, which was a bit annoying as I thought the kids could have done with seeing Ruben. I did suggest we popped over there, but Rose just met me with a stony look and a 'stop going on about them, Mummy.' She'd obviously started to grow away from playing with two toddler boys, instead preferring to sit on the iPad for as much of the weekend as I'd allow her to.

It was now Monday morning, and we were rushing through breakfast when the letterbox clanged. Immediately freezing with the spoon halfway to my mouth, I barked "sit down!" as Ted rose to go and get the post. He sat back into the chair without argument, his little arms wrapping around his legs and his head buried into them too, but not before I caught sight of his quivering lips. Rose leant over to give him a hug, shooting me a cross look as she did. Suitably chastised, I moved round to their side of the table, and gathered them both up to me, kissing the tops of their heads and murmuring 'sorry, sorry.'

I left them chattering away once more and padded swiftly down the hallway. A bunch of envelopes were sticking out of the metal, taunting me with their undisclosed terrors. Shaking my head to stop myself being so dramatic, I grabbed them and glanced quickly at one after the other, my pulse rate slowing as bill after bill became apparent. I even smiled a little inside at the thought of being happy to receive summons for money. But after all, when the alternative was creepy stalker gifts, who wouldn't be?

"Guys, come on! Teeth and hair, we're going to be late!" I chucked the bills carelessly on the kitchen side as I re-entered the room, watching as both kids scraped their chairs backwards and escaped up the stairs to the bathroom. Slurping my now lukewarm coffee, I started chucking fruit and snacks to join Rose's sandwich in her lunchbox. Upstairs I could hear the faint sounds of Rose and Ted arguing over the stool to reach the mirror above the sink. Everything was as normal as a school day could be.

I'd completed drop off and was speeding across town towards the nursing home when my phone began to ring. The ID said withheld. I never answered numbers I didn't know; they were usually marketing or cold callers anyway. But this time I wanted to be sure that's all it was.

"Hello?" I said, my voice striving to sound normal and carefree.

"Hello, is that Marnie South? It's Detective Sumner regarding your recent break in." My fingers gripped a little on the steering wheel. *They'd found something.*

"Yes, this is Marnie. Have you found them? The person doing this?"

"I'm sorry, nothing's come up our end. I just wanted to check some facts with you; is this a good time to talk?" I felt my pulse rate drop dejectedly as I pulled slowly into the nursing home car park and straight into a space. The officer's timing was impeccable.

"Yes, that's fine."

"Great," he said. "Can you firstly please confirm your full name and date of birth?" I answered the questions almost without thinking about it, watching as the first group of the day appeared from the main doors, waiting for their nurse to cross them over the road to the green space.

"And when did you first realise it was your fault that your mother died?" I jolted as the words hit my ear and I gripped the steering wheel.

"What did you say?"

"I said, when did you first think these packages and letters might be connected to the night your mother died?"

"Oh, I thought...erm, never mind." I felt hot, sweaty and confused. "The football stub was from a match that was on the day she died. And the magnet was of Wimbledon tube; she died outside the station. I have actually already explained this all when I first reported it." I tried to stop my tone from becoming confrontational; I could feel myself getting upset, something I never allowed myself to do over Mum.

"Sorry, a football stub?" I realised that maybe I'd never reported that part; what with Lula dismissing my fears, it'd seemed pointless. But now they were on the line, well… "I know it must be hard to talk about, I'm just trying to get everything down for the report."

"Yes, sorry, I received another hand delivered letter, it had a note and a ticket stub from the football match at Wimbledon the night Mum died. I didn't ring you as I thought I might have been being a bit dramatic, you know?"

"Yes, but with the added angle of the items you've received being linked to your mother's murder it's just important we know it all. I've logged the extra letter so that's in your file, ok? Please let us know if anything else arrives; it'll be important if we ever have enough to build a case. Thanks for your time, Ms South; we'll be in touch."

I hung up but stayed in the car, feeling too vulnerable right now to be mistaken for my dead mother by a demented old man. Instead I watched as another group of the elderly emerged from the building, their bodies hunched as they paused before crossing the road to the grass. A few of them were smiling, their mouths seeming too big for the shrunken features surrounding them. The absent sadness that I felt for most old people suddenly crystalised itself into something much more sinister; one day I would be this frail. This old. This forgotten.

Speaking of the frail and infirm, I'd better get my act together and go in to see Dad. Now I'd calmed down a little I was almost looking forward to a familiar face. Entering the building, I signed in and quickly made my way down the corridor towards his room. Just as I reached Dad's door Devon came out, and catching sight of me, he seemed to grimace before rapidly closing it behind him.

"Marnie!" he began, a weirdly large smile playing about his lips. "How nice to see you, we weren't expecting you in today."

"Hi Devon," I replied, moving a little closer so that I'd be able to open the door when he stepped away. Instead he stayed where he was, and I looked at him questioningly, nervous anticipation beginning to bubble away. This was the moment where he told me Dad was dead, I just knew it. Suddenly I was just desperate to hear it. "Is something wrong?"

"Oh, no, nothing's wrong," he replied, still guarding the door from me. "George has just managed to fall asleep; he had a bad night."

"Oh, ok," I smiled, the relief at the thought of not having another dead parent quite yet almost dripping off me. I went to grab the door handle next to him. "I'll just pop in and sit with him for a few minutes, then."

"Actually, I think it'd be best to leave him be," Devon replied, still not moving from his sentry post. "He's been quite distressed the last few days, and this is the first time he's managed to fall asleep naturally."

"Naturally? So, you've had to sedate him? Has he really been that bad?" I felt unbelievably guilty for not visiting over the last few days, but it had just become habit not to when it was my weekend with the kids. Devon looked at me sympathetically.

"He's been very upset and asking for Judy a lot. He seems to think he's in some sort of prison, and we're keeping him here against his will. We only sedated him because he was getting himself so worked up; I'm sure he'll be ok again in a few days, Marnie. He just needs a bit of rest, that's all. Maybe ring tomorrow and see how he is instead?"

"Oh. Yeah, I suppose I could do that. Are you sure I can't just pop my head round?"

"Best not," he responded. "Come on, I'll walk you out." I allowed Devon to take me by the elbow and steer me towards the exit once more, my confusion making me mindlessly docile. As we passed the desk, I intercepted a loaded look that the receptionist shared with him, and she waved me on, saying she'd sign out for me instead. Devon walked me right out to the car park, his hand cheerily waving at a group of residents in the gardens when they raised their own hands to him. He was so popular with the old folk, and I'd been so happy when we'd ended up with him as Dad's key carer.

"So, shall I give you a call tomorrow, Marnie? Let you know how he's getting on? There's no point in you coming all the way over if he's still not himself, is there?" Devon was giving me his usual beguiling smile, and I began to return it when I found myself really looking into his eyes. Hard brown spheres stared back at me, without an ounce of warmth or compassion to match the honeyed tones with which he spoke. I gave myself a mental shake, trying to stop the crawling cold up my neck, and looked at him again.

His usual compassionate mask radiated back as he waited for a reply. I smiled and murmured my agreement before sliding into the driver's seat.

I gunned the engine, deciding to go straight home and go to bed for a bit. I hadn't been sleeping well at all the last few weeks and it was clearly making me paranoid. Glancing back in the rear-view mirror, I saw that Devon was watching me leave, an appraising expression filling his face. He turned, and as I watched his retreating back, I tried to get rid of the odd feeling that Devon was hiding something. I couldn't get that split second of malice on his face out of my mind. I'd imagined it. I must have. It was Devon; the man I trusted the most with my aging father, and the only one that Dad ever seemed to recognise on sight these days too.

Devon preoccupied my thoughts for the entire journey but at last I was nearly home, pulling into our new-build estate. As a shift worker, I'd always enjoyed the lull of the mid-morning, when most of the population were either at work or at school. I could see that today was no exception, with more driveways empty than full as I passed. My house was at the end of a Cul-De-Sac and looked exactly the same as the others. The uniformity was what had comforted me when I picked it; another by-product of my early life was that I hated to stand out in any way.

Climbing into bed it was welcoming, and I felt my body begin to relax almost instantly. The good thing about working night shifts was that I was used to sleeping at random times, and so I could actually be in with the chance to get a good couple of hours rest here. I started to drift off, my thoughts circling the weirdness of the last weeks before I consciously swerved my brain onto the banality of the upcoming Christmas shopping that I needed to do. There was no point in getting myself all worked up for no real reason, and I drifted off, arguing mindlessly with myself about whether Ted really was old enough for a Nintendo Switch or not, and also whether Rose's pleas for makeup should finally be granted.

My eyes opened with a suddenness and my brain whirred immediately. I sat up in a panic, trying to remember where I was. As I focused on the chest of drawers across the room, I realised with some relief that I was in my own bed, the weak late autumnal light flickering through the gaps in the blinds. Flopping back down onto the pillows, I grabbed my phone from the side table to check the time. To my immense satisfaction I noted that I'd managed to sleep for almost three hours straight; more than I had in days. Adjusting the pillows behind me into a more upright position, I wiggled towards the head of the bed until I was sitting comfortably and pulled the duvet around my waist.

Automatically I opened Instagram and mindlessly began to scroll through the stories running across the top. I was just watching some random woman cleaning her oven while a stroppy toddler had a tantrum on the floor behind her, when the stories flicked to the next account. My screen was filled with phone footage of a busy street, the usual sounds of car horns and general busy-ness making me think it was a city. I glanced up to the top to see who's story it was. The name 'Judy South' shone back. I flinched at the sight of Mum's name, and my automatic reflex to chuck it meant that my phone almost launched across the room. But instead, with morbid fascination, I watched. The camera zoomed in towards a building in the near distance. I knew where it was now; a place I would never be able to forget.

The camera got closer and closer to Wimbledon tube, and I tried desperately to see more than it was showing, to try and work out who was behind it. It was useless of course, and the screen went suddenly blank. Perplexed, I carried on staring at the darkness and my hands made a jarring movement when headlines began to pop up, one after the other. *'Mother killed at tube station,' 'Football match tainted with knife death,' 'Daughter, 8, kills own mother'.* Wait, what? I pressed the left-hand side of the screen to go back to that screen again, sure that I'd read it wrong. The phone remained resolutely black. I began stabbing the screen in frustration; trust it to stop bloody working now. Weird, almost childish writing popped up.

'Wouldn't it be awful if everyone found out the truth about what happened to your mum, Marnie? Poor little Rose and Teddy would be taken away. They're not safe with a murderer like you.'

I took an involuntary sharp breath in. Whoever this was knew my children's names. I needed to ring the police back right now, this had gone way too far.

'In fact I think I'll take them. What if you snap again?'

This time I couldn't even breathe. Fear was sliding from my neck right down my spine, making me clammy and nauseous.

'I'll be coming for them soon. For their own good.'

The screen went blank once more before colour bounced onto the screen, and the inane chatter of another Insta-mummy filled my vision. Really chucking my phone across the room this time, I leapt up and ran, only just making it to the toilet in time.

TEN

I was moving agitatedly around the kitchen, my hands impatiently swapping the phone from one to another as I silently willed them to get here. After throwing my guts up I'd wasted no time ringing 999, resolutely ignoring my innate need to apologise for bothering anyone. This nutcase was now threatening my kids and that was where I drew the line. The emergency operator tried to persuade me to ring 101 because, in his words, 'it wasn't an emergency,' but I refused to be bullied down. The panic was coursing neverendingly through my body, and it was taking all I could not to drive straight to the school and to bring them home. I kept myself at home to wait, telling myself that this was too big for me now; the police needed to deal with whoever this psycho was, and fast.

An hour later I was still pacing, anger at the shockingly slow response of the police now rising to the same levels as my panic, both emotions vying for attention like siblings. I glanced at the clock. It was almost time to get the kids now anyway, and with a cross growl, I grabbed my keys and headed for the front door.

I sped through the quiet streets, my mind on nothing else but collecting Rose and Ted and getting them to safety. Visions of turning up at the school and being told they'd disappeared filled my brain with such agony that I almost didn't see the little boy skipping along the path. Teddy's gleaming hair was bouncing along with the half-jumping skip that he did to copy Rose, as he held the hand of a slight, older woman in jeans and a leather jacket.

I swung the car erratically over to the side, almost mounting the pavement as I did. I'd barely put the handbrake on before I was out and in front of them, my hand stretched out to grab Ted's arm in a panic. The older woman screamed and jumped forward too, her hand coming down on his other arm while she clawed at the back of my hand.

"Get off him! Get off!"

"Teddy? Teddy, it's Mummy. It's ok sweetheart, I've got you!" The woman increased her scratching, my skin burning with the fire of jagged nails as she tried to push me roughly aside to unbalance me.

"Get off him, you psycho!" She screamed, the panic in her voice mirroring mine. Just as her words resonated, Teddy looked up at me. Big brown eyes full of tears met my blue ones.

"Nanna?" He quavered, turning from me to look at the older woman. I immediately released him, and trembling, stared wordlessly at them both. The woman had gathered the boy to her, his tiny little shoulders heaving up and down as he sobbed.

"I'm sorry," I whispered. "I'm sorry, I thought it was my son. God," I knelt down and tried to find the boy's face in his grandparent's chest. "Hey, look I'm really sorry. I didn't mean to scare you." The boy increased his screams, and I felt a harsh pressure push me away.

"What the hell is wrong with you? You've scared the life out of him!" I looked up from my prone position on the ground to find the woman apoplectic with fury just above me. "Get away from us!" I realised she was shaking too and got up to face her.

"I'm so sorry, please..." I trailed off as she gave me one last glare, tears glistening in her eyes.

"You should be locked up. I'll be calling the police about you!"

"No, it was a mistake. Look, I'm sorry, this isn't like me! I'm not a weirdo I promise, I've got kids! I've just had a bad week and I thought he was my son. I mean you can understand why I panicked can't you?"

"All I know is you've frightened him to death. And me! You nearly run us over, and then you're screaming and shouting and pulling a poor little boy around. I'm sure all these people will be willing to be witnesses. You're a mad woman!" Suddenly, at her words, the rest of the world came into focus. There were people gathered uncertainly in a circle around us, a few with buggies or clutching tightly to their own toddlers, staring at me as if I were a monster. I felt the heat rush to my face as I recognised a couple as school parents. The waves of accusation washed over me, and I felt my own eyes begin to fill. I stood stock still, not knowing what to do next, tears pouring down my face and sweaty with the residual panic and shame that now flooded every cell of my body.

"Marnie, they said you nearly ran them over and then got out and tried to abduct the child! I mean, what the hell were you playing at? The kids were terrified when you didn't turn up to get them! And I thought something truly awful had happened to you!"

I listened wordlessly as Steve berated me for the fright I'd given him and the kids. After the woman had gotten her phone out to ring the police, my flight response had kicked in and I'd tried to get back in my car to leave. Several of the bystanders blocked my way, telling me I had to wait. I hadn't resisted; the shame of what I'd done was too great. Instead, when the police turned up ten minutes later, they found me sitting with my back to my car and staring at the ground. I didn't even have the strength to stand up and argue the toss, instead letting the irate woman have her say with no rebuttal. In the end, and seeing that no harm had come to anyone, the police let me go with a stern warning. By the time I pulled up at the school the playground was deserted, and Rose and Ted were gone.

Running into the school Reception with panic truly consuming me, I was informed that one of the mothers who had witnessed my humiliation had ratted me out to the school. The school had then rung Steve to collect the kids in my stead, pulling him away from work and ensuring my humiliation was complete. My cheeks reddened even further at this, and I had sloped back to my car before ringing his mobile. Now that he had finally run out of steam I took my chance.

"I'm really sorry, Steve. It was an honest mistake. Look, are you at home? I'll come and get them now. I'm sorry you had to leave work and everything. I'll make it up to you I promise!"

"Fuck work, Marnie!" He shouted, shocking me with the expletive – Steve had probably sworn three times in our entire marriage; the legacy of a teacher. "I couldn't care less about leaving work early. And just for the record, Ted and Rose are the ones who need an apology; it's all over the school playground what you did. Some of the boys were shouting horrible stuff about you as we left, calling you a 'psycho' and all that. Rose is in floods of tears, she's so embarrassed. And poor Teddy doesn't know what's going on, just that Mummy didn't turn up when she was supposed to! How do you think that made him feel? God, don't you ever think before you do anything?" He went silent and I felt the tears sloping down my cheeks, my throat hurting with the humiliation. I knew how it felt to have people talking about you at school. After a moment Steve audibly sighed down the line and spoke again, this time more measuredly. "Look Marnie, it's you I'm worried about. What's going on with you? You're all over the place at the moment."

"It's all this stuff going on with Mum and what happened. I'm not sleeping well, and I'm worried about the kids. I didn't want to panic you, but I think you should know; this thing came up on my Instagram today," I explained, filling him in on the stories that had flashed before my eyes this afternoon. When I finished, he exploded again.

"What!? Why haven't you called the police? Christ Marnie, These are my kids too you know!"

"I have!" I exclaimed, stung that he was shouting at me all over again when all I'd been doing was giving him the heads up. It was so unlike him. "But they didn't turn up and I had to get the kids..." I trailed off, not wanting to highlight the fact that in my shock and embarrassment I'd neglected to actually fill the police in on the reason I was so panicked when I thought that boy was Ted. Steve sighed yet again, and this time it felt patronising.

"Well who was it? Who's stories?"

"Well, that's the thing. The name was my mum's." Silence again greeted me. It felt odd to have so many silences with Steve, he was the ultimate conversationalist who always filled gaps with jokes, facts or stories to make whoever was with him feel at ease.

"That makes no sense, Marnie. Why would someone do that?"

"Steve, none of it makes sense! But someone's out to get me. First the magnet, then the ticket stub. Then note about Sarah, and now this! I'm so scared someone's going to do something to take them away from me. Maybe even hurt them! Please. I know you're cross with me about today, but please, I'm begging you to help me figure this out." I sat with the phone cradled in my shoulder and balled up both hands into fists, pressing them hard into my eyes to stem the flow of helpless tears cascading down my cheeks.

"Marnie you know I'm always here," his voice was gentle now, caressing, and reminding me of all the times he'd rescued me from a situation of my own making. "But you're making it hard with all this stalking stuff.

You know Instagram as well as I do, and you wouldn't suddenly not be able to go back on the stories. It's ridiculous. And people don't just send you things from something that happened twenty odd years ago, and the police don't suddenly accuse you of killing your mum." I sat, stung into nothingness as he continued. "And there's all the drinking stuff too. Do you even remember Rose having to call me to come and clear you up the other day? No, I didn't think so. It's not on; Rose has seen too much already and there's no way I'm letting Ted go through the same. It's getting really similar to how you were before, isn't it? Before I got you the meds you needed? I think you're having some sort of breakdown to be honest. Are you seeing a counsellor or anything?" I still couldn't answer, shocked by his disbelief of me. Steve had always, *always* had my back.

"No, of course I'm not. There's nothing wrong with *me,* it's the nut job who's threatening me!" I ignored the drinking accusations as the righteous anger bubbled now. That just wasn't true; I *never* drank around the kids. "Look, are you at home? I'll be there in ten minutes; we can have a proper conversation." I started the ignition and prepared to turn around to head to his.

"No Marnie. No, they're too upset to see you at the moment, and I don't know what else to say. I'm just going to keep the kids for the rest of the week. You need to get some proper help. Making a nuisance of yourself with the police isn't going to get you anywhere, is it? I think you need to really have a good think about whether all this stuff is truly happening, or whether it might just be in your head." His voice had dropped a few decibels, and the old kindly Steve seemed to be back in charge.

"I don't need help. I need to know my kids are safe. I'm coming to get them," I bit out, struggling to keep my temper now.

"Marnie, you need to realise they're not just your kids. Remember that" he replied, making me wonder at the hint of warning I thought I could hear.

"Well Rose then. I'll come and get her."

"Rose wants to stay here with us for a few days. Look, where's the problem?" He continued, pre-empting my protest. "You leave her with me all the time, she's happy with us. You get a break, which I think we can both agree you desperately need. What do you think is going to happen to them? Am I going to kill them or something?" He was laughing at me now, and for the first time I thought I could detect malice from my ex-husband.

"There's no problem, I just want them home," I replied in a small voice.

"And they can come home on Sunday. If they want to, of course. It's our weekend for Ted anyway, and I'll see if Rose wants to go to Dan's. You need a break, Marnie. You're losing the plot. A bit like before, isn't it?" I swallowed, taking note of the shakiness of my hands on the steering wheel, and whispered in agreement before hanging up. I needed to get to the bottom of this all. Maybe it'd be best if the kids weren't caught in the crossfire anyway.

ELEVEN

Wednesday morning found me staring at the ceiling before my alarm had gone off. I dragged myself out of bed, heading for the shower before work. I'd purposely re-jigged my shifts to do the daytimes this week. If I wasn't allowed my children, then the best thing to do would be to keep busy. I'd rung the police station several times after getting off the phone with Steve, and every time I was fobbed off, told to come in if I really wanted to, but that they couldn't do anything about something I couldn't show them proof of. In the end I'd given up, resolving to take their advice and go in person to get some answers.

Now, twisting my wet hair up into a towel turban, I reached for my phone to ring Steve before he left to take the children to school. His mobile rang and rang and, annoyed, I scrolled down to find his home number. After a couple of rings, a woman's voice answered.

"Hi Addy, it's Marnie," I said, trying to keep my voice mellow and modulated. "Are the kids there please?"

"Hi Marnie, how're you doing? Sorry Steve's already left for work with them. He had an early meeting, so they've gone to breakfast club." I growled under my breath. So, he was allowed to keep them from me for the week, but he couldn't even be bothered to rearrange his schedule to take them to school at the right time?

"Oh right. Well, he could have dropped them to me. I'd have taken them if he was too busy." I wasn't being as successful as I hoped I would be about keeping the tone light, and Addy's reply matched a little of my stiffness.

"He offered to change the meeting actually, Marnie, but Rose insisted on going. Her best friend Ruby goes you see."

"Yes, I do know that *actually*, Addy," I replied through gritted teeth. "But I'd have loved to see them this morning. As I won't be for the rest of the week, will I?"

"Yes, well, Steve thinks it's safer for everyone that you have a break. Have you managed to make an appointment to speak to someone? I know of a wonderful therapist if you're stuck for choice."

"Safer? What's that supposed to mean? Who on earth isn't *safe?*" I was spitting my words out, shocked at the pure gall of Addy to be behaving so holier-than-thou, when we'd always worked on the principle that the kids, and me for that matter, were absolutely none of her business and she was not to get involved. "And actually, Addy, I'd appreciate it if you and Steve stuck to discussing the kids and kept your stupid opinions about me to yourselves. Because, for the last time, THERE IS NOTHING WRONG WITH ME." I slammed the phone down, my towel slipping aside and unravelling its strands of damp hair all over my face. I glanced in the mirror, and a mad woman stared back.

All the way through my shift, and afterwards, the conversation with Addy replayed in my head. I was a people pleaser by nature; I hated confrontation as a rule. And Addy and I had always got on so well; she'd never overstepped the boundaries like that before, where she felt she had a right to an opinion on my life. It made me wonder what Steve had been telling her, as she was obviously hearing things that were making her think she could join in with the witch hunt. Michal gave up on me after half an hour of little response, and I could tell by his clenched jaw that he was hurt and confused by my reticence.

I decided to send Steve a text just to let him know how unimpressed I was with the way that Addy had spoken to me, and that he should have dropped the kids to me if he couldn't be bothered to take them in without resorting to breakfast club. His reply was rapid, blunt and to the point; he didn't want me having the kids this week while I was so obviously going through 'a mental health issue' and that was the end of it. It made me so angry that I responded with a few cuttingly choice expletives, and, not too surprisingly, hadn't got anything back after that. It annoyed me that I'd resorted to swearing. I knew Steve would be feeling superior.

The shift crawled by but eventually I made it home. I had a desperate need to hear their voices, just to remind myself that they still needed me. Swallowing my pride, I rang Steve's mobile and prayed that he'd pick up. I didn't fancy having to ring the house phone and go through Addy again. My luck was in, and his familiar voice came clearly through the earpiece.

"Hi Marnie," he said, sighing a little. I was getting sick and tired of the sound. "Ringing to give me a bit more abuse?"

"Of course not," I replied, irrationally upset at his obvious disinterest in speaking to me. Steve had always paid me the most attention, even after I'd left him and he remarried. There was no hint at all now of that normal, playful ex-husband of mine. "I just want to speak to the kids. Can you put them on please?"

"They're out at the moment, Addy took them round to the park."

"What? And why haven't you gone? I though you wanted to spend some time with them this week, but so far it seems like all you've done is dump them with other people!" I felt it sharply, as the familiar hurt of feeling left out hit me.

"Don't be ridiculous, Marnie," Steve said scornfully. "Addy's taken them to the park to meet one of Rose's school friends, Ruby? Well, Ruby's mum collared Addy at pick up today to ask if everything was ok at home. Apparently, Rose had said a few things to make her think you were struggling. So, Addy's gone to meet her to find out more. You see," he continued, raising his voice when I tried to interrupt. "It's not just us who are concerned by your behaviour. And how embarrassing's that? Rose is so worried about you that she's been telling her friend's mum about it? It'll be all around the gates in no time." He paused but I stayed quiet. I had absolutely no idea what to say back. My cheeks were flaming, and I wanted to cry. Rosie was so worried about me she'd been talking to Ruby's mum? What was she worried about?

"Why are you being so horrible to me?" I whispered, feeling the all too familiar lump in my throat expand and burn upwards. Steve chuckled a little unkindly.

"You sound like a child," he replied scornfully. "This isn't all about you, Marnie. The kids are the important ones here, and Rose particularly is clearly taking it hard. You need to think a little more about them in all this; think about how stressed they are, not knowing what's happening to their mum. You're behaving like you did when I first met you, you know; a petulant young girl who didn't know how to look after herself, let alone a child."

"Rose and I were fine then!" I replied, shocked at the tangent the conversation had gone off in. "We were doing ok Steve, you know we were." He snorted disbelievingly.

"Marnie, when I first met you, you were an unmedicated mess. Your anxiety and depression made you miserable, you were completely skint, you weren't eating properly, and you struggled to keep everything afloat for Rose. And I was the one who saved you from that, didn't I?" His voice took on a silky tone. "Let me save you again, babe." His voice was caressing, a light hand dancing across my back. "Let me come to the doctors with you. Maybe get you back on those pills? They could probably refer you to someone to talk to and try and sort your head out too."

"I don't need doctors, or pills, or talk, Steve! I just need everyone to stop treating me like I'm crazy and help me find out who's behind all this mad stuff. Please, can't we..." I stopped as my phone beeped, putting Steve on loudspeaker to look at the screen. Instagram was telling me I'd been tagged in a story. "I need to go," I said, hanging the phone up on Steve without waiting for a reply. I waited for the app to launch with a burning feeling in my stomach, my fingertips trembling on the sides of the metallic rectangle. Pressing the notification, my screen went black once more, with only my Insta-name tagged, and the fire began to travel up my throat, forcing me to swallow back the vomit. Bold writing faded in and out before becoming still on the screen; the lunatic was even using effects now. Music started in time with the words. With a painful pang I recognised it. 'You are my Sunshine.' It was the song I used to sing to the children when they were babies.

I told you they'd be better off without you, Marnie.

They've got a great mother in Addy, wouldn't you say? Even the other parents like her better than you. You wouldn't be missed if you just...disappeared..

Just a friendly warning....

Next time you have them, I'll be paying you all a visit.

Just like last time, the stories flicked onto the next person, and I watched blankly for a few seconds as a former soap actress began to demonstrate her make up routine. Whirling into action, I frantically swiped my finger back across the screen, but it stubbornly refused to reload the story. Without wasting any more time, and with Steve's word echoing relentlessly in my head, I spun on my heel, grabbed my bag off of the kitchen side and headed out of the door. I was going straight to the police now if they couldn't be bothered to come to me. Steve was right; I needed help.

I drummed my fingers agitatedly on the desk, glaring at the sergeant behind the glass who was staring passively back. I gave it another thirty seconds before it became unbearable.

"Hello?" My voice was louder than I'd expected. "Can you hear me? I need to speak to someone about my stalker NOW." The man kept looking measuredly at me and I slammed my hand against the glass, all remnants of control lost. The man didn't flinch, only now something bordering on humour danced across his expression. I hit the glass again in a rage, noticing that the spittle-flecks I'd left on the surface jumped with the bang every time. Whirling around, I caught a strange woman staring back at me. Her hair was brown but unkempt, her eyes wide and red rimmed, her mouth swollen and sore. A typical junkie, I thought with a frisson of middle-class fear, dismissing her as I tried to control my temper. I began to turn away, ready to repeat my demand that someone see me, when in my peripheral vision I saw the woman turn too. Her gaze met mine straight on, and the more I looked into her crazy eyes, the more I recognised. She was me.

With the shock of my appearance my agitation drained, and fear replaced it as naturally as if it were breathing. I forced myself to stop staring and turned my attention back to the front. The desk sergeant was still watching me, and as I approached again, he seemed to draw himself upright, clearly ready to intimidate me.

"Please. Could I just speak to someone? It is urgent. I promise." I gazed at him beseechingly, and only when he didn't relax and smile, did I realise how often I must use my normally well-kept appearance to get what I needed from strangers.

"As I've already told you, Ms South, the officer in charge of your case is tied up at the moment. I'll get him to ring you as soon as he's free."

"I told you. I don't want to wait for a phone call! I want to speak to someone now! I'm being threatened! Why isn't that important enough for you?"

"It's not that it isn't important," he said placatingly. "It's just that we have limited officers available to see walk ins. Budget cuts and the like, you see? Now why don't you go home and wait until someone can give you a ring? It'll be a lot comfier you know."

I shook my head. "I'm not leaving. I'll wait." I chucked myself into the nearest plastic seat, my phone clenched in my fist. The sergeant merely shrugged at me and continued to work, his face concentrating on the screen.

"Suit yourself," he replied without bothering to look at me again.

I banged into the house, so cross that I didn't even care if the psycho was at home. In fact, right at this second, I'd relish it I was so angry. I could quite happily commit a murder, just bring it on. The officer who finally spoke to me had been more than useless and were clearly subscribing to the same school of thought as Steve and Lula; that I was just a crazy person who was making things up for drama.

Storming noisily to the back of the house I flicked the kitchen light on before clocking him. Steve was sitting at my kitchen table with a cup of coffee in front of him. There was another one in front of the chair opposite, and he gestured that I should sit down. I stood where I was, looking gormlessly at him.

"The police rang," he began, answering my silent question. "They're concerned about you, and as you gave them my number as your emergency contact, they thought they'd have a chat with me. Do you want to know what I told them?" I nodded, my mouth too dry to answer. "Well sit down then!" He was smiling malevolently at me.

"You'd think I was dangerous, the way you're behaving! Come on babe, I won't bite." I placed my handbag quietly on the worktop before walking over to him, my phone still wedged in my by now sweaty paw. "Coffee? I've already put two sugars in. Some things you never forget, eh?" I gave him a wobbly smile as I slid into the chair. Steve was all of a sudden threatening, his usual exuberance stripped and leaving a complete stranger in its wake. "There we are," he said, pushing the cup towards me. He seemed to be waiting for me to drink it, so I picked it up and took a sip, burning my entire mouth in the process.

"How did you get in?" I asked thickly, my tongue feeling swollen against my teeth and the roof of my mouth on fire. He grinned at me, his face breaking out into the usual Steve.

"With my key?" He started laughing at my stricken face. "God Marnie don't tell me you've forgotten that I have a key?! You really have lost the plot, haven't you?" He leant back on his chair and stretched his legs out while I sat trying to keep up with the sudden change in his behaviour. He continued to grin easily at me whilst I floundered.

"Oh...yes. Sorry, I forgot." I was whispering without meaning to, annoyed at myself that the goalposts seemed to have moved, and suddenly my ex-husband seemed to have the upper hand yet again. "So, what did you tell them?"

"Well," he began, shooting suddenly forwards onto all four legs of the chair so that they banged abruptly onto the tiled floor and resonated around the room. "They had a few things to tell me too actually. What would you like to hear first?" My hands were trembling on my mug and even I couldn't work out if it was anger or fear.

"Just tell me what happened," I said quietly.

"Well," he repeated, leaning his elbows on the table and taking a sip of his own coffee. He's enjoying this, I realised. He's enjoying freaking me out. "They rang to say that they had you in the police station. You were refusing to leave and raving about this person who's supposed to be stalking you! Honestly Marnie, the officer could barely stop laughing while he was telling me. You were rambling about magnets, letters, random Instagram stuff. I told them you'd been saying the same thing to me."

"Why was he laughing?" I asked, astounded. "It's true. Someone is stalking me. You saw the magnet yourself after the break in. You're the one who told me to ring the police in the first place!"

"No idea what you're talking about Marnie. You rang me drunk and raving about a break-in and a magnet. I came to get you because Addy was worried that you'd do something stupid. But there was no broken window when I got there. No magnet either."

"Don't be stupid Steve. I had to get a bloke in the next day to replace it, didn't I?" Laughing silently, he shook his head.

"Don't you get it yet? It's all in your head, Marnie! Let's look at the facts," he continued, adopting what I assumed was his teacher persona, needing to explain something simple to a child who just couldn't get it. "You say someone sent you a magnet. There is no magnet. You say someone broke your window. There was no broken window. You say someone sent you a ticket stub, but no one's seen that either. Then you attack a poor grandmother and her grandson and try to kidnap him. And now you're claiming someone's sending you secret threats on Instagram, but you can't find them again to prove it, and no one else has seen them? Have I left anything out? I mean, just think about it!" He began to laugh in earnest now, his face creased up into what I had always thought was the kindest of expressions, but I could now see was only judging and ugly. I stood up, the anger bubbling righteously inside me.

"You saw the broken window yourself! And no magnet or ticket stub?" I stormed over to the drawer of the dresser, ripping it open to pull the objects out. "What are these then?" I was shouting as I rooted around for them, so cross that I was having to explain myself yet again when my children were being threatened. My fingers brushed against all of the items that I shoved in there every couple of days; sewing threads, birthday candles, random letters, and a huge variety of pens. I pulled it out more violently; my eyes frantically searching now. Where were they? They were here this morning; I'd checked.

The drawer had been an unhappy beacon for me every single time I was in the house, whispering softly to me to open it, to handle each painful reminder of the worst day of my life over and over again. Behind me I could hear Steve laughing softly while his chair scraped excruciatingly across the tiles. Eventually I wrenched the drawer too hard and it came completely off of the runners and fell with a bang onto the tiled floor. Falling to my knees, I moved amongst the debris, impervious to the sharp scratches of sewing needles digging into my fingers. Steve rose from his chair so that he towered above me.

"Right, well I'll leave you to it then. Christ Marnie, I didn't actually think you'd go this far. It's a good job the kids have other homes to go to. As I told the police earlier, I'd be worried about their safety if they were with you." As those last words pierced my consciousness, I lost it. I leapt up and took a running jump. Suddenly my legs were wrapped around his midriff as my fingers clawed aimlessly at whatever flesh I could reach. His laughter had turned to shouts now, and I felt the wet sensation of drawing blood before powerful hands had my wrists in a vice, my body being pushed easily away. Ending up in a slump on the floor once again, I looked up at the scarlet droplets gathering on both sides of Steve's face. He was panting from the counterattack as he met my gaze. Suddenly he smirked.

"And I told Dan it was going to take months for us to get custody from you. Well done, Marnie," he continued, reaching for his phone. "You've just lost the last two people you love. You seriously need to check into the nuthouse." I watched helplessly as he put phone to his ear. "Hello, detective? Steve Houghton here. I want to report an assault please." He left me on the floor of the kitchen, my name wafting back to me as he continued his conversation.

As I heard the front door slam behind him, silence took over the house, with only my ragged breathing interrupting its slumber. For thirty seconds I stayed where I was, with Steve's parting words ringing uninterruptedly in my ears. Suddenly they clicked into consciousness and bolting upright, I sprinted to the door and wrenched it open. He was gone.

TWELVE

I was almost starting to believe Steve when he said I was going mad. After his abrupt departure I immediately tried to get hold of Dan to find out what was going on. He answered for once, but only to tell me he was having Rose for the weekend and to leave them alone. Sarah didn't answer any of my frantic calls, and nor did Addy or Steve.

Eventually out of desperation I rang Lula. After a few static sentences, it became clear that she agreed that I needed a break, not seeming to understand the seriousness of what Steve and Dan were doing to me. As we argued back and forth that I was being unreasonable not letting Steve and Dan keep the kids for the weekend, I realised; it had to be them. All this time it was them doing this to me. It was the only thing that made sense after all; they both knew the details of my past, and Steve had easy access to my house. How simple would it have been for him to come and remove the evidence before I could take it to the police? They were setting me up, making me seem crazy enough to take my kids away from me.

"It's them Lula!" I interrupted her berating of my 'drama queen' personality mid-flow.

"Who?"

"Steve and Dan!" Quickly I explained. "I've got to go, Lula. I need to ring the police." I'd almost hung up when I heard her tinny voice shouting back.

"Marnie! Marnie!"

"What?" I said impatiently.

"Don't ring the police," she said, causing my jaw to drop momentarily. "Marnie, they already think you're mad. You're not going to be doing yourself any favours by making a nuisance of yourself, and if the boys really are planning on going for custody, you'll be playing right into their hands." I protested but she ignored me. "I mean it Marnie. And I think maybe Steve's right; you're not yourself." I hung up on her. I didn't have time for this.

The next time I opened my eyes my head felt like it was being slowly but surely crushed in a rusty vice. I sat up gingerly, trying to make sense of my surroundings and work out where I was. The floor was hard and cold, and light streamed relentlessly in, piercing my eyes painfully as the room came into view. I was on the kitchen floor, the tiles seeping their freezing hands into my back and bruising the back of my skull with their unrelenting rigidity. More than one wine bottle lay next to me, glinting in the sunshine and laughing at my folly.

Panic swept over me, and I rolled quickly onto my knees in order to get up, before the wave of intense nausea bombarded me and I collapsed to the ground again. After a few moments of mental perseverance, I felt ready to try again, and grabbing the handle on the kitchen cabinets besides me, I wrenched myself onto my knees again and upwards. Finally upright but leaning heavily over the side, I waited for another wave of nausea to wash over my now overly hot and sweating body. My hand scrambled across the worktop until my fingers found the kettle and flicked it on. While waiting for it to boil I rested my head on the cool countertop and thought about my next move.

I couldn't ring the police anymore, that was clear to me now. At the end of last night's phone call, they said that they would charge me with wasting police time if I called again. I checked my watch. It was already eleven, and Rose and Teddy would be at school and nursery. It was Friday though, which meant no clubs after school. I'd simply go to pick up and bring them home, I decided. They couldn't stop me; the school knew I was their main parent after all, and it must have been odd to them that I hadn't done this week's school runs anyway. I mean, Dan had never done a pickup in his life! And Steve wouldn't be there because of work so he'd probably send Addy. And let's face it, I thought confidently, I'd be given my kids over that bitch any day.

I drank the by now temperate coffee, contemplating heading over to the nursing home before school. I hadn't managed to see Dad for days now, but with everything else going on I hadn't given it as much thought as I should have. Suddenly though it seemed unusual, and maybe even sinister, that they weren't allowing me access to him. Briefly I toyed with ringing Lula again and asking if she'd been denied entry too, but I found I was too cross with her after last night's conversation to try and be civil.

Mind made up, I chucked my mug in the sink and, trying to ignore the pounding ache that was resonating from head to toe through my body, I picked my handbag up off the side from where it'd been since Steve invited me to sit down. I'd almost reached the front door when I caught sight of myself in the hallway mirror. My eyes were ringed with bags so dark that I looked like I'd been punched, and my skin had broken out in spots and cold sores. Some were weeping, likely infected. I literally look like a druggie, I realised, and not for the first time. No one would let me see an elderly old man or pick my kids up looking like that.

I scooted around on my heel and headed for the stairs, lifting my arm to smell myself as I did. It was rancid; musty and mixed with alcohol sweats. Now I came to think of it, I probably hadn't washed since Steve took the kids, so that was a good four days now. I hadn't really had a reason to; after that first day when the kids were gone, shift control had told me to take the week as holiday. Apparently 'my mind wasn't on the job,' and it had been hinted at that they'd heard I was having a hard time. Briefly I wondered whether Michal had complained about me after the last shift. I found I didn't care too much; work was a lifetime away from me now. But after they'd told me that there seemed little point in taking too much care of my hygiene. I wasn't seeing a soul, no one cared what I smelt like.

As I waited for the shower to warm up a little now, I moved through the top of the house opening every single window to let the air in. The sudden chill made me shiver but feel alive and maybe even hopeful. I couldn't have Rose and Teddy coming back to a hovel, and they needed to know everything was back to normal. I was their mum, and their place was here. With me.

THIRTEEN

I was being paranoid. There was no way that every single parent in this playground knew anything about what was going on, but it didn't stop me feeling like everyone was staring. Even those mums that I knew well enough to talk to seemed to be whispering to their compatriots behind their hands and taking sneaky glances at me whenever they thought I wasn't looking in their direction. I stayed where I was, right at the front of the crowd, and kept my eyes trained on the door that I knew Rose would be released from. My arms were aching with the frenzied cleaning spree I'd embarked on before coming, and I scratched the top of my hand compulsively where the bleach had irritated it. Suddenly I felt a cool hand rest lightly on the top of my forearm and a gentle voice stage whispered over to me.

"Are you ok, darling?" It was Ruby's mum, her eyes meeting mine with a look of concern on her face. "That looks really sore, look, you've drawn blood." She picked my injured hand up in hers, holding it for me to see the damage while the other mums craned their heads to watch. I flushed with embarrassment, now definitely the centre of attention in the crowd. Wrenching my own hand back out of hers I took a step back and dropped my shoulders.

"I'm fine thanks, Grace," I replied, projecting my voice as confidently as I could. "Just having a deep clean and the bleach on my skin, you know…" She stepped forwards, still with that look on her face and reached out towards me. "I said I'm fine!" I shouted, recoiling, and moving a step further away. "And you can stop spreading rumours that Rose is unhappy while you're at it. Nothing's wrong except people like you sticking their nose into our lives!" The playground was almost silent, broken only by a few sly sniggers and murmurs. Grace took a step back again and dropped her outstretched arm, looking wounded.

"I was only checking Marnie," she said quietly now. "I only wanted to check. And I haven't been spreading rumours, Rose was upset the other day, and said some things were going on with you at home. I know parentings hard. I just wanted to offer a friendly ear, that's all."

"I don't need it! We don't need you offering anything to us, ok? Stay away from me and stay away from Rose if you know what's good for you!" She shrunk back, and looking into her eyes I saw something new; fear. Just as I registered this another parent stepped in front of Grace, coming to her defence.

"For God's sake Marnie! She was only trying to be nice! What is wrong with you?"

"Me? There's absolutely nothing wrong with me, except you lot! Don't think I don't know you've all be talking about me for weeks; you don't exactly hide it, do you? You all think you're better than me – well you're not! You're just sad, pathetic, middle-aged women who don't have anything better to do than gossip about something you know nothing about!"

Just then the bell rang faintly from inside the building, and I felt my shoulders tense up. I turned back to the school door now, the glaring woman in front of me now completely forgotten. This was it. Risking a quick scan either side of me, I was gratified that there was no sign of either Steve or Addy. A tiny bit of self-satisfaction began to glow slowly within, warming my stomach. At least I could arrive on time to collect my children, which was clearly something they struggled with. The kids began to troop out of the red brick building, and I strained to pick Rose out of her line as my anxious heart thumped. It gave a leap of relief as I found her, nearly at the back and laughing with Ruby as usual.

As she made her way towards the front of the queue, I saw her scan the crowd for me. She spotted me easily, and I gave her a happy wave, my face breaking into its first proper grin since last weekend. She turned away quickly, carrying on her chatter with Ruby. Only I had noticed the rainbow of uncertainty and worry that crossed her features. I lowered my hand, a little hurt that after nearly a whole week without me she wasn't jumping for joy at being reunited. Then I gave myself a mental wobble; this was a seven-year-old girl that I was expecting to behave in a certain way. And she'd probably been listening to God knows what being said about me at Steve and Addy's, not to mention Grace the saviour. I knew that once we were all home normality would resume. Eventually it was her turn to be handed over, and I watched with confusion when she didn't point in my direction. Instead, she scanned the crowd some more until her face broke into a huge smile and she pointed. But not at me.

"Rosie!" I shouted, waving frantically to get her attention. I could feel the heat of the teacher's gaze on me, but I ignored her. "Rose! I'm here! Come on, we need to get Teddy." My daughter's face was going red, and she looked up at her teacher. "Rose!" My voice had taken on a bark-like edge. I felt so shamed by her. Why was she behaving like I was some random stranger? I began to walk towards her and her teacher, keeping my eyes on my daughter's red face and trying to ignore the fresh whispers that were emerging behind me. Reaching them both, I held out a hand to her, my temper now fraying with humiliation. She wouldn't meet my gaze, or take my hand, instead looking around the side of me. Suddenly her face lit up with relief for a second time. I didn't even have time to whirl around before my hand was knocked carelessly aside by another. Rose took the proffered hand and I put mine on her arm to stop her, about to protest.

"Let her go, Marnie," a low voice to the side of me muttered. "You're making a scene." I went to pull her to me, raising my eyes to glare at Dan. My words melted in my throat at the furious anger etched on his face. "Let. Go." He bit out once more. "You're embarrassing Rose. Jesus Marnie, look at the state of you." I looked at them, Rose tucked under her dad's arm as he shielded her protectively from me. In my peripheral vison I could see everybody staring at me, and a weird silence now pervaded the playground where normally there was none.

"She needs to come home with me," I said, trying my best to keep calm. "Dan, I need her to come home with me." I turned my attention to Rose herself, crouching down so that my face was level with hers. "Darling, come on. Let's go and get Teddy, eh? We can order Dominos if you like. And ice cream? And you can choose a film, that'll be good, won't it?" I went to take her hand automatically, as I had done every day since she could walk, taking on the role of her greatest guardian as naturally as I breathed. She flinched and turned her face into Dan's side, refusing to meet my gaze. A tap on my shoulder made me swing around. Rose's teacher was standing beside us, her expression unreadable. Behind her, I saw that the teaching assistant had taken over distributing the last few children to their parents.

"I think it might be a good idea if we moved this discussion inside to somewhere more private. You're welcome to use my classroom? And I could sit outside with Rose while the two of you discuss whatever you need to." She motioned back towards the double doors, and I began to move before I noticed that Dan was going nowhere.

"That won't be necessary, Mrs Davies. I think Marnie here has just forgotten it's my week to have Rose. Isn't that right, Marnie?" He gave me a none too gentle nudge when I didn't immediately reply and I glared at him and drew myself upright, no longer caring who was watching.

"Actually Dan, it's not your week, it's mine. You don't do weekdays, remember? Normally too busy in the pub or out with your mates. Now come along Rose, we'll be late to get Teddy." I spoke loudly and with as much authority as I could, used to being in control when it came to the kids. Dan smiled nastily and raised his voice too.

"That's low even for you Marnie. She's not coming home with you, and nor is Ted for that matter." He wasn't trying to keep the volume down either. "Rose," he bent down, speaking in a gentler tone but still at full volume. "Who do you want to go with, Mum or me?"

"You," she replied immediately and distinctly, causing my face to flame and my heart to break.

"There we are then." Dan smiled triumphantly. "Sort yourself out, Marnie. You look like some sort of junkie. Back on the gear, are you?" With one last malicious look at me, he and Rose turned away without a goodbye. I stayed standing where I was, humiliation, indignation and heartbreak mingling interchangeably. The crowds were thinning, and I turned to Mrs Davies.

"Sorry about that," I said, pasting a responsible adult smile on my face. "Rose's dad…well…he's not very reliable. And he can be quite spiteful. I mean what he said about drugs just then, well obviously you know that's not true. I'm a paramedic for God's sake!"

"Don't worry about it," Mrs Davies replied, returning a ghost of a smile. "Are you sure all's ok at home though, Ms South? It's just that Rose has seemed very out of sorts the last few weeks, and when we've asked her if she's ok…"

"What?" The teacher looked awkward.

"Well, she seems to think that you're having a hard time just now. All that business with the boy in the street earlier this week too. I know it was mistaken identity," she continued, waving my explanation away. "I just want to make sure all is ok. We're here to support the entire family, you know. Not just the child. We could put you in touch with people who can help if you're not coping?"

"There is nothing wrong with me!" I was shrieking now, the acute sense of unfairness coming to the fore. "I have single-handedly brought my children up, you know. Especially Rose. And now her dad waltzes in, makes a few remarks, and you decide I need help! I am SICK of people saying that to me! All I need is my kids back home and I will be FINE!" I turned around, not trusting myself to stay here any longer and be patronised. I steamed across the playground in the direction of the Pre-School, the blood thundering in my veins. How bloody dare the school turn against me? How could they take Dan, of all people's, side over mine?

I reached the deserted pre-school entrance in record time, my anger making me faster than usual. There were no staff members milling about anymore, and I realised how late the altercation with Dan had made me. Poor Ted must be wondering where I was; I was never late to pick up. I rang the bell and waited impatiently for someone to answer it. I jiggled on the spot, for the first time noticing that I'd forgotten my coat in my eagerness to get to school. I heard a few scraping sounds as someone began to unbolt the door. Finally. It opened to reveal the setting manager's bulky figure.

"Ms South, hi." Even as I looked around her body for Ted, I noticed the awkwardness in her tone. I went to take a step forward, pasting a smile on my face in anticipation of seeing him. She didn't move, and for the first time I looked squarely at her.

"Where's Ted? Getting his stuff?" I kept my tone light, even as the reality sunk in. If even Dan had managed to pull his finger out and be a father for once, then Steve was guaranteed to have made sure I couldn't get Ted either.

"Teddy was picked up earlier, Ms South. By his stepmother?" I felt my face begin to colour. "She is one of the people named as an authorised adult to collect," she continued, clearly keen that I knew her staff were not in the wrong for letting him go. "We're very careful about who our children go home with. Of course, we checked she knew the password before they left."

"Yeah, she would know it," I agreed flatly. A beat passed and I just stared at her blankly, all of the fight and energy limping slowly away. I nodded a goodbye, my throat too constricted with unshed tears to speak. They'd won.

I spent the entire drive home from school with tears of humiliation streaming down my face, paying no attention whatsoever to the road. I'd ended up standing outside the pre-school in silence for so long that the nursery worker had awkwardly tapped me on the shoulder and asked if she could help me with anything else. I didn't need help. She'd refused me entry to the building while she told me that someone not even related to him had my child. How in the hell was she going to be able to help me?

I was almost at the opening to our estate when an off-licence on the side of the road caught my eye. I rarely made an appearance in there; I normally bought my weekly bottle of wine in my food shop. Today though, there was ample reason to top up. I swung the car suddenly to the right, pulling up on the pavement and causing the car that had been travelling behind me to swerve to avoid going into the back of me, beeping at my sudden manoeuvre. I flipped the bird at them as I emerged onto the street.

The shop door chimed as I opened it, a sound that I'd always loved but nowadays seemed relegated to the past. It reminded me of vague memories of being little and going to the local shop with mum for groceries, and I never heard it anywhere anymore. Off licences seemed to be an institution immune to the changing of time. Once over the threshold I paused, relief creeping over my face. Every single surface was piled with booze of all kinds, and homing in on the gin section, I made my way over.

"Can I help you?" A pleasant voice came from my left side, where an elderly man was standing politely waiting with his apron on over his shirt and trousers.

"Oh, erm no thanks," I replied. "I'm just looking for a couple of bottles of gin. Party, you know?" His face broke into a delighted smile.

"Ah well what sort of flavours do you like? We've got some fantastic ginger ones, or lemon? Or how about this orange flavoured one? It's on offer too. Would you like to try it?"

"Ok, I mean no I don't need to try it. I'll just take it though." I felt flustered by his questions. I just wanted to get home and get blackout drunk.

"Ok so two of the orange? Or one orange and one something else?"

"Oh, you choose." I just wanted to get home and sink into alcoholic oblivion.

"Fabulous, I'll give you the ginger one too. Now, let me show the tonics we carry; this one for example goes well with the orange gin?"

"Ok, yes fine." My voice was getting more abrupt, and I just wanted to get out of there now.

"Ah, it doesn't go with the ginger though." He began to rummage, "but this one does?"

"I'll take two of each then." I was desperate to leave and very much doubted I'd be needing the tonic anyway. I followed the man over to the till, where he took about ten minutes to scan them through. My debit card tapped impatiently on the wood as I silently willed him to hurry up.

"So that'll be £42.40 then please love." I proffered the card but he waved it away, continuing; "would you like to round it up to £43.00? We're raising money for the local hospice and every little helps."

"Yes, yes ok, that's fine. Look can we?" I held my card up. "It's just I've got to be somewhere."

"Ah, the party?" He asked, nodding knowledgably towards my booze.

"Yes, exactly." I shoved the card into the reader, and mercifully, the experience came to an end. I rushed back out of the door, the tinkling of the shop bell now annoying rather than nostalgic. I jumped into my car, barely shutting the door before I'd put my foot on the accelerator and reversed carelessly into the road.

Two minutes later I was pulling into my own driveway, already opening the bottle of orange gin in my head, and taking those compassionate first gulps. I'd almost reached the front door when Lydia, my middle-aged neighbour, opened her own one and called out.

"Marnie!" She wrapped the big cardigan she was wearing around her to cover the fact that her generous chest was braless and padded across our boundary in her slippers. Reaching me, she held out a small package. "Here," she said, waiting for me to take it. "I had to sign for it for you." I flinched, and the bag of bottles swung noisily against my leg with the sudden movement. She smiled at the sound. "Tough day? That's kids for you, eh?" She peered around me towards the car. "Where are they, not with you tonight?"

"Erm, no. It's their night to be with their dads."

"Oh lovely. A good break for you then sweetheart." I nodded and turned back to my door to unlock it. "Don't forget this, love!" She pushed the package into my free hand, waving and smiling as she turned away.

The paper felt cold and alien, already seeping it's malevolent contents into my palm. I flung it on the kitchen worktop and stared at it for a few moments, trembling with sick anticipation. There was no way in hell I could open it. One more horrible surprise would probably send me over the precipice, and I didn't want to find out what was waiting for me there. Instead, with one last glance at it, I grabbed a bottle of gin and went into the living room.

I gulped it down straight, enjoying the pain of my throat being on fire. With my free hand I rummaged on the shelves and, retrieving the first photo album that I touched, sat clumsily on the nearest side of the sofa. It was dated six years ago, right around the time I met Steve. He'd always thought it was weird that I printed photos in this day and age, but there was something so satisfying about palpable evidence, a bit like turning pages of an actual book rather than a Kindle. Owning hard copies made me remember that my life was real; that these children were mine; that I'd once been a part of a happy family.

Over and over again I raised the bottle to my mouth, until I'd downed half of it neat, and I knew I was going to be sick if I carried on without a mixer to dilute it. Heaving myself up to grab it I found that the door handle had moved a foot to the left, and I bounced off it, smacking ungracefully into the wall before managing to get over the threshold. Meandering down the hall it took a few more bumps into the walls to realise that I was more than just pissed; I was teetering on the edge of paralytic. But still, I decided, not as drunk as I wanted to be. My hand fluttered uselessly on the wall as I tried to find the kitchen light. I hadn't noticed how dark it'd gotten while I'd been wallowing in memories.

Eventually my finger made contact, and the light blinded me momentarily. Just as the haze of green spots and stars cleared from my vision, there it was. Taunting me, right next to my gin supply. I purposefully turned my face away while I picked up the big bottle of tonic and a glass, ready to head back to safety. But I stumbled, and my fingers momentarily stroked the brown package. Without wanting to, without even looking, I grabbed it too and gingerly made my way back down the hallway.

The living room felt like a friendly refuge I was now invading as I placed it carefully on the coffee table and began to pour myself another drink, this time diluted ever so slightly. The shopkeeper hadn't needed to try to sell me on the flavours I thought to myself; by this point I could barely see, let alone taste. But I had an uncontrollable urge now to find out what this next torturous chapter entailed. Taking a deep breath, I ripped the small package apart, shuddering at the prospect. Several shiny photos fell out. I gathered them together, turning them over but somehow already knowing what they'd be. It was the next step. Rose and Ted's figures were achingly familiar even when not in sharp focus. Rose's long hair was flying carelessly behind her as she tipped back on the park swing. Ted's cheeky face was scrunched up in laughter as he skipped along the pavement right outside his nursery holding Addy's hand. Steve had to be behind this. And it wasn't about me after all. It had always been about my kids.

My heart rate increased as I flipped over to the next photo, the alcohol making my fingers shake so much that it was hard to focus for long. I immediately recognised Steve's back garden with the treehouse and climbing frame he'd made from scratch in full view. Both Rose and Ted were sitting on the patio steps. I peered closer. Rose was crying, her face red and scrunched up. Ted had his head in her lap, his hair facing the camera so that I couldn't see his face. My own tears dripped onto the surface of the picture as if hoping to mingle with my daughter's but sliding as easily away as they fell. I felt so hopeless. My children were in pain, were in danger, and I couldn't do a fucking thing about it.

No, I could. I could go to Steve's right now, with these pictures, and force him to confess what he's been doing. It made so much sense to me now, that I couldn't believe I'd not worked it out before. Steve's wife, Steve's garden. And if it really wasn't Steve...well then he'd be as worried as I was and be calling the police himself. I felt determined now that I had a plan. I got my bag, shoved the photos in, and, banging into the wall one last time, headed for the front door.

FOURTEEN

I woke up on the doormat with my keys in one hand and an empty bottle of gin in the other feeling like I'd been subjected to a stampede. Everything ached. Confused, I looked around to find a clue to explain why I had ended up here. After a beat I remembered the photos! In a wild panic I jumped to my feet, before swiftly falling back down in agony. I held my head in my hands and willed my brain to stop banging against my skull so that I could concentrate.

Forcing myself to my feet more slowly, I ignored the pain as much as I could. I needed to get to Steve and show him the pictures before this escalated any further. After roughly five minutes of crawling up the wall I was finally upright. I looked all around the hall for my bag, but it was nowhere to be seen. That was weird. The last thing I remembered was heading to the door on my way to Steve's. I must have passed out before I managed to get outside, but I would have had my bag, wouldn't I?

I peered into the living room, and quickly recoiled. It looked like someone had ransacked the room, with the shelves' contents pulled messily down. Hundreds of pictures littered the floor, and empty bottles of gin and tonics were laying sideways on the coffee table, some still slowly expelling their contents onto the carpet. Rose and Ted's faces beamed up at me from every single angle, interspersed here and there with Steve, or with my dad, and occasionally, with me. The urge to give up and sink myself back into happier times was overwhelming as I stared at them, but I needed to keep in the present. I needed to work this out. I pulled the door shut on my memories and headed for the kitchen instead.

The weak October light streaming into the kitchen made me want to die. Or more accurately, made me feel as if I was actively dying. I made myself ignore every single nerve ending that was screaming at me to get into a dark room and lay down, and instead forced myself to focus. There my bag was, right on the worktop next to the surplus bottles of tonic water from last night. I grabbed it and ran to the car, barely thinking about what might happen if I got pulled over as I gunned the engine and reversed haphazardly out into the road.

The roads were almost deserted as I sped towards Steve and Addy's, which was strange for a Saturday morning. It was only when the news jingle cracked through the speakers of the radio, and the newscaster announced the seven am news that it made sense why.

I'd barely parked before I was steaming up the path towards their front door, ignoring the curtains that were still drawn across the two bay windows. It was a matter of life and death, and Steve would soon understand that when he knew what I knew. I pressed the doorbell several times. After ten seconds, and when nothing had happened, I put my finger on it and held it down, using my other hand to bang on the door too. As I did so I noticed my knuckles were cut and bruised, the livid red and purple at odds against the rest of my pale skin. Absently I wondered how I'd managed to do that before a silhouette began to grow on the other side of the door and all thoughts of my hand flew out of my mind. The door was wrenched open, and Steve glared down at me, his face screwed up with rage.

"What?" He barked. I didn't have time for this.

"Steve, I need to talk to you, it's urgent." I went to walk into the house as I always had. It wasn't until I nearly fell over from bouncing off of his chest that I looked up, shocked. "Let me in then, I need to show you something." I held up the bag. "Hold on, what happened to your face?" I asked, as he moved forward and the bruise under his right eye was highlighted in the weak morning hue.

"None of your business," he barked again as he took a small step backwards into the shadows. "Go home, Marnie. Christ, even for you this is getting out of hand. It's seven in the morning and you've woken the entire household up. Teddy's hysterical, he thought we were being burgled. Yet another thing I gather we have you to thank for; scaring him to death with all that talk of a break in."

"There was a break in. You know there was, Steve," I retorted, stung. "But anyway, we haven't got time for arguing, I need to show you these pictures that were delivered. I know what you did." I was rooting in my bag while I spoke. "Pictures of the kids, taken by someone from the bushes in the park. There's even some of them in your garden. You need to tell me the truth! I promise I won't stop you seeing Ted or anything, but you need to own up to this before I make things difficult for you." My hands were brushing left and right in the depths of my handbag, trying to find the package. Eventually I gave up looking blindly and peered into the dark interior, tipping it slightly to allow the early slivers of light to illuminate. A myriad of lip-glosses, forgotten toy cars, snack bars and wipes greeted me. No package, no photos. "No," I whispered to myself, moving stuff frantically out of the way until eventually I lost patience, crouched down, and tipped the whole lot out onto his doorstep. Steve was watching me with contempt. "They're gone," I acknowledged in wonder, sitting back on my heels.

"Finished?" Steve said, going to shut the door on me. With a speed that made my bones jar, I stuck my arm over the threshold and grabbed the door frame.

"Steve, I know it was you! It all makes sense, the whole thing. I get it now; you're upset over the way I broke the family up and you're trying to get back at me! Look, I can't say I'm not upset and angry, but we can work it out, ok? I won't tell the police it was you, and we can just go back to how things were. I'll just take Ted now, collect Rose, and then we'll have a good talk about everything when we've all calmed down." Again, I went to step over the threshold, before being rebuffed by Steve's hand pushing against my chest.

"Marnie, please. Please stop this, for the kids' sake. Please." Steve sounded like he was going to cry but I knew him better now. I hadn't forgotten our conversation at the kitchen table. I hadn't forgotten the way he looked at me and smiled at my pain.

"I will if you'd just admit it and leave the past alone!"

"I haven't sent you anything Marnie," he replied, still not letting me in. "I swear on Teddy's life, ok? This is all in your head and someone's going to get hurt if we can't get you the help you need." He sounded sincere, but an edge of warning had crept into his tone.

"You didn't send me anything? Or call me? Or post any stories on Instagram?"

"No. I keep telling you. No, Marnie. Why would I? I want the kids to be happy; both of them. And I want them to have a mum who's stable enough to take care of them."

"Ok," I said slowly, pretending to believe him. "But if it wasn't you, then I'm telling you, someone is stalking them! Or don't you care?" I was working my way to a standing position as I spoke, which was quite tricky when I couldn't risk letting go of the frame. "My neighbour came out after I'd got back from the school, and she said she'd signed for a package. And when I opened it, all these photos fell out of Rose and Ted at the park and in your garden, loads of them!" Steve exhaled loudly and closed his eyes for a moment.

"I know you, Marnie. If that was true, you'd have been round here like a shot. It's just another story of yours. Just like all the rest. Anything to make yourself centre of attention, eh?" Steve took a step forward and began to peel my fingers of off the frame, his skin hard and unyielding against my sweaty digits. "Look I'm tired of this now. I'll give you one last chance to leave, or I'm calling the police myself for harassment. And from the smell of you," he gave a dramatic sniff, "I'd say they might be arresting you for a little more than you bargained for."

"What?" I said, truly confused now.

"The booze, Marnie. I could smell you as soon as I opened the door, and judging from the state of you, I'd say you probably shouldn't be driving, wouldn't you?" He smiled unpleasantly. "You're a disgrace. It's a good job you've not got the kids, isn't it? Who knows what sort of danger they'd be in with you." The words resonated alarmingly around my brain, trying to anchor onto the origin. Just as something began to make its way fuzzily to the front, my gaze was pulled towards a movement through the banister behind Steve's head. Two little blue eyes peered out at me, a thumb stuck in the rosebud mouth, and tracks of his recent fright still evident down his cheeks.

"Teddy!" I exclaimed, forgetting completely about the door frame and holding my arms out for him. Steve whipped around and growled at our son.

"Ted, go up to Addy. Now!" His words made our son flinch, and he looked uncertainly between the two of us.

"Baby, come here," I crooned, desperate to feel his warmth in my arms. "Let's have a quick cuddle, Teddy Bear? I've missed you so much!"

"Ted I'll be up in a minute, mate." Steve had modulated his tone to match mine, the caressing honeyed tones reaching out to Teddy's uncertain frame. "Don't worry," he continued when our son didn't move. "Mummy's going now. She's sorry she frightened you, but remember what I told you? Mummy's not very well at the moment. She's going to get some help." I watched in cold horror as my child nodded his head, his eyes suddenly lighter, and without a second thought and a relieved smile, he turned and scampered back up the stairs to Addy, who had appeared at the top. Tears filled my eyes as I watched them embrace and move out of sight. Steve now turned his attention back to me, his eyes glittering with triumph.

"Bye then," he spat in my direction, taking the opportunity that Ted had given him when my fingers left the doorframe to reach out for the hug, and slammed the door in my face.

Somehow, I managed to get myself home, negotiating the car through much busier streets than when I'd arrived. The only moment I remembered clearly was when someone stopped suddenly in front of me to let a couple cross the road, and I only just avoided going into the back of them. Slamming my foot on the brake I made the wheels screech in protest. The couple crossing had shaken their heads at me in disapproval. It took a massive amount of willpower not to scream at them out of the window. Only the nagging thought that I was probably at least five times over the limit stopped me. I didn't need to get arrested today too.

As soon as I got back home, I carelessly chucked my keys and bag onto the hallway floor and began pulling every single room downstairs apart to find the photos. The precise moment I located them I would be straight back to banging on Steve's door, and this time he would have to listen to me. Half an hour later I was close to admitting defeat. Someone had been in here. Someone had taken them. The thought sent a sliver of goosebumps down my spine before I impatiently shook them off. I needed to find those pictures to prove once and for all that I wasn't going mad, and dwelling on who had or hadn't been in my house wasn't going to help me. I was sitting back on my haunches to concentrate when I had a flash of inspiration; maybe I'd hidden them in my dresser? I didn't remember doing it, but occasionally I'd found bills or important letters in there, hidden for safe keeping.

I ran upstairs, still a little fuzzy and unbalanced, bouncing off the walls. Rushing into my room I wrenched the drawers open with such force that they fell to the floor, one of them catching the lamp's lead and causing it to crash onto the carpet so that flecks of the glass shade ricocheted everywhere. I upturned the drawers onto the bed, my manic hands feverishly searching through the piles of paper as the soles of my feet impatiently ignored the sharp slicing of flesh underfoot. Still nothing. Panting from the exertion I dropped to my knees and sat back on my heels, fishing out my phone. I needed help and there was only one person left who would be able to do it. Even if she wasn't talking to me.

"Lula? Hi... no! Look just listen! I haven't got time to argue. Please? The kids are in danger and the police think I'm crazy! Steve and Dan have the kids and won't give them back and you're the only person left on my side, and I need your help!" My voice was reaching a pitch of panic. "Lula? Lula, can you hear me?" Crackles interrupted the silence on the other end. "Hello?" I was just about to hang up when a loud beep exploded from the other end and the line went dead. I immediately rang back, but the line wouldn't even connect this time. Growling in frustration at my little sister's total lack of support, I ran back down the stairs, smearing blood as I went. I needed to find evidence. No one was going to believe me without it.

My second round of ransacking was as fruitless as my first, and I still hadn't come up with a single piece of the evidence. I ripped through the DVD shelves for a third time, just in case something had been caught up in between, and found I was starting to second guess myself. Maybe they were right, and I was losing my mind. If what I thought was all true, then why couldn't I find the evidence I needed to prove it, and why was everyone so determined to tell me I needed help; that it was all in my head?

FIFTEEN

The light was streaming through my closed eyelids, causing my stomach to churn and the vomit to rise right up to the top of my throat. I only just managed to roll onto my side before the hot, acidic and chunky liquid poured, uncontrollable and uncontainable, out of my mouth and onto the carpet. I tried to stand and get to a sink, but the force of the vomiting and the shakes still pacing through my body made it impossible. Instead, I sank further into a ball and let go.

When I woke up again, I was surrounded by my children's faces, smiling at me from every angle. My mouth felt like someone had stuffed tissue into it, so that all of the moisture had been stolen from me. I ignored my pounding head and kept my eyes on their faces, all my fight now extinct. I'd had enough. Teddy's scared eyes yesterday and knowing that I was the cause of his worry, had sucked away the very last of my certainty that I was going to win them back. Steve had managed to turn him against me, and Dan and his mum had been trying to turn Rose against me since the day I took her and left. I closed my eyes again. I was done.

The final time I woke it was cold. Gingerly I raised myself into a sitting position, cold, wet hair trailing onto my cheek and causing me to shudder as I realised it was in fact covered in sick. I looked around. The living room was behaving as if it had been the setting for an illegal rave. Furniture was upturned, DVDs were strewn all over the floor, empty drinks on the table, and sick covering the floor. I sat in the pool of my own vomit, trying to piece together how exactly I'd ended up in this state again. The last thing I could properly remember was feeling like I was going mad.

I'd grabbed my keys after Lula's phone call, determined to track her down to see if she could help. I knew I'd gotten into the car and driven haphazardly through the estate. But the next thing I knew was that I was here in a pool of my own sick, and it was Sunday morning. Angrily I forced my battered mind to think; what had happened in between? I couldn't get anything to link up properly and it was so frustrating. Why couldn't my life just go back to the normal monotony it'd always been; where the school run and work were the boring, never-ending routines, and no one felt the need to threaten me or to send me reminders of those memories that I'd rather not re-live.

It was strange, now that I thought about it, that whoever it was behind it all was determined to entwine Mum's murder with my kids and my life nowadays. There was no overlap whatsoever; I was the only thing to link them. After all, there were over ten years between Mum dying and Rose being born, so why were the two separate parts of my life so important to whoever was behind it? If it really was Steve and Dan trying to mess with me to get hold of the kids, then why bring Mum into it?

There was a nagging feeling lingering just out of sight that I was missing something important, some information that would show me exactly why my past and my present kept colliding. I needed to talk to someone about Mum and what had happened that day. Maybe there was a detail I was missing that would show me exactly who was behind it all.

Lula was, as ever, my first thought, but on balance would be useless. We'd gone over and over all the information we could remember over the years, and she'd been in the car with me. She'd only seen what I had. It needed to be someone who knew more, and the only person I could think of who knew the entire story had unfortunately lost his mind. But I had to try. Without a backwards glance at the destruction I was leaving behind, I decided to head straight to the nursing home and see if I could glean anything from an old man's addled brain.

I was just signing in and trying to ignore the receptionist's wary looks when Devon approached the desk. He looked a little puzzled to see me.

"Hello, Marnie. What can we do for you?" I looked up at him, now unsure myself.

"I've come to see Dad," I replied, leaving the 'obviously' unspoken as it was probably a little rude.

"Oh. I thought when we spoke yesterday that you understood what had happened." I stared at him for a moment.

"Yesterday?" I repeated, the query clear in my voice. Devon nodded.

"Yes…when I asked you to come in for a chat, remember?" He was looking a little uncertainly at me, and too late I caught a whiff of the drying sick on the side if my head. I really should have had a shower.

"Of course I remember!" I retorted, anxious not to be thought of as mad. "But *I* can still see him, surely?"

"I'm afraid not," Devon said, shaking his head slightly as he tried to hide his disgust for me from his expression. "He really is too frail at the moment."

"For God's sake, Devon, I'm his daughter! What right have you got to say whether he can see me or not? I'm the one paying for him to be here, after all!" I exploded, causing several other visitors milling around the entrance hall to look at me askance. Devon's expression darkened and he moved slightly closer to me.

"I'm afraid I'm going to have to ask you to leave," he said quietly. "You're upset at not seeing him, Marnie, and I understand that. But he's not well enough, and you're upsetting our other patients." I'd had enough of being palmed off and tried to move past him towards Dad's room. He moved to block my path and nodded to the receptionist as he addressed me again.

"No, I'm sorry but you need to leave. Tracey is calling security, so I suggest you let me walk you out to your car, go home, and calm down." We faced off at one another, each silently urging the other to give in. I dropped my eyes, and sensing his victory, he moved towards me to take my arm. Seizing my opportunity, I ducked under his outstretched limb and began to run, my only thought getting to Dad. "Marnie!" I heard him shout as rapid squeaking behind me told me he was giving chase.

I skidded round the corner, Dad's door just in front of me, when rough hands grabbed me from behind and I was stopped in my tracks. I struggled against them trying to escape, but they were too strong. With a man on either side of me I was frogmarched back down to the entrance and through the double doors, just managing to catch sight of Tracey the receptionist's open-mouthed stare as I went. Within thirty seconds I had been deposited next to my car.

"Go home," Devon, who had followed our three-legged race to the car park, said. "I understand your dad being poorly is upsetting, Marnie. But we need to think of all our patients and visitors, and you're causing distress. Ring tomorrow and we can talk a bit more. For now, I'd suggest making sure your kids are ok."

"What did you say?" He looked confused.

"I said go home and we'll talk tomorrow."

"About my kids," I said, louder now. "Why wouldn't they be ok? What do you know? Is it you? Is all this you?" I was shouting at him now, spittle flying from my mouth in panic. Devon's expression had changed again, and he looked at me, a level challenge in his eyes.

"I have no idea what you're talking about," he replied calmly, clearly buoyed up at the fact that he had his two gorillas next to him still. "Now you will either leave the premises, or I will call the police. Ring tomorrow when you've calmed down." With a last contemptuous look, he turned and headed inside again, leaving me with no choice but to get in my car and leave while the security men looked on.

SIXTEEN

I drove around aimlessly until four o'clock, willing the hours to fly past in droves until it was finally time for me to get my babies back. Hurrying up Steve's path, I'd almost reached the front door when I realised that probably for the first time ever, Ted's face wasn't beaming from either the front window or the doorstep at my approach. The thought caused me to pause in my tracks, a little ridiculous kernel of hurt brewing slightly in my chest. Shaking my head in consternation, I continued to stride purposefully until I reached the door. Pressing the doorbell and waiting for them to answer I began to bounce impatiently from one foot to the other. I was so late thanks to Devon; only God knew what state Rose would be in by the time I got over to her too. I just knew, without her having to tell me, that the shine of having Dan looking after her would have dimmed somewhat.

I pressed the bell again, leaning in to listen carefully for the chimes to check it was working. The tune played itself out and I peered through the frosted pane of glass, waiting for some movement to signal they were coming. I was beginning to feel a little frustrated now; both Steve and Addy knew the rules. I was so used to them being easy going and taking anything that I had to say or do in their stride. Even after this week's arguments, it felt a little weird not to be catered to immediately.

Fishing out my phone I pressed Steve's number and waited for him to answer. As I did, I noticed that there was only one car in the driveway. Of course, Addy was allowed to leave the house, but on a Sunday afternoon they were usually all at home to greet me. Steve's phone went to voicemail, and I growled in frustration, not being able to help it when a little panic set in. Surely Steve would've have rung to say they wouldn't be home, even after the way he'd treated me? Horrific accidents were racing through my mind as I decided to go and get Rose first instead.

I raced through town, pressing both Steve and Addy's numbers alternately and letting them ring out. I was seized with the certainty that something bad had happened. By the time I reached Dan's estate the panic was actually physical, and my hands were shaking uncontrollably as I tried to swallow as much of it as I could. I screeched to a halt at Sarah's back gate, not even bothering to park properly against the kerb and causing a rough looking woman across the road to shout at me to move it. In her anger she almost dropped the phone in her hand onto her baby.

It was normally the sort of encounter that would have me apologising profusely and hoping not to get my head kicked in, but my terror was too great right then and I ignored her, bowling up the path and wrenching the handle of the door instead, desperate to get to Rose. It was locked. Frantically I began to bang on the kitchen door. Still no response. I thought I might faint with adrenaline as I pounded the glass over and over so that it shook beneath my fists.

Just as I was on the point of helplessly sliding down to the doorstep a shadow suddenly appeared on the other side of the frosted glass. I let out a huge sigh of relief, even lifting a foot ready to step forward over the threshold. The door stayed shut.

"Who is it?" a croaky voice asked from the other side of the glass. Sarah.

"It's Marnie. Open the door! I need to get Rose. Now! Ted's gone missing; I need to find him!" I tried my hardest to keep my voice from betraying my dread. I didn't want to worry Rosie. Ted would be fine; I knew that really. It was just all this stalker stuff going on that'd gotten inside my head. But a tiny voice argued back; Steve wouldn't have gone out without good reason when it was time to pick Ted up, the tiny little voice resonated. Unless he was trying to freak me out more that is, really push me over the edge. "Sarah? Sarah, can you open the door? I really need to get going!" There was a pause, enough time to allow my blood to boil a little more. The door remained closed. I raised a fist to bang on it.

"They aren't here," the same croaky tone came from the other side, momentarily stumping me.

"What? Where are they? Sarah!" I was firmly in panic mode now, and banged once more on the frosted glass. "Sarah, open the door! Rose? Rosie it's Mummy, open the door sweetheart. We need to find Ted."

"I told you." Came Sarah's voice again, stronger and now with a hint of malice. "They aren't here."

"Where are they then; at the shop or something? Look, tell me where, and I'll go and meet them. I need to find out what's happened to Teddy. There's been some really weird stuff going on, Sarah. I'll explain when I've got more time, but right now the kids are in danger." Silence greeted me yet again and I let out a snarl of frustration. "Can you just open the door and have an adult conversation with me please?"

"No. You need to leave us all alone now, Marnie. Rose is better off here, with me and her dad to look after her. You're not right, all this pretending with the stalker and everything. Steve rang Danny this morning and told him all about your visit yesterday. Screaming and shouting at seven in the morning on their doorstep and terrifying your own child? He's worried about you, and neither of them think the children are safe with you at the right now. I'm sorry love," her voice had taken on its usual motherly chimes. "But it's for the best." I physically reeled away from the door as if she'd smacked me. A voice that couldn't belong to me replied.

"You can't do that," I said, feeling like I was whispering, with no energy. She could hear me though.

"We can. It's for Rose's own good. And there's no point in ringing the police," she rang out, pre-empting me. "He's her father. He's got rights too. Now take care of yourself. And get some help." With that her outline began to recede as she walked away back into the house, leaving me on her doorstep without any idea of what to do next. A shout from behind made me flinch.

"Oi! You guna' move this car or what, posh girl?" It was the woman who'd been using her baby as a phone holder, although I realised there were now three of them. Funnily enough, the terror of being beaten up didn't even come into the equation; my agony at my children being missing was too strong for anything else. But it did at least galvanise me into action, and I fled back down the path towards my car, chucking my bag onto the passenger seat and turning the ignition. "Yeah, off you go then. Don't worry about us lot tryin' to get through or anything." The women all stared intimidatingly at me through my open window. As I gunned the engine and screeched off, I just about had enough wits about me to flick them the V sign out of the window.

Almost mounting the kerb on the corner of the estate, I fumbled with my phone to find another number, barely even bothering to check anything was coming before I pulled out onto the main thoroughfare.

"Lula? Lula can you hear me? Something bad has happened. Steve and Ted are missing, and Dan's taken Rose somewhere and no one will tell me where, and... Lula? Lula are you there?" Static silence greeted me from the other end of the phone, and I almost hung up thinking she'd gone, when a voice so harsh that I almost didn't recognise it came down the line.

"Don't be stupid, Marnie. They're with their fathers'. They're hardly missing." I swerved blindly towards the edge of the road, breaking so suddenly that the car behind gave a loud honk and I vaguely heard swearing as they screeched past my window.

"Lula? That *is* you isn't it?" I said uncertainly, not understanding why she was speaking to me like this. She responded with a bark-like laugh.

"Of course it's me. *You* rang *me*, remember? Honestly, you need help. Sarah's right, you really have lost it." She was sneering unpleasantly, and even in my heightened state of fear it stung.

"You've spoken to Sarah?" I whispered, shocked. There had never been any love lost between my sister and my ex-boyfriend's mother. Lula had always said (rightly it turned out) that she let Dan get away with murder, and often at my expense. She laughed derisively.

"Well of course I have. We've been speaking to each other all week, trying to work out what to do. You've completely lost your mind, Marnie. Did you really think that we'd leave you to it, put the kids in danger like that? In fact," she continued, a hint of arrogance now entering her words, "it was my idea that they take the kids away for a bit and let you to sort yourself out." I felt my heart shatter, and I pulled the phone from my ear to stare at it stupidly, as if it could explain to me exactly what was happening. The sense of betrayal was bigger than I'd ever thought possible. They had all decided to take my kids away, and my own sister had orchestrated it? Distantly I could hear her calling my name still from the speaker. I put the phone back to my ear, anger coursing through my body like never before.

"Tell me where they are." I managed to bite out between taking huge gulps of air to try to calm down enough to focus.

"You don't understand, Marnie. We aren't going to let you do this to them anymore. They're scared of you. I spoke to Rose on the phone yesterday and she was in tears, saying that you'd told them some crazy person was after you all and was going to hurt them. She said that you've started sleeping with a knife under your pillow. You've lost your mind. Ring me when you've sorted it out. 'til then none of us are having anything to do with you. And don't even think about trying to see Dad; I've told Devon you can't be trusted with anyone vulnerable. You're not to be allowed near him. Goodbye, Marnie."

A faint click showed she'd actually hung up this time. I flinched as if she'd slammed the phone down on me, when in reality she'd just flicked her fingertip across a screen. My entire body began to shake with shock, the panic and anger coursing through me simultaneously. My entire world had crumbled in the time it took for my sister, for my only real family left, to tell me she'd been in on the betrayal. I couldn't work out what to do now. I was so used to bouncing ideas off Lula, for her to tell me in her forthright, direct, and even sometimes rude manner what the best thing to do next was. She'd been the one to tell me when enough was enough and I had to leave Dan.

She was the one who told me that it was obvious I didn't love Steve and that we both deserved to find better, and it was Lula who told me it was time for Dad to go in a Home. I realised in that moment, sitting at the side of the most familiar of roads, that my life had completely and utterly imploded. And I would be lucky to find enough scraps to piece it back together. Gunning the pedal, I veered out into the flowing traffic aimlessly, with nowhere left to turn.

The last thought I had was that I'd never thought about how loud car crashes were. A searing whiteness ran up and down my side and sparks filled my vision as the metal intruder barrelled through my protection and into my soft, supple skin. But all I could think was how noisy it all was. I looked down towards my stomach as the edges of my picture darkened, moving inwards in ever decreasing circles. I was surprised that all I could see was buckled greyness, no sign of my jeans or plum T shirt to be found. An odd wetness was damping down the white-heat that had been running through my body, and vaguely I realised that it must be blood. As the darkness became too powerful to fight, I suddenly understood with a clarity that was at odds with the rest of my muddied head. This was it; I was going to see my children.

PART TWO

SEVENTEEN

I could hear them before I could see them. The faint chatter that had been the background to my life for seven years was finally back and I couldn't be happier. Even in the complete darkness my body relaxed, and I drifted off once more, comforted that they had been returned to me.

The next time I woke all was still, and instinctively I knew it was night-time. Eager to see the kids, I reached out towards my bedside table to grab my phone and switch the torch on, opening my eyes in the dull darkness and waiting for them to start to adjust. My hand banged into something cold, metallic and unfamiliar, and it made me flinch in alarm. I blinked rapidly as I pulled myself, with difficulty into a sitting position. Sharp pain shot through my right hand and I took a sharp breath. I peered down to find the source, and my slowly adjusting eyes could just make out a bulky outline. I balled my hand into a fist. Tight pain, as my vein was stretched against the needle inserted in the back of my hand, seared through me. I realised that I must have a drip, now aware of the cool feeling around the site, as the saline was pushed steadily into my body.

A door opened to the left, the dim light that it afforded giving me a chance to take a sweeping view of my surroundings; it seemed I'd lucked out with a private room. As the door closed a figure walked over towards me, the soft padding of their feet a sure sign of experience. It was funny, but you did actually develop a 'hospital' walk in the healthcare game. You learnt to run almost silently and to be unobtrusive on your travels. As the person came closer, I could see it was a man. Probably in his 40's. He was almost within touching distance when he glanced at my face, meeting my eyes in one swift movement. Weirdly his expression changed to wary, and he immediately took a few steps back to the door. Opening it I could hear him calling softly outwards. Confused and opening my mouth to ask what was going on I was suddenly confronted by three more heavily built men entering the room, all dressed in hospital scrubs and approaching the bed cautiously.

"Good evening, Marnie. My name's Jamie. How're you feeling?" This came from the first man, the one who'd entered alone. He was hovering about a foot away from the bed and waiting for me to answer.

"What's going on?" I asked, ignoring his question and getting to the important stuff. "Where am I? Are the kids out there? Can you bring them in?" Jamie took a cautious step forward and began fiddling with something on the other side of the bed railings. He took a deep breath before looking up to meet my eyes. Suddenly I was sure he was going to tell me bad news, terror gripping me. "What?"

He didn't speak, and I began to get agitated, pushing myself further against the top of the bed so that I could sit up properly, pain shooting through my hand and stomach once more and causing me to flinch. "Where are Rose and Teddy?" I demanded, flashes of that last day filling my head. "Where are Steve and Dan? Where did they take them? They've brought them back now, haven't they?" I had been so sure I'd heard them earlier on in my sleep, but now I began to wonder.

I saw Jamie glance towards his colleagues, still shadowed from me. When he turned back a shutter had come down over the nurse's eyes and he abruptly moved to be right next to me, taking my hand gently in his to check I hadn't ripped the canula out.

"Everything's fine, Marnie," he began, continuing to hold my hand, stroking it gently. "Steve and Dan brought them back. The children aren't here now though; it's late and past their bedtime. Can you tell me what you remember?" At his words, I'd slumped back into the pillow, the relief that the kids were fine almost overwhelming me. Suddenly I felt very, very, tired.

"I was in an accident?" I posed it as a question, slurring in my effort to stay awake now. "A van, I think. But Rosie and Ted?" I was fighting against my body now, willing myself to stay for just a moment longer. I lost, and the world faded into black as I felt Rose's hand slip into mine, the warmth of her skin a blanket, her soft breath on my cheek a kiss.

EIGHTEEN

The next time I woke it was daytime, and the light streamed in through the un-shaded window. It was so bright that I was astounded I'd managed to sleep in the room at all. Excitement fizzed inside me as I realised that daytime would equal visitors, and Rosie and Ted would be here soon no doubt. Having learnt my lesson from last night, I gently pushed myself upwards into a sitting position, carefully folding my drip-fed hand over the other in my lap and stared expectantly at the door for someone to come in and tell me what was going on.

From somewhere in the distance I could hear crying; a true heartbroken sobbing, and my stomach contracted immediately as I imagined what must be happening in that person's life to be making a sound like that. The swishing of my door opening distracted me before my thoughts dived too darkly, and I grinned, expecting the kids to be standing in the doorway. Instead it was the nurse from last night, although his name escaped me. I kept the smile pasted on even in my disappointment.

"Hi," I said brightly. He smiled a little as he came over, picking my hand up again in his huge one and studying the bruised insertion site carefully. I allowed him to carry out his checks with as much patience as I could muster; being in healthcare I knew how annoying it was when the patient distracted you by asking inane questions all the time. Eventually he laid my hand carefully back in my lap and began to fiddle with the drip. I couldn't take it anymore. "So," I began, striving to be polite. "Are my children here yet? Can I see them please?" Jamie shook his head slightly, his eyes full of kindness.

"They aren't here Marnie, but one of our doctors would like to have a chat. Do you think you're feeling up to it?" I didn't reply for a moment, a little more confused than I was already. Doctors didn't ask to come and speak to you, did they? They just turned up, as far as I was aware.

"Well, yeah I suppose so," I agreed. "But I really need to see my kids. Can you pass me my handbag so I can ring and get them brought in?" I glanced around the room, noticing for the first time that there was nothing personal in the room at all. "Wait. Where's my bag and clothes and stuff?"

"Oh, all that's been stored safely for you, don't worry. We just didn't want it all out while you were so poorly and not able to keep an eye on it." The nurse wouldn't meet my eyes. He's lying, I realised with a start, panic starting to build ever so slightly. He's lying to me.

"Hey," I called as he got to the door, opening it with one swift movement. He turned to look at me. "You'll get my bag now though, won't you?"

"Sure," he agreed easily, both of us now aware he wasn't telling the truth. "The doctor will be in shortly. Try and rest." As though his words were a command, I felt my eyelids immediately begin to grow heavy and my retort died on my lips, the world crumbling away as I silently screamed for my children.

The next time my eyes snapped open it was bright still, but I knew that it was a different day. Every muscle in my body had that grogginess you only got when you were stationary for a decent block of time. As my eyes adjusted, I noticed a slight movement from the corner of the room. As far as I could recall this was where the huge visitor's chair was stationed, and I blinked eagerly to encourage my eyes to focus on what I was certain would be their faces. Just then the blurry mass stood, and I fell back onto my pillows in disappointment. It was an adult. A woman, I realised, as her heels clacked on the shiny floor towards the bed.

"Hi, Marnie," she began when she was close enough to touch me. "How're you doing today? I'm Dr Roberts. Do you remember me?" She seemed to be studying me carefully, even while she glanced down at the papers in her hand, pretending not to. Foreboding was filling me again and I knew she was about to tell me something horrific. There was something familiar about the woman too, now I came to think about it, but for the life of me I couldn't place her. But maybe I'd worked briefly with her? As a trainee paramedic I interacted with a huge number of doctors and nurses on the handover, but often for only a few minutes in a lifetime. Although now I came to think about it, this room didn't look like any that I'd seen in St Martin's in the time I'd lived and more recently, worked in the area. Hospital rooms were a little generic though. Just because I'd never been in this particular room didn't mean anything really. So instead, I composed my face into polite anticipation and met the woman's eyes straight on.

"You do look familiar but I'm so sorry, I can't seem to place you." I sounded weird even to my own ears. I waited for her to fill me in. She didn't speak, just continuing to look at me. When the silence got too awkward I felt I had to say something. "Erm, did you hear me?" I began, fully expecting her to apologise for being so rude.

"Yes I heard you. Are you sure you can't place me?" The woman was being deliberately obtuse, and I had a hard time swallowing my frustration.

"No," I bit out, hanging on to my last strand of cool with everything I had. "I already said. I can't place you. Did we work together?" She looked knowingly at me, and I was uncomfortably aware that she knew I was about to lose it completely. I swallowed. Thankfully she spoke.

"No, we didn't work together. Do you know where you are?" She changed tack and I gave an impatient snort.

"I'm in hospital. Now, maybe you can tell me straight what exactly is going on? Where are Rose and Ted? I need to see them; the last thing I remember is that Steve and Dan had disappeared with them, but one of your nurses said they brought them back? So where are they?"

"You're in a safe place here," the doctor said, as if I'd not spoken. "If there's anything you can remember you can speak to us any time." Her tone was so full of faux sympathy that I glared at her, the anger bubbling up and almost overwhelming me.

"What I *remember* is that my kids were missing, and no one will tell me where they are or get them here. I *need* to see them, why can't you understand that?" I glared at her for a second longer before I was suddenly galvanised into action. As I swung my legs out of bed and pushed forward onto my feet, I was gratified that the doctor took a startled step back. I just had time to feel the cool lino under my feet before the room was suddenly heaving with bodies, and I was pushed firmly back onto the mattress. I yelped, my protests dying in my throat as a heaviness on my chest began to push all of the air out of my lungs. A voice whispered in my ear.

"It's ok, Marnie. Don't fight us; we're trying to help, you know." I managed to focus on the face beside me, the doctor's eyes glinting in malice as she smiled. I wrenched my head forward towards hers in a headbutt, wanting to knock the smug look off of her face. For the briefest second I made contact, her wisps of hair stroking my face before I was dragged back into blackness again.

A rush of sound and colour filled my head and my ears, with flashes of images that I couldn't understand racing past, not giving me enough time to focus on them. Rose's voice was high pitched, her obvious terror only heightened by Teddy's cries of pain. I reached out to pull them away from the horror that was holding them, my hands scraping against the fabric of her jacket, of his little shorts.

But I was too late; they began to fade before I could get a good grip, and as they slid away helplessly, all I could hear were them whispering my name. My eyes snapped open, and the hospital room came into focus unsparingly quickly. It was night again, and the lights had been dimmed. A hushed atmosphere penetrated through the closed door.

"Hi Marnie." I jumped in shock; a difficult thing to do when you're apparently tied to the metal railings of a bed. My eyes swept the room, landing on the big armchair in the corner. It was a woman, with a familiarity about her that was impossible to ignore. Suddenly it clicked. It was the woman from before.

"You're the doctor," I answered, my voice still a little slurred from whatever they kept pumping me with to knock me out. She nodded but didn't speak, instead continuing to watch me. Feeling like an experiment, I swallowed my brewing temper; I needed answers, not to be knocked out again. "Where are my kids?" I asked as politely as I could.

"Where do you think they are?" She replied, leaning forward and studying me intently.

"I don't know, that's the problem!" I replied, real anguish overtaking my impatience. "Sarah said Dan and Steve had taken them somewhere safe, away from me. We need to call the police, or have you already done that?" She watched me for a moment, and when she replied her answer was measured.

"They were found by the police, Marnie. You know that don't you? The police found them." She was speaking gently, and finally on her feet, approached me slowly as you would a wounded animal. When she finally reached my side, she placed a cool hand over mine. "Marnie, do you remember the police coming?" I stared at her for a moment, confused and trying to work out what she was asking me. I shook my head.

"Well obviously not. No one told me the police had found them. Can you get them in to see me? Have Steve and Dan been arrested? It was basically kidnap. I'd have expected this of Dan, you know, but Steve? I thought he was on my side! He knows what I've been through recently, with all those letters and photo's and stuff." I was vaguely aware I was rambling on to myself, the injustice of those idiots thinking they could just take my children from me still rankling.

"Why do you think Steve and Dan took the children away?" The doctor deflected my question yet again with one of her own.

"How would I know? We had a few arguments last week, and there's been all this crazy stuff going on; I thought they were the ones behind it but…" I threw my hands up in exasperation, forgetting about the restraints and wincing as my wrists jarred against them. "All I know is what Sarah told me. She's a spiteful cow too. If you want to know so much, why don't you ask them?"

"Do you remember why you're here Marnie? Can you tell me in your own words what happened?" I felt like my head was about to explode with anger now.

"Are you people stupid? I was trying to track them down when some van just crashed straight into me. Next thing I know I'm here. Are we done with the ridiculous questions now? And when are you going to take these things off me? I need to leave! God knows what state the kids'll be in with not being able to see me." I glared at her and proffered my remanded arms as far as they could go. Dr Roberts' composed mask slipped a little for the first time.

"Ok," she said in a falsely confident tone. She was scrabbling to regain the high ground and it gave me satisfaction. "I'll tell you what we'll do, Marnie. If we let you out of your room for a bit, I'd really like you to come to a group session with me. We have some other patients in here who have been through similar things to you." I looked dumbly at her, for once so completely confused that I couldn't speak.

"What do you mean?" I asked. "They were in car accidents too? Why would I need to talk to them?"

"No, not car accidents," Dr Roberts began gently. "They've been placed here with severe PTSD like you. Marnie," she took my hand in hers again. "You do know that you're on a psychiatric ward, don't you?"

NINETEEN

When I next woke up in the sterile room, I thought that I might die of humiliation. Me; in a mental ward? After the doctor revealed that I was on a psychiatric ward I lost it big time. In fact, to my secret satisfaction it had taken no less than six of the doctor's big, burly nurses to hold me down, even with my restraints, while they sedated me.

After that, every other time I'd gotten close enough to break through the surface and begin to hear the voices around me, they topped me up, dragging me back under to a world that I didn't want to inhabit. This twilight world of sounds and colours was torturous. Rose and Teddy screamed non-stop in my ears, their hands wrenched from mine by the unseen stalker over and over. Blood sometimes bloomed from their mouths as they were taken. It was bone-scrapingly excruciating.

Eventually they must have forgotten to give me more meds, and I now here I was, delivered back to reality with a slashing clarity. As I took in my bare surroundings again, I scratched my nose with my finger, and in doing so realised that I was free. The soft looping restraints had disappeared, as had the canula in the back of my hand. I lay stunned for a moment, before a shot of adrenaline electrified me and, eager to take advantage of my sudden freedom, I pushed the sheets back and swung my legs over, determined to get out of this room and find some answers. But as my feet finally made contact with the floor my legs collapsed beneath me, leaving me in a sad little pile on the scuffed lino. My eyes shot to the door, expecting the big idiots to come bundling in at the crash and put me back in my prison. Nothing.

I crawled painfully slowly over to the exit, finally able to stand by pulling myself up the door frame. I was gripping the handle so tightly that even the bruised skin on the back of my hand from the needle was bright white and sweat was pouring down my back from the effort. Summoning all the strength I had, I put my entire weight into making the steel hook move. Fully expecting it not to budge, I almost lost my balance when it swung easily down, the door clicking to permit me to leave.

I slowly opened it, hugging the doorframe again as I did and peered cautiously out, still expecting to be tackled and sedated. Instead, I was greeted by the sight of a young woman walking sedately past and chattering animatedly with one of the gorilla-type men that had kept me in my torture chamber before. She wasn't in a gown like me, and, hoping she was being shown the way out, I slid behind them as quietly as I could while keeping the wall pressed tightly against the left-hand side of my body to keep me upright. The woman was now laughing at something, and I felt a sudden pang of envy at her happiness.

As they reached the end of the corridor they slowed, and a large desk came into view. The two of them had come to a stop, I assumed to sign out, and, out of breath from my first exertion in days, I paused to watch. Another nurse appeared on the other side of the desk, greeting the woman warmly. Leaning forward to try to hear the conversation that the three of them had settled into, I jumped in shock when a voice whispered into my right ear.

"Ah Marnie, there you are!" I whipped round so speedily I felt my neck crunch painfully as I came face to face with Dr Roberts. The woman's eyes were searching mine intently, and for the first time I detected a genuine warmth there. We both regarded one another in silence; each waiting for the other to speak. When it became obvious it wasn't going to be me, she smiled.

"Would you like to come and meet some of the other patients? Group is just about to start I think, but you have time to get changed into some comfier clothes if you want," she said, checking her watch.

"Group?" I repeated, my voice gruff and harsh from disuse.

"Yes. It's a safe space I told you about; for everybody to share their stories. Have you done anything like that before?" She was watching me carefully.

"Well of course I haven't!" I blustered, offended. "What d'you think I am, a drug addict or something?" The doctor looked a little dismayed at my reply.

"I know you aren't recovering from addiction; not that there'd be anything shameful in that even if you were. But group therapy is used as a treatment for lots of other conditions too. Like PTSD for example." I summoned the strength to roll my eyes at her.

"Oh I see. We're back on this then; you've clearly heard about my past. Listen, I had a counsellor when all that happened and I'm fine now. Or I would be if I could just see my kids. I don't suppose they'll be allowed in today? And you still haven't told me where they are?" I asked, forcing myself to use a different tactic and be polite; anger had gotten me nowhere so far. She watched me for a moment too long before answering.

"Not today, Marnie, no. The children are being cared for. Now, shall we?" She gestured towards the door on the other side of the desk; the one the woman had exited through moments before, and that I had assumed led to freedom.

"Wait, that woman is imprisoned here too?" I asked, putting as much scathing into my tone as possible. "But she's allowed to wear her own clothes?"

"She is," she replied calmly. "Like I said, you're welcome to get changed before we go anywhere; a bag of clothes was dropped in for you. Or you can stay as you are, whatever makes you happy. And just to be clear, we prefer patient to prisoner. So, group?" She moved her head in a slight nod. I gave a dramatic sigh.

"Do I have much choice?" I asked, disgruntled. For the first time she truly grinned at me, seemingly delighted at my show of spirit.

"Not if you want to be discharged at some point. After you," she swept her hand across her body and into a slight bow.

"This is ridiculous," I muttered as I moved back towards my room to get changed. The doctor left me at the door. "

I'll be back in ten, ok? Jamie's just grabbing your stuff now." I glared at her before sitting heavily on the edge of my bed to wait. "See you soon," she said with a smile as she left.

"I don't know what Steve and Dan told you but they're liars. There's nothing wrong with me. I just need my kids," I tried to explain. She didn't bother replying, the soft click of her heels on the polished floor the only sign she was still with me. She'd been true to her word, collecting me after ten minutes, and I was now walking back down the corridor dressed in a pair of grey trackies and a jumper that I wouldn't have been caught dead in in the outside world. We reached the door and I pushed against it, unsurprised to find it was locked.

"Now you're up and about I'll give you the code for it," Dr Roberts said as she moved forwards to unlock it.

I was already acting institutionalised as I stood obediently to the side and waited silently for her to enter the passcode into the keypad. A small click and a push later, and we found ourselves in another corridor, this time bustling with traffic.

I paused, startled and already unused to crowds. Laughter was drifting along the hall and punctuated by an occasional cry or shout. There was a small huddle of women leaning against the wall while they chattered, their hands wrapped around their steaming mugs as they giggled and whispered. With a jolt I realised. This was exactly like the old days. The days of never-ending playgroups with the mums herded together to share the mundanity of life over a coffee while their kids played about at their feet. I glanced down, almost expecting to see Rose or Ted wrapped about my legs or toddling away, the déjà vu was so real.

"Where are we?" I whispered so quietly that I thought the doctor would have a job to hear me. She did though.

"This is the communal area, Marnie. Do you want to have a look around? We've got a few minutes before group starts. Look, there's the kitchen. Everyone's free to make themselves a drink or snack." She was pointing at the room just to the left of the group of women, who all fell silent as they looked at me. God it really was like playgroup; cliquey and bitchy. Brilliant. I ignored them and peered uninterestedly into the room. Just as we were about to move off, I caught the eye of a frail looking woman who was still staring blatantly. She immediately dropped her gaze to the floor.

"And here's the TV room, she pointed to an open door through which most of the laughter seemed to be filtering out from. I looked in and immediately wished I hadn't; it was as depressing as the common room at Dad's dementia home. I went over to join the doctor as quickly as I could, my legs already aching from being upright for so long. "And up here," she gestured to two more closed doors, "are our group rooms. I think," she paused, clearly judging something silently, "I think we'd be best in this one today. After you then, Marnie," she said, smiling and nodding at the door on her left. Apprehension caught me like a force field, threatening to throw me over the edge.

"Erm, you know what, I think I'll leave it for today," I said, backing back down the corridor as quickly as I could.

"That's your choice of course," the doctor said quietly, piercing me with her gaze. "But I'm afraid all you're doing is prolonging it. There's nothing to worry about you know," she continued, her smile turning sharky. "They're a friendly bunch. You might even learn something." We held one another's eyes, both wondering when she would inevitably win. After a few moments I sighed, dropping my eyes, and moving grudgingly towards the door.

The handle felt sweaty and hot, completely at odds with its cool metal appearance. Looking down at it I realised it was in fact my hand that was sliding slickly across the surface, burning with anxiety over what I was about to experience. Taking a deep breath in I pushed down, for the first time willing a door in this place to be locked. It clicked smoothly and opened of its own accord. A sea of faces turned hostile stares in my direction. I flushed with anxiety, already taking a stumble backwards when I felt the doctor's arms steady me.

"Come on now," she said, a hint of steel souring the caring tone. "You'll be fine once you sit down." She pressed a little more firmly on the tops of my arms, and fleetingly I thought of the way you squeezed a horse to make it go. It obviously worked on humans too, because before I knew it, I was padding as quietly as I could towards the only empty chair left in the circle. Already the other patients were turning their gazes away, as, with my compliance I had become boring, and I sunk gratefully into obscurity before realising that the doctor hadn't followed me over. Instead, she stepped around the other side to pull another chair for herself and address the group.

"Hello everyone," she began, her smile seeming so kind and generous to the unknowing eye. "I'm glad to see we've got a full house again today! We'll begin where we left off yesterday. Cally," she turned to address a slight black woman on her right, "did you want to carry on or would you like us to come back to you later?" Looking frightened, the woman shook her head.

The doctor smiled. "That's ok. Ah. Amy?" A rustle to the left side of me signalled that someone had stood up and was apparently called Amy.

"Yes, I'd like to share," she said in a voice that could never be described as timid. The doctor nodded at her encouragingly.

"Great. You can sit down if you'd prefer you know, Amy. We don't make a habit of making people feel like they're in the spotlight here."

"I'd prefer to stand thanks," Amy replied. I got the impression that this woman enjoyed being centre stage. Just as she began to speak, I flicked my gaze over to Doctor Roberts. To my surprise she was looking straight back at me, and when our eyes met, she grinned conspiratorially. This was all getting weirder and weirder. Confused, I turned to study Amy.

She was holding court, speaking loudly about having been diagnosed as bi-polar as a teenager, but kept flicking back to her earlier life full of stepfathers who liked her a little too much and truancies, so that by the time we'd gotten to her mid-twenties I'd tuned out completely. Instead, I furtively began to study the group members one by one.

To my immediate left was the confident Amy, a tall brunette who, judging from the thighs in my eyeline, was powerfully built, and spoke with a booming but melodious Welsh twang. I glanced down to be greeted by beautifully manicured feet encased in sliders with the word Gucci emblazoned across them.

"...And that's when I took the overdose. I just couldn't handle it anymore." My head snapped up and I stared at the woman beside me. Her story had come to an explosive conclusion, and just like that I felt awful for judging her. What sort of person tried to kill themselves anyway? I'd always wondered how anyone got to that stage. Maybe it was because mum was taken from me, but I couldn't understand how, especially if you had kids, you'd willingly leave the people you love to fend for themselves. With that thought my heart started aching badly for Rose and Ted, and I hastily locked their presence away again to focus. Doctor Roberts was speaking now.

"Thank you for sharing your story, Amy. As one of our longest standing patients we know how much work you've been doing on coping with your feelings; maybe you'd like to give our newer members some extra support over the coming weeks?"

As Amy began to reply I decided to make my exit. This was all getting a bit too serious for me now, and I felt like a complete fraud for intruding on this poor woman's mental problems. I'd just go back to my room and wait for the doctor I decided. Then when we were alone, I could just explain to her all about Steve and Dan suddenly wanting custody, and that whatever they'd told her to get me in here was lies.

I rose and I felt the room fall still and silent. Amy stopped mid-sentence and glared at me, and too late I realised my chair had scraped long and loudly against the lino.

"Sorry," I said to the large woman. "I'm just going to go..." I trailed off, for some reason waiting for the doctor to give permission for me to go. Instead, she was watching me, a neutral expression on her face. I tried again. "I'm just going to go to my room I think," I said, my voice getting stronger as I spoke. "Sorry to interrupt you," I continued, directing myself straight at Amy this time. "But this just isn't for me, this...stuff." Amy looked offended and I didn't blame her; she struck me as the sort of woman who wouldn't forgive my interruption of her baring her soul very easily. Doctor Roberts was still watching me. "Is that ok, Doctor Roberts?" I asked, hating myself a little for needing her validation. She waited a beat before replying.

"Marnie, as I've told you many times, it's your choice to come to group therapy. You're free to go back to your room of course. But you never know, what Amy has to say might be helpful." I bit back a snort of derision.

"Why would it be helpful? I haven't tried to kill myself. I wouldn't do that to my kids," I countered, too late realising that this wasn't the most tactful thing to say to a room that was obviously full of attempted suicides. And what did she mean, 'many times,' anyway?

"Something someone else shares might end up being the one thing you need to hear," the doctor replied, her voice not increasing in volume but a hint of steel entering her tone again. "And it's a little rude while someone's in the middle of sharing. Why not wait until Amy's finished if you're so keen to leave?" I flushed with embarrassment at this discreet dressing down, sure that every other person here had heard the telling off as I had.

"Ok, sorry. Sorry Amy," I muttered, bowing my head and sinking back into my seat and keeping my face firmly averted to the floor. After a beat, Amy's strong and lilting voice filled the room once more.

In the end I stayed for the entire session which went on for *hours*. I didn't have the balls to try and leave again in front of everyone, so I had to endure three more self-pitying tales of woe; children taken from them, suicide attempts, addictions, the works. Every single person here was on their knees, and a couple had even committed crimes because of their problems. I listened as sympathetically and politely as I could, but quite honestly, I didn't get it.

Dr Roberts ended up next to me as our small stream of people filed out and down the corridor. Everybody else peeled off as we moved; some to the tv room, some to the tiny kitchen. At last, just the two of us remained, and as we reached the locked door that separated this area from the bedrooms, the doctor touched my arm lightly to pause me.

"Wouldn't you like to go and make a hot drink or watch tv or something? You don't have to go straight back to your room, you know." I shook my head.

"No, I want to go back. Look, can I speak to you properly? About why I'm here?" She looked concerned.

"Why do you think you're here?" She returned my query to me in the softest of tones. "Actually," she held up a hand to stop me before I'd even opened my mouth again. "This would be better somewhere more private. Shall we go back to your room together now? Or we could go to my office if you'd prefer?" I was just about to accept her offer when I noticed that one of the gorillas had materialised next to us, standing silently and watchful. The doctor was a second too late in hiding her summons of him and I clamped down. I felt idiotically betrayed by her.

"Why do I think I'm in here?" I began, my voice rising with my anger so that other patients began to turn. "Oh, I don't know. Maybe because you lot are so fucking gullible that you believe two jealous men over me. I don't know what they must've told you to make you think I needed to be locked up. In fact," now I'd started I couldn't stop. "I'd like you to tell me right this second why I'm on this nutty ward!" Having to stop myself from actually stamping my foot like Teddy does when he's annoyed, I stood flushed and glaring. The doctor and her chimp glanced briefly at one another.

"Marnie, Jamie's going to help you back to your room, ok? You're very frustrated, and I get that. But it's not going to do you any good talking while you're so worked up. I'll tell you what," she continued, looking at her wristwatch. "It's half past twelve now, go back with Jamie and have some lunch and a rest in your room. I'll get you to come to my office at three, and I promise we can talk then, ok?"

The bile in my throat was reaching dangerous levels, but realising I was getting nowhere, it took all I had to swallow it back down. With a sharp nod I turned on my heel and waited for the security door to open.

The door to my room closed behind me, the latch gently nestling into its resting place with a small click. I waited for the additional noise of the key being locked. Thankfully though, they seemed to have stopped locking me in. I looked dismissively at the bed and turned towards the armchair in the corner instead, slumping down as all of the adrenaline of the last few minutes drained out, leaving me sluggish and depressed. Before I understood what a mistake it would be, I closed my eyes.

Images of the kids danced across my flickering lids, their laughter filling my head and silencing for a moment the torturous present. My longing to hold them was excruciating, and I dug my nails into the palms of my hands to allow me to think of something else; anything else. It was all just too much, and the hot tears escaped, rolling unchecked down my cheeks and pooling uncomfortably in the hollow of my neck.

Why was no one standing up for me and getting me out of here? Why couldn't I get back to them? Where was Martha, my supposed best friend? Where was my sister? With a guilty jolt I thought about Dad. Even he might have been able to explain I was a good daughter and mother, and not some crazed lunatic.

The images began to change, and suddenly all three of us were laying in my bed, their sleeping faces pressed sweetly into either side of my chest, my arms encircling them both. I felt myself relaxing into sleep, my breathing deepening into a world of content and happiness. Just before I dropped off, I squeezed them ever so slightly to me, relishing in the feeling of their warm little bodies.

I was shunted awake by a loud bang, instinctively gathering the kids to me in panic as my newly opened eyes darted around. The clinical surroundings of my room greeted me, my arms empty of my children. The disappointment was so acute that I almost burst into tears there and then. I looked up to find the security guy from earlier was standing just over the threshold, one of his meaty arms holding the door open for me.

"The doctor's ready for you Marnie," he said in a surprisingly mellow voice. I rose eagerly from the chair and joined him, the memories of my dream with the children giving me a renewed determination to get out of here. As we both padded along the hallway to the security door, I felt something that I'd almost forgotten even existed; optimism.

This was going to be my chance to explain properly that Steve and Dan were out to get me, that they had to have been trying to make me lose it with the magnet, the notes, the photos and stuff. They wanted me to be crazy enough to take my kids away.

After being scanned through the heavy metal doors we immediately went right, down a little way from the hubbub of the kitchen and recreation rooms. Jamie stopped at the third door and knocked sharply. A 'come in' was heard wafting underneath and I was ushered forward, reaching out for the handle and pushing it down. The first thing that greeted me was the smell. Faintly flowery, but almost laundry-like in the way it enveloped me. It felt homely and reassuring.

"Marnie!" The doctor beamed at me from behind her desk before rising. "Shall we sit over here? A little more comfortable I think." She was gesturing towards a battered leather sofa and chair, set out just to the right of the desk. I nodded and sank onto the sofa, surprised and comforted by the feel of the ancient hide enveloping me. She nodded approvingly and came to join me on the chair. "Thank you, Jamie," she said as she lowered herself. "If you could wait outside for Marnie, please?" The man nodded and disappeared, closing the office door almost silently as he did.

"So!" The doctor began when it became apparent that I wasn't sure how to begin. "How're you feeling? You look a little calmer now." I looked hard at her, trying to decipher any malice in her tone. Detecting none, my hackles lowered, and I nodded.

"Yes, I'm feeling a bit better thanks." When she didn't respond I continued. "You must understand why I'm so angry though? I'm going out of my mind not knowing where my kids are, and no one will let me see them." My voice was beginning to rise as my panic rushed once more to the surface. "Please," I continued, actually wringing my hands together like they did in films, "please just help me get out of here so I can get them back." The doctor surveyed me for a moment before seeming to decide something.

"Marnie, can you tell me about the last time you saw Rose and Ted?"

"Of course I can!" I replied, baffled. "I dropped them to school one day, and next thing I know, Steve's telling me I need to get help, and that he and Dan were having them for the week. This is what I mean; they're trying to make out like I'm crazy."

"And did you speak to them over the week?" She asked as if I'd not elaborated.

"Well, of course! I mean, I tried. But they weren't letting me speak to them directly. They said they didn't want to talk to me. I ring them every day that they're not with me. I worry, you see. Especially about Rose with Dan. His mum's ok but you can't trust him."

"And Steve? Do you worry about him?" I almost smiled at the ridiculousness of that comment before remembering the Steve of the week before the car accident.

"I did trust him. Completely. Him and Addy. But I was wrong, wasn't I?"

"Why do you say that?"

"Well look at me!" I spluttered, waving my hands expansively. "He's put me in here just as much as Dan has. They're making out everything's in my head when it's not! And that old cow, Sarah," I continued with more venom than I'd thought existed. "She had no right at all not to tell me where they'd gone. If she'd just been straight with me, I wouldn't have been driving round like a lunatic, and I wouldn't have had that accident, would I?"

"I suppose not," the doctor agreed carefully. "So, the last time you saw or spoke to them was dropping them to school? And you don't remember seeing them again?"

"Well of course I don't! I told you all this when I got here; I went to pick them up Sunday afternoon as usual and they were gone. Where did the police find them? Can you tell me exactly what Steve and Dan have said for me to end up in here?"

"They were found, Marnie. And you say there was strange stuff going on before the weekend they disappeared?" I glanced at her sharply, her question startling me with its obtuseness.

"Yes! Yes, there was," I repeated to try to calm myself into being coherent. "I was getting sent all kinds of weird stuff, all about my Mum dying, and then they started threatening the kids. It took me a while to work it out, but it must have been them doing all that stuff to me; driving me crazy and making me think I had a stalker. Bastards! They both knew exactly what happened to mum!" I finished and shut my mouth tightly, angrily certain that they had been behind it all.

"What sort of things were happening? Why do you think it was them?" I thought back to that very first parcel, with the magnet.

"Well, it had to be someone who knew me, who knew about the way my mum died. At first, I thought it was just one of those weirdos, the ones we used to call our 'fans' when we were younger. But then I started wondering how they'd found me. I've only recently moved back you know, ever since Dad's been ill. Lula's been struggling to cope all alone. I lost touch with a lot of my friends when I left, so it's not like many people know where I live now. But obviously Steve and Dan do." The doctor looked down, consulting a notepad that I'd only just noticed was cradled in her lap.

"Can you tell me more about Lula?" she asked.

"Well, there's not much to say really. She's my sister. My little sister, two years younger than me. We've always been close growing up, especially since Mum...well, Dad didn't cope very well after she died. So, me and Lula looked after ourselves, and each other."

"I see. And are you close to her now? Do you see a lot of each other?"

"Yeah, I see her all the time now I'm back in town. She's got a little boy too, and Teddy and Rose adore Ruben! Actually," I said, an idea suddenly making me lean forward eagerly. "Could she come and visit me? I'd feel so much better if I could hear from her that the kids are ok. And Dad too." The doctor made a few marks on her pad before replying.

"I'm not sure it'll be possible for her to come just now, Marnie. I don't think you're quite up to visitors yet. Now," She continued, firmly closing the conversation on Lula visiting down. "I'd like to go back a bit. You mentioned your mum died when you were a child. What happened to her?" My fingers played irritably on the hem of my jumper.

"You know what happened. We spoke about this last time I was in here."

"Last time?" The doctor repeated, looking intensely at me. "Have you been in my office before today then, Marnie?" I gazed back in confusion, my mind playing tricks on me.

"Well, no. I can't have been, can I? You've only just stopped locking me in my room! I just thought, for a moment..."

"What did you think?" The doctor prompted a little when I stopped speaking. I shook my head.

"I don't know. Forget it, I just had a little déjà vu. My mum was murdered when I was eight, outside Wimbledon tube station. Me and Lula were there; we saw the whole thing." I said it baldly, so used to it being the most interesting thing about me as far as strangers were concerned that the words themselves no longer meant anything.

"You saw it? Can you tell me exactly what happened?" I sighed impatiently at the thought of going over it yet again before remembering that it wasn't the doctor's fault she didn't know.

"If I tell you, will you tell me more about how the kids are?" I took her silence for a yes. "Right. Well, we were going to pick my dad up from the tube station," I began matter-of-factly. "He worked in The City then, and Friday nights were the only night of the week where me or Lula didn't have a club on, so mum insisted we always picked dad up on a Friday and went for a pizza." I glanced up from my fiddling fingers, meeting the doctor's eyes looking sympathetically back at me. I lowered my gaze; sympathy was not welcome; I'd learnt long ago it solved nothing.

"We were parked opposite the station, where we always waited for him. No," I said, suddenly remembering something else. "No, actually we were parked a little further down than normal. Wimbledon were playing a football match at home and the road was really crowded, so mum couldn't get as far up as normal. The window kept fogging up. It was freezing. November, you know? And me and Lula were playing hangman on them with our fingers while we waited. I kept getting annoyed with her because she couldn't spell." A quick look showed the doctor frozen and looking at me.

"Mum was singing along to something on the radio. She kept the car running to keep the heating on because it was so cold." I paused for a moment, remembering. "And then Lula and I started arguing; she wasn't putting the right letters down and she was hanging my man even though I'd got it right. I remember fighting in our seats. I pushed Lula off and into the foot well." I paused again as her shriek filled my present, her body brushing mine as she fell with a thump. "Mum told me off. She was between the front seats, pulling Lula back up, and she told me off. It was the last thing she ever really said to me." I glanced down at my hands again. The sleeves on the threadbare jumper they'd found me were beginning to fray.

"And then suddenly she was out of the car and over the road. She told us both to stay in the car, so we did." I didn't really know how to go on. This was when the person asking me normally began to recite the bits of the story they'd read, or the rumours they'd been told. In the years since she'd died, my mum had variously been innocent, guilty, protector, antagonist, hero and attention seeker, depending on who's opinion you got. But every time she was still dead by the end of it.

"And that was when she went to help?" The doctor prompted.

"Well, yes," I agreed. "Depending on what you think happened, I suppose that is when you could say she went to help." I sighed loudly, risking a look at the doctor, and hoping that she'd think it time to call it a day for now. No such luck.

"Depending on what you think? I think you can agree she went to help, didn't she?" Doctor Roberts probed. I snorted a little derisively.

"Oh yeah, she really helped sort that situation out. Sticking up for some random woman she'd never met before, and then getting herself killed!" The feeling of the unjustness of the events that usually lived so deep inside me that I barely felt it anymore was rising. I swallowed, hard. "She should never have got involved," I said quietly and tonelessly. "She should have stayed with us." The doctor didn't speak but looked sympathetically into my eyes.

"Go on," she encouraged.

"You know what happened, don't you? You must be a poor doctor if you haven't even bothered to read my history. I mean come on; I know for a fact there are notes about it in my medical file. The amount of counselling they made Lula and I have, raking over every stupid, horrible detail. I'm not going to be able to tell you anything new."

"Of course I've read your old notes. But I'd like to hear it in your own words now, as an adult, if you don't mind? You never know what your mind can uncover when you think about things from a different perspective." I gave her a hard stare. Did she really think that I'd happened to forget anything about that night? "I know, I know," she said, able to read my mind easily. "How could you forget anything about that night? But humans are funny things; sometimes when something is incredibly painful our brains choose to delete or rewrite parts of it to make it easier to cope with. So, if you feel up to it?"

I gave another loud sigh. It was so tedious, having to go over the same things again and again. Every single doctor or counsellor I'd encountered had thought they'd be the ones to unbury more to the story, trotting out the old 'your brain's protecting you' line. None of them seemed to understand that there was simply no more to it than that. They all wanted to be the one to 'crack me'.

"There's nothing I've forgotten. Believe me. I've thought about what happened for the past eighteen years every single day." She simply fixed me with a measured gaze that brooked no argument. "Fine." I said, abruptly choosing to humour her.

"There was an argument going on, straight across the road from us, outside the station. It was between a woman and a man. Me and Lula didn't notice anything until mum suddenly jumped out of the car and ran across the road. She locked the car so we couldn't have followed her even if we'd wanted to. We watched her through the window, but we had to keep wiping the mist off and it was a bit blurry. Anyway, mum started arguing with the man instead. She was standing in front of the woman, and that's when we saw that there was a little girl there too. It all happened really quickly after that. One minute mum was in the middle of them, and the glass all steamed up. By the time we'd wiped it off again she was laying on the floor. The man had stabbed her. The ambulance came and took her away. And Dad finally came and got me and Lula out of the car."

The room was silent, and I left it like that. I'd had enough of talking about old news today. To break the tension, I leant forward and poured myself a glass of water from the low table between us. Slurping noisily in my need to both break my thirst and the silence, we regarded one another and waited for the other to speak. Eventually the doctor gave in.

"You saw it all from the car?"

"Yes," I replied. "Like I said. We were locked in." Briefly a flash of noise and smells shot through my mind, the sirens, the cold, the smell of blood. It was so strange that I almost told her.

"Shall we leave it there for today, Marnie? You must be exhausted. Could you come again tomorrow? Say," she checked the front of her notes before continuing, "9:30? Then we can both go to group straight afterwards." I opened my mouth to argue the pointlessness of this before the realisation suddenly hit me.

"You're the one who's going to decide when the kids can come in to see me aren't you? And decide when I'm going to be able to go home?" The doctor inclined her head slightly. I sighed, defeated. "Fine. Will that gorilla come and get me again?"

"*Jamie* will come and get you, yes. Please remember Marnie that we're only here to help you, nothing more sinister." She watched me get quickly to my feet and cross over to the office door. When I turned back, wordlessly waiting to be dismissed, she smiled ruefully. "Off you go then. See you tomorrow."

After being escorted back by my security guard I found myself at a loose end and pacing endlessly about my room, not able to settle. I'd been ready for a nap on the way back after my day of listening to other people's problems and having to regurgitate my own, but instead I was agitated. Speaking about Mum always did this to me; it was one of the many reasons why I usually avoided doing it.

Flashes of memory pinged about in my brain, unfettered and flying freely. Noises, colours and smells, all now having been pulled to the forefront, were unwilling to let themselves be pushed back into the comfortable oblivion of subconscious. I remembered the noise of the traffic as I ran across without looking, dragging Lula behind me. The aching cold was whipping about my face, the already congealing darkness around her coat as I bent over her still warm frame.

Wait. That wasn't right. By the time Dad got to us we didn't need to run, we didn't need to watch as her life drained from her into a gigantic pool of red beneath because she'd had already gone. My mind was going into overdrive; dredging up the past was making me misremember things and I didn't like it. Angry at the doctor but exhausted all the same, I climbed slowly into bed and pulled the covers over my head. All I wanted was to see Rose and Ted. I still didn't understand why we were dragging up my past instead of concentrating on my present; my willingness to appease the doctor was faltering. Finally, I fell into an uneasy doze.

TWENTY

The colours were becoming sharper and the noises more familiar. With supreme effort, I wrenched my eyes open and looked up at the woman beside me. A burst of adrenaline shot through me as I realised it was Mum. I grinned up at her, beaming. She wasn't dead anymore. I'd just opened my mouth to praise her when I noticed that she was arguing with someone above my head. The other person, a man, was wild eyed and spitting as he shouted back at my Mum. I could feel that something really bad was about to happen, and I moved closer to her, noticing as I did that I only came up to the other two's chest.

I glanced down at myself, taking in my bright white woolly coat, the one that had been my pride and joy when I was eight. The bad feeling was bubbling faster and faster, racing towards flashpoint as my panic rose exponentially with it. I felt a rush of warmth as dampness began to spread slowly into my woolly tights, my bladder responding directly to my fear. I grabbed Mum's hand urgently and pulled it, trying desperately to get her attention. She ignored me, and suddenly a strange glint of metal appeared in the crazy man's hand, the feeble artificial lighting of a cold November's night shining momentarily on it before he took a purposeful step towards me.

The ground was freezing cold and wet when I found myself unceremoniously flung onto it. A little dazed, I sat up, expecting Mum to scoop me off the pavement while telling the horrible man off for pushing me. Instead, there was just an empty, dark sky above me, and the arguing adults had disappeared. Urgent voices were rising and falling above me, the words that I couldn't make out rapid and fierce to my small ears.

Sirens were suddenly screaming, getting louder and louder as I sat where I was, the chill seeping upwards from my soaking bottom. I began to cry. I looked around for Mum, but I couldn't see her. There was a surge of people next to me, more racing over to join the crowd by the second, and one accidentally stood on my fingers as they ran past. I howled in both pain and terror, desperate now for Mum to find me. Suddenly someone scooped me up, standing me upright and holding onto my arms as they bent down to look into my face. It was a man dressed in a suit, his briefcase lying carelessly on the floor next to my feet.

"Are you ok?" he said, his voice distant under the sirens and the crowd. "What happened? Is that your Mum? Are you hurt?" His voice was clearer now, and he was gesturing towards the crowd.

"I can't find my Mum," I said, the tears streaming hot and heavy down my cheeks. "The bad man pushed me and now I've lost my Mum!" I gulped back the horribly burn-y feeling that was coming up from my tummy. The man looked at me for a moment before cupping both of my hands gently in his.

"Is your Mummy wearing a white coat, a bit like yours?" He asked quietly, his voice cracking with something I couldn't understand. I nodded, relieved that he had seen her. His face changed, and for some reason he looked panicked. "Ok. Ok," he repeated, clearing his throat and seeming to change in front of my eyes. "What's your name, sweetheart?"

"Marnie," I replied.

"Right then, Marnie. Mummy's had a little fall, a bit like you did, ok? Why don't me and you go and sit over there," he gestured inside the tube station entrance to a small bank of seats, "while we wait for the ambulance to come and make Mummy better? Do you know your Daddy's number?" I shook my head, worry taking over.

"She fell over?" I repeated. "Where is she? She'll be worried about me. She'll be worrying that nasty man hurt me." I followed the man's glance at the big crowd, and suddenly I knew where she was. "She's there!" I shouted, bolting from the kind man's grip as I took him by surprise. My eagerness to get to mum carried me through people's legs, their coats and bags banging against my body and head without me feeling them. Suddenly I was at the front.

A heap of red and white clothes was piled on the floor and two people were kneeling on each side, pushing down firmly on top of the fabric. Confused, I looked around for mum, glancing back to see if she was on the other side of the crowd. My eyes dropped to the pile of fabric on the floor, meeting her desperate gaze at once.

Her mouth moved, and I knew she was calling me even though no sound came out. I thought I screamed her name too as I dropped to my knees, my hands brushing against her coat and slipping as I tried to hold her face.

Rough fingers were clawing at the back of my arms to lift me away from her. I burrowed my face into her soft neck where her coat didn't quite reach up to, inhaling the most familiar thing to me, my first scent and the smell of home, as deeply as I could. All around me there were noises, more sirens, and another metallic odour invading my nose. Eventually the grabbing from behind stopped and I closed my eyes, concentrating only on the slight flicker of my mum's pulse against my left cheek.

TWENTY-ONE

When I woke up the doctor was sitting in the armchair in my room. She glanced up, and seeing I was awake, smiled at me.

"Welcome back Marnie. How're you feeling?"

"My head hurts," I replied, failing to return the smile. "I've had the weirdest dreams too. How long have I been asleep?"

"You've been in and out since we had our session yesterday. It's exhausting reliving our past, so I thought I'd come to you rather than make you come to me," she replied. "Apart from your head, how're you feeling?"

"Sad," I replied, a lump forming in my throat at the inadequacy of the word.

"Yes, that's understandable, you've been through a lot," Doctor Roberts agreed. "I hope you're feeling up to talking?" She waited for my small nod before continuing. "I thought today we could speak some more about what happened the day your mother died." I glared at her.

"Is it going to be too much to ask that you tell me how my kids are first? I don't really care that much about what happened the day my Mum died anymore, to be honest." Doctor Roberts fixed me with a stern look of her own before relenting.

"I promise you, they're safe and being well looked after. But before we can discuss what happened with the children, I need to help you to address your trauma. The past always influences our futures, you know."

"What? What does that even mean? I've never shied away from Mum's death. Not even when it happened. I told the officer everything I saw as soon as they got me out of the car."

"That's sort of my point Marnie. From all of the witness statements and police reports, you weren't actually *in* the car when your mum was killed, were you?" I opened my mouth in astonishment.

"Come on, Marnie. This is in your head somewhere. You need to find it." My head skipped immediately to my dream last night.

"But no, that's not right," I stuttered, shaking my head in disagreement. "Me and Lula; we were stuck in that car for ages before Dad came and got us out. Lula was so desperate for the toilet she wet herself." Past senses flashed unbidden, electrifying me. The coppery smell, the cold wetness of her neck as I burrowed my cheek into her skin. Then, unbidden, new memories; Rose's soft arms clinging to my neck, her sobs warm and breathy in my ear, Teddy's body burrowed into mine as he cried for his daddy. My legs curled up in agony at the sounds of them, my babies, scared and afraid.

"You weren't in the car, Marnie," the doctor repeated, eager now for me to take hold of this revelation. "The police, they couldn't peel you away from her, after. You wouldn't let go until your father arrived and managed to pull you away." Rose and Ted were still crying in my ears, and I was finding it impossible to concentrate on the present conversation. I raised my hands to them and, cupping them, pulled down sharply to try and right myself.

"Yes, Dad did get us," I agreed. "From the car."

"No Marnie, not from the car. You weren't in the car!" She sounded a little frustrated. Keeping my head encased in my hands I tried to follow her words but kept tripping over the shrill cries of my children bearing down on me.

"Ok," I said, realising that she wasn't going to let this go until I got to the end. "Ok, say we were with Mum outside the station. Wouldn't I remember something like that? Wouldn't Lula?"

"Ah. Lula." The doctor said, leaning forward and focusing even more closely on my face. "Tell me about Lula." I lifted my head back up, startled and confused at the sudden change in questioning.

"What do you mean, tell you? Lula. Tallulah. My little sister. I already told you this." I scoffed a little, feeling lighter. She didn't know all the facts after all.

"And what's Lula like? As a person I mean?" She asked.

"Erm, well, she behaves like she's still a teenager," I began, finding my mouth turning up in an attempt at a smile at the thought of my little sister. I continued at the doctor's encouraging nodding. "She's funny, like really funny. And confident too. Everyone has the best time when she's around; the party never starts until she's there!" I smiled fondly at the thought of her.

"Confident?" The doctor questioned. "In what way?"

"Oh you know…she wears really out there clothes, clashing bright colours, cycling shorts and fishnets together with a massive coat, things like that. She doesn't care what anyone thinks and just goes for what she wants. Even when it upsets other people," I continued wryly. "When she first met Rashid and decided she was going to marry him, he wasn't really given a choice about the matter." Now I found myself grinning. "Poor guy, he didn't stand a chance. But she's a really good mum," I continued, eager to make sure the doctor didn't think she was just out for herself. "She adores Ruben." Doctor Roberts smiled back at me.

"When your mum died, where was Lula?"

"With me. In the car."

"Marnie!" The doctor said my name warningly. "Not in the car! You weren't in the car!"

"Fine!" I glared at her for a moment. "Not in the car. With me I suppose. With Mum." The doctor looked at me, expecting me to say more than I had to say. My mind was assaulted again by the feel of mum's blood seeping through my clothes. I looked down at my arms, the whiteness of my coat, the one that eight-year-old me was so proud of, slowly turning pink, then ugly, nasty, red. Strong arms had eventually come from behind me, unwelcome and enclosing and ripping me away from mum, allowing her to slip away, to leave me all alone.

The smell was what I recognised. The familiarity of our washing powder cut with the faintest whiff of whisky. My Dad. I struggled, kicking him and hitting him, wanting desperately to get back to the prone figure on the floor. I knew that if I could just touch her again, she'd be ok. The paramedics were sitting back on their heels, the urgency of their movements seeming to stop as suddenly as I was lifted away. All at once I knew she'd left us, and as Dad tried to hold my face in, to block out the world for me, I stopped fighting and buried into his chest. Even at eight I noticed the difference. Dad's skin was so warm.

Back in my hospital bed, the was doctor looking at me curiously.

"You remember?" She was almost whispering, unwilling to startle my thoughts back undercover. I nodded, the lump in my throat returning painfully. I knew without having to live through it, that it would remain there for the rest of my life.

"I was there with Mum. Dad pulled me away." She nodded in agreement and waited. "I knew she had died. She was so cold and wet."

"And where was Lula?"

"She wasn't there."

"Why?"

"I don't know. Maybe she was left in the car?" The doctor shook her head, warning me again.

"Marnie, you have to understand that the trauma you suffered, watching your mum be killed in front of you, was huge. Do you remember why she was attacked?"

"She was arguing with the man," I replied, the feeling of terror and my mum's hand in mine palpable. "He was shouting at another woman. She had a little girl too. He hit her." The doctor nodded, waiting for me to continue. The memories flooded in now, the barrier well and truly broken for me. "Mum stepped in front of the woman. She let go of my hand. She was trying to talk to the man. He was screaming at her. I wanted to try and help."

"Go on," the doctor encouraged gently.

"He started coming towards me," I said, the past fear making me shiver now. "She saw and she came too. Then she fell."

"That's right," the doctor agreed. "According to the witnesses she jumped in front of you to protect you, and that's when he stabbed her. He was a paranoid schizophrenic who was suffering a mental break. He didn't even know the other woman and child; he had approached them just before you and your mum arrived. Your mother probably saved their lives."

TWENTY-TWO

It was dark again, I realised idly. The doctor must have left hours ago, dropping her bombshells, and then leaving me with them.

I had been upset enough at the time that she called in reinforcements, and they came in spades, strong-arming me onto the bed and injecting that blissful nothingness back into my bloodstream, just letting me fall off the cliff and into the black. The dose can't have been huge though because now I was awake, knowing it was still the same day; that it was only this morning that the truth about my mum's death had been exposed.

Without moving my body at all, I carefully began to examine my feelings. Everything I had remembered, and everything the doctor had confirmed and told me was true. Now that I knew the whole story, now the memories were firmly back in place, I was only astounded that I'd managed to paper over them for so long.

Dr Roberts says it's a coping mechanism, that my brain couldn't take the impact of watching Mum die, so it had put me in the car when it happened instead. She kept asking me to try and remember more details, but I couldn't, stupid things like what colour coat was the man wearing, did I speak to the other child who was there, did I recognise her at all? All details that my stupid brain couldn't figure out. I desperately wanted Lula to come in tomorrow for the session; maybe she could remember more than me.

I didn't expect her to remember much really; Lula had never once contradicted what I had thought had happened. Although now I came to think about it properly, I'm not sure we ever really discussed the minute details of what happened that day. Every time I brought it up my little sister would shut down, refusing to even acknowledge my obsessive train of thought. Mum was dead and two little girls had lost her forever. To a six and an eight-year-old, that had been all that had really mattered.

I decided to strike now, and swinging myself out of bed, I stuck my feet into the slippers on the floor and padded out into the corridor. Jamie was sitting at the admin desk, his head resting on his crooked arm and his face turned away from me. My mood lifted a little at the sight of him as I realised how glad I was that I wouldn't have to talk to a stranger. Stockholm syndrome was taking me for its own, I thought ruefully.

"Jamie?" I said quietly when he didn't turn at the sound of my footsteps. His head jolted on his hand before he whipped his face around towards me, and he was halfway out of his chair before I could open my mouth again.

"Marnie! You ok?" He said, blinking rapidly as if trying to focus on me. I'd obviously woken him up, and immediately I felt bad; did he ever actually go home?

"Yes, sorry. I woke you up." I stated, feeling weird that I had to think about someone else's feelings; something I hadn't had to do since I'd first woken up in this hospital.

"No no, I'm awake. How can I help? Do you need something?"

"Actually, I was wondering if I could talk to the Dr Roberts quickly. Not for ages or anything," I carried on quickly as he opened his mouth to say no. "I just wanted to ask her a question about tomorrow's session." Jamie nodded his head.

"Ok. She's gone for the day but let me see if I can reach her on the phone." He picked up the receiver on the desk and I turned away for a moment, pulling my sleeve down into the palm of my hand and nibbling it a little. Mum had always told me off for doing that to my school cardigans, threatening to send me in rags before inevitably spending her evening mending it instead. Once she died, I really did end up going to school in ragged clothes – no one left at home knew the first thing about sewing.

A side door next to the desk opened and a slight girl came padding out into the corridor before turning the other way. I hadn't even thought about having neighbours before, too wrapped up in my own problems to care. I wondered for moment what trauma must have befallen her to end up in here.

"Marnie." Jamie's voice broke my reverie, and I turned back to the desk. "The doctor's on the phone for you." I took the receiver from him, the weight of it feeling strange in my hand.

"Hello?"

"Hi Marnie. How're you doing?" Doctor Roberts' familiar voice picked me up a little and I had another uncomfortable flash of recognition that I was relying too much on my captors.

"Yeah, hi. Look, I was wondering, as we're talking about Mum and what really happened and everything, could Lula come in tomorrow for our session? It's just I really want to see her. I want to know why she never disagreed about what I thought happened. Or maybe she doesn't know either. I mean if she's confused too then maybe she should have some counselling or something?" I was garbling in my eagerness for her to agree.

"So. What'd you think?" I said when she hadn't responded. I thought I heard a brief sigh, a tiny exhale of air.

"If you really think it'll help?"

"Oh it would!" My voice rose several octaves in relief that she had agreed. "I really think it'll help both of us to understand if we can talk to each other about it."

"No problem. Now try and get some sleep and I'll see you in the morning." I handed the receiver back to Jamie, a smile on my face for what felt like the first time since I'd gotten here.

That night in my head I was eight again, back with my old family; the family before Mum went and died and defined our lives forever by that moment. Finally, dreaming only of them, I slept peacefully.

TWENTY-THREE

The morning routine of breakfast and staring strangers barely even registered the next morning. Jamie was shadowing as usual but I only I went through the motions, having trouble staying patient. I just couldn't wait to see Lula again; to see the one person that understood, the only one that had been through the same thing as I had.

I didn't even say hello to the doctor as she opened the door, my eyes instead scanning eagerly for Lula's familiar figure. The room was empty. Impatiently I crossed over to the sofa and sat down, sinking into the cosy leather as I scanned the room again.

"So where is she? Late again?" I asked, grumpy that even when I'd been locked up for weeks, Lula still couldn't be bothered to be on time. I picked up the blanket that was neatly folded next to me and wrapped myself up, feeling a faint pang that I was much too familiar with the routine already. The doctor came and took her usual seat on the low table beside me, her face close by and closed off.

"Let's talk a bit more about Lula," the doctor replied. "Just while we're waiting for her. I want you to lie back and relax. We're going to try and find out a little more about your lives together."

"I can tell you about our lives right now," I retorted. "I don't need your therapy for that; I didn't forget about *her*, did I?" I gave her a look but was already lying back against the cushions, my body relaxing into the fabric and my eyes closing. "You'll stop when she gets here though, yeah?" I felt a little shy about being caught in a weird trance when Lula got here; she would find it hysterical and never let me forget it.

"What's your first memory of Lula, Marnie?" When I stayed silent the doctor continued. "Do you remember when she was born?" I thought for a moment before shaking my head.

"I would only have been two, wouldn't I? I don't remember. But Dad always said I adored her as soon as I saw her. I'd 'help' mum with the nappies and everything." I grinned with my eyes still shut.

"But what's the earliest thing you can actually remember?" She persevered. I shrugged.

"I don't know really. I don't remember much before Mum died. I feel like that took over everything else when it happened. Obviously I remember her being there in the car." I corrected myself, my eyes opening momentarily. "Not in the car."

"No," the doctor agreed. I closed my eyes again, but the right pictures refused to come into my head, instead just showing me alone, burrowed and blood-soaked, into my mum's neck.

"Where was she then? Or was she in the car? Maybe that's why I always thought I was too?" I swallowed, my thoughts confusing me enough that I wanted to get out of them for a while. I sat up. "Where is she? She'll be able to tell you."

"Marnie, you know this. You know. Where was Lula?"

"In the car. She must have been. I mean where else? We always went to pick Dad up on a Friday altogether. It was our thing, you know? Get him, grab a pizza or a burger, talk about our week." I opened an eye again to find the doctor staring intently at my face.

I suddenly felt vulnerable, a stranger watching me relive my worst memory. "Can you stop staring at me?" I bristled, opening the other eye and glaring. "It's making me feel really uncomfortable, you watching me like that." She leant back into her chair, removing the physicality of her presence but refused to look any less intense.

"Sorry, I wasn't trying to make you feel uncomfortable, Marnie. Is this better?" The movement had broken the tension but the feeling of being exposed lingered. I closed my eyes and tried to focus again. The memories swirled, slightly too quickly to pin down, but always coloured in blood-red and white. I felt myself lie once more on the broken body of my mum, her hair whipping against my cheeks in the freezing November. I glanced up at the frantic heads moving above me, the semi-darkness of the London evening fragmented by blue flashes while the sirens blared relentlessly, adding to the chaos.

The faces surrounding me came into focus; the paramedics leaning back on their heels and calling time on my mum's last moments on Earth. The kind man in his suit who'd tried to shield me was lingering at my side, gesticulating towards me as he spoke urgently to a police officer who had tear tracks down his face. I scanned the sea of faces for my baby sister, for Lula's wild curls that drove mum crazy because she refused to let her brush them. She was nowhere. My father appeared, the dull regularity of his work suit at odds with our trauma.

He bent down and picked me up, the scent of his aftershave overwhelming me, the warmth of his body comforting and protective. Dad's voice was breaking with tears as he murmured the same words over and over; "Come on darling. Come away with me now."

As he turned me away from the prone figure on the floor, I caught sight of our car, parked and waiting across the road. No face appeared at the window, no smears marked the games I'd been playing on the windows with my little sister. No sister anywhere to be found. Snapshots of life before the murder pinged without remorse through my head; holidays, birthdays, Christmases. Mum and I baking a surprise birthday cake. Dad and I shovelling snow. Mum, Dad and I having a diving competition somewhere hot and sunny. No Lula.

"Marnie. Where was Lula?" the doctor repeated, her tone caressing and low; just as you'd speak to a frightened horse.

"Not there," I croaked, hating the truth that was slowly dawning on me, the catastrophe of real life seeping ever closer to the present.

"Why not?" The doctor's eyes were kind now, sympathetic. She gripped my hands in hers, the warmth reassuring in my icy cold realisation.

"Because she's not real?" I said, my voice blunt and quiet.

"Because she's not real," the doctor confirmed gently.

"But she is. She's got to be!" I exclaimed, half laughing as I tried to recall her childlike face to me. It wouldn't come now; all I could picture was the little girl at the tube station, her curls bouncing in the wind as the man screamed in her face. The curls that Lula has, I realised, my heart fracturing. "She's not real?" My voice was breaking with grief and loss for my sister.

"What's wrong with me?" The doctor squeezed my hands again before leaning forward a little more.

"Nothing's wrong with you!" For a moment the doctor looked frustrated through her sympathy. "Marnie, you need to understand this. You have been through unimaginable trauma, an event that anybody would have found hard to survive! Taking what you've told us before along with the newspaper articles and police reports written about your mother's murder, we think that 'Lula' was what you christened the other child there that day; the one your mum saved from the man with the knife."

"But, why?" I whispered. "How can I be so messed up that I invented a sister?"

"After talking to you for the last few months, we think that your mind created 'Lula' as someone for you to share both the grief and the survivor's guilt that you still feel about your mother. Do you remember much about your dad after she died? What he was like, things like that?" I shook my head without speaking. "Well, you have remembered before. And when we include the conversations that we had with your father before he died, it's clear that he was absent as a parent, unable to deal with your grief as well as his. So, Lula became your comfort and your family, once your real one was no longer around."

"But...hold on, before he died? Dad's not dead, he's in the Home." I smiled, suddenly sure that the doctor had me confused with another patient.

"Marnie, your dad died a few months ago, just before you were admitted here. As you know, he had dementia. It ran its devastating course." She gave me a moment to digest this before continuing. "We think that this was the trigger for your mental breakdown, coupled with the anti-depressants you had been taking." Grief was slamming into my chest like a sledgehammer, making it hard to breathe properly. In the space of two minutes, I had lost both my sister and my father. Coupled the fresh knowledge of the part I'd also played in Mum's death, I was in serious danger of being overwhelmed.

"He's not," I whispered, sinking back into the sofa and closing my eyes. "He's not dead. Lula's real." I was shaking all over. Images flashed through my mind; the last time I'd seen Lula when we went shopping and had lunch, and the last time I'd been to see Dad when Devon had refused me entry. Unbidden, recollections began to creep into my brain; the hug Devon gave me as I left the Home for the last time after Dad passed away in his sleep, the mindless drive from the Home to pick up the kids afterwards, the silent sobbing so as not to wake them up that night as I'd realised that the last tenuous link with my past had left me here alone.

TWENTY-FOUR

I slept for a long time, and quite possibly days, my body completely exhausted by the revelations. I dreamt only a little and was ridiculously thankful that the blood and gore had left me at least momentarily, replaced instead my whispers of happier times with Mum and Dad. The staff left me alone, only bringing food and water three times a day and shadowing me discreetly as I made occasional trips to the bathroom. Despite the upheaval of recent days, I found I was more at peace with myself, no longer feeling guilty for what happened to Mum, or shocked at Dad's death. I only felt gladness that he was released from a life of confusion and pain, and that he'd had such a peaceful exit, especially when I knew how violent the ending of a person could be.

The day eventually came when I was collected by Jamie and unceremoniously dropped off at the group session door. I gave Jamie a withering look and he returned it with a grin.

"Doctor's orders," he said. "She must think you're getting better you know. And if I were you, I'd try to share this time. She likes it when you guys open up to the other patients. I really think you might crack it this time, Marnie."

"This time?" I repeated his words sharply back to him, and his face fell.

"This group session I mean. Now go on." He gave me a gentle nudge towards the door. "Make me proud." I gave him one more suspicious look but entered the room with no more argument. Strangely I was beginning to rely on Jamie as my only ally here. He also definitely knew more about the kids than he was letting on, so I needed to keep him happy; he would be a much easier nut to crack than Doctor Roberts.

The room was already pretty much full, and as I walked over towards the empty seat next to Amy with everybody watching me yet again, I told myself that I was going to have to have a word with Jamie about his timekeeping. The doctor waited until I'd sat down before smiling at me. I looked a little stonily back. It was pathetic, but I'd gotten used to having her undivided attention and being in a room with her other patients wasn't going to help me in any way.

"Right, I think we're all here now. Today I'd like us to talk about the importance of taking responsibility for our own actions. Does anyone have any thoughts they'd like to share to start us off?" She waited a few seconds, ignoring Amy's waving hand and looking around before locking eyes with me. Please God no. "Marnie? Anything you'd like to share?" She asked me pleasantly, her head tilted to one side. It felt like she was laughing at me. I shook my head, but she just sat there, waiting.

"No," I said gruffly. "I'm not talking to anyone about anything else until you tell me when I can see my kids." I still felt too raw from the revelations about Dad and Lula to share, and after the annihilation of my perceived history my focus had landed squarely back on the family I knew were still living. We sat and stared at each other for a moment in a stalemate. She pursed her lips.

"Marnie, group therapy is designed to help. The more you're willing to share the more you'll heal." With one last disappointed glance she dismissed me. "Amy?" The Welsh woman stood up again, and as her draining voice began to fill the room, I tried to work out what it was the doctor expected me to share; especially the part about taking responsibility for your actions.

If we were talking about the past, as sad and fragile as I was, I finally felt absolved from the guilt I'd carried around from Mum's death. If it was the present the doctor was alluding to, the only people who needed to take responsibility for me being in this place were Steve and Dan for taking my kids away.

The group ended without much drama, with the only point of interest the fact that Amy had ended up driving into a wall to try and kill herself after she'd lost her family and job. And another woman, Zara I think her name was, had been put here after attacking her mum while off her medication. I was surrounded by a bunch of basket cases. I just wanted to go home. Jamie came and took me in for lunch. As we were walking to an empty table with my tray, he suddenly stopped me.

"Hey Marnie, I need to go and see another patient quickly. Here," he took my elbow and guided me to a seat where Zara was sitting alone. "Have a chat with Zara. I'll be back soon." I sat down without a fight, a little shocked at the thought of having to speak to someone else. I glanced up at Jamie and opened my mouth to protest but he shook his head slightly, smiled, and turned away. I looked down at my jacket potato, suddenly not hungry in the slightest. It reminded me of school days where you'd fall out with your friends, and suddenly be the loser that no one liked, sitting at a table with a random stranger. I pushed the food around, determined not to make eye contact.

"It's Marnie, isn't it?" I looked up unwillingly. Why had she spoken? Couldn't we have just sat here in mutual silence and waited for him to come back? I nodded. "I noticed you in group. It does help you know. To talk about everything that happened to you. Especially the stuff that you're ashamed of and want to take responsibility for? I felt like I was still going crazy before I came to terms with it. We're sick. Not evil. You know?" I murmured something non-committal and looked back down at my potato. I could feel her eyes on me, waiting for me to respond. After a few more minutes I heard her chair scraping. "See you around then," she said. I looked up just in time to see her walking away. My appetite gone, I followed in her wake, dumping my full plate of potato into the bin and heading back to my room feeling utterly defeated. I curled up, fully clothed on top of my bed and closed my eyes. I just wanted my kids.

The deodorant and perfumes stood messily on my dresser along with trails of cheap necklaces that had been discarded after the odd occasion when I'd actually been bothered to wear one. The tv on the wall was off, a dark and cold spot in the otherwise pale landscape of the walls. The curtains were drawn, with soft light coming through and dappling against the walls, the dreamlike state of early evening.

I prepared myself to truly study my children as closely as possible, sure now that these memories were all I would have for myself. On my left was Ted. He was tucked facing into my body and curled up into a cuddly little ball, the same way he slept every night. My hand encased the curve of his spine, and it lifted rhythmically in time with his breathing. Smiling in delight at the feel of his little body curled into mine I turned my attention to Rose over on the right. She was facing away from me, curled up on her right-hand side with her hand jammed underneath her cheek. I smiled at her profile, so calm and serene. Awake my children were like any others; loud, argumentative, cheeky, and most importantly, never still. Only asleep did I ever feel like I could study them and gloat over my perfect creations.

I moved my hand to Rose's cheek to stroke the stray bit of hair aside, thrilling at the softly cool skin. Wait. Not cool. Cold. I sat up, craning over her to see properly. Her eyes were closed; she was sleeping peacefully. My heart began to slow in relief as I began to relax back against the pillows, my eyes sweeping across her face as I did so. Her lips were wrong. They were pale, almost translucent looking, her cheeks without the bloom for which she was so aptly named. I put my trembling hand to her nostrils, waiting for that tell-tale warmth as she breathed out. Nothing.

Roughly I rolled her over onto her back. Her head moved from side to side from the motion, coming to a stop for a split second before I grabbed her shoulders and shook her.

"Rose? Rosie, wake up. It's Mummy, wake up!" I grabbed her face, having to stop myself from squeezing it in my panic. "Oh my God," I whispered to myself as my eyes panned down her still form to her chest. My fingers carefully stroked my baby girl's skin, the blood long since congealed as a darkness onto her front, the moist chill of it still penetrating my fingers and speeding as a bullet to shatter my heart. "Rosie," I whispered, gathering her to me as even then I noticed a new stiffness to her form I'd never felt before.

Placing my lips onto her forehead, I kissed her as if I could never stop, and wished that I was dead too. Gently placing Rose back onto the mattress, I took a deep breath before I turned once more to Ted, both knowing and fighting with every ounce of my being what I was going to find.

But he deserved my heartbreak too. Slowly I rolled Ted onto his back also, this time my eyes going to straight to his torso and the darkness covering my baby boy from neck to waist. It took all my courage to look at his face. This time my mind wasn't playing tricks on me, and as I studied his angelically long eyelashes, ones that I had always thought were a waste on a boy, resting on his pale cheeks. In front of my eyes his cherubic lips were growing muted and greying. I pulled him up to me, kissing him softly before laying him gently back down. Pausing to survey my world one last time, I grabbed the knife that was waiting for me on the bedside table, and happy to be going with them, plunged it as far into my stomach as I could. The agony took my breath away, barely allowing me to turn onto my back and gather my babies to me as I shut my eyes and prepared to join them wherever they had gone.

Jamie came running at my screams, bolting into the room and flying over to the bed to grab hold of me. He ended up having to get me in a bear hug to take control. I was panicking so much I couldn't breathe, and my body convulsed as it desperately clamoured for oxygen. Shouts were assaulting my senses and Doctor Roberts suddenly appeared in the doorway, her eyes wide with surprise.

"Marnie! What's wrong? What's happened?" I tried to get the words out but my lungs were protesting. I fought valiantly to take a breath, and with it I forced the words out.

"They're dead! Rose and Ted! They're dead!" My eyes were darting wildly, looking for an escape. I needed to find out where they were. I struggled some more against Jamie and felt a dull thump as another body was added their body weight to imprison me further. The doctor was in my face, her words blurred and untuned against the overwhelming grief. She shouted still more loudly, her hands now gripping my shoulders and pushing her face inches from mine.

"Marnie, they're not dead. Marnie. Marnie! They're not dead!" I finally found her eyes.

"What? What did you say?" I was panting with the adrenaline.

"The children are fine, Marnie. Why do you think they're not?"

"I saw them. I fell asleep and I saw their bodies on my bed. They were covered in blood and cold and grey. You who keeps telling me my dreams are trying to tell me the truth after all!" I was suddenly angry with her. She'd *told* me to listen to my dreams and now they were wrong?

"Marnie. I promise you now, they aren't dead, ok? They're safe and well."

"Do you promise?" I asked, falling still as my eyes bored into her brain. "They're really ok?" Doctor Roberts nodded, her hands on my shoulders now giving gentle pressure to comfort me.

"So why can't I see them? Why can't they visit me or even just ring me?" Doctor Roberts glanced at Jamie. "Look, can you just give me a straight answer for once?" I asked impatiently.

"The problem is it's not really a straight answer situation. Fancy coming for a chat now? If you're feeling calm enough that is?"

"Fine, but I need to know the truth now. I can't handle this anymore. I feel like I'm losing my mind. You'll tell me where my children are? And why I can't talk to them?" Doctor Roberts nodded.

"Yes of course. I think we need to straighten out exactly what happened. Especially if you're having these sorts of dreams."

We walked along the corridors as a strange threesome. The doctor led, her low heels clicking along the polished floor in a reassuring rhythm. Jamie and I came behind her together, he in his regulation scrub trousers and T shirt. And then me. Basket case extraordinaire and mental patient. If Lula could see me now, I thought with a wry smile, before remembering she wasn't real.

As we walked over the threshold of the office, I suddenly felt apprehensive. The visions of the children cold and bloody persisted and lingered, I couldn't quite believe that they really were ok. I took a deep breath and crossed over to the sofa as usual, keeping my focus in taking one step after another rather than what I was about to be told.

"Strong enough to go through this?" The Doctor asked when I'd settled myself frailly onto the fabric. I nodded. "Are you sure?" She leant forward in concern. "You really don't look well this morning." I gave her a withering look.

"Are you surprised? I need to know what's happened to them. It's driving me crazy. And those dreams…I think it happened. I remember finding them."

"I want to see if we can unlock the truth, Marnie. I know it's in there somewhere, and it'd be much better for your recovery if you can find them yourself rather than me tell you. Look, lay back and get yourself comfy. Here." She chucked the familiar blanket over to me and I swung my legs up onto the sofa. "Close your eyes, Marnie. Take me back to that day. The day you went to collect the children and they were gone." The lights began to dim as she shut the blinds and turned on the side lamps. I did as I was told and soon my muscles began to relax and my heartbeat slowed. "Start when you're ready," Doctor Roberts said.

TWENTY-FIVE

I was sitting in the car outside Daniel's, waiting for Rose to come out. Sarah had asked me to stay away from the house while Daniel was there. Apparently, he thought I was 'unstable' and didn't want to deal with me anymore. 'Fine by me,' I'd retorted to Sarah. I was sick of dealing with his deadbeat parenting too.

I drummed my fingers on the steering wheel impatiently and stared meaningfully at the three of them grouped on the doorstep. Sarah and Daniel seemed to be talking intensely to Rose, her little face, so like the flower for which she was named, upturned and carefully listening. Eventually she nodded and gave Dan a cuddle before walking down the garden path towards me. I beamed at her, although I was a little perturbed by her expression, which seemed anxious as she met my gaze. Sarah followed her, with Rose's little bag swinging from her hand. As Rose opened the passenger door and slid in, I went to envelope her into a hug.

"Hi sweetie," I said, leaning over. Rose moved out of my reach at the last second and I ended up grasping thin air. Feeling foolish, I withdrew quickly as Sarah appeared after putting the bag in the boot. She leant down through the open window and wrapped Rose up, whispering swiftly in her ear as she did. "What was that?" I asked, trying and failing to smile for Rose's sake.

"Oh, nothing Mum. Bye nan, see you Tuesday then?" Rose was clearly eager to separate her grandmother and I.

"It was obviously something," I replied, stung that Rose was being made to keep secrets from me. Rose looked stricken at the tone of my voice and Sarah looked hard at me.

"I was just reminding Rose that she can ring me and her dad anytime, especially if she's worried about anything at home. That's all."

"And why would she be worried?" I retorted. "Rose? Is there something wrong with being at home with me and Teddy?" I demanded, not waiting for a reply from Sarah.

"No Mummy," she stammered, bright red and looking miserably at her lap.

"See," I replied to Sarah, my voice rising in anger. "Nothing's wrong. We just need people to stop following our every move, and Steve to stop his stupid little mind games."

"Marnie," Sarah said a little more gently. "You're scaring the kids with all this talk about someone stalking you. Rose has been talking to us this weekend about it and she's worried about you, aren't you love?" Rose's little curls bounced as she nodded, still looking down into her lap. "You need to get some help," she said, even more gently, opening the door and reaching through to try to hold my hand. I moved away so she couldn't reach, and her voice hardened a little.

"You need to get some help, Marnie. All this stuff you're imagining is going on, thinking Steve's somehow trying to drive you over the edge. It's got to stop. Look," she took a deep breath, "why don't Daniel and I keep Rose for this week too? Let you have some time to yourself to go and speak to someone? Steve said he'd do the same with Ted." I glared at my ex-mother-in-law, realising what that meant.

"You've been speaking to Steve behind my back? Shut the door, Rose." I gunned the engine, my face heating up with anger. "I don't need any of you to 'help.' If you're with Steve and his campaign to try to fuck with my head then you're against me too, and you're a danger to Rose. You won't be having her again." I began to move off even before the door had been shut, forcing Sarah to slam it to keep Rose safe. We sped off down the road, the young mothers on the corner shouting at me to slow down

I opened my eyes to find the doctor once more seated on the low coffee table beside me.

"Well done, Marnie. Can you remember when that was?"

"That weekend. The last weekend." I murmured. "The Sunday; I always pick them up on a Sunday. But they weren't there when I went to get them? Remember, Sarah wouldn't open the door, and I was panicking. That's why I crashed."

"You picked Rose up as normal?" she replied, ignoring my question. I sat for a moment, puzzled. The car crash was the last thing I remembered before I ended up in here, and that was because I was in such a state that they were gone.

"I. I don't know," I replied, confused. "That's the first time I've remembered that. Or made it up, or dreamt it, or whatever the hell that just was." The doctor studied me.

"Shall we carry on?" She asked after a moment. When I didn't respond she continued. "It really is up to you, Marnie. We'll go at your pace." I heard pity in her tone.

"Let's do it now," I said, giving my head a dog-worthy shake. "I need to know the truth. No matter what...well no matter what." I laid back down and prepared myself to continue.

I was running through our front door, the kids just ahead of me as I pushed and shoved them over the threshold, slamming the door shut behind us as we all collapsed into a heap. I scrambled to my feet, my hands shaking with adrenaline as I tried to slide the chain lock across, the increasing shadow on the other side inducing more panic and causing the smooth silver disc of the lock to slide out of my hands repeatedly.

"Come on. Come on!" I muttered to myself, pure fear giving way to focus for a split second. The lock slid across, and I fell with relief back onto the floor with the children, pulling them both to me tightly as the pounding on the door began.

"Marnie!" The voice screamed from the other side. "Let me in. I swear you will regret this! Open the door before someone gets hurt!" Through the anger and violence in his tone I barely recognised Steve's voice until Teddy shouted back through the glass.

"Daddy!" He screamed, the terror at his father's presence palpable. He ran towards the door instead of away, obviously in a panic, but I managed to grab him and pull him back just in time. The pounding got more intense.

"Teddy, it's ok! Marnie, for God's sake you're scaring the kids, let me in!" My terror was reaching such a height that I couldn't reply even if I'd wanted to. I slid backwards towards the stairs still with a child under each arm. Rose was struggling against me, her horror even greater than mine.

"Shh, shh, it's ok," I whispered, finally succeeding in pulling her tightly into my chest. I felt her go limp for a moment. "Come on, upstairs quickly. I'll call the police." I grabbed Ted up into my arms and sprinted with difficulty, his sobs wracking through my body. Dumping him unceremoniously onto my bed, I dashed back down to help Rose. She was sitting right by the front door, her face pressed against it. "Rose, get away from there!" I screamed, visions of Steven's hand breaking through and raining down shards of glass onto her. My scream had alerted him.

"Rose? Rosie, it's me, it's Daddy Steve. Remember?" His voice was softening, the edge of anger still there but under control. She sobbed in response. "Hey, don't cry angel. I know you're scared, but I'm here now. Come on, open the door and I can help you. I can help Mummy too, ok?" Realising almost too late that I had been paralysed on the stairs while I listened, I sprinted to reach my daughter. Her hand was on the latch and pulling it down by the time I got there and with Steve's weight on the other side, the heavy wood flung forcefully inwards, catching with a resounding thud as the chain lock fully stretched.

"Marnie!" Steve's voice was much louder with the door open, and his fingers were scratching against the back of the chain lock as he tried desperately to dislodge it. "Open the door! You've lost it, can't you see that? Rose," he moved downwards to what he must have judged to be her level. "Rose, get a stool and slide this lock for me, babe." Rose's hands slipped through the gap in the door before I could stop her, and he enclosed them for a moment.

"St-addy?" She said softly, a name she had purposefully stopped using for Steve since the divorce. It had been her beautifully innocent mixture of Steve and Daddy. Her own special name for him.

"Rose, get away from him!" I screamed as I pulled her up, the terror making me reckless and rough. "He's trying to hurt us! Get upstairs now!" Rose was wrenching her body from me, her panic making her go in the wrong direction. I chucked her towards the stairs before putting all my weight on the front door to try and close it. Steve pushed back, his superior strength meaning that had the chain lock not been on, I would have gone flying. His fingers were still snaking around the door frame and fiddling with the metal.

I screamed without words, my last desperate push making no difference whatsoever to him. Finally, I cut my losses, sprinting after Rose who was still standing at the bottom of the stairs, tears streaming down her face as she watched. I half carried and half pushed her in front of me as Steve's voice carried on after us.

"Marnie, Marnie, please. Just let me help you. I swear I won't hurt anyone." There was a tremor to his voice as he called me now. Almost as if he was crying.

The room came back into focus. I was sitting up and panting while the doctor poured water in front of me. "Here," she proffered it to me. "Sip this. Slowly," she added as I gulped down the cold liquid, my heart hammering against my chest.

"He *was* trying to hurt us," I stated bluntly. "I told you so." The doctor watched me for a moment.

"Was he? Because he was trying to get in the door?"

"He was trying to break in. He wouldn't give Teddy back to me. He said I'd lost it, so I had to grab him and run! He's psychotic." The doctor nodded as if in agreement, otherwise waiting silently until my breathing steadied a little and my sips of water became more measured.

"But he must have given Ted back to you, mustn't he? And what about what he said at the end? You said he said was just trying to help you. You said he sounded like he was crying."

"He was lying," I said, non-plussed. "God, he's good, he's even getting you to believe him through me!" The doctor shook her head.

"I think that's enough today, Marnie. Let's continue tomorrow."

"No!" I shouted, banging my hand on the coffee table at the side of me and causing Jamie to stick his head round the door to check we were ok. He closed it again on some signal of the doctors. "Please," I continued in a quieter, and what I hoped was calmer, appeasing tone. I lay back down and closed my eyes, not giving the doctor much choice but to let me continue. Instead I heard her sigh.

"Ok. But I'm warning you, this part's going to be rough. You know that?" I nodded, not letting myself think about what the next part must entail even while knowing that reliving it once would be all I could take.

With difficulty and a lot of swearing under my breath I'd eventually managed to get the chest of drawers from under the window to in front of the bedroom door, shoving it as closely against the wooden frame as I could manage. I was trying my best to ignore the whimpering from the bed as the constant banging from downstairs tremored through my body. Finally, after running over to the window and yanking the curtains closed, I flung myself onto the bed and gathered the children to me with one on each side.

"It's ok, it's ok," I said, dropping kisses on each of their foreheads in turn. "Here, drink this," I continued, offering them both a glass of squash. "This'll make it all better, I promise. Shh, shh, I won't let him hurt you, ok? It's just us three; we'll stay together."

I felt, rather than saw, Rose's muffled nod against my side, as she drank deeply before handing it back and burrowing into the bedding. After both had had a drink and seemed calmer, I reached over past Ted to get the kitchen knife I kept in my bedside drawer for protection out. The banging seemed to be coming from the back of the house too now, and I instinctively knew that Daniel had arrived. The sudden sound of shattering glass made me jump, the children clinging tighter to my body under the covers, and I gripped the knife handle to the point of painful, ready to defend.

Footsteps pounded through the house, muffled shouts of the men seeping through the floor and into my bedroom. Carefully I moved the children off of me a little so that I could sit up more. The blade glistened even in the dulled light of the room, slick and almost wet. My mouth was aching with pure horror and panic, my lips dry. I could feel every single hair on my body stand up on end as the voices became clearer, the footsteps came closer. The bedroom door began to rattle, inch by inch opening more, the dresser helpless against the man's weight.

"Rose! Ted! Are you in there? If you can, get to the door. It's going to be ok." The mounds beside me were still, the children too terrified to move. "I'm coming in!" The voice screamed, as with a final shove the dresser moved a foot. The door flung open a bit and Steve's face appeared over the drawers, pulling himself through the gap. He grinned at me. "Too easy, Marnie." The room swirled with action, and the glint of the knife in my hand was the last thing I saw before everything went black.

I couldn't breathe, even with the doctor's hand on my back, coaching me through it, her voice deliberately calm as she counted in and out for me. I was retching repeatedly, my body trying to expel every part of itself. When I could eventually control my gagging enough, I spoke hoarsely.

"He killed them. I was right."

"You said you blacked out, Marnie. How do you know what happened?" I glared at her.

"He knocked me unconscious. I woke up and they were dead!"

"Were they?" She refuted me softly. "I've already told you they're alive, Marnie. They're ok. That was a dream."

"It all makes sense now." I said, awed. "He broke in, he stabbed me. Look!" I ripped the blanket off and yanked my top up to reveal the still red and angry scars running across my stomach, intertwining with the silvery traces of my pregnancies. "This was him, wasn't it? It wasn't a car accident; He did it! He did this to me!"

"Oh Marnie," the doctor whispered softly, before sighing a little, almost in defeat. "I'd hoped this time it would work, and you might get there yourself, but I think I'm going to have to tell you the last part. You just don't, or maybe you just won't, remember. Jamie," she called, raising her voice so that he opened the door enquiringly. "Can you come in for a second, please?" I whipped my head around to face her.

"I thought this was all confidential," I accused. "I don't want him listening and judging me too!"

"I understand that, but I think it's going to be for the best. Don't worry; Jamie is well-versed in confidentiality." She nodded her head for him to come closer.

"Now listen to me, Marnie," she continued more gently. "Steve's the one who called the police because he was concerned about you and the kids. You turned up at his house after making a scene when you collected Rose." I almost wanted to laugh. "I've got his statement here. Do you want to hear it?"

"No. I've just told you what happened!" I felt the anger burning up my throat and into my mouth. "Ok. Yes." I bit it out. "Tell me what lies he's told to get me locked up in this dump." I was sitting up now but now I wrapped the blanket even more tightly around me. Doctor Roberts picked up a file and rifled through for a moment before she cleared her throat.

Witness statement of Steven William Houghton given to Detective Julia Sommers and Detective Kari Patel.

On the afternoon of Sunday 16th October at approximately 4pm, my ex-wife turned up at my house to collect our son, Teddy. She was ranting about me, saying I was threatening her and that the children were going to be kidnapped. I told her that she was in too much of a state to take Ted and that he was going to stay with me. I could see that she had her elder daughter, Rose, in the car. Rose was crying.

My wife, Addison, tried to take Ted upstairs so that he didn't have to watch us argue, but Marnie managed to push past me and grab hold of his arm. She pulled him down the path and practically chucked him in the car without even strapping him in. I chased them, but she managed to pull away before I could get the door open and I was worried if I opened it while the car was moving, Ted would get hurt.

I got in my own car and went after them. I managed to keep up with her practically the whole way back and she was swerving all over the place – I think she'd been drinking. I lost them at the last set of traffic lights. They turned red and I didn't want to cause an accident so I stopped, but I wish I'd just gone through them because by the time I pulled up at her house they had just gotten through the front door.

I ran and banged on it and asked her to let me in. I told her I wasn't there to hurt them, but she's got it in her head that someone's stalking them and that it's me. I could hear the kids crying and begging me to help them.

Rose managed to get to the door and open the latch, but the security chain was on and I couldn't get in. I was begging her to let me in to help. Rose pushed her fingers through the gap to me. She needed my help.

I rang the police and then I went round to the back of the house to try to find an open window. There weren't any so I smashed a panel in the back door with a rock and unlocked it. By the time I got up the stairs they were all in Marnie's bedroom and she'd put something heavy across the door. I could hear the children crying and Marnie telling them I was trying to hurt them and that she'd make sure it was just the three of them. I begged her to let me in and I kept pushing against the door.

"This is absolutely ridiculous!" I interrupted. "How would I have managed to move it if Steve couldn't? I'm not superhuman, am I?" Doctor Roberts ignored me and carried on.

I managed to push it enough that the door moved, and I could get my head through to see in. The kids were both on the bed and they looked a bit drowsy. When I called their names, they didn't really respond. Marnie was sitting in between them but a little in front. She had a kitchen knife in her hand. She told me she was going to make sure the three of them were safe. I knew she'd really lost it and that she might hurt them so I kept on pushing the door and finally the space was big enough that I could crawl onto the chest of drawers and squeeze into the room.

Marnie began screaming at me to get out. She was getting really close to Rose's back with the knife and I knew I only had a few seconds. I ran to the bed and tried to get the knife off her. She was swiping it at me, trying to get me. I was trying to get it away from us both but somehow she managed to turn it. I let go because I didn't want her to be hurt, and that's when she stabbed herself in the stomach. The children were pretty out of it by then so I checked they were still breathing before I left them and applied pressure to Marnie's wound until I heard the police break down the door.

They called the ambulance and it came and took them all away. She'd given the kids some sort of sedative so they needed to be under observation too.

I truly believe that Marnie would have killed them if I hadn't gotten there in time. She'd been acting erratically for weeks, and her father's death pushed her over the edge. I tried to help her, by taking the kids, so did Dan but she'd become convinced that someone was stalking her and the kids, sending her creepy gifts and messages related to her mother's death years ago. She called me in the middle of the night once to say someone had smashed her kitchen window. When I arrived there had been no break in, and we couldn't find any sign of the magnet she was raving about. I decided she was drunk and took her home to my house because I was worried about her.

"The chest of drawers was still half barricading the door, and the room had been trashed when the police arrived. It seems that you must have done that looking for the missing photo's, remember? Everything Steve said in his statement matched up with what the police found." My mouth dropped open.

"Don't be so fucking stupid," I bit out. I'd long since trained myself not to swear out loud; for both the kids and my job it was important, but the white-hot anger was making me careless. The doctor didn't even react as I continued. "You know what happened. I've told you what happened. Why are you messing with my head like this? Why are you trying to make me think I'm mental?" In my peripheral vision Jamie moved slightly closer to us.

"I'm not making anything up, Marnie. I'm telling you the truth about what the police found – you with a stab wound that Steve was applying first aid to, and the children beside you, unharmed but sedated. Do you understand what I'm saying? Marnie?" She began to look a little worried as I stared blankly at her.

"You're wrong."

"Marnie, I'm so sorry but…"

"Don't." I said in a low voice. "You. Are. Wrong." I stood up suddenly, taking the doctor by surprise so that she jumped back a little on her knees; a random bunny hop. I strode over to the door without looking at her again. Trying the handle, I realised with some trepidation that it was locked. "Open it, I want to go back to my room," I said, without looking at either of them. When no one moved I tried again, louder. "I said I want to go! Open this fucking door. Now!" I began kicking it, such rage filling me that I couldn't see for the red mist. Once again I found myself scooped into Jamie's sturdy body, his arms easily picking me up and moving me away from the door. "And stop doing that!" I shrieked, using his manhandling as a reason to be even more incensed, kicking backwards to try and get him to let go.

"Listen to me!" the doctor continued, no longer the soft and malleable person I had thought her. "If you don't calm down do you know what will happen to you?" She didn't even wait for me to reply. "You'll have to be sedated. It'll be days before you're able to come and talk to me again, and all this progress will be wasted. You are *so* close now, Marnie. You want to be better, don't you? You want to know the truth; to understand?" After a moment I reluctantly nodded.

"Good," she said decisively. "Let's go back over there. That's it, sit back down on the couch. Jamie?" The man moved across the room to sit next to me, and the doctor perched on the low table in front of me. "Ready?" The doctor asked, when we were in position. I gulped, razor blades scratching at my throat.

"I need you to think about what I've just read. Really think about it. The police searched the house when they broke in. They didn't recover any of the items you said you'd received when you reported the stalking behaviours to them." Flashes of screams, bolts of colour, the knife swinging in the air were ripping through my consciousness.

"I wouldn't have hurt them," I whispered, my body shaking uncontrollably, my hands icy cold as I screwed them together. "I would never have hurt them. Or me. You said that was a dream, not real. I didn't stab them. I didn't stab myself either. I've never wanted to die; I'd never leave my kids. It was him. He did it. He wanted me dead!"

"Dead?" The doctor offered gently. "Marnie he was giving you first aid when the police arrived. Why would he have done that if he'd wanted you dead?"

"Why do you believe him?" I screamed in her face, suddenly done with being painted as a maniac who tried to kill herself and her children. "Why is what he says the truth and I'm in a fucking psycho ward? It wasn't me," I choked out. "I would never hurt them. I would never leave them without a Mum. I know how badly that can fuck someone up." I half laughed in despair through my tears, the irony not lost on me as my children's cries rippled through my ears. "I was trying to save them. I called the police for help, but no one believed me. Not one of them believed he was stalking us. Not Devon. Not Addy. Not Dan. Not the police. Not Lula." My voice caught on the last word and the Doctor looked at me sympathetically.

The cries were getting louder now, and each one was like another knife stroke through my body. Barely aware that I was in the doctor's office and not on the bed with them, I shoved my hands against my ears, a childish attempt to block them out. The metallic edge of the knife caught the dull light, slicing through the air, over and over, again. "I didn't do it. I didn't do it," I whimpered, repeating myself while my clamped ears made no difference to the terror that I now realised would never leave my head.

"Marnie, stop!" The doctor's voice was rougher than I had heard before, and the bark-like quality of it made my visions pause. She was closer than I had realised, and as she leant even further in, I could smell the coffee that she'd been drinking. I reached out with my hands, beyond control now, and clawed at any part of her I could find. Distantly I could hear screaming, but whether it was me or her, or even Rose and Teddy, I could no longer tell.

Alarms were ringing in my ears, reminding me for a moment of the monotony of the weekdays, of dragging everyone out of bed and to school. My left hand closed around something soft and malleable, and I yanked it towards me, sure it must be the door, sure that I could escape. Rough hands grabbed every inch of my body, wrenching me apart. A sharp scratch in my arm made me inhale quickly, before finally, mercifully, it all went black.

TWENTY-SIX

When I opened my eyes, my arms were strapped to the metal bars of my bed and the Doctor was waiting for me in the armchair. She smiled when she saw I was awake.

"Nice to see you again. We were worried you were going to do more damage to yourself the way you were fighting us off." She moved off of the armchair and poured me a cup of water. As she carefully poured it into my mouth, I noticed the livid bruises dancing circularly around her wrist. She looked at me wryly. "Yes, that was you. So," she started once more. "You remember our session?" I nodded and slurped thirstily from the cup. My mouth felt like it had a full arsenal of razor blades shoved in there. As I carefully used my tongue, loosened from the liquid, to explore, I realised every millimetre was covered in ulcers. I winced painfully as my tongue poked a particularly big one.

"My children are ok," I stated. That was all that really mattered.

"They are ok physically, yes." Doctor Roberts agreed with me. "But mentally they're still quite fragile, Marnie. Especially Rose. She's been quite badly affected by the entire thing. Obviously being that bit older, she was much more aware of what was going on in the weeks preceding that afternoon in the house. But she's having regular therapy. My colleagues are pretty confident she'll be ok."

"So when can I see them? When can I get out of here? That was the deal, wasn't it? I remember what happened and then I can go?"

"Do you remember what happened?" The Doctor's question threw me off.

"Is that not what our whole session was about?" I asked, confused. "I remembered taking the children. I remembered barricading us in. I remembered Steve stabbing me."

"Did you? I thought everything went black? As I told you, Steve's account is very different there. And he is backed up by the police reports."

"I wouldn't have hurt myself." I felt like I was a never-ending record. "Why can't anyone see how dangerous he is? Oh my God," I had a sudden, terrifying thought. "He hasn't got them, has he? Rose and Ted? Please tell me you haven't actually given my children to that psychopath?" I tried to scramble up before remembering I was still restrained. The Doctor caught my eye.

"I'll take those off once I know you're calm enough, ok? And yes, Teddy is with Steve and Addy. They have Rose a lot too. I believe he and Dan have made the arrangements between them so the children can see each other." I began to cry. Tears of pure heartbreak began to drip down my cheeks. They were all a family without me?

"When can I see them?" I asked again. I needed to see them before my heart imploded on itself.

"They don't want to see you yet, Marnie." The doctor spoke quietly, her eyes full of sympathy. "I'm sorry but they were very frightened by the events. Both Steve and Dan don't believe it's in their best interests just at the moment. And we do have to respect that."

"We have to *respect* that?" I hissed at her. "Why do we have to respect what they think? What about what I think? What about what Rose and Ted think? There's no way they wouldn't want to see me. After all the shit Dan and Steve put us through, and we have to *respect* them? They're MY children!" I was fully shouting now and trying to get up. "I'M the one who's loved them and looked after them and dealt with all the sleepless nights and tears and nappies and worrying about money to give them the best life! ME!" The bars on the hospital bed were rattling with my rage.

"Yes, we have to respect that," the Doctor replied quietly and ignoring my outburst. "They've got custody of them currently, and they don't believe it's in their best interests. What we really need to concentrate on is getting you to accept the truth. Then we can begin to get you better. Do you see?"

I stopped struggling and turned my face away from her, allowing the tears to pool under my cheek and soak the pillow.

"Marnie? Do you understand? You need to accept the truth before you can get better." I didn't answer and I heard her get up quietly, her clothes rustling a little as she went to leave.

"But that's not the truth," I half whispered, half sobbed, just before I heard the door gently click shut.

A few days passed before I saw Doctor Roberts again. Jamie said that she was off on annual leave, but I didn't believe him. She just didn't want to see me. I tried to talk to Jamie about it, thinking maybe he could be convinced of the truth, but he just blandly agreed, and never giving any answer besides an agreeable murmur.

After a while I couldn't even be bothered to talk to him, I was achieving nothing if he didn't at least take part. I wanted him to fight my corner with the doctor, but it looked like he wasn't going to be doing that; even he wasn't around as much. I spent most of the day in my room or else wandering the corridors when I got kicked out to 'socialise'. I avoided the dining room as much as possible. There was no chance I wanted to be accosted by that Zara, or even worse, Amy, again. Instead, I waited like a patient dog for my master to deign to see me.

On the third day I finally got the message. As Jamie walked me down towards her office, I found my stomach was bubbling excitedly. I'd had the last few days to let everything sink in and had been silently (and not so silently with Jamie) practicing my defence. I'd begun to piece more of what happened that together as the initial shock wore off, and now I could almost see what had happened second by second. Snatches of dialogue between Steve and I had come back to me too, and I couldn't wait to tell her.

At the familiar 'come in' Jamie opened the door for me, and I walked through. The doctor watched me with a big smile on her face.

"Hi Marnie, lovely to see you. You look happier today?" She posed it as a question, and I willingly replied.

"I am! I've remembered more about what happened."

"Fantastic! Come and have a seat then, and we'll have a chat. Sorry I've not been available; I've had a few days off. It does everyone good to have a little break to recharge, wouldn't you agree?" I nodded and went to sit down on the sofa. I couldn't wait to begin; with any luck I'd be out of here by this afternoon, and Steve would be locked up. I watched impatiently as she poured us both some water and settled herself into her armchair opposite me.

"So how have you been doing?" She asked pleasantly. "Have you managed to make any friends? Jamie told me you spoke to Zara once. She's a good person to speak to Marnie. Very level-headed, and popular with the other patients too."

"What's she doing in this nuthouse then?" I grumbled, not impressed we were talking about another patient; this was my time.

"She spoke in group last week. Don't you remember?"

"I was too busy trying to find out what'd happened to my kids!" I felt my ears reddening a little with embarrassment.

"Well, it's her story to tell. But she's good at sharing. Why not ask her over lunch today?"

"Yeah. Yeah, maybe. So, can we talk about the kids?"

"Go ahead." Doctor Roberts sat back and looked at me, the epitome of calm and composed.

"Ok. So, I've been thinking, and I think the first thing you need to do is take them away from Steve. God, I'd even be happy for them both to go to Dan until I get out. But you need to understand; they are in danger with him." I paused, expecting something from the Doctor, who just looked passively back at me. "So, will you take them off him?"

"Why do you think they're in danger? Apart from what you've said before about him being the stalker. After all, you said the stalker was threatening you, not them. Whoever it was wanted to save them, didn't they?"

"Well, yes. Steve was threatening to take them away from me. But I've remembered more about the day he broke in. Once he'd gotten into the bedroom, he spoke to me."

"And what did he say?"

"He admitted it. He was coming towards me and saying he'd never need to worry about me again. He said he thought the threats would have worked, but now I'd gone too far, taking the kids and putting them in danger. He said he was going to fucking kill me. And then he grabbed the knife, and he stabbed me."

"You actually remember him stabbing you?"

"Yes," I lied. I remember it all now. "So, you can let me go. The police should really go and arrest him. He tried to murder me. He needs to be locked up."

"Oh Marnie." She looked sad as our eyes met. "I thought you might really have cracked it this time."

"This time?" I repeated sharply, reminded of Jamie a few weeks ago. She swiftly changed tack.

"Marnie, can I ask how long you think you've been staying with us here?"

"Well...a few weeks, I suppose. Since I woke up here."

"You've been here with us for six months now," she replied in a low voice. "Since your dad died, and you suffered your mental breakdown."

"Six months!" I repeated disbelievingly. "But that makes no sense! The accident was only a few weeks ago; I only woke up a few weeks ago."

"This is the third time we've gotten to this point with you now. Me and you; we've been talking about your life for a while. All about your mum, your children, Lula even; for months." My hands began to turn white as I balled them up in my lap, and she gripped them, intense and understanding. "Marnie, I know this is a lot to take in." Tears fell onto our entwined hands, my heart so painful that I couldn't get it to make sense.

"But...how? How can we have been talking about it for months and me not know? You're lying to me." I stood up, suddenly angry, and Jamie appeared swiftly next to me.

"I'm not," the doctor replied, her voice louder as she tried to make me listen. "I promise I'm not," she continued more gently. For some reason she sounded like she wanted to cry too. Jamie put his arm around me, a caring gesture on the surface, but with steel that left me in no doubt that I had little choice but to go with their flow.

"We have been talking for months, I promise you. Look, I can show you proof if you like." She waited for me to give her a curt nod before walking over to her desk and grabbing something from its depths. She swiped her fingers a few times, and then handed the iPad to me, startling me into taking it before I'd realised what I was doing. A video was playing, taken from above of two people.

"It's us," I said, dismissing her as I passed the tablet back. "So what? That could have been from yesterday for all I know." The doctor nodded.

"It could have been, but that was our first meeting. Look." A long list of video files had appeared on the screen, each with my name followed by a date. As the doctor's fingers gently scrolled the touch screen downwards, the dates got further and further away, until she clicked on the last one, six months ago, and the video she had just shown me popped up once more.

"It's not proof. You could have put any date you like in," I said, trying to remove my fingers from hers.

"We could have, but we didn't. This is a hospital. We aren't in the habit of making stuff up to trick patients," she said lightly, clearly in an attempt to make me smile. "Please just listen a moment, then you can go back to rest." She cleared her throat and started again.

"When you arrived here you were in a dreadful state. From what you've managed to tell us, and from Steven and Daniel's accounts of what happened, you'd been living as if your father was still alive for those last few weeks. In fact, according to them, you didn't tell anyone he had died, you simply stopped contact with the Home, forcing them to arrange the funeral without you. We think that his death and the loss of the last link to your family, coupled with the new medication, was too much, and you began to live as if it hadn't happened." The doctor stopped and looked at me for a moment, obviously deciding that she was ok to continue.

"That's when we believe that your mind began to 'remember' a different narrative, and Lula was brought into the equation. According to both of your exes, as well as your friends, you've never once said that you had a sister, and you've always talked about your mother's death consistently with what happened. But after your dad died, your behaviour changed. You began to believe that someone was stalking you, sending you things to do with your mother's murder, like breaking your window, and sending the magnet, photos and the Instagram posts.

The Nursing Home told the police that you found some old bits in your dad's room the day he died, and it seems that your mind then filled in the blanks with a story." The doctor stopped again, sharing a glance with Jamie. "Do you want to stop?" I shook my head. I needed to know.

"According to Steve you became so erratic that he was concerned about you and the children. After discussing the children with the school, he and Daniel agreed to have them more. They believed that if you had a bit of a break, you could get back to normal. Seemingly you did initially agree to this, but then became distressed, believing that they had been behind the 'stalking' all along. There were certain other…incidents that were causing alarm too. Do you remember trying to take that other little boy? You thought it was Ted." So that bit wasn't a figment of my imagination, I thought, humiliated.

She leant in a little more, meeting my eyes. "It's not your fault, you know. Your mind just couldn't take any more trauma. Instead, it made up stories, and even Lula, to protect you."

"Your illness made you believe that Steve was stalking you all and that he was going to hurt the children. We think in doing what you did, you thought you were protecting them from him. You did give them the sedative after all; you weren't going to let them to suffer."

"But I'd remember! Come on, if I'd tried to kill myself or drug the kids I think I might have a recollection of it! Just like I have about Mum, about Lula. Even Dad now…" I tailed off, taken back into his room, holding his tissue paper hand while he slipped gratefully away. But the memories of the children still refused to change or evolve. "It was Steve!"

"Marnie, he didn't do anything." The doctor was aiming to soothe, but for the first time I detected a little patronisation in there too, like I was the thick kid who couldn't work it out. She doesn't believe me, I thought suddenly. "This is your stumbling block," she continued. "This is where we get to every time. You remember everything until that day; we untangle all the fake and real memories about everything else, but your mind simply won't let you remember this part. It is completely understandable," she continued kindly, "but we can't get you better and we can't treat you properly. Until you take responsibility and remember your actions that day, we can't get you mentally healthy again."

Her mask had slipped now, allowing her contempt for me to shine through. Unless I admit that I was going to kill them, and that I tried to kill myself I was stuck here. I closed my eyes and thought hard, dragging myself back to the day I lost everything. The images flashed through on fast forward, the desperate slamming of the front door as Steve tried to enter, the grabbing of Rose and bundling them both up onto the bed. The juice on my bedside table I'd given them to calm them down as the pounding of feet were racing up the stairs. The knife in my hand as he busted through the bedroom door, the blade not pointed downwards to the bundles on either side of me, but aimed directly at him as he advanced, his face screwed up in a menace that I had never seen on him before. The words he spat at me before the knife was wrenched from my grasp, the handle coming down forcefully onto the side of my head, and the world went black.

"It wasn't me," I whispered again, opening my eyes to find the doctor and Jamie both watching me. "It *was* him. He wanted me dead." The doctor shared another look with Jamie before they both slumped back in defeat.

"You're tired. We'll continue this tomorrow. But don't worry," the benign mask was back. "We will get there eventually, I promise. Now," she raised her voice as I began to protest; there was no way I wanted to stop now, not now I knew. The bastard, I thought. He's managed to get them to believe him and now he has my children. "Jamie is going to give you a little more sedative, to help you sleep, ok?" I shook my head.

"No I..."

"I insist, Marnie. Get a good night's sleep and then things will be clearer tomorrow, ok?"

"I don't want to sleep; I want to carry on! It wasn't me; don't you see? Everything else has come back, all those other memories. But I know the truth. My memories haven't changed." The hope that began to flow threatened to overwhelm me. *'It wasn't me,'* I whispered to myself, relief momentarily flooding as the first layer of self-hatred began to peel away.

"You need to go and rest," the doctor repeated, iron filtering into her tone. "Jamie." She nodded to him, and he put a hand under my elbow, raising me to my feet.

"No! Please. I'm ok. Really. I just want to talk about this."

"Rest, Marnie. We'll speak again tomorrow," she continued, pre-empting me by putting her hand up to stem my protests. "I've got other patients to see today." Terror seized me. I began to struggle from Jamie's grip, almost succeeding in getting out of his grasp when suddenly I stopped. It was pointless; all they'd do is pump me full of drugs again, and then who knew how many days I'd lose. I made the decision, I was going to do as I was told. For now, at least.

"That's it," she said as I stood, breathing deeply to bring my temper under control, her voice sugary with the relief that I wasn't kicking off. "Thank you, Marnie. We'll talk again in the morning, ok?" I nodded and was swiftly escorted from the room.

TWENTY-SEVEN

I watched the sky lighten on the ceiling of my cell, curled up tightly into a ball on my bed. I'd convinced Jamie not to sedate me, and so the long night had given me ample opportunity to reflect on my situation, with the revelations of the last few days, and just how fucked up everything was.

I ran through each event repeatedly, and every time they became more solid, as if now that the fog had lifted my brain had been jolted back into reality. With a surgeon's precise movements I turned each memory, every single person involved, over in my mind, allowing them to settle into wherever their correct position should be.

The day of Mum's murder was crystal clear now, so much so that I was shocked that I could ever have thought it different. The smells and sounds that had assaulted my nightmares for weeks were now grounded in pure fact, and I found I had made my peace with it.

Dad's recent death was also back in its rightful place. I now appreciated what a relief it was that he was no longer here, confused and thinking that I was his dead wife, come back to see him after all these years. Because that had happened more than I'd cared to admit. For months, maybe a year even, he'd forgotten I existed, and was instead seeing the person who should have been there to grow old alongside him. I couldn't remember his funeral. I knew for certain I'd never been to the funeral; the doctor had been right about that.

The revelations about Lula out of the lost members of my original family was weirdly the most painful. I knew that she wasn't real, but I did remember her. She'd been my imaginary friend after Mum died, taking on the appearance of the other little girl there that day, the one I hadn't even known I'd taken so much notice of. All the counsellors and doctors back then had assured my father an imaginary friend was normal, healthy even, and had said to allow me to play out a fantasy that was clearly helping me to cope. Don't get me wrong, I hadn't spent my entire life believing in her; around my mid-teens, she had been regretfully packed away with the rest of my toys, when real life friends came into my life.

But it was Rosie and Ted that hadn't allowed me to sleep last night, and whose absence meant that I would never sleep peacefully again until they were back with me. I sensed it should be guilt that was making me feel like this, and in a way it was. I laid on this bed wracking my diseased brain, searching desperately for the moment that I apparently plunged that knife downwards, trying to snuff out my own life. I knew it was my only way out of here, but it wouldn't come. If I couldn't convince these people of the truth, then Rose and Ted were lost without me to protect them from Steve.

Instead, I could only relive the terror as Steven chased us in his car, and as I dragged Rose away from the door in the certainty that he was here to kill us. And I remember the moment he came twisting through the door like a serpent, the knife raised in my hands in self-defence, and the pain of something granite-like crashing down into my skull.

Every moment was clear. Every single event that Dr Roberts and I had unravelled was lodged firmly back into place, and much as I knew it would take me time to properly process and to properly grieve, I was at peace with the past. But not this version where I tried to kill myself, where I would have killed them too, had I been given the chance. It wasn't possible. Every single fibre of my being had been programmed to protect them at all costs from the moment they entered the world.

By the time Jamie came to wake me I was dressed and determined. I would be listened to today, I vowed it. I walked down to get some breakfast, confident that today was going to be the turning point to getting the hell out of here. I didn't have too long to wait.

"Steve would like to see you, Marnie. Do you think that would be ok?" I looked up from the puzzle I was working on in the common room after my silent breakfast, to find the doctor and Jamie standing over me. Steve wanted to see me? I glanced up at Jamie. He looked a little dubious about this turn of events, and I found I was happy to have an ally. I opened my mouth to tell them Steve could go to hell when I caught Jamie's eye. He gave me an almost indiscernible nod, as if to say, 'do it.' Out of everyone I'd met so far in this nut house, Jamie was the only one I even slightly trusted.

"He wants to see me?" I repeated the doctor's words back to her, looking down at my puzzle and playing for time to see if I could get any more information. "Why?"

"Well, I think he'd like to speak to you about how the children are doing, and generally just check in on you. It would be fully supervised of course," she continued diplomatically, but whether that was supposed to be a comfort to me or a warning not to do anything stupid, I didn't know. I looked up again, a big smile pasted on my face.

"That would be great," I replied easily. "When?" She looked wrong footed for a moment at my apparent levelheadedness.

"He's here now actually," she said, her face screwed up in anxiety while Jamie grimaced at her side.

He was in the doctor's office, lounging around on the sofa as if he owned the place, as we opened the door. *My sofa. My place.* I bit down the urge to tell him to move and let the doctor usher me into her own usual chair. She grabbed another from across the coffee table, moving it closer to Steve's sofa and facing me alongside him. It felt like a firing squad as I levelled my gaze at the two people most responsible for my imprisonment in this place. Steve met my eyes, grinning happily momentarily before looking down. I'd never so much wanted to rip someone limb from limb with my bare hands. The doctor cleared her throat.

"Hi, Steve. Welcome. It's great to have you here in person rather than speaking on the phone. Marnie and I are glad to see you, aren't we?" She stopped speaking, waiting for me to respond. I stared at her blankly, willing for her to carry this conversation because at the sight of him I seemed to have lost all logical thought. I watched him gift the doctor with a big smile. It was his work smile; his 'you can trust me with your kids' smile. The smile that had fooled me all those years ago, the one I'd believed was genuine until just a few months ago.

"Doctor Roberts, hi," he purred, his hand outstretched to shake hers. "We've spoken at length on the phone of course, but it's nice to put a face to the name." I could feel the atmosphere soften as she reached out, their hands meeting in a firm handshake and the doctor reciprocating with a beam of her own. I'd quite happily punch the both of them.

"Nice to meet you Steve," she said more tenderly. It was like watching a couple of drunk strangers meeting in a bar. Jamie cleared his throat and the doctor seemed to remember where she was before collecting herself. "So," she repeated, her hand abruptly dropping his and forcing her eyes to focus elsewhere. Unfortunately, the next thing they rested on was me. "Marnie! Why don't you tell Steve all about the great work we've been doing recently?" I reddened with embarrassment, feeling like I was five years old again and bringing my dad to the classroom to look at my work. I reacted in the same way I did then.

"No. You tell him," I muttered sullenly, my own eyes on my lap as I fiddled with the soft cotton of my sleeve. Hospitals were always boiling; you never needed anything more than a long-sleeved vest. Idly I wondered why they didn't install a bit of air con, but then again it was probably another punishment for us lunatics. As I picked a loose thread, I could feel the doctor's eyes on me, but I refused to meet them. I heard a familiar exhale of disappointment before she started talking once more.

"We've made a huge amount of progress with Marnie in her programme, Steve," she started, her voice a more melodious pitch than it had ever been with me. "Obviously I can't discuss the details but suffice it to say we're really very proud of how well she's doing this time." I chanced a glance at Steve. His gaze was fixed firmly on me, and when he saw I was looking back, a gleam of triumph shone in his eyes.

"Well that's very good to hear, Doctor Roberts. I'm so glad she's doing well." I glared at him, itching as I never had before to rip him apart. He smirked again at me, his eyes crinkling with cold humour. My hands clenched into balls as I imagined putting one of them straight through his face. Maybe the doctor noticed, because she reached over to the jug of water between us and poured me a glass before sliding it in front of me.

"Marnie," she spoke softly but there was a hint of caution in her voice. "Have a drink, you look thirsty." I tore my gaze from the evil sitting opposite me and met her eyes. The usually sympathetic gaze was tinged with warning. I picked the glass up, gulping the liquid down in one in a fruitless effort to dampen the rage building. The doctor had turned her attention back to Steve.

"Now like I said, Marnie is doing really well with us. In fact, we're hoping that in a month or two she may even be ready to leave us, if she keeps it up." A shadow of shock flitted across Steve's face before he arranged his features back into his ingratiating smile.

"That's fantastic news. Well done Marnie!" Steve replied. I wondered if I was the only one who could see the small clench of his jaw; a sure sign he was pissed off. I could feel the tension rising from my ex-husband.

"Yes, exactly, she's done so well! And with that in mind, the reason I invited you in today was to discuss the possibility of getting Rose and Teddy in to see Marnie. As I'm sure you can imagine, she's very anxious to see them, and I really think it would push Marnie's recovery on even further if she could just have half an hour or so with them. Just to put her mind to rest that the children are happy and healthy, you know?"

My heart began to beat rapidly as the doctor's words hung expectantly in the air between the three of us. I could really see Rose and Ted? I would be able to touch them, to kiss them, to listen to their stories, worries and excitement after all this time? I turned my attention to Steve in that moment, all my hope and delight written over my face. Too late I realised my mistake. Immediately Steve's jaw relaxed itself and he leaned back into his chair, his entire countenance changing in that instant.

"Steve. Steve, *please*," I whispered, already knowing that I had lost. He glanced at the doctor before fixing his attention back onto me. His eyes bored into mine as his smile returned full bore. He winked ever so slightly in my direction.

"I'm so sorry," he said, helpless appeasement oozing from every syllable, "but I just don't think the children are ready for that. They really are very traumatised by what happened." Doctor Roberts nodded.

"I understand that completely Steve," she replied. "But Marnie has come so far, and it's been a long time that they haven't seen each other now. They would of course be supervised closely; no harm would come to them. I just think it would be good for all of them to begin the healing process, don't you?" I cringed silently, feeling like the two of them were my parents arguing over something naughty I'd done whilst pretending I wasn't even there.

"Quite frankly, no I don't." Steve was reddening now, the clench back in his jaw and his body tensing for a fight. "Ted is still having nightmares; did you know that? Every night he wakes up screaming for me and Addy to rescue him from that bedroom. He's petrified *she's* going to come back." My body was shattering at his words, each slice a slash against my heart.

"And Rose? Don't even get me started." He glared at us both, one after the other, daring us to argue back before resting his stare on me. "She wouldn't speak to me for a month, Marnie. A month! She wouldn't come near me, she wouldn't go to school, she wouldn't see her friends. Dan had to stop working to look after her. And all because of you! All because of what you did. If you think for one single moment, I'm going to let you come back in and turn their world upside down again, you're completely wrong." He reached across, draining the jug of water into his own glass before leaning back in his chair and sipping it composedly, the matter firmly closed to his mind.

"But I didn't do anything to them, Steve! Please. Please tell the truth so I can get out of here. I can't function without them. I can't cope. I can't…" My voice trailed off as the huge wave of grief at being separated from my children threatened to overwhelm me. "Please," I whispered, my voice scratched with emotion. "We need each other, the kids and I. Please." I reached over the coffee table to where he was putting his glass down. I just managed to scrape the back of his left hand before he yanked it away, coldness emanating now from the man who'd only ever shown me affection. He studied me with a steady detachment of emotion, torturing me, before glancing over to the doctor.

"Do you think we could get some more water please?" he asked politely, holding the empty jug out. Doctor Roberts rose from her chair and took it from him.

"Of course. I'll ask Jamie." I watched as she moved quietly over to the door, before I flinched at the sharp pain on the back of my hand, still resting on the table from Steve's rebuff. His nails were digging into my paper-thin flesh and I tried to yank my hand away. He gripped me tighter. I raised my eyes to meet his.

"You won't see them again, Marnie." His voice was a whisper but strangely echoing in my ears. The freezing contempt in his eyes was chilling, and coupled with the pain and sound distortion, I felt disorientated. I pulled away again. The murmurs of the doctor and Jamie were making it hard to focus. "No, Marnie. You don't get to choose when to leave me this time." He smiled. "And you won't see the kids because I won't let you, got it? I'm the one who decides what happens now. You should never have left me; look what you've become without me to look after you - a nutcase who's a danger to her own children. I told you over and over again you weren't strong enough to be alone; look how easily I proved it."

"You proved it?" I stuttered, momentarily stopping my struggle to get my hand free. "What do you mean?" He snickered softly.

"You know what I mean, Marnie. They're always going to believe me over you. You didn't really think you had some crazed stalker, did you? I mean who'd be that interested in someone as pathetic as you? I guess the death of that sad old vegetable you called a father really did manage to fuck you up." I ignored the slight on my dad, too intent on learning the truth.

"You sent me all that stuff? You made me think my kids were in danger? But why? Why would you do that? Why would you do it to Rose and Teddy?"

"You don't deserve them," he replied bluntly. "I told you all along you were nothing without me, and look, I was right, now you're just that. Locked up here with no hope. You're nothing." He released my hand and sat back again, his victory making his features strangely grotesque.

A drumbeat was pounding through my veins and the world diminished to just the figure in front of me. I leapt across the table, smashing into him with a force that would have winded me if I had been capable of feeling anything else. My shin bone clashed painfully with the solid wood but I felt no pain. I vaguely heard Steve take a sharp intake of breath before my fists rained down on him, my screams barely audible to my own ears. I could feel his arms trying to grab onto mine to stop the onslaught but for once he lost, my anger making me superhuman. The hammering was only getting louder, and my body became attuned to its rhythm, using it as a baseline for my attack.

As suddenly as it started it stopped. My arms were wrenched roughly behind my back, and I gave an involuntary yelp of pain as they were pushed towards my shoulders. I stumbled upwards as I was half-lifted from Steve's lap and pulled forcefully across the floor. The excruciating pain in my shoulders that pulsated up and down my arms was reaching a crescendo as I fought desperately to get free.

"He did it all! I'll kill him. I'll fucking kill him!" With a last wrench I freed myself, feeling my right shoulder pop out of its socket as I closed the distance between Steve and I once more. Steve raised his arms in defence, but not before I managed to find his throat with my left hand. I squeezed as tightly as I could, his taut neck muscles twitching under my touch before a sharp blow knocked me off balance and I fell to the floor, howling as my dislocated shoulder rammed into the ground.

Immediately I felt a heavy weight on top of me as Jamie once again rendered me immobile. The sudden stillness focused the world suddenly, and I became aware of shouts and an alarm pitching relentlessly in the corridors. From my prone position I could only see Steve, the doctor now standing over him, still in his chair, her hands cradling his face as she checked for damage.

She moved and his face came into full view, bruises already forming on his left cheekbone and neck and a bloodied lip adding to the gore. Steve and the doctor were murmuring to one another, and from his tone he seemed to be reassuring her he was ok. She nodded and moved away to allow Steve to get up. He put both hands on the arms of the chair to stand. Just before rising he met my eyes and winked before sauntering gingerly over to the door.

I screamed, intelligible and guttural in his direction, fighting Jamie with every ounce of my being to be released so that I could tear the monster apart. Just as Jamie's grip was loosening against the barrage of my assault, the door flew further open and bodies poured into the room, providing Jamie with the strength to hold me. From my prone position on the floor I saw a glint as the sunlight caught the metal of the syringe in one of the nurses hands.

"No!" I screamed. "No, please! You can't leave them with him, he's a psycho. He did this! He did this!"

But with that by now familiar sharp scratch, my racing mind was immediately beginning to slow down with the clouds of grey covering my eyes, and even while I fought the inevitable, I sank, perversely thankful, into the arms of my babies and the darkness.

TWENTY-EIGHT

I flung myself back on my bed, quivering with anger. "Bitch!" I screamed over and over, with tears of rage coursing down my cheeks. They were coming for me, I could hear the alarm that Jamie had pulled, the running feet coming closer. This time I welcomed the inevitable oblivion. She didn't believe me. She would never believe me. I was never going to get away from here. A flash of fire scorched through my flesh as I realised there was a real possibility that I was never going see Rose and Ted again; that they were going to grow up in the house of the man who tried to murder their mother.

Every day I tried. Every day I pulled myself out of the fog that they forced me into, the need to be heard stronger than any drug. Every single time they denied the fragments of memories that painted a different picture. No one believed what Steve had admitted to me. The police had evidence and witnesses to prove I was crazy, even the school had given a statement about the fight that Dan and I had. When I argued back, when I tried to make them understand that I couldn't remember because the memories weren't there to find, the doctor got angry with me. When I demanded to see the evidence that had forced me into this place, she looked angrier than I had ever seen her.

"You aren't trying! You aren't trying like you should be Marnie, and we need you to admit the truth, we can't afford to keep going backwards! You keep getting to this point, and then that's it. You snap right back to remembering nothing again," she said this afternoon, throwing her pen down onto her notepad in frustration. I stayed still on the sofa, watching her try to regain her composure. I had recently been trying a different tactic, where I would be as subversive as I could to begin with, lying on the sofa whilst the doctor tried to unbury the truth. It always descended into chaos.

I tried to keep hold of my composure now. "I am trying! But I can't remember something that isn't there, can I?" The conversation eventually got as heated as it always did. "Why won't you believe me?" I had ended up shrieking as they carted me off again. "Stop putting me to sleep and believe me! Please." My last word was choked out in a sob. It made no difference, and now as I checked the clock, I saw that I'd been out cold for four hours.

Making a mark in my make-shift diary, I counted up. It had been over a month now since I'd discovered that Steve had played his winning hand. The hope that had flashed that day in holding onto my innocence was now in tatters. And with each hopeless argument it was ground further into oblivion.

I tried to stay up all night, unable to sleep for fear I would dream about their blood-soaked bodies again. Even now that I knew it was a false memory, my diseased brain decided to torture me repeatedly with it anyway. As always, I eventually fell into an uneasy doze in the early morning hours, so that when Jamie came to get me for breakfast he had to wake me, doing all he could to persuade me to move, and threatening me with a feeding tube if I didn't. It became the pattern of our lives. I would sit, unwashed and unspeaking in the dining room, while Jamie chattered away in a fruitless attempt to get me to respond.

I'd lost interest in speaking to Dr Roberts now. All she wanted was get me to admit something that I knew for a fact wasn't true, and the sessions had become too painful. My early morning vigils began to be filled with the nagging doubt that the children were indeed dead, what with her utter refusal to let me speak to them or to see them, supposedly on Steve's say so. I begged her to let me hear from the police about what they had found but she said I wasn't well enough. Sometimes she reminded me of the nuisance I'd become to law enforcement before I ended up here, as if trying to humiliate me would make me believe I'd been crazy enough to hurt anybody. I had no one left on my side who believed me. I asked for Dan, or Sarah; I'd even have taken Steve again at this point. Anyone. She almost laughed.

For the last few days, I'd simply sat in silence, ignoring any questions that she asked me until she sighed and gave Jamie the nod to take me back to my room. They always sedated me now at my own request; consciousness was unbearable.

Whenever I was forced to be in the real world I tried to concentrate only on the happy moments that I could recall with clarity, mostly with Rose and Ted, but sometimes with Mum and Dad too. I became so comfortable there, and so at peace, that I began to spend more time with them in my head, replaying holidays, picnics, even cosy nights snuggled up on the sofa together. I was blocking out the present so successfully that it was now true reality that seemed dreamlike and fantastical. Jamie, the other patients, even Dr Roberts; they all became unimportant, unrealistic figures beyond the horizon.

The gaps between living my life in memories and living in the real world were becoming smaller as the injections came more frequently. One day a sudden noise jolted me from pushing Rose on the swings at the park, and I realised that it had been a long time since I'd been shepherded by Jamie to the doctor's office. In fact, it'd been a long time since I'd been shadowed by the man to go anywhere. Now, I wandered of my own accord throughout the wing, sometimes coming back to the present and finding myself in the dining room or sitting mindlessly in front of the tv.

None of the other inmates spoke to me, their eyes sliding over my silhouette as if I was completely invisible, entirely irrelevant to them. On the few occasions when I begrudgingly was present on the wing, I studied them, idly interested in what they had done to get themselves locked up in this forever prison. I took care never to stay in this world long enough to find out. If I was ever unable to get myself back into my dreamworld alone then I would scream, shout and kick, until they were forced to send me back into welcome oblivion with the needle that I now looked on as an old friend.

I awoke one morning to immediate reality. With a grunt I went to roll over to try to go back to sleep. It was then that I noticed that Jamie was sitting in the armchair next to my bed. He was watching me, and, meeting my gaze, raised his eyebrows knowingly.

"Are you back with us this morning?" He asked softly, leaning forward so that my own gaze couldn't disconnect from his. "Or are you with them?"

"You," I replied gravely, my voice hoarse with lack of use. "How long have I been gone?" He almost smiled at that.

"Depends on what you mean by gone," he said. "You've been completely sedated for twelve hours; you had a bit of an argument with another patient. You bumped into her; she took offence." I nodded listlessly, having no idea what he was on about. "But you've not had a session with Dr Roberts for about two weeks now if that's what you mean. She stopped them when you stopped talking. From experience, we know that we can't bring you back by this point, but I asked her if I could just try one more time.

"What did you want to try?" I didn't care. I just wanted it over with so I could get back to the reminiscences in my head. He cleared his throat, looking a little nervous.

"Well, I wondered if you knew how long you've been here now?" I nodded impatiently; this was old ground. "I know the doctor told you you've gotten to this point before. But...do you know what happens after this each time?" I shook my head, still not overly interested. Why would I care? It's not going to be that come to believe I'm innocent, was it? Jamie took a deep breath.

"You go all the way back, Marnie. You go back to living in your head again, to believing all the stuff you've managed to unravel so far." I stared at him uncomprehendingly.

"I don't understand," I croaked. "I just forget everything?"

"They don't think it's a case of forgetting. They just think the strain on your mind when you try to acknowledge what you did to yourself and would have done to the children is too much for you to handle. Instead, you simply go back to living in a world where it never happened. You go to live in a place where you have a sister to share the grief and guilt with you over your mum's death, and where your dad is still alive. Where your children are still with you and life is normal. Then we begin the whole process again. Sometimes it's days, sometimes it's weeks, but eventually you 'wake up from your accident' and we start to unravel your mind and memories again. Do you understand?" I looked at him blankly.

"Marnie, you've gotten here three times so far. Each time you begin to retreat, just like you are now, back into your head, until eventually we can't get you back to reality even for a moment. You become completely mute, apart from the nightmares, then you scream for them all. We need to try to help you while you're still lucid enough, before your mind snaps under the pressure. Before we lose you again and it's too late. Do you see?"

I nodded without caring. Not really. Finally I spoke, the urge to go back to them was far too strong to fight.

"I understand. Jamie, I'm tired. Would it be ok to give me something to help me sleep?" I looked trustingly at him, knowing instinctively that he would oblige. With a sigh and a rustle, he turned to the tray that he'd bought in, now resting on the side table, and I rolled over slightly to give him ready access to my flesh. Just as he picked up the needle, he paused to look at me.

"I've grown fond of you, you know," he continued, awkward now and looking just over my head rather than meeting my gaze. "And to be honest, I think I believe you. You know, about all the stalking and stuff. Your story never changes on that. It's the same every single time." He seemed to have run out of things to say, and I had no bright ideas either, stunned as I was. After a few moments I spoke.

"You believe me?" I repeated, scarcely able to comprehend his words. "You think I'm telling the truth?" Jamie met my gaze steadily this time, placing the needle back down and nodding.

"I do. But the problem is Marnie, that no one else here does, and eventually you're going to lose the fire in you, and we'll have failed you all over again. What we need to do," he continued, leaning forwards from his chair, his eyes boring into mine, "is get you out so you can prove it."

TWENTY-NINE

Jamie's plan was simple in words, if not in action. The single most important thing that he said I needed to do was to fight against the urge to become insular and detach from real life. Jamie had heard Doctor Roberts speaking to another colleague about my case the other day, and they were discussing the possibility that the next step would be to transfer me out of here and see whether other professionals could make any headway.

The idea of leaving here to be locked up somewhere unfamiliar filled me with absolute dread, and Jamie certainly didn't help my anxiety by agreeing that this would almost certainly mean an even longer hospital stay as they would inevitably want to start treatment from the beginning again. So, I needed to win the fight of my life, with my opponent none other than my own mind.

Jamie had decided to tell Doctor Roberts that I had become responsive again, and that I wanted to see her. I waited impatiently, pacing relentlessly, counting the steps I was taking over the ugly linoleum floor, with scuff marks from years of the furniture being moved around my markers in keeping me sane.

Reality was far too connected to me now, the conversation with Jamie lighting an uncomfortable but undeniable spark in my brain. I was painfully aware of my surroundings, and as I listened to the noises coming from outside my room, I realised it had been a long time since anything like that had penetrated through the fog. I stopped abruptly halfway towards the window and pivoted. If the doctor wasn't going to come to me, I'd go to her.

I'd put my hand on the door handle by the time the fear caught up, and I shuddered involuntarily, flinching and letting go at the clinical coldness of the metal. If I opened this door, if I took that step out into the corridor, I was going to have to leave them behind. All those happy memories of Mum and Dad. All the good times with Rose and Ted would have to be erased while I fought for my freedom. I knew Jamie was right; if I wanted to get out of here and fight for the truth then I wouldn't be able to risk even a single moment of reminiscence. His talk of regression had scared me. My own mind was the biggest enemy here, and if I even wanted a fighting chance, I had to put everything I had into combatting it.

I put my hand back on the handle, swallowing hard as the room seemed to suddenly fill with the ghosts of family bonds. Mum's perfume intertwined with the soft scent of whisky, flocking to my nostrils with unending familiarity. Ted's laughter rang in my ears as I felt the affectionate touch of Rose's fingers finding their home in mine. The metal under my hand was alien and unyielding, and the only thing I wanted to do was to relax back into a world where I was enshrined in love and peace. I gripped the metal harder, forcing them all back from me. I swung the handle down until it clicked, whispering goodbye to my ghosts.

The corridor was a hive of activity, with patients and staff alike walking up and down purposefully. I joined the slipstream towards the common area until I reached the security door, which was propped open with a doorstop. The noise levels were even higher down here and I faltered a little feeling overwhelmed. I forced my feet forwards towards the kitchen. I needed to keep busy, I needed to keep them all at bay and the only thing I could think of to do was to make a cup of tea. There were two other women in the kitchen chatting to one another as I entered. They fell silent, watching as I crossed to the cupboard for a teabag. I could see the moment in their eyes when they dismissed me, probably used to the shadow that I'd once more become in the last few weeks. Their conversation continued over my head as I moved quietly between them, nothing more than dust.

I finished making the tea and stood awkwardly with my back leaning against the counter, taking small sips of the burning liquid and trying to work up the courage to join in. If I was going to do this, I needed to do it properly, and Jamie had said that included showing I could socialise with others. One woman, a slim lady in yoga pants and an oversized T-shirt, was moaning about her daughter's attitude towards doing her homework. I smiled in solidarity, working up the courage to open my mouth and agree that Rose was the same. The woman caught my eye and gave an uncertain smile back before looking at her friend.

Suddenly both women began to move towards the door, their hands wrapped around their own mugs and their chatter continuing as they exited, leaving me excluded and alone once more. I blew out a frustrated breath. This was going to be a bigger challenge than I thought.

I stayed there in the kitchen until I'd drained my entire mug, watching as various women came in and out to make themselves a drink or get something to eat. None of them were familiar to me from the groups, making me wonder if those lucky people had found their way out of this hell while I rotted inside my own head. Not one of them acknowledged me, and I felt too shy to try and approach anyone else after my first attempt.

I walked out, turning right and finding myself outside the common room. There were groups of people seated at tables, some with cards in front of them, some with games, some just with tea and biscuits. Peering in I caught sight of a very young woman seated alone, a pack of cards spread out in front of her like a clock. I fought the urge to turn and run back to the safety of my room, where the only people there were spirits who'd welcome me in. I needed to keep busy to prove my sanity was intact. Instead of fleeing, I swallowed and pushed the door open making a bee line for the lonely girl.

"Hi," I said, dropping into the chair opposite. "Clock patience?" I asked, nodding towards the cards. "My nanna taught me to play that." My companion looked up at me and I realised she was even younger than I'd thought, surely not more than nineteen.

"Mine taught me too," she replied, her voice barely more than a whisper. "Do you want to play something together?" She asked, her hands poised to scoop the nearly complete clock up off of the table.

"Oh no, it's fine!" I said, shaking my head before she could do so. "Do you mind if I just watch? I'm Marnie, by the way," I added as an afterthought.

"Florence," she replied, smiling gently again before reaching out towards her cards. The long sleeves of her jumper rode up and I caught sight of her heavily bandaged wrists. She quickly pulled them down, flushing red with embarrassment as she glanced back at me and saw that I'd seen.

"It's ok," I said softly, feeling an almost maternal tug in my chest. "Honestly, we're all in here for something, aren't we? Do you want to talk about it?" She shook her head. "Ok. I don't want to talk about my problems either, so shall we just play cards?"

Jamie found me there half an hour later while Florence and I were playing Go Fish. I was concentrating hard and didn't notice him until he'd approached the table.

"Hi Florence," he said when we both looked up. "Do you mind if I steal Marnie for a bit? Her doctor would like to see her." Florence shook her head smiling, and I noticed Jamie's expression was gentler than it had ever been when he looked at me. I pushed myself up from the table.

"Ok. Well erm…bye then. Thanks for letting me play," I said as Florence gathered her cards up again, this time taking care not to stretch her arms out too far. "I'll see you around, I guess."

"Bye Marnie," she replied, already busy shuffling. "See you around."

Jamie didn't speak to me again until we were outside. I went to turn left towards the Doctor's office, but he steered me right instead.

"Back to your room quickly, Marnie," he said tensely, his hand on my arm as he guided me. "Doctor Roberts has agreed to a session, but we need to get your story straight first, ok? And," he continued, stopping me for a moment to look me up and down, "a shower and some clean clothes might go a long way too."

I entered one of the shower rooms with my hands full of clean clothes and a towel, Jamie standing guard outside. I hated these rooms with a passion, which probably at least partly explained why my personal hygiene was not up to scratch. There were no proper locks for obvious reasons, and the rooms were sparse and unwelcoming. I undressed quickly, wanting to get back out as soon as possible, and turned the water as hot as it would go.

Not even ten minutes later I appeared in front of Jamie, my dirty clothes wrapped up in the wet towel and my skin and hair feeling strangely light now they were grimeless. Jamie and I walked back to my room in silence, and he wafted me through the door before entering himself and closing it silently. I sat down on the edge of my bed while he took the chair and we looked at one another for a second before he began to speak.

"I spoke to Doctor Roberts. I've told her you seem lucid, really with it, and that I think you might have finally had a breakthrough. To be honest,

Marnie, she's a bit sceptical at your sudden recovery from where you were starting to go."

"But she'll see me?" I asked eagerly. "She'll start the sessions again?"

"She said she'll see you today to see what she thinks. It's a start, Marnie, but I think this is going to be harder than either of us thought it would be. You're going to have to convince her you've remembered the truth." I couldn't help rolling my eyes a little.

"I *have* remembered the truth, Jamie. You know that."

"I mean about hurting yourself. If you've got any hope of her signing you off as fit and healthy, your story is going to have to match theirs."

"You mean I'm going to have to say I stabbed myself and tried to hurt the children?" I asked, my voice rising with the sudden anger. "You mean I'm going to admit I've lost my mind?" Jamie put his hand on my trembling one for a moment.

"Calm down. I've told you I believe you, Marnie. But to get out of here, to prove you're telling the truth and get to the kids, I think it's going to be the only way." I stared at him for a moment, realising he was right.

"But…how? I'm not an actress, Jamie. And I've never been much of a liar."

"You need dig deep and find your inner Meryl Streep then. Remember, everyone wants you to tell this story, and Doctor Roberts has given you all the information you need. You just need to tell her what she's already told you, ok? But be careful, she'll expect you to be angry about it, not just accepting. This is going to take a while, and it's important you don't rush it." I nodded, my resolve building at the thought of Rose and Teddy's faces.

"Ok," I replied, my voice strong even while my hands shook. "Let's get on with it."

Doctor Roberts welcomed me in with a smile, her relief at seeing me seemed to be genuine. She ushered me over to my normal spot and poured us both a glass of water from the jug that I'd wanted to wrap round Steve's head only a few weeks ago.

"Marnie. It's lovely to see you looking so alert. How are things? I was pleased that you'd asked Jamie to see me again."

"Yes I, well, erm, the thing is, I…" I trailed off, picking at my sleeve. I couldn't find the words to start. I was going to fail.

"Jamie said you've remembered more?" The Doctor prompted gently after a few moments. I'd forgotten for a second what he'd told me. She wanted this to happen.

"Yes, that's right. I've remembered how I got hurt." I silently pinched the inside of my wrist at the lie, the pain making my eyes glisten. I kept pinching until I could barely stand it anymore, before looking up.

"Oh Marnie," she said, reaching over the table to touch my hand. Bingo. "Are you feeling strong enough to tell me about it?" I moved my hand away. I couldn't lie to this woman while she was touching me.

"I hurt myself didn't I?" I asked in a low voice. "With the knife. I gave Rose and Ted something to make them sleep." Doctor Roberts had sat back now, looking at me appraisingly.

"Go on," she said, her eyes never leaving mine. I pinched my wrist again, the pain helping to mask the absolute disgust with myself. I continued.

"Jamie, come on! I don't want to do this anymore. You promised I'd be out of here by now." I was pacing around my room, ignoring going near Jamie who was waiting patiently at the door. We were three weeks on from my initial confession and belief that I was going to be released was slowly dripping away.

"I know, I know. You're getting there, I promise," he replied, his voice even and his countenance unruffled. "She even told me the other day how impressed with you she was. Just a few more group sessions and I think you'll be free!" I rolled my eyes and continued to pace. I'd graduated back to group sessions last week, meaning that not only did I have to announce to the Doctor I'd tried to kill myself and my kids, but also to a load of strangers who looked at me with pity and judgement in equal measures. I knew they were secretly all just glad it wasn't their story.

"I'm sick of being judged, Jamie. I'm sick of people thinking I'd ever try to do anything like that."

"It's the only way, Marnie. Now get your shoes on and let's go." Jamie had taken a step into the corridor without so much as a glance, confident that I'd follow. After all, what choice did I have? After a few pointless sighs I begrudgingly followed in his wake.

The group had changed since I'd attended before, the population transient by its very nature. Gone was the loud-mouthed woman whose woe is me act had got on my nerves so much, but all in all they were still the same self-obsessed idiots as before. I'd now become one of them, baring my story for their entertainment and comments as I pinched my by now raw skin over and over again. Today's session was no different, with strangers prodding at my wounds and judging me on my supposed actions, some with empathy, but some with horror. And I let them. The anger that Jamie had asked me to show initially had melted into a willingness to make amends. It was all a part of the plan.

Eventually the hour was up, and as I got to my feet I saw Doctor Roberts moving towards me.

"Well done, Marnie," she said quietly. "I'd like you to come to my office quickly, if you have the time? I've got some news for you."

"Yes, of course. Now?" I immediately began walking towards the door, afraid she was going to change her mind. This was it; I could feel it. She put her hand on my arm to still me briefly.

"Give me ten minutes. Grab a coffee or something with some of the others." I nodded and watched as she glided across the emptying room. Grabbing a coffee was the last thing on my mind, but I needed to do something. I joined the slip stream, allowing it to push me along in the direction of the kitchen. It was full now, the group ending always seemed to be a general signal to put the kettle on. I hung around in the door frame watching as they chattered quietly, the weight of their problems momentarily lifted from the atmosphere. I switched my attention to the wall clock, willing the spidery hands to turn faster. At last the ten minutes were up, and I turned on my heel without a word of goodbye to anyone.

I knocked before entering, finding Doctor Roberts seated behind her desk.

"Marnie! Come in, take a seat." I moved towards my usual spot on the sofa by the coffee table. "No, here," she said, gesturing to the hard back seat on the opposite side of the desk. My blood was fizzing with anticipation. I couldn't shake the feeling that this was going to end badly. Gingerly I lowered myself into the assigned seat, my hands planted firmly on the sides to stop the shaking. Doctor Roberts looked at me before smiling.

"I asked you to come and see me because I've got some news." She stopped speaking, her smile getting wider.

"You already told me that," I replied tersely.

"Sorry, yes. Well, I'm so pleased to tell you that the mental health tribunal had a meeting about your case yesterday. I attended, along with the social worker and other services assigned to your family's case. Your progress over the last few months has been astounding, Marnie, particularly in the last few weeks. The medication you've been taking seems to be working really well, and your mental health is better than I've seen since you first came here. We discussed everything, and we've come to the decision that you are to be released from your involuntary section order."

"Released? That's it? I can go?" My body felt hot and cold at once, the adrenalin coursing through my veins as I tried to get my head around it all. I'd come in expecting to fight for this, and she was giving it to me on a plate.

"It means we're no longer holding you involuntarily, Marnie. But there's still a long way to go, you do understand that, don't you? You're still carrying a lot of trauma that will need to be resolved for you to get completely better again. My advice would be for you to choose to stay here a little longer on a voluntary basis, allowing us the time to do this." I shook my head.

"I need to get out of here. I'm sorry, I know you've done a lot for me. But I need to go. I need my kids back."

"It's not quite that simple, Marnie," she replied. "While you can discharge yourself now, and we legally can't stop you, the children are a different matter entirely. Their social worker believes that the best thing to do will be to set up supervised visits in a centre in the first instance. This will give them, and you, the chance to adjust to seeing one another again slowly and safely." I opened my mouth to protest but the Doctor held her hand up to stop me.

"Believe me, I know how much you love them and want to go back to normal. But the courts are the ones who will decide what's in Rose and Teddy's best interests, not me."

I opened my mouth yet again to argue before realising the futility of it. She was right. I'd admitted to trying to kill myself and insinuated that I also intended to harm the kids. No one in their right mind would give them back to me. Well, not until I'd proved Steve had set me up in any case.

"Ok. Ok great. I want to discharge myself. Can I go now?" Doctor Roberts gave a small sigh.

"If you're really sure you don't want to stay a little longer, then yes. We need to get your medication organised, and you'll be discharged to the local mental health team, who'll want to see you regularly to check on your progress. But yes, you're free to go." I jumped up from my chair, the tears forming and reaching across the desk to hug her.

"Thank you. Oh God, thank you so much!" I repeated as I closed my arms around her back, feeling the fragility of her spine under my palms. She reached up and gently detangled herself.

"Don't thank me, Marnie. You did it," she said, her eyes also suspiciously glinting in the afternoon sunshine. "Now, go and pack." I grinned at her with genuine happiness, the tears now threatening my clothes as they coursed their way down my cheeks.

Jamie was waiting outside in the corridor, his expression changing from anxious to delight as he read the news in my face.

"You're leaving?" he whispered, as we fell into step together towards my room. It was taking everything I had not to sprint.

"They've agreed to discharge me. I can't have the kids back, but I'll be able to see them again." The thought of holding their hands, of watching their faces as they told me their stories was almost too much joy to bear. "I need to get packed. I need to get going." Jamie grabbed my hand and gave it a brief squeeze before dropping it.

"Let's get you out of here, Marnie," he said.

THIRTY

The close looked exactly as I'd left it when the taxi pulled up outside my house. I rummaged for cash through the bag that the hospital had relinquished to me on my departure. As my hands zoned in on my purse, I realised how strange it felt to be touching money after so long, and it took me a moment to calculate what notes and coins I needed. The taxi driver got out to get my bag out of the boot, and as I reached out to take it my medical bracelet slipped out from under my jumper. Hurriedly I pulled my sleeve back down, my face burning and muttering my thanks before turning away from him in the hope he hadn't noticed.

The garden path was untidily littered with fallen leaves, and with no one to take care of it, my car was also covered. Apprehension at what state I'd find the house in filled me with dread, the memories of what had happened last time I'd been here threatening to overpower me.

Warily I placed the key in the lock and turned. The door pushed up against the inevitable pile of letters strewn across the door mat. I'd be spending a good week of my life sorting that out, I thought, but first things first; a good shower and a pair of scissors were needed to remove any trace of that place.

I had wanted to get the taxi straight to Steve's, happy to camp out on the doorstep for as long as it took to get him to confess, but Jamie had strongly counselled against it while he helped me to pack. The kids were there, he reminded me. I'd scare them if I just turned up, not to mention it would be against the custody court order. If I wasn't very careful about how I played this, I'd end up back in the hospital, or even in prison. It had taken a five-minute argument, whispered back and forth as we packed my scarce belongings into a bag, but he'd eventually won.

I crept up the stairs of my house now, dreading the mayhem that was going to greet me at the top of the stairs. Nothing was out of place. The doors to the bedrooms stood open, spotlessly hoovered carpets visible through the doorways and beds made neatly. I paused on the landing in confusion. I turned to enter my own bedroom, the scene of the crime. The chest of drawers stood in its rightful place against the wall, and the upturned drawers had been neatly packed away inside. I reached out and ran my fingers against the door frame, the jagged edges where the paint had been chipped off the only remnant of that day. I entered the room slowly, a solitary glimmer on the carpet catching my eye. I picked the earring up, studying it intently before placing it carefully on the dresser. Martha. It had to have been Martha. She wouldn't have wanted me to come back to a smashed-up house, no matter what she believed had happened here. My chest expanded with the breath I hadn't realised I was holding, and I sat down on the clean sheets heavily.

I stayed where I was, absently watching the softly burnished leaves of the tree in the driveway kiss my windowpane as they swayed slightly in the breeze. My mind was racing as I relayed to myself the plan Jamie and I had come up with. Firstly, I needed to get the contact meeting set up with the social worker. The end goal was prove to everyone that Steve was the psychopath. Jamie had put a few extra steps into the plan, warning me that any unpredictable or aggressive behaviour could set me back.

I removed my mobile from my pocket, reaching across to plug it into the same charger that six months before had been part of my monotonous nighttime routine. Now I relished the ability to control something so small. I sniffed, the clinical smell of the hospital assaulting my nostrils and making me grimace. Shower time, I told myself, enjoying the softness of the carpet beneath my socks as I padded across to close the blinds against my amorous tree neighbour.

I took my time under the gushing water, soaking up every single moment of warmth as I doused myself head to toe with all of the products I could find littered about the windowsill. The steam escaped eagerly back into the bedroom as I finally opened the door and followed it out. I dressed speedily, glancing at my phone that had begun to light up with unread texts. I wasn't sure I could take whatever was on there, instead clicking onto Martha's contact details and pressing call. The phone rang several times before my best friend's voice became clear.

"Hello?" She said warily. "Is that you, Marnie?"

"Hi Martha!" I responded, happy to speak to someone who wasn't a paid accomplice. "How are you? Listen, I just wanted to say thank you for…"

"Look, Marnie," Martha's voice interrupted me, "I can't speak right now, ok? Actually," she went on, her voice dropping to a whisper, "I think it's best if we don't speak for a while. People are still upset about what you did, and I've got a lot going on right now with the PTFA and stuff." The background noises became clearer as she paused, and I realised she was out and about, from the clanging and random chatter I'd guess at a café.

"Oh, ok," I stammered, not sure how to reply. "Well how about we grab a coffee sometime-" The soft silence told me she'd hung up. I sat down on the bed again, stung but maybe not that surprised. Martha's life had carried on after all, and considering what I'd supposedly done, it can't have been easy to be the best friend through all that.

The phone suddenly rang in my hand, piercing the quiet with its combination of noise and vibration and making me jump. It was a number I didn't know but with a local area code.

"Hello?"

"Hi, is that Marnie? This is Patrick, your family's social worker. Is now a good time for a quick chat?"

"Yes, yes of course!" I replied, automatically smoothing my damp hair, and rising to my feet as if he could see me.

"Great! So, I just wanted to call to introduce myself and see how things are going. I understand you're at home now?"

"Yes I'm fine. I've been back for about an hour. How are the kids? Can I see them soon?" I clenched my free hand in anticipation of his answer.

"Well, that's another reason I wanted to call you," Patrick said as my heart sank into the ground. I wasn't going to be allowed. "I wondered whether you were available this weekend at all. We've got a slot at the contact centre, and I think it would be great if we can get things moving. Marnie? Hello?"

I was frozen, a writhing ball of anxiety and ecstasy, incapable of speech.

"Marnie?" He said again. "Are you still there?"

"Yes! Yes, this weekend would be great! Sorry, I'm just a bit shocked, I think. I wasn't expecting to be allowed to see them so soon." He chuckled gently.

"Of course, I completely understand! But like I say, we'd like to start the process as soon as we can. The children have been asking after you."

"They have?" I queried, my smile stretching unchecked across my face.

"Yes, they have. I think they're ready. Me and you can have a chat beforehand on to go over a few things first though, if that's ok? Does two o'clock on Saturday suit you? The centre is in Woodley, about twenty minutes away."

"I know Woodley. Yes, Saturday at two. Can you give me the address?"

"I'll email you a confirmation with all of the details on there now. There are also a few sheets that I'll attach; ground rules, helpful strategies, what to expect, that sort of thing. Ok?"

"Yes! Yes, I'll make sure I've read it all, thank you so much!" I was gabbling, I knew it, but I couldn't stop. "Can I bring them presents or anything? Maybe I could bring them McDonalds too? They love that."

"A small gift would be good for now, but don't worry about food. And just to let you know, Steve and the children have already visited in preparation so that they're familiar with the centre. Steve will be bringing them but will be in another room while you have your session. You probably won't see him, but I wanted to pre-warn you that this is how it works."

"Ok," I replied quickly, biting back my quick anger at the thought.

"Ok, good. So I'll see you at two on Saturday? We'll have a quick chat and then the children will arrive ready to see you." We ended the call and, chucking on some old tracksuit bottoms and a jumper, I moved downstairs while I refreshed my emails impatiently. I couldn't believe I was going to see them. All those months of torture and soul baring had been for this.

For something to do while I waited for the information, I picked up the post strewn all over the floor and carried it through to join the neat piles already assembled on the kitchen table, seemingly sorted by obvious bills and others. Martha might not want to speak to me right now, but you had to hand it to her, she was good at organisation.

I picked through the bills first, sadly grateful that at least Dad's move into the residential home and the gift of some of the house sale proceeds had provided a buffer in the bank for me to stay on track. Everything looked as it should, and I moved my attention to the smaller pile. There were a few appointment reminders for the opticians and the dentist, and I wondered whether Steve had kept on top of any of that stuff. It had never been his job after all, maybe it hadn't even crossed his mind. I opened a few cards, grimacing at the 'get well' embossments on the front. I rolled my eyes. Get well? Well, I was certainly trying to.

I refreshed the email app again as I opened the second to last envelope. Another 'get well' card. I sighed and flipped it open to read.

'Love, Steve, Addy, Rose and Ted.'

Instantaneously I crumpled it beneath my fingers, chucking it in rage at the kitchen wall. It bounced off harmlessly, and I picked it up once again, storming to the side door and throwing it into the outside bin. The nerve of him was astounding. I flung myself towards the front of the house, grabbing my keys from the shelf and had even opened the door before my head caught up with my temper. I couldn't go steaming over there. Jamie had specifically warned me against this; any trouble and I'd ruin everything before it had even begun. I needed to see the kids, that was the most important thing. Play the game. Play the game.

I spent the next few days holed up in the house, sorting and cleaning to keep my mind off things. By Friday night I had a respectably large pile of toys and clothes to take to the charity shop by the dining table and every room in the house had been aired and cleaned to within an inch of its life. I'd ordered a food shop so that I didn't need to brave society, and now, with a piping hot microwave carbonara and a glass of coke I settled myself onto the living room sofa and reopened the email attachments from Patrick. I read them quickly, mouthing along to the words I knew almost by heart.

The centre was 'designed to provide a safe space for the non-residential parent or other family member to spend time with their children with support from professionals.' Even though they were well intended words, it rankled that I would ever need support to talk to my own kids. The ground rules were pretty simple too; no alcohol or drugs and no aggressive behaviour. It made me wonder what sort of club I'd unwillingly become a part of when things like that needed to be spelt out.

I woke abruptly on Saturday morning. Lying there in semi-darkness my mind began to race with the expectations of the day. The road was silent, with only a dog barking in the distance to prove there was life outside. Leaning over, I grabbed my phone only to discover it was only six o'clock. I groaned, sinking back into the pillows and shutting my eyes tightly in the hopeless attempt to get back to sleep. Seven whole hours to kill before I needed to leave, and I didn't think I could spend it conscious.

Twenty minutes later, the dog had gotten louder in sync with my inner monologue. I sat up, holding my head in my hands to try to still it. What if they didn't want to talk to me? What if they screamed? God, what if Ted didn't even recognise me after so long? He was only three after all, and he'd been living with Steve and Addy exclusively for months now. Maybe he called her Mummy, ran to her from the pre-school door, climbed into her lap like a cat looking for respite when he was tired? I swung my legs out from under the covers with purpose. The urge to see him was overpowering my common sense.

The drive round to Steve's was uneventful, with barely any cars on the road so early on a Saturday morning. I pulled up slowly, trying to make my car as unobtrusive as I could in their silent close. The blinds upstairs were still drawn and the hedges at the front made it hard to see through the bay window. I killed the engine and quietly opened my door before padding gingerly up the path. Finally reaching the front of the house, I crouched down and peered through into the living room.

Ted was sitting on the massive corner sofa, his mouth rhythmically moving like a cow chewing cud as he stared unblinkingly at what I knew was the TV, his hand reaching into the bowl of cereal propped on his lap every so often. I was so close to him that I could see his beautifully long eyelashes, the secret envy of both me and Rose, curling gracefully onto his little cheeks.

The pain in my legs from my prone position was barely noticeable as I drank in every single aspect of his being. My baby.

Suddenly his head whipped to the right, and he began speaking to someone not in my line of vision. I moved like a crab to get a better view. There was Addy, with pristine matching pyjamas and a fresh face walking into the room and plopping herself down next to Ted. She put her arm around him and he snuggled into her side. I sat on the cold ground, fighting the renewed urge to storm to the front door and demand my child be returned to me.

Instead I stumbled back to the car, no longer focused on stealth. The hedges were my friends now, sheltering me from prying eyes as I sat with my head on the steering wheel. A noise made me look up in panic that I'd been caught. It was just a neighbour across the street, with his slippers on and filling the wheelie bin with recycling. Some people were so productive at the weekend it sickened me. Sighing, I turned on the engine and made a slow U turn before leaving the close.

I arrived at the centre an hour before I was supposed to meet Patrick, unable to sit in that empty house for a moment longer. The carpark was busy, and I idly watched as people came and went, sometimes alone, sometimes with children in tow. I mentally tried to match them up; was the well-dressed older woman with a full face of make up there to reconnect with those two red haired children who had walked in front of my car? Or was their mother the painfully thin woman in her thirties who, despite her highlights, had a definitive strawberry blonde tint?

The minutes ticked by. When I was finally within ten minutes of my allotted timeslot I got out of the car, hoping no one I knew was going to see me. It was pointless to be embarrassed, I reminded myself with a shake. I'd just spent months in a mental hospital - the capacity for embarrassment had already topped out.

The reception was bright and airy, with kids' drawings and paintings adorning the walls. I nervously approached the woman on the desk, who looked up at me with a welcoming smile.

"Hi there!" She said, for all the world as if I was just the person she wanted to see. They must vet them for cheerfulness here. "Can I help you?"

"Erm, hi," I responded, eventually reaching the high wooden frame. "I've got an appointment with Patrick?" I lowered my voice. "He's a social worker." Her grin turned into an understanding smile.

"Of course," she replied. "Can I take your name please?"

"It's Marnie. Marnie South." She keyed something into her computer and rose from her chair.

"Great. He's ready for you. I'll take you through." I followed her through a security door, trying my hardest to keep the sudden flashbacks of the hospital at bay. This wasn't the same. I wasn't going to be locked up here. She drew to a stop a couple of doors down and knocked before opening it. "Patrick, Marnie's here," she said to the unseen man in the room. She moved back to allow me the space to enter, giving me a view of a cluttered office, files adorning the walls and the smell of strong coffee wafting towards me. Patrick was at his desk but rose as I entered.

"Marnie, hi! Nice to see you. Come in and have a seat." He gestured to the chair in front of him. I moved towards it, not really knowing what to expect. The door closed softly behind us as the receptionist left. Patrick sat back down. "So, I just thought it would be good to have a bit of a chat before you see Rose and Ted today, just to go over what to expect, what we find works well, things like that. Ok?" I nodded, my nervousness bubbling in my throat.

"Now firstly, I wanted to check in with you. How are you finding being back at home? Have you managed to see any friends or family or anything?"

"Yes, yes fine," I mumbled, the bubbles making me sound gruffer than I usually did. I cleared my throat. "I mean, yes, it's fine at home. I haven't spoken to anyone though. I tried to ring my friend but..." I trailed off, not wanting to admit that Martha couldn't have wanted me off of the phone any quicker. Patrick nodded understandingly.

"Well, these things can take time. Have you checked in with work at all? Colleagues?" I shook my head.

"No, not yet. I will though. I'll ring them Monday," I offered, suddenly worried I'd failed at something. Truthfully, I didn't think I'd be able to contact anyone at the ambulance service ever again.

"That's fine. No rush! Now, about today." He sat back in his chair and drummed his fingers slightly on the top of the desk. "As I told you on the phone, Rose and Ted will be brought in by Steve and Dan."

"Dan?" I interrupted. "I thought Steve would be bringing them both. Dan's never been very good at all that appointment stuff." I stopped. Maybe I shouldn't be slagging him off right now.

"Yes, Dan's bringing Rose and Steve's bringing Ted. I think they both wanted to be here for the first time."

"Ah, ok. Makes sense I suppose." I didn't want to sound bitter even if this was the first time to my knowledge Dan had been sober enough on a Saturday to take Rose anywhere.

"Ok. Now onto what to expect today," Patrick continued, shifting slightly in his chair as he leaned forwards and met my eyes. I felt my body relax under his kind gaze. This man was one of the good ones.

Half an hour later we were ready. Patrick had explained that I would be taken to one of the contact rooms where I would wait for the kids. He'd taken me down himself, and had gestured to a large and airy room, full of toys, games and even a craft table. It reminded me of a reception classroom, full of hectic colour and cheeriness. I stood for a moment on the threshold, unsure of where to place myself. Patrick had advised me to sit rather than stand so that the children didn't feel intimidated, so I headed over to a sofa in the corner and perched uncertainly on the edge.

I clasped my hands together, digging my nails into the soft palm of the other hand to quell the anticipation. This was it. The moment was finally here. Just as I was beginning to worry that they'd point blank refused to meet me, I heard high pitched voices floating down the corridor. Ted's unmistakeable laugh was bouncing against the walls and I heard Rose's murmur in response. As they became louder I almost got to my feet before remembering the rules.

Suddenly there they were. Patrick and another staff member appeared in the doorway flanking my babies. My face broke out into the first genuine smile I could remember for a long time, and my arms automatically opened to gather them up. They had come to a complete stop in the doorway, just like I had minutes before. For a moment there was silence, and the three of us stared wordlessly at one another.

"Hello," I whispered, my voice so strangled with emotion that I struggled to even get the word out. Ted glanced up at Rose and I watched as she put her arm over his shoulders protectively. A rainbow of emotions were sweeping across my daughters face as I watched her; uncertainty, fear, anger. This was going to go the wrong way, I realised, almost lowering my gaze in failure. Just at the last moment I saw a small upturn of her lips as she gazed straight at me. Hope was there too I realised. Maybe even love. I smiled at her again, more gently this time, and lowered my arms so as not to appear threatening.

"Hi guys," I whispered again. "Would you like to come in?" It felt so alien to me that they weren't fearlessly running and jumping into my lap, bundling me as they'd done for their entire lives. Ted looked up at Rose again and she nodded before taking a step into the room. Teddy mirrored his big sister's actions and met my eyes again as he shyly approached me. When he got within two feet of the sofa I lay my hands out on my lap with my palms up in a reconciliatory action. Rose was still standing back a little, her fingers twisting upon themselves in a way that was synonymous with whenever she felt anxious.

"Hi Teddy," I said gently. "I've missed you." He was sucking his thumb but took another step towards me. "I've bought you a little present. Would you like to open it?" The bag lay at the side of the sofa, and I reached down, drawing out the gift-wrapped car that I'd ordered on Amazon as soon as Patrick had arranged our meeting. I held it out to him, silently willing him to take it. Slowly he reached out, his little chunky fingers brushing mine briefly and causing my heart to expand with adoration. We all watched in silence as he opened it, ripping the paper off and letting it float harmlessly to the floor. He gave a squeal of glee as the car became visible, and immediately began to tear at the cardboard packaging.

"Would you like me to open it?" I asked tentatively. Ted thought for a moment and then handed it to me. I felt like I'd won the lottery. Carefully

I removed it from its wrapping and gave it back. Ted smiled at me, his thumb back in his mouth. He got down on his hands and knees and began to chug it up and down, making vehicle noises as he went. I turned my attention to Rose.

"Hi babe," I said softly. "I've got something for you, would you like it?" She shook her head wordlessly, her eyes following Ted and her cheeks rosy like her namesake. "Ok. That's ok darling," I replied, moving my hand back from the bag and expelling a small, disappointed sigh. We both trained our attention back onto Teddy while I racked my brain for the right thing to say.

"So, how are you? How's school?" I began, injecting some false cheeriness into my tone.

"Ok," she replied, still not looking at me.

"How about Ruby? Is she still your best friend? Has she still got Jack as her boyfriend?" I was embarrassed listening to myself wittering on to try and make her talk. But we'd always gossiped about her school mates, it was one of the things I liked most about having a daughter.

"Yes," she said, still only on the one-word answers. She began dragging one of her trainers back and forth across the floor, and I realised she felt like she needed to be dismissed as if I was her teacher.

"Ok. Do you want to have a look at the craft table?" I asked lightly. "I'll just stay here with Ted." She nodded without meeting my eyes and turned away. I lowered myself onto the ground beside Ted, noticing that the other staff member, a woman, had followed Rose over to the craft table and was chatting to her quietly. Even though Rose wasn't particularly enthusiastic, the fact that she was replying in full sentences to this stranger felt like a stake to the heart. I grabbed another car from the box, and Ted and I began to push them up and down in sync. For a little while he said nothing to me, merely making his car noises as we moved faster and faster.

"Can we race?" he suddenly said, sitting on his haunches at looking up at me with an open expression.

"Yes!" I replied, too loud in my enthusiastic response. "Shall we build a track?" I asked, gesturing to the box of plastic next to us. For the next ten minutes we built a side-by-side track, Ted, rummaging through and handing the pieces for me to assemble. Finally he was satisfied.

"Ready?" I said, holding my car on one side. He reached up and placed his on the other.

"Ready Mummy," he replied, causing my eyes to well up with happiness.

For the rest of the visit Rose kept her distance from me while Ted and I played. I ventured towards the table a few times, leaving Patrick to take my place racing, but each time Rose became still and unresponsive, not willing to entertain my questions or even presence. As the hour came to an end, Patrick approached me and Ted to quietly tell me it was time to say goodbye.

Much to Teddy's dismay, we dismantled the track and put away the spare cars, with him only agreeing to help when I told him we could play with them again next time. When we were finally finished I turned to him, still on my knees.

"You're going to go back to Daddy now Teddy bear," I said softly. "But I'll see you again soon, ok?"

"Ok Mummy," he replied quite cheerfully. "And we can do the cars again?" He confirmed.

"Of course, baby," I responded, struggling hard to keep my composure.

"Great!" he said. "Bye bye." He suddenly leaned forwards, climbing into my lap and tucking himself in against my body just like he used to. I wrapped my arms around him immediately, burying my face in his soft hair as I breathed in deeply. He smelt just as he always did, and for just a moment I didn't think I was going to be able to let him go. I glanced over above his head where Rose was standing with Patrick, still with those rosy cheeks and burning eyes, and gently I released Ted from my grip.

"Rose?" I said, still kneeling but proffering my arms out to her too behind Ted's back. She turned away, looking like she was about to burst into tears. I got to my feet and moved towards her, stopping to give her a little space. "Bye babe," I said tenderly to the back of her head. "I'm so glad I've finally been able to see you." She turned her head fleetingly towards me, giving me enough time to see the tears now flowing freely down her face.

"Bye Mum," she replied quietly, before walking straight out of the door, not even waiting for Ted. I let them go, leaving me standing alone in the colourful room and suddenly feeling even more bereft than I thought possible.

THIRTY-ONE

I spent the next few weeks in solitude apart from the weekly contact centre visits. I'd done all my organising, and now I was busy with planning. The contact centre visit had been the strike of the match to spur me on; watching Rose's internal conflict when she saw me was breaking my heart, but yesterday she had had actually graduated to full sentence answers about school, friends and sports. She clammed up if I even mentioned Steve, Addy or Dan, immediately going to another activity in the room and leaving me hanging.

The problem was that I didn't know quite how to prove my innocence. Steve wasn't going to confess, Ted was too young to really remember what had happened, and Rose was still reluctant to discuss anything of consequence.

After a week of pacing around my empty house and concocting plans that ranged from probably getting me arrested on anything from stalking to murder, I realised the only thing I could possibly do was find the evidence that led to my breakdown in the first place; the magnet, the photos, the ticket stub; all of it. And the only place I was going to find any of it was at Steve's house.

It was now Sunday morning. Ted had told me at the contact centre yesterday that they were going to visit Steve's parents today for lunch, with Rose going too. They lived a good hour away from here in a dull little village where, as the reigning couple amongst all of the other middle-class pensioners, they spent their time inserting themselves into every little squabble with the magnanimity of royals bequeathing unsolicited advice to their subjects.

They'd never warmed to me. The fact that their only son had chosen to marry a woman who already had a child was not a match they had been able to boast about. They were discreetly hostile to me in that underhand way that only that generation had, and while they tolerated Rose at least outwardly, it was always tense. Once Teddy was born Rose and I may as well have been invisible for all the use we were to them. Ted was promenaded around the village for hours like the young prince they thought him to be while my daughter and I played the role of servants to the family.

I knew they'd be gone for hours as Melanie and Clive didn't tend to let their precious Steve go too easily. It was the opportunity I'd been waiting for, and nervous energy was fizzing through my veins as I pulled on my black yoga pants and the darkest hoodie I could find. I slid my feet into a pair of old trainers and wedged a pair of sunglasses on my face before grabbing the car keys from the hallway mantle. The car purred into life, and I gripped the steering wheel for a few seconds to steel myself before reversing slowly out into my cul-de-sac. The man opposite (I'd never actually learnt his name) was outside trimming the low hedge that dictated his land from the path, and I raised my hand in greeting. He watched me motionlessly as I turned and moved away. Notoriety was something I was getting used to. But not for long.

I trundled through town with Pink playing as loudly as I could stand. The energy matched my mood, with the crashing drums and forceful lyrics spurring me on to task. I sang along, willing a little of the independent and strong woman vibes to embed themselves under my skin and give me the strength and prowess to pull this off.

Steve and Addy's house was, as usual, immaculate from the roadside. The bay window blinds were open but tilted so that from my position on the road I couldn't quite see through. My heart pumped painfully for a moment as I registered Addy's car was still on the driveway, but common sense took over. Obviously, they'd have gone in one car, probably picking Rose up on the way for a lovely family day out. My teeth bit down weightily together as I imagined them all having their idyllic day out, culminating in one of Melanie's 'famous' roast dinners. I had to hand it to my ex-mother-in-law; she may be a classist idiot, but she was a good cook.

I waited until the road was clear of any activity, with a dark blue range rover gliding slowly past me as it headed towards the main road. I kept my face turned away, not sure whether the occupants would be interested in checking out who I was, but not wanting to find out. Finally it was silent.

I exited the car and pushed the door as gently as I could. It closed but not properly. Grimacing, I opened it and pushed it shut again with a little more force. The slam seemed to echo like a gunshot, and I glanced manically about to check no eyes were glaring in my direction.

All was still silent, the distant sounds of machinery, which sounded like either a mower or maybe a leaf blower, setting the scene for a wholesome Sunday in a leafy home county town. I crept as quickly as I could to the boundary of my quarry, keeping my eyes fixed on the bay window for any sign of life. After what felt like an eternity but in reality was probably only thirty seconds, I reached the front door.

I'd reached the first checkpoint, and now I just needed to gain entry without causing any damage. I tried the front door first, hoping in vain that they'd left in a hurry, perhaps having the sort of mundane domestic about getting everyone out on time that Steve and I used to have, and had forgotten to lock it. Of course it was properly locked. Addy would never have been the sort to lose her temper over something as stupid as getting out of the house.

I moved quietly towards the window now, double checking as I passed that there was no convenient crack that I could squeeze myself through. The best option that I could see was to get round the back of the house. At least there I'd be away from prying eyes while I worked out a plan. The side gate was locked under my hand, and, swearing under my breath, I took a small step back to study it. It was a six-foot fence with a neat little yale lock for entry. Steve had never been one for lax security, so why would I be surprised?

I leant against the house's wall for a moment while I assessed my options. There was a food bin to the left of me, it wasn't a full size one but maybe it would give me enough height to swing myself over. I glanced out towards the road. Voices were flowing through the airwaves in the distance and I was visible from here. If I didn't move soon it was only a matter of time before I was spotted.

I gave myself the internal go ahead. This was the best I could come up with, so I needed to try. Carefully I moved the small bin into position right next to the gate and gingerly put one foot on. Silently praying that it would hold my weight, my other foot followed while I waited for the inevitable crack of plastic under too much duress. It didn't come. I grabbed the top of the fence quickly, and without thinking too much about the unlikelihood if me being able to actually swing my leg high enough up, pushed powerfully off of the plastic lid and extended my arm to full lock.

The crack I'd been waiting for sounded as my right leg flew up and over just as my arms gave out from the weight and I collapsed, one leg half over and my chest buried painfully into the top of the un-sanded wood. I gave a grunt of pain and forced my arms to cooperate, pushing up once more until I had enough space to manoeuvre my leg all the way over. Now sprawled and half upright, I glanced down at the other side. There was a mish mash of boxes and old tools laying to greet me, an old skill saw glistening menacingly up at me just where I knew I was going to land.

The voices from the road were becoming clearer, and, with a deep intake of breath, I pushed up and flung myself over the precipice. As I pushed myself off I aimed away from the metal disc of the saw, going for the cardboard boxes stacked against the side of the house. I landed hard, my right ankle grazing the rough render of the building and landing heavily through the cardboard while rolled onto its side. I gave an involuntary welp of pain as I reached solid land, putting my hands out against the wall to steady myself. Taking a few steadying breaths, I looked down the small alleyway towards the garden. Washing was flowing on the string line in the steady breeze and inwardly I marvelled at Addy's optimism that it wouldn't rain while she was gone.

The side door was to my right. I kept my back to the wall as I slid towards it, picking my way through the cardboard boxes that littered the slabbed path that were probably chucked out there for Steve to take to the recycling bin at some point.

I tried the side door. Locked. What was I supposed to do now? Finally I cracked and rang Jamie.

"Marnie, hi!" He answered the phone as if I was the one person he'd wanted to hear from, and it made me wonder for a moment just exactly what was in it for him. "How are you doing? How are the kids? What's been going on?"

"Yeah, yeah I'm good I guess," I replied quickly to stop the flow of questioning. "Listen, I've come to Steve's house and…"

"Marnie, no! What are you thinking? No confrontations; ever! It's just going to make things worse for you. And what about the kids? They'll stop you seeing them!" Jamie's voice flooded my ear agitatedly.

"Jamie. Jamie!" I shouted, trying to make myself heard. "No one's here, it's fine!" The line went silent. "They've gone to Steve's parents' it'll be empty for hours. I've got into the garden, but everything's locked up. How do I get in?" A deep exhale of breath came down the line.

"It's not a good idea, Marnie. What if the neighbours see you? What if you're caught?"

"Well I haven't got a lot of options now, do I?" I retorted, trying to keep my voice to a whisper. "I need to get evidence, and as I'm not allowed to even *speak* to anyone, this is my best chance! Now, have you got any ideas about how to get inside or not?" My foot was still throbbing, and I leant heavily on the wall to raise it off of the ground.

"Look I really don't think this is the best idea. But if you're determined, well are there any open windows you could squeeze through?"

"There were none open at the front, I looked," I replied as I hobbled down the alleyway and peered around the corner to take in the full extent of the back of the house. Everything was flush, no telltale pieces jutting out from the vista to give me an easy way in. "Nope. None out here either. Any other ideas?" My focus scanned the garden, resting on a pile of bricks stacked up neatly to one side. "Hey, I could break a window! There're bricks here," I continued as I gingerly crossed the patio towards them.

"No! No, you can't break in! Someone's bound to see you and you'll end up arrested! Look, you're not thinking straight. Just get back in your car, send me the address, and I'll come to you. We can go for a coffee and talk about this sensibly, ok?" I reached down, the rough edges of the brick niggling uncomfortably at my palm. I straightened up.

The bi-fold doors that I knew led straight to the kitchen were imposingly solid sheets of glass, seemingly impenetrable and laughing at my small piece of brick. Steve and Addy had only had them put in last Summer and they'd told me how much they cost. I pictured myself launching my missile straight into one of the panes, watching it shatter into a thousand pieces, all that money wasted in one hit. The urge was strong.

To the left-hand side were a small set of older double doors with a full length pane of glass in each. I knew these led into the small study that they had created for Addy's job. She was a social media something or other, working fully remotely and part time. Steve was very proud of her; he never passed up an opportunity to marvel at her skills, and more importantly, her wage, to me. I approached the doors quickly, ignoring the steady stream of words beating relentlessly down the earpiece of my phone. There was a woman's face in the glass gazing straight at me. I jumped, almost dropping my phone. The woman jerked too.

"Marnie? Marnie!" Jamie was shouting through the phone, his voice tinny when not pressed against my cheek. I lifted it back to my ear. The woman did the same. It was my reflection, I realised, with a shaky laugh. "Marnie! Are you still there? Please, just give me the address and I'll be there in twenty minutes, ok?"

"21 Broomleaf Close," I replied before arching my left arm back and launching the brick straight at my image. The pane fragmented where it stood. In slow motion I watched as more and more fractures appeared across the smooth surface before finally, with a satisfying crunch, it shattered. The tiny pieces hit the floor with more force than I'd anticipated, bouncing off the hard patio slabs and ricocheting in every direction imaginable.

"Marnie!" Jamie's voice was distant now even though I knew he was screaming. I clicked to disconnect the call and stepped forwards, taking care to avoid as much of the shimmering mayhem that littered the floor as possible. The large sheet of glass was gone but had left behind it some jagged edges just patiently waiting for me to brush against them and rip my flesh. Instead, I reached through the now gaping wound in the frame to find the key, nestled gently in its pigeonhole, enticing me to turn it. With a soft click it turned easily in my hand and the door opened fully.

The soft carpet muffled my steps as I padded quickly into the cosy study, marred by even more flecks of razor-sharp glass that had fallen through into the sanctuary. I looked around. The desk was neatly minimalistic, with only the computer monitor and a pot of pens for show. Files were neatly stacked beside each other, each a different shade of pastel and creating an Instagram-worthy vision. Photos of the family, *my family*, adorned the walls. I gritted my teeth, fighting the urge to rip every single one down, and headed for the door on the other side.

The house was quiet, with that underlying hum of a building left to its own devices. I slipped my shoes off, feeling like any noise I made would alert it to intruders. I padded carefully up the stairs, every nerve ending alert for a sign of life. Steve's own office was upstairs next to Teddy's room, and if he was going to hide anything it would be there. I thought back to all the times I'd spent in this house before, when Steve and Addy would invite me for Sunday lunch or barbeques in the Summer. I would often end up here until late, tucking Ted into bed while Steve went to do a bit of work next door and Addy cleared the downstairs of our festivities. Back then I could never believe my luck; I'd broken up my family but had somehow been invested into a new, more wholesome one. It was a bit like that eighties film, Three Men and a Baby. Mum and I had loved that one.

Ted's door was slightly ajar as I passed, and I couldn't help myself. I stopped on the threshold, pushing it further afield so that the entire room came into view. His little bed with his Spiderman sheets was neatly made, a row of teddy's propped up as a guard at the end. A rug made into a car racing track lay on the floor with his box of vehicles to one side, just waiting for him to come back. I closed my eyes as his sweet and distinct scent washed over me. Without even knowing it, I'd crossed to his bed, sat down and buried my face into his pillow.

I wasn't sure how long I'd been there, taking deep inhalations in whilst the tears soiled and soaked his little dream pad before a sudden rap jolted me back to the present. I sat up, frozen with anticipation, as I waited for the front door to inevitably open. Another bang forced me to my feet, and gingerly I crossed the landing to peer over the banister towards the front door. There was a silhouette on the other side of the frosted glass, moving from one side to another as if trying to see through.

"Marnie?" A muffled voice shouted, accompanied with another sharp tap. "Marnie, are you in there?" Jamie. I should never have given him the address, what was I thinking? Growling in frustration with myself I thumped down the stairs.

"What are you doing?" I hissed, both wrenching the door open and ushering him inside. "The neighbours are bound to have heard you screaming my name! What if they call Steve?" I shut the door with more force than I intended and stormed back up the stairs. "I need to keep looking. If you're not going to help, then stand there and keep guard. If you are going to help me, well, take your shoes off."

I was already in Steve's study when I heard Jamie's careful tread behind me. I was so familiar from our walks along the hospital corridors that I could have picked him out of a line up without ever seeing his face.

"Try that cupboard over there," I said, pointing to the right of me as I knelt in front of the desk drawers, papers already strewn about. "Any photos, any tickets, anything like that, ok?" He sighed before following my directions.

"It's not a good idea," he said quietly, even while he opened his own task and started pulling stuff out.

"It's all I have," I replied just as quietly. "If it makes you uncomfortable you can go."

"I can't," he muttered under his breath. "I can't leave you now." His words lurched in my chest, awakening a long-buried feeling. We both continued in silence, his embarrassed, mine wondering. Finally, with the entire room torn to pieces I had to admit defeat. There was nothing here but school stuff and bills. I sat back on my heels in frustration before jumping up. Jamie was watching me warily.

"Maybe their bedroom?" He held my gaze for a moment before swallowing and nodding. I moved swiftly, conscious that an hour must have passed since I'd first arrived. I led the way to the end of the corridor, opening their door to a clean and aesthetically pleasing room in soft greens and greys. The faint smell of Addy's perfume pervaded the air. I crossed impatiently to the large built-in wardrobe and began to rummage.

I glanced back to see Jamie still in the doorway. He was staring around the room, looking nauseous.

"You ok?" I asked, pausing for a moment. He didn't reply, instead looking horrified with the kind of look you'd expect on someone who had witnessed a car crash. "What is it? Jamie!" Uttering his name seemed to bring him back to the room.

"What? Yeah fine, I'm fine. I'm going to look downstairs, ok?" He backed away without waiting for my reply. I stared after him for a moment, confused about what had spooked him. A distant car horn put me back on task. Time was running out.

Twenty minutes later their gorgeous bedroom lay in tatters and still I'd found nothing. I raced down the stairs.

"Jamie? Where are you? Have you found anything?" He didn't answer me as I ran from room to room calling him. The living room was deserted, so was the kitchen. "Jamie!" I shouted again, pausing in case I was covering up his replies. Still no shout pinged back to me. Maybe he'd left, washed his hands of me, gone back to a normal life that didn't contain a messed-up outcast and her plans?

I headed to the last room left; the study I'd entered through. Pushing the door open I found Jamie kneeling on the floor, his shaking hands creating a bowl full of stuff that I couldn't see. He turned at my footsteps, proffering the spoils upwards.

The achingly familiar underground magnet was sitting in pride of place atop a sheaf of papers. Carefully I reached forwards and picked it up, rubbing my thumb across the singular word that was risen and emblazoned across the front. Wimbledon. I reached again with my other hand to take the worn ticket stub, my eyes straining as they hyper focused on the information I knew by heart. Again and again, I reached for another item from Jamie's trembling grasp, the notes that I'd once received were bare in their brazenness, the photographs of my children a sharp reminder of what had gone on. I glanced past Jamie into the garden, the scene where the pictures had been taken.

"Steve hid them here? All this time they were here in Addy's study?" I'd spent the last few months envisioning the moment the proof of his plot came to life, but now that I had, I could barely believe it was true. Jamie nodded.

"There's more." He got to his feet and pulled out the keyboard on it's little pull-out from beneath the desk. The monitor came to life, with a vibrant collage of my children's faces, interspersed with Addy and Steve's. He clicked onto the file icon. "You said about the Instagram stories that disappeared? Look at the names of all these. I bet something in there will tell you how he did it." I moved to be behind him and scanned the list. 'Footwell Instagram', 'Footwell Facebook', 'Titanite Twitter', and on it went.

"Addy's client list?" I said, confused.

"Look here," he replied, pointing to the very bottom of the list. 'MS Instagram.' MS. Marnie South.

"Click it," I said, leaning even closer over his shoulder and catching a small trace of aftershave. He double clicked. More files appeared. "Click on one!" I said impatiently when he paused. He clicked and the screen filled with a video, the first one I'd watched. We watched it to the end before he pressed on the second one.

Just as it began to play a slammed door made us both whip our heads around. Footsteps were coming steadily down the hallway towards us. Jamie looked at me in panic.

THIRTY-TWO

"Quick!" I hissed. "Outside! Through the door, let's go!" I pulled him up and shoved him in front of me, dropping the things still in my hands in my panic. He jumped over the doorstep and onto the patio, swiftly disappearing around the side of the house. I followed him, my blood pumping in fright. I took a running step over the threshold, landing hard on my injured foot and releasing a sharp cry of pain. I tensed up and caught my following limb on the step, tumbling hard onto the patio.

"Marnie?" A voice came from behind me and I turned on the ground to look up at Addy. "What are you doing? What's happened to my study? Oh my God, what's happened to the door?" She went to come outside. In my peripheral vision I could see Jamie standing with his back against the outside wall. I scrambled to my feet, wincing at the battered body I was now inhabiting. I moved as quickly as I could, blocking her from coming onto the patio.

"Addy, what's all this doing here?" I asked as calmly as I could, gesturing to the spilled pile on the floor. "Did you know about this?" She followed my lead, gazing down for a moment as she took in the evidence we'd uncovered. She paused before raising her eyes defiantly.

"What do you mean?" She challenged, her back straight and her eyes cold. Her beautiful dark hair was flowing in its usual Hollywood waves about her shoulders before she tossed it back with a small shake. There was no trace of the nurturing woman I'd grown to trust with my children. Instead waves of resentment emanated from her and I took a small step backwards from the heat.

"It's the stuff. It's all the things…everything I said was happening to me. All of it." I was stuttering, pure confusion at the rapid turn of events making me inarticulate. "Why is it in here? Addy, has Steve made you do something? Forced you to hide this it?" A small smile appeared on her face before she broke into a huge grin and laughed.

"Steve? Don't be silly, Marnie. As if he'd ever have the balls. You've been married to him. You know he's all mouth." I was suddenly aware that my mouth was hanging gormlessly open, my brain racing to try and connect the dots. "Oh, I know I know," she continued, "he likes to think he's in control. All those little trips to the doctors to put us on pills, laughing at us with the kids, all of that. Quite honestly, I found it funny to begin with. Now he's just a bit irritating. The upstanding educator who secretly rules with an iron fist. He used to tell me you what he used to do to you, you know. I knew you were weak; I knew it would be easy."

A distant bang temporarily distracted both of us. Addy peered out into the hallway. She must have decided it had come from outside the house. As she went to close the office door I inched backwards again, risking a glance behind me in the hopes that Jamie was going to appear.

"It was you? But why? Why would you do that? I thought you liked me." I sounded petulant; a little girl in the playground whose friend had ditched her for someone else. The door clicked softly behind her, and she took a step forwards, closing the distance between us again.

"You're not a child, Marnie," she said softly as she bent down to pick up the strewn photos, assembling them neatly in her hands. She extended them to me. "Here," she said. "There's some nice ones of Rose and Teddy, isn't there?" She was laughing under her breath. I shakily took the sheaf from her.

"I don't understand though. Why? What have I ever done to you?" She sighed and moved towards the desk chair, sitting down gracefully and crossing her legs. She leant down again and picked up the magnet, caressing it between her slender fingers.

"Well I suppose you might as well know, before I get you locked up again. Did Steve ever tell you how we met?" She asked, watching me with intensely dark eyes even whilst her fingers worked.

"At the park, wasn't it?" I replied. "But what does that have to do with anything?" I continued with confusion.

"We met at the park, yes," she confirmed. "But what Steve doesn't know is that I picked him out." She didn't wait for a response before continuing. "I was walking through the park to get to the station one Saturday and he was there with Rose and Ted. Ted was in the swing and Steve was laughing at how happy he was. But little Rose? She was sitting by the railings, picking daisies, just watching them with those big eyes of hers. I smiled at her when I went past. She smiled back. She offered me a daisy chain through the bars." I stood still, still completely clueless about where this was going.

"Ok, so you saw them at the park once. So what?" She grinned.

"Oh no, not just once. I left and got on the train that day, but I couldn't stop thinking about Rose, that beautiful little girl with sad eyes. I wanted to see her again. I started walking through there every Saturday, hoping to see her again. Finally, after two weeks they were back. Steve and Ted were ignoring her again, having their own fun while she sat at the side. I waited until Steve was facing the other way. I passed some chocolate through the bars to her. Honestly Marnie, you should have seen her smile after that! I put my finger to my lips, and she copied me. She's just so smart, isn't she? Even at five she knew we were going to be secret friends. I mean, I bet she's never told you about that, has she?"

"No. She didn't," I bit out, feeling pure rage boil in my throat. The woman was a psycho. Addy smirked.

"I knew she wouldn't. Well anyway, after that I used to drop her some sweets every time they were there. Sometimes she whispered to me. She told me Steve wasn't her real dad. I asked her where Mummy was, and do you know what she said?" Addy grinned at me again. "She said you were probably out with your friends having wine because Mummy and Steve had broken up and that's what you do when they're not there. Oh, she told me all sorts of things over the next few weeks. All about you, Steve and Teddy. And Dan. Steve didn't notice us, not once."

"You're actually crazy! What the hell are you doing, talking to a little girl in the park?" My protective instinct had kicked in fully, and I stopped being scared, moving quickly towards her chair and making her flinch back. When my face was centimetres away from hers, I grabbed her throat. "If you ever come near my family again, I promise I will kill you!" I said harshly, flecks of spit hitting her cheek with the force of my words. She stood, motionless, until I let go.

"Well come on then, tell me the rest!" I barked, my hands balling into fists. "You were stalking my five-year-old. Then what happened?"

"I didn't *stalk* her," she said quietly. "We were friends. I felt sorry for her; you two don't love her as much as Teddy, and she knows it." I laughed disbelievingly at the woman's gall.

"How dare you tell me how my own child feels!" I exclaimed, taking a step forwards.

"I couldn't stop thinking about them," she replied. Suddenly she got to her feet. I flinched as she moved, certain she was going to attack. "Do you know how lucky you are to have them, Marnie? And you didn't even mean to get pregnant either time, did you? It just happens for you; no thought, no effort, nothing!" The fight seemed to leave her momentarily and her shoulders slumped.

"I always wanted a family, but I can't seem to get pregnant. I've never even been on birth control." She tittered wryly. "I kept hoping and hoping there'd be a consequence; something I could pass off as an accident. A bit like yours were. Before I met Steve, I was with someone for a long time. I thought he was going to be the One, but there was never a sign of a baby. So, when I saw Steve, a man who had kids already, I decided that he would be a good bet. I approached him in the park, pretending I'd lost an air pod in the grass and was looking for it." She broke for breath, and I impatiently wait for her to continue, horribly fascinated.

"It was easier than I'd anticipated to be honest. He helped me look; even got Rose and Teddy involved. Rose was a star as usual. She didn't give him any indication that she'd seen me before. She caught my eye and put her little finger to her lips like I'd shown her. Steve and I started chatting. He asked if we could meet for a drink the weekend after as he wouldn't have the kids. And that was that. We got married quickly and I kept waiting to be pregnant." She glanced down at her wedding rings, the diamonds glistening in the light as she twisted them softly around and lost in her own head.

"But you didn't get pregnant," I prompted. She looked up at me with hard eyes.

"No, I didn't," she bit out. She composed herself. "But I did get the next best thing. I got Teddy, and, thanks to your horrible choice in men, I got Rose too. We became so close! She'd tell me things she couldn't tell you, like how worried she was about how you were acting after her Grandad died.

She said you started talking about him like he was still alive. When she asked about the funeral, you told her to stop being stupid; you only have a funeral when someone dies. She told me you kept mentioning some woman called Lula, behaving like Rose knew who it was. I knew it was the right time. You'd lost the plot; you didn't deserve those children."

Tears sprang up as I realised how hard that must have been for Rose to watch me spiral after Dad died. I also knew now, thanks to the doctors, it was the trauma coupled with the medication and so wasn't really my fault, but for a seven-year-old it must have been terrifying, and I could never forgive myself for putting her through that.

"The right time for what?" I asked, wiping my eyes so that I could concentrate fully on what she was saying.

"To get rid of you! Steve kept banging on and on about how he wished we could have the kids full time, but he never did anything about it! I told him we should fight for custody of Ted, after all we were a married couple with two incomes against you, a single mum barely getting by. But he wouldn't. He moaned about you constantly, but he always said the kids needed their mum. He couldn't see that I would be that person if he'd just get on with it."

"You'd never be their mum," I said quietly, swallowing the bile that was threatening to spill out of my mouth.

"I would be if you couldn't get to them," she retorted. "And you'd gone mental! Even Steve was worried about what was going to happen to the kids. The things Rose was saying were really concerning and Steve still just sat there slagging you off! I was the only one who seemed to care enough to sort it out."

"So you thought you'd drive me insane by sending me all this stuff?"

"Steve had filled me in on your Mum's murder. I made him tell me everything he could remember when he first mentioned it. I mean, it's intriguing, isn't it? The woman trying to help out gets stabbed in the middle of London and her young daughter watches the whole thing? I was fascinated. I looked up all the news articles, I read all about your family. I even thought about asking you, but Steve said you never spoke about it."

"I started looking for stuff I could use as reminders online. The magnet was easy to find; Amazon have got so much rubbish on their site, haven't they? But I wanted something more personal, something that would really shake you up. So I looked for memorabilia from that date, and the football ticket came up. It wasn't expensive. I mean Wimbledon aren't exactly Chelsea or Man United, are they?"

"What about the letter? The one about Sarah behaving like my mum? Why would you send that?" She laughed, a tinkling chime at complete odds with the situation.

"Ah that was good, wasn't it? I thought it would freak you out and I was right! You started thinking Sarah might have something to do with it after that didn't you? I know how much she meant to you growing up, and I didn't want her sticking her nose in and finding out what was going on."

"You're actually mental! Jesus Christ, they'd have a field day with you in that hospital." I shifted my body around slightly so that I could risk a quick glance out of the door. Where the hell was Jamie? If he could hear all this, why wasn't he coming to help me? I needed to play for time. "The problem is, Addy, you don't really know me at all. If you did, you'd know I stopped obsessing over my mother's death a long time ago." She smiled again, seemingly delighted at my defiant tone.

"Yeah, I realised that after a while. I'll tell you what, I reckon it was the Instagram stories that really made you sweat though, wasn't it? You went absolutely ballistic after those."

"I just didn't understand how you managed it? How can I have seen them and then the next second they were gone?" Addy gave me a pitying look.

"I'm a content creator, Marnie. Even if I wasn't, it's so simple. You really can't figure it out?"

"I really can't," I confirmed, gritting my teeth. "Why don't you tell me?" She sat back, getting comfy in the desk chair.

"Well, ok. You know how you can see who views a story?" I nodded. "I made an Instagram account and added you as a friend. By the way you probably want to set your profile to private in future." She grinned and the temptation to punch the smug look off her face was palpable. "Then it was easy; I made the videos, posted them to my story and watched the views until I knew you'd seen it. Then I deleted it so you couldn't go back. Simple, huh?"

"Very," I breathed. "You're fucked up, do you know that?" She gave a tinkling laugh.

"Yeah, I have been told that before, believe it or not. So that's all of it. You got locked up and we got the kids." She smirked again. "And now I'll call the police, and you'll go right back to where you came from. You know, in a way I'm glad I got to tell you all about it. Now while you're wasting away in that hell hole, you can picture Teddy calling me Mum. All I need to do now is get Dan to give Rose up; shouldn't be too hard with all the photos of his drug dealing I've got on my phone." She'd pulled her mobile out. "Want to see?"

Before I knew it, I'd closed the five feet between us, my hands reaching for the most vulnerable part of her body. She gave a small whimper as the air expelled from her throat once again under my touch.

Suddenly my hands were ripped away from her neck, and I was forced across the room. I looked up from my crumpled heap, disorientated. Steve was standing next to Addy, cupping her face in his hands and talking softly, asking if she was ok.

"Where did you come from?" I asked, shakily getting to my feet. Steve and Addy both ignored me, their eyes locked firmly on one another's. "Steve! Where's Teddy?" I said again. He looked over at me, his arm still protectively around Addy's back.

"I came back early. Addy said she wasn't feeling well this morning, and I was worried about her. Ted's at my parents; they'll drop him off later. Now what's going on? Why are you in my house?"

"Ask her," I retorted. "Look Steve! All the stuff that was happening to me, it's all here, the photos, the ticket, the magnet. Everything." Steve's gaze took in the magnet that Addy was still holding and the photos now littering the floor once more. He reached gently down and took the magnet from his wife.

"Addy?" he said softly. She had buried her face into her arms, now curled up like a ball on the chair; submissive and perfectly still. "Babe?" Hearing him use the caressing voice that used to convince me of my safety was jarring; I knew how he could turn. When she didn't answer I decided to.

"She used it all to make me think I was crazy, Steve! She wants to kidnap my kids. You've got to call the police." He looked at me from across the room with a closed expression on his face. "Steve!" I yelled again when he didn't respond. Instead, he looked down into Addy's face with such tenderness it took me by surprise.

"I know, Marnie," he eventually replied, ducking his head and placing a tender kiss on his wife's hair.

"Wh...what?" I stuttered. "You know?" I gingerly got to my feet, placing my back against the wall again for self-preservation. "How? What? You let her do this to me?" I stumbled over my questions. Steve looked at me with a little sympathy now.

"I didn't know at the time. But I was looking for some Sellotape a few months ago and I came across this stuff. Addy didn't want to tell me what she'd done, but in the end I got it out of her."

"And you let me stay there in that hospital? You let them keep me locked up and trying to make me admit to hurting the kids? You even came in to taunt me, and you knew all that time? What the actual fuck is wrong with you, Steve?"

"I had to, Marnie. I couldn't face losing Addy, not after you walked out on me. She just wanted Rose and Ted to be happy and safe, and you'd lost it when your Dad died."

"I was grieving, Steve!" I was shrieking now, the unfairness of the situation making me lose control. "Like any normal person! My God, I actually can't take this all in! So your wife torments me to the point where I'm locked up, and you do nothing? That's it, I'm out. I'm going straight to the police. The kids are coming home and you two will never see them again!"

I went to walk out of the broken door and back into the garden but Steve had charged at me, grabbing my arm so that I couldn't move.

"I don't think so," he said quietly. "I don't agree with what she did but she's my wife and I won't let her be arrested for this. I'll be the one to call the police. Addy and I will tell them you broke in ranting and raving. They'll see you're still sick, Marnie."

"You're the sick one," I said hoarsely. "And you can't do this!" I began to struggle against my captor, letting out a scream as my arm came into painful contact with the jagged glass in the door frame. Suddenly something rushed past me, and I was released. I looked around to find Jamie panting in the middle of the room, having just barrelled into Steve. He turned around to face me.

"Are you ok?" he asked me, putting a reassuring hand on my arm. I nodded back and he spun around to face my aggressors.

"Who are you?" Steve spat out in rage. "Why are you here?" Before Jamie could answer Addy rose from her perch.

"Jamie?" She said, walking forwards as if in a daze and reaching for him. Both Steve and I gaped as they embraced hungrily. Addy's hands were caressing his back, and his face was buried in her hair. I felt like I was intruding on something intimate. Finally, Steve stirred into action, and he leapt forward, pulling Addy away.

"That's the guy from the hospital, isn't it, Marnie?" he said, spinning her around to face him. "What's going on, Addy?" Her wrist was going white with the pressure he was applying. He gave it a little shake when she didn't respond, instead she was staring at Jamie as if he was the Sun itself. Jamie answered.

"Yes I'm Jamie," he confirmed. "I work at the hospital. I came to help Marnie because she rang me."

"But how do you know Addy?" Steve cut him off impatiently. "Why are you standing in my house and cuddling my wife? How do you know her?" I could tell I was of absolutely no interest to Steve now; his possessiveness had well and truly come to the fore. It was Addy who answered this time, her eyes never leaving Jamie's face.

"He's the love of my life," she replied quietly. The room went still as all three of us registered her words. Jamie looked shocked but gratified, while Steve's face began to darken with anger.

"He's what?" he ground out.

"The love of my life," she repeated, her voice stronger now. "I've loved him for the last five years, Steve. Ever since we met at the hospital."

"The hospital? My hospital?" I said, my brain whirring frantically to try and connect the dots. "You know each other from the hospital?" Jamie nodded even while Addy replied.

"I was a patient there five years ago," she said. "I'd been sectioned after several violent incidents including suicide attempts. I never told you, Steve, but I didn't have a very good life growing up, what with the way my parents were, and things just got too much. Jamie had just started working there and we grew close. He hung out with me every time he was on shift. One thing led to another, and we started a relationship. I got healthy, got discharged and moved in with him." Steve had released her arm now and was just staring at her, listening intently. "We started trying for kids straightaway. We tried for two years straight before we went to the doctors. They did some tests and told us there was a problem with me and it was unlikely we were ever going to be able to get pregnant. We kept trying but it just wouldn't happen for us. That's when I saw Rose. I fell in love with her. I left Jamie. He was heartbroken and so was I, but I just had this insane need to have a family, you know? So, I married you."

"After a few months, I bumped into Jamie in the supermarket, and we started chatting. It was like I'd been hit by a car. We met up a few times, just to talk. Eventually the meetings led to going back to his place. We started sleeping together. I kept on hoping this would be it and I'd get pregnant with his baby. Even if it'd been yours, Steve, I'd have taken the baby and gone back to Jamie. And then all this happened. Jamie knows me so well. He put two and two together and realised what I'd done. He broke it off. For you, Marnie! I couldn't believe it. He said he couldn't be a part of what I'd done to you, that he'd grown fond of you. He said you were being tortured daily and it was all because of me."

My mouth wasn't just gaping but fully hanging open now as my gaze flitted from Addy to Jamie and back. Finally my eyes landed on Steve. He was still staring at Addy but now with a broken expression. Addy moved towards Jamie again, softly laying a hand on his arm. "I miss you," she said quietly. "Can't we just leave the two of them to sort it out now, start again?" Jamie swallowed and glanced towards me; his expression conflicted. Equally gently he removed her hand from his body and took a step back.

"I'm sorry," he said quietly, confusing us for a moment about who he was talking to. "I can't do that to Marnie. I told you this when I found out what you'd done; I can't be with someone who can inflict this sort of damage." Addy was stock still.

"What? What do you mean? We're made for each other, you and me. Please babe, come with me." She held out her hand to him and Steve and I watched as he slowly shook his head.

"I'm sorry, Addy. I can't," he repeated quietly. "I need to call the police. You need to admit you need help. What you've done isn't normal. You need to see someone." He approached her now and put his hands on her arms, looking deep into her tearful eyes. "Ok?" he said, now rubbing her sleeves with his palms. She met his gaze and from my perspective I could see the moment her expression changed.

"No!" she screamed, launching herself backwards away from his touch. "I did the right thing for those children, just look what they have for parents! Marnie's lost her mind, and Steve's a misogynistic bully who thinks he has the right to dictate everyone else's lives! They need me. They need someone who cares about them, who'll look after them properly! I deserve to have my chance to be a mum!"

Not one of the three of us saw the glint as she suddenly barrelled towards me. The last thing I saw was the blade travelling downwards toward my scarred belly as she tumbled on top of me, forcing me to the ground. The blur of Jamie rugby tackling her sideways and away from me gave me a moment to catch my breath before she rolled back, surprising Jamie with the quickness of her movement and then slamming my head into the floor.

This time it was Steve who pulled her away, his hands roughly tussling with her to gain control.

"No Addy! Not again, no!" He threw her into the desk chair and, by pressing his legs forwards between hers and his hands gripping her wrists, managed to pin her down. The air was filled with heavy breathing as they both fought the other for power. With a final vicious swipe to her head with his hand, Steve wrestled the knife from her, and Addy was finally subdued. For a moment no one spoke.

"Again?" Jamie asked quietly, approaching the prone figures on the floor. "What do you mean 'again' Steve?" My ex-husband didn't answer, his eyes darting to meet Addy's briefly. "Steve!" Jamie barked, the suddenness making us all flinch.

"That day, at Marnie's. I found her standing over Marnie and the kids. She'd stabbed her." Steve replied quietly, talking to Steve but looking straight at me.

"What?" I whispered hoarsely. "But how? The bedroom was barricaded until you arrived. How could she have been there?" I glanced down at the woman on the floor, her eyes hardening as she met my stare.

"I was in the en-suite when you came in. I'd been swapping your medication over the last few months with painkillers, and I was in the middle of doing it when you arrived home. Steve's got a spare key, so every week I'd pop in and change them over. Very handy that you decanted them into that little pill tray to be honest! I thought if you were off your meds, it might make things easier, and I was right, wasn't I? You turned into an absolute nutcase without them." My brain was struggling to comprehend what she was saying.

"Hold on, so when I was in the hospital and the doctor said the medication had caused the breakdown when Dad died, that wasn't true at all? It was because I wasn't on anything?" I didn't know whether this made me feel better or worse; on one hand I could no longer blame the drugs, but on the other hand, did that mean I couldn't trust my own mind? Addy nodded.

"That's right. You were on painkillers but nothing else. It was all you. That's why I had to do it you see? Rose and Ted weren't safe anymore. I'd decided that was the night I was going to call the police and get them to do a welfare check. So, when Dan dropped Rose to us earlier that day for an hour or so, I gave them both a sedative in their squash. I thought if the police turned up and they were drugged they'd give them back to us, at least for a while. But you coming home and locking yourself in the bedroom gave me a better opportunity."

She stopped and grinned at me, and suddenly I could see her face over mine that day, my shout of terror as she appeared, the knife glinting as I wrestled her for control before she plunged it into my stomach. The scene was full of clarity in my mind, the banging on the door as Steve tried desperately to get in against the dresser, the warmth as the blood began to spread across my abdomen. The edges beginning to fade as a sudden yell wafted through the air, the images turning black slowly as two people fought above me. I turned my glare to Steve, still pinning his wife down.

"It was *her*?" I spat out, blind rage building in me. "You knew she tried to kill me, and you still protected her? She drugged our kids, and you've still let her be alone with them? What the actual fuck, Steve?" I grabbed my head to stop it exploding. He reddened before my eyes, his grip still tight on his wife while he looked from me to her.

"I couldn't tell anyone, Marnie," he replied quietly. "I'm sorry, but she's my wife. I love her. She made a mistake. She only wanted to make them drowsy to help us get custody, she explained it all to me." He gingerly got up off of the floor and held a hand out to Addy to help her up. They stood facing me, their arms around each other united.

"A mistake? A *mistake*? Forgetting to put the bins out is a mistake, Steve! This was attempted murder and child abuse! Jamie, call the police," I commanded, "this ends now."

Jamie pulled out his phone but before he had a chance to do anything Steve strode across and put his hand over it too.

"No! No, please don't. She thought the kids were in danger, she just wanted them safe. You can understand that, can't you? Didn't you love her once? She's not a killer, Jamie, she was just trying to protect the children." Jamie glanced over at me before setting his gaze on the silent Addy. She smiled gently back at him, her expression full of affection. He lowered his phone before glancing at me.

"Jamie?" I whispered. I couldn't believe this was happening. "She's a murderer, Jamie! She's unhinged; you've got to help me." He dropped his eyes to the floor, and I knew it was lost, it was three against one. "Please," I whispered, tears filling my eyes at the unfairness of it all. Addy smiled wickedly in my direction.

"I'm sorry," Jamie muttered, pressing his forefinger on his phone and lifting it to his ear. "Police please. I'd like to report a break in. There's a weapon involved."

Tears were streaming down my face as the minutes ticked by, despair and grief washing over me in constant waves of terror. Jamie stood beside the broken garden door with his back to me while Steve and Addy stood at the other end of the study guarding against any chance of escape I might have had. They didn't need to worry; the fight had gone out of me with Jamie's betrayal.

Eventually sirens could be heard in the distance coming ever closer, and I sunk to the floor, wrapping my arms around my knees and burying my head in my lap. I didn't want to see them; any of them. Jamie said my name softly, but I didn't raise my head. It was over, I'd tried to play the detective game and I'd lost. No more cosy mornings snuggled up in bed with my kids, no more contact centre visits. Rose and Ted would be lost to me forever.

I could hear the doorbell chime its tinkling tune and still I didn't move. Let them scrape me up off of the floor, let them lift my dead weight before they throw me back into the loony bin. Voices and footsteps were coming closer, I could hear Addy's peal of laughter as she spoke to someone, a viper ready to deliver the final blow to me once and for all. The study door clicked open and still I stayed put.

"Marnie South? I'm PC Waters." I could feel the disturbance in the air as someone knelt down next to me. "We've been called to a report that you've broken and entered this property with a knife. Your ex-husband has given us the weapon, but we need you to come with us to the station. You're under arrest on suspicion of breaking and entering with a deadly weapon. You do not have to say anything, but anything you do say may be given in evidence in a court of law."

I stayed where I was until I felt an arm on each side loop around my own and hoist me to my feet. Opening my eyes I took in the scene. Steve looked like he was going to be sick as he stared across at me from the doorway. Jamie was next to me, holding me up on my left-hand side. I thrashed away from him, his traitorous touch disgusting me even in my depression. He hung on, wrenching me back into place with a hiss.

"Officers?" He said, his voice buzzing strangely through my head. "I'm Jamie Saunders, I'm the one who called. Look, I think I need to explain something to you before you take Marnie here." He paused to clear his throat, and I risked a look at Addy, her smile frozen in place as she stared at her former lover. The officer not holding me stopped on the threshold and inclined her head, indicating for him to continue. "I did call you because Marnie broke into this house, but there's a bigger problem here than that. You see we have just been told about an attempted murder."

"I'm sorry, sir? An attempted murder here, with the knife we recovered?" PC Waters tightened his grip on the other side of me.

"Two attempted murders, actually," Jamie continued strongly, his former tentativeness forgotten now. "One six months ago, and one right here today, one with that knife."

"She tried to kill someone? Who?" PC Waters asked aggressively. I could feel his fingers digging into my flesh.

"Not me, her!" I screeched, galvanised by Jamie's sudden disclosure. "She stabbed me six months ago and tried again half an hour ago!" The two police officers looked at each other in confusion before Steve moved swiftly to stand between the two. In my peripheral vision I could see Addy trying to slip past the second officer into the hallway.

"She's lying," he blustered. "She's not mentally well! Look," he dropped his voice into his teacher tone, reasonable and sincere, "Marnie had a breakdown recently. She ended up being sectioned and the police were involved. I'm sure if you look her up, you'll see all of the reports. I can even give you her doctor's number at the hospital if you'd like to speak to her too?"

"You're lying, Steve!" I shouted. "Addy was torturing me. She nearly killed me; she's just admitted it to us all. You can't let her get away with this, please!" Addy was nearly past the other officer when she put her arm across the doorway, blocking her escape.

"Hold on," she said slowly. "You're admitting you broke into this property, but that someone tried to kill you? Can anyone corroborate this story Ms South?"

"Yes, yes! Jamie and Steve can, they heard it all! Tell them the truth. Tell them what she's been doing to me." I looked beseechingly back and forth between Steve and Jamie. Steve wouldn't even meet my gaze as he answered.

"Look she's clearly sick. I'd like you to arrest her for breaking into my house and threatening us with that knife. I mean I have kids who live here; I need to know they're safe from her turning up again!"

"Stop lying, Steve!" I was bellowing now. "You and her, you're both psychotic!"

"Me, psychotic?" Steve retorted. "You're the one who's just spent six months locked up because you tried to kill yourself!"

"That was her," I bawled, throwing my head back in frustration. "She's admitted it to all of us! She's not getting away with it a second time, she…"

"Stop, stop, stop," PC Waters, said, letting go of me and holding her hand up. She turned to the silent man by the back door. "Can you corroborate this?" Jamie didn't speak for a moment, scanning the room in silence. I held my breath.

"I can," he said quietly. "Marnie did break in, but everything she says about Addy is true. She's admitted to mentally torturing Marnie for months before stabbing her in an attempt to kill her."

"Prove it," spat Addy for the doorway, still trying to get past the officer who had now moved to block the exit completely. "It's my word against yours, Jamie, and she's got previous, remember?"

"Oh but we can," continued Jamie, smoothly pulling a phone out of his pocket. I looked in confusion from one hand to the other. Two hands, two phones. "I started recording when you came back, Addy. I called the police to arrest Marnie because I knew you'd run away if you suspected I was going to give you up. I'm sorry I had to do that to you, Marnie," he continued gently, turning to me. "Here," he pressed the new phone into PC Waters' hand. "Everything you need is on there."

Addy moved before the officer had time to react, barrelling into her and knocking her roughly into the door frame. We could all hear Addy's manic footsteps along the hall before the slamming of the front door. All at once all hell broke loose. Steve was wrestling with PC Waters as he attempted to follow his erstwhile wife, the police radios had burst into life with rapid descriptions of Addy being shouted through and repeated by different voices with varying urgency.

PC Waters finally managed to subdue Steve to the ground, face down with his arms behind his back so that he looked like a trussed-up turkey waiting to be cooked. The other officer was now rapidly barking instructions to her colleague, sirens were screaming, voices pitching, and I was forgotten in the mayhem.

EIGHTEEN MONTHS LATER

The hot water was pounding down onto my shoulders, the heat making me shudder with something halfway between pain and pleasure.

"Mum! Mum, Ted's taken my iPad, and he won't give it back. Tell him! Muuum!" The pounding on the door began, fists bouncing off of the woodwork in frustration. With one final soaking I shut off the water and gingerly stepped onto the mat.

"Ok Rose, just coming!" I trilled as I wrapped a fluffy bath sheet around me, still so stupidly happy to hear her voice no matter what tone she was using. Opening the door, my daughter's beautiful little mouth was set in a pout.

"Mum, you need to tell him to leave my stuff alone! He's gone on my game now and messed it all up!" I wrapped my arms around her, not caring that she huffed at the dampness of my body. Dropping a butterfly kiss on the top of her head I closed my eyes and inhaled for a second the unique scent of my first born.

"Ok, ok I'll tell him," I agreed as I drew back. "Now go and get ready for school, we need to leave in thirty minutes. I went to let go of her, but she tightened her grip and pulled me in, just for a moment, before releasing me. We smiled a little at each other before I nudged her gently with my bare foot. "Off you go then, babe," I said, allowing my face to break into a full grin.

Eighteen months had been enough time to completely and utterly change the fortunes of me and my children. After the arrests of both Steve and Addy and the subsequent searching of their property, the police informed me that they had found sufficient evidence to charge Addy with my attempted murder and stalking. The knife she had used, which turned out to be her own rather than the one I used for self-protection at home, was found hidden in the loft, Addy's fingerprints still clearly on it, and her computer and files had been seized. During questioning, she apparently broke down and confirmed the story that she had already told Jamie and I that day.

I had been dreading the day where the case went to trial. The media circus surrounding the case only intensified once the press put two and two together and connected my mother's murder to the present, and I had spent months imagining the strain that reliving the last year was going to put on my health, when her defence put forward a plea of diminished responsibility due to her mental state. The judge accepted it, and Addy once again became an involuntary inmate of a high security hospital to begin her sentence.

Steve had been charged with perverting the course of justice, thanks to both Addy's admission that he was the one to hide the knife, and Jamie's recording, and was currently serving a sentence of thirty-six months in prison. The thought of being free of him for three years was liberating, but I had worried about how the children were going to cope with yet another absent parent in such a small space of time. So far, and probably in no small part due to their ongoing therapy sessions, they seemed to have accepted the new status quo.

Surprisingly Dan had really stepped up to the plate now that Steve was gone, holding down a steady job and spending his weekends with Rose rather than down the pub. We were on civil terms on drop offs and pickups, and he had actually voiced his intention to come to parent's evening last time I saw him, which was something I'd never imagined I would say.

Jamie and I had lost touch with one another soon after the showdown at Steve's. As much as I was grateful for all he did to free me and clear my name, the revelations of his past with Addy were just too much for me to overcome. I felt confident in my decision when I heard through the grapevine that he had left the hospital I had been in, finding work at another nearby to where Addy was being held. I couldn't be sure, but I would be willing to bet that the two of them were still in contact; their lives seemed destined to be intertwined, and I was far happier out of it all.

I hadn't yet returned to work, savouring the freedom that had for so long been denied to me, and living for now off the remaining proceeds from Dad's house sale. Michal, my ex-mentor, had been in touch though, and after a few months of texting and hour-long phone calls, he had shyly asked me to go for a drink. Almost a year later, and despite being wary of putting a proper label on it, even I had to admit we were something of an item. I smiled slightly to myself at the thought, already looking forward to today's lunch date at the local pub.

In the present, as I smoothly pulled into a parking space a road away from the school, the kids chattering away about their forthcoming days, I allowed myself to take a deeply relieved breath. We were on time again this morning, beating the bell for a record-breaking three-week streak, and as they scampered off into their lines I happily sauntered back through the playground.

"Marnie! Hey, Marnie!" I turned around quickly to be greeted by Martha and her PTFA crew. "We're going for a quick coffee at the pottery place around the corner, do you fancy one?" Martha locked eyes with me, and I saw only affection in her gaze. I found myself nodding.

"Sure," I replied, glancing at my watch to check I wouldn't be late for lunch with Michal and smiling at the entire group. "I've got time."